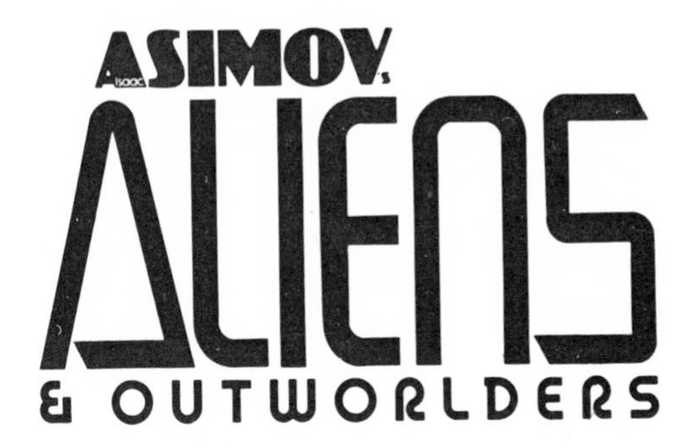
Isaac Asimov's
ALIENS
& OUTWORLDERS

Edited by
Shawna McCarthy

The Dial Press

Davis Publications, Inc.
380 Lexington Avenue, New York, N.Y. 10017

FIRST PRINTING

Library of Congress Catalog Card Number: 78-60795
Printed in the U. S. A.

COPYRIGHT NOTICES AND ACKNOWLEDGMENTS

CONTENTS

EDITOR'S NOTE

It's long been an assumption, on the parts of those not connected with the field, that science fiction (or sci-fi, as they are wont to call it) is "about bug-eyed monsters, little green men, and spaceships." Those of us who actually read SF usually respond to those charges with a heavy sigh. After all, how can one explain the breadth and depth of the ocean of ideas to be found in SF? It's *not* all critters and spacecraft.

But some of it is. And, of course, those of us who read SF regularly know that there are a host of wonderful concepts explored (and still waiting to be explored) in these areas. For instance, there's the old (and by *old* I mean in years, not in freshness of ideas) Aliens Taking Over The Earth theme, the Aliens Among Us theme, the We Are The Aliens theme, the We Meet The Aliens theme, and many, many more.

To classify themes so flippantly may sound as if the stories themselves are easily dismissed—not the case at all. As in "mainstream" fiction, themes are merely the looms on which skilled writers weave their cloth. And the writers represented in this collection are masterweavers all. Kate Wilhelm, Isaac Asimov, Larry Niven . . . when they pick up the thread of a story, you're likely to get so entangled in their web of ideas that you'll never want to break loose.

And let's not forget that you needn't be an alien to be an extraterrestrial. Humans living on lost colony planets, or in spaceships, or even in L5 habitats are by definition *extra*terrestrial. So we broaden our tapestry even further.

We think you'll enjoy the mix of stories and ideas found in this volume, and for those of you who happened upon this book at your local library, bookstore or newsstand, here's how you can get more of this calibre fiction thirteen times a year. This collection is called *Isaac Asimov's Aliens and Outworlders* because all the stories herein are taken from the pages of *Isaac Asimov's Science Fiction Magazine.* Subscription information is available at: Subscriptions, Isaac Asimov's Science Fiction Magazine, Davis Publications, 380 Lexington Avenue, New York, New York 10017.

So now, without further ado, I hope you'll turn the page and meet our fabulous collection of Aliens and Outworlders.

WITH THIMBLES, WITH FORKS AND HOPE

by Kate Wilhelm

art: Janet Aulisio

Kate Wilhelm won a Nebula
award for "The Planners" in 1968.
Her major novels include
Let the Fire Fall (1969); *Margaret and I* (1971);
Where Late the Sweet Birds Sang,
a Jupiter and Hugo Award winner (1976);
The Clewiston Test (1976);
A Sense of Shadow (1981);
and *Oh, Susannah!* (1982).
A new novel, *Welcome Chaos*, is forthcoming.
Together with her husband, Damon Knight,
she teaches SF writing every year
at the Clarion workshops.

". . . beware of the day,
If your Snark be a Boojum! For then
You will softly and suddenly vanish away,
And never be met with again!"

"They sought it with thimbles, they sought it with care;
They pursued it with forks and hope; . . ."

The Hunting of the Snark
—Lewis Carroll

I.

The farm house glowed in the late afternoon dusk, like an old-fashioned Christmas-card scene. Low evergreens crowded the front porch, the sidewalk from the drive curved gracefully; it was all scrubbed looking, the white clapboard freshened by rain that had started to fall. Charlie felt a twinge of guilt at the cleanliness and the comfort of it after spending most of the day in New York. He parked in the garage and entered a small side porch that led into the back of the house. The porch was a catch-all for the bottles to be returned to the store, newspapers destined for a recycle center, some wooden seed flats that had got only that far on their way to the barn, an overflowing woodbox. When the clutter got so bad that he could no longer make his way through it, he cleaned it all up, but not until then, and he never had finished cleaning everything—the seed flats had been there since June.

Inside the house the fragrance of soup was tantalizing; there were the odors of wood fires, of onions, of cats—three of them—cedar paneling, and other things he had not been able to identify, left-over things from when the house was built, or from the first seventy years of its occupancy.

"Hello," he called out, but he knew Constance was out. The house felt empty when she was outside. Two of the three cats stalked over to sniff his shoes and legs, checking credentials before they accepted him. The third one, Brutus, glared at him from on top the upright freezer. It was Charlie's fault, obviously, that the rain had started again. Brutus turned his back and faced the wall.

Charlie went through a narrow hallway, through the utility room, all the time dancing to avoid squashing a cat. He heard the soft plop Brutus made when he left the freezer, and he knew the evil old tiger cat was following along, his tail rigid, daring either of the other two to get in his way. They would keep an eye on him and scamper if he got near. Brutus was a New York cat; he had not, would never approve of country life. In the kitchen there was a copper-colored electric range with a stove-top grill, a dishwasher, a disposal that had never been used since they had moved in—meat scraps went to cats, and everything else went on the compost; there were rows of hanging pots and pans, all gleaming copper-bottomed, seldom used. What was used every day for nine or even ten months of the year was a forty-year-old wood cookstove. On it now there was the iron kettle with soup simmering so low that a bubble broke the surface once every five minutes or so.

The orange cat rubbed against him and complained about things generally. He rubbed its ears for a moment, then said softly, "She's going to be mad as hell, Candy." Brutus swiped at the gray cat, Ashcan, in passing and settled himself on the rocking chair nearest the stove. His eyes gleamed yellow as he narrowed them in the way that made him look Mephistophelian. Candy went on detailing her awful day, Ashcan licked the place where Brutus had nabbed him, and Charlie tried to think of a way to break the news to his wife that he had practically taken on a job for them both. She would be mad as hell, he said again under his breath, and he put down the briefcase filled with reports that he planned to read that night, and have her read.

On the slope overlooking the house and yard Constance was on her knees planting daffodils under the half-dozen apple trees that made their orchard. Next year they should start bearing. Goddamned rain, she muttered, had to do it now, couldn't wait another fifteen minutes, had to be right now. Rain trickled down her neck, icy fingers that made her skin flinch, trying to turn itself inside out. She plunged the bulb planter into the yielding earth, twisted it viciously, lifted out the plug and laid it down. With one hand she scooped up wood ashes and bone meal and sand and tossed the mixture into the hole, with the other she groped in her pail for another bulb and dropped it in, no longer taking the trouble to put it right side up. She returned the column of dirt topped with newly cut grass and jabbed at the ground a scant six inches away to repeat the process. It was impossible now for her to summon the vision of apple trees in bloom on a golden carpet.

She had heard the car and knew that Charlie was home. She had known when Charlie left that morning that when he got home he would hem and haw around for awhile and finally blurt out that he had taken the job, that it would be a milk run, nothing to do, nothing dangerous, etc., etc. Her stomach would churn and her blood would chill, making her fingers cold, and she would nod silently and try to find words that would tell him she hated it, but she was willing for him to do it because she knew he couldn't just quit the business cold turkey. She knew that now and then he would go see Phil Stearns and come home to tell her that he had agreed to do just this one job, this one last time.

But it wasn't fair, she muttered. For twenty-five years Charlie had worked on the New York City police force, and he had come out scarred but intact, and it wasn't fair to risk everything again.

The worst scars were the ones that could not be seen. Invisible scar tissue had formed, protecting him where he had been hurt too often. In the beginning he had been possessed by zeal, a sense of mission, holy justice; over the years that had become cynicism and simple dedication to sharpening his skills of detection. Then he had become different again, had developed a cold fury because nothing changed, or if there were changes, they were for the worse. His rage at the criminal began to extend to the victim. Constance had known then it was time for him to get out. Surprisingly, he had agreed, and three years ago, at forty-seven, he had retired.

She looked with dismay at the pail: at least twenty more bulbs.

The rain was coming down harder; there was a touch of ice in it. Her fingers were red and swollen-looking and her nose had started to run and she couldn't wipe it without smearing mud across her face. "It isn't fair!" she cried, looking at the house.

By the time she finished the job and put away her equipment, the rain was a downpour and the day was finished with the gray sky lowering to the ground. Charlie met her at the back door and drew her inside, pushed her gently into a chair and brushed a kiss across her nose as he leaned over and pulled off her muddy boots. He helped her out of the sodden jacket and then took both her hands and pulled her across the kitchen through the hallway to the bathroom that was steamy and sweet smelling from bubblebath.

She sighed and did not tell him she would have preferred a shower in order to wash her hair also. Since her fingers were stiff with cold he ended up undressing her and then held her elbow firmly until she was in the tub, only her flushed face and wet hair above water.

Charlie was perplexed about the hair; she was not the image he had anticipated, with mud on her cheek, and her hair dripping and clinging to her cheeks and her forehead.

"Be right back," he said and left, taking her wet clothes with him.

As soon as he had vanished, she stood up and pulled a towel from the rack and tied up her hair. It was silly for Charlie to baby her; she was taller than he was, and almost as broad. Her face was wide, Slavic, her eyes pale blue, her hair almost white it was so blond. The gray that was already showing here and there blended in and no one but Charlie knew she was turning. She knew she neither looked nor acted like the kind of woman a man would baby. She sank back into the suds and thought again it was silly for him to go through this to ease his conscience, but she was glad he did. Sometimes he babied her, sometimes she babied him, it worked out.

He came back carrying a tray with two frosted martini glasses, the shaker, a plate of garlic salami, the kind you could get only in a good New York deli, and strips of cheese. He sat down cross-legged on the floor so that his eyes and hers were level, poured the drinks, handed her a towel and then her drink, and began to tell her about the job. While he talked he ate the salami, and held out pieces for her to bite.

Constance watched him and listened and she thought: he was night to her day, all dark and brooding and secret. His hair was a mop of tight black curls, his eyebrows so heavy they made his face look out of proportion. There was a gleam of gold in his mouth when he laughed, one gold cap. His teeth were crooked, an orthodontist's nightmare, but they were the whitest teeth Constance had ever seen.

"Lou Bramley," Charlie said, eating cheese, "will be fifty-one November first. That's Saturday. He's got a wife that he cares for, two good kids, treasurer of Tyler and Sacks, Incorporated, no debts, everything going for him. And Phil's sure as sin that he's going to suicide before the end of the day Saturday. And leave him, Phil, holding a five hundred thousand dollar insurance policy."

"So why doesn't he just not issue the policy?"

"Because it's too big to piss away without more than an itch to go by. And nothing's come up. He's had his best working on it for the last three weeks and they haven't come up with anything. No motive. No problem. No woman. Nothing."

"Why does Bramley say he wants that kind of insurance?"

"His story was that at a party a screwball astrologer told him the next six months are the most dangerous of his life, that unless he takes extreme care the odds are good that he will be killed in an accident." Charlie poured the last of the martinis and laughed. "Phil even hired an astrologer to do a horoscope for Bramley. Nothing to it. He's riding a high wave, nothing but good things ahead. Can you imagine Phil going to an astrologer?"

Constance laughed. They had known Phil Stearns since Charlie's college days. Phil believed in nothing but actuarial tables. "Charlie," she said then, "it's an impasse. In time a good psychologist or psychiatrist could give Phil his answers, but if his people couldn't find anything in three weeks, what does he think you can do in three days? He has to gamble, or cut loose."

Charlie nodded. "I more or less told him the same thing. Midnight Friday the policy goes through automatically if he doesn't reject it. By midnight Saturday we both think Mr. Lou Bramley will no longer be with us, and Mrs. Bramley will come into a sizeable fortune. Phil is ready to cut him loose, but he wants a back-up opinion from a good psychologist. From you."

She shook her head. "I'm retired. And you are too, if you'd just remember it from time to time."

"Bramley's gone down to a flossy resort in Florida, in the Fort Myers area. That raises the possibility of a vanishing act instead of suicide. In either case it has to go down on the books as accidental death for the big payoff. All Phil wants you to do is go down there and observe him, talk to him, and on Friday give Phil a call. He needs something more than an itch to refuse a policy like that."

Constance glared at him. "You can't take jobs for me. I'm not an indentured servant or something."

"I didn't tell him anything definite," Charlie said reproachfully. "I did say that if we agreed, we'd want a week's vacation at the flossy resort after we finished this little job. On Phil, of course."

She shook her head. "Go stir the soup or something."

As soon as he was gone, she opened the drain, pulled the towel from her hair and turned on the shower. She hated bubble bath; this was a gift from their daughter. Of course, Charlie would be hooked on Lou Bramley; they were the same age. He would never admit it, but the idea of stopping everything now when there was so much to do, time enough finally to do it, that would frighten him. He was not a coward, he had survived too many encounters with near death, and had gone back too many times, but he was cautious. He was not ready. His own unreadiness would make it impossible for him to sidestep Lou Bramley who evidently was ready. Charlie would have to know why. He would have to stop him if he was stoppable.

Constance had called Charlie late in the afternoon of her first day at the luxurious hotel. She had managed to talk briefly with Lou Bramley, she reported. "He's withdrawing, Charlie," she had said soberly. "Anyone with half an eye could spot it. He's not eating, not sleeping, doesn't finish sentences. He stares and stares without moving, and then jumps up and walks furiously on the beach. Nervous energy. He's so obsessed he doesn't even realize he's got two women pursuing him."

"Two? What do you mean?"

And she had told him about the woman who was openly stalking Lou Bramley. The bellboys and waiters were betting on when she would land him, it was so obvious.

Charlie did not like having a woman appear. It was possible they planned to skip out together.

He was going to like it even less, she thought. The woman was June Oliveira, from Brazil, and Lou Bramley was the first man she had paid any attention to in the week she had been in the hotel. Wherever Lou Bramley went, she was so close that she might as well have been attached to him. Constance had watched her sit at a table next to his, and start edging her chair toward him. When she got within whispering distance, he apparently had become aware of her for the first time, and he had moved out to a beach chair in the sun. His action had been almost absent-minded. The woman had continued to watch him intently, and moments later when he jumped up and started to walk, she had followed.

It would have been easy to miss, Constance knew. The terrace was usually a busy place, especially during the late afternoon happy hour. Waiters were rushing back and forth, groups forming, breaking up, reforming. If she had not been watching closely, she might not have noticed, partly because the woman was so brazen about it; somehow that screened her intentions even more than secrecy would have done. When she first mentioned the woman to Charlie, Constance had realized she could not describe her beyond the most obvious features—long black hair and slender figure. Her face was smooth and unreadable, expressionless; she wore no jewelry, no make-up, no nail polish. Probably she was in her thirties; she was too self-assured to be younger, but there were no visible signs that she was older.

Up to this point Charlie would be willing to accept her assurance that Lou Bramley and the woman were strangers. And then she would tell him that last evening the woman had moved to a room next to Bramley.

The bellboy who was willing to sell information had rolled his eyes when he told her that. Later last night Constance had gone for a walk, and in the shadows of a seagrape bush, she had stopped and looked back at the hotel, studying it until she found her own room, counting up and over from it to Bramley's. On the balcony next to his, she had made out the dim figure of the woman as close to the joint rail as she could get.

Constance remembered the chill that had shaken her, and she felt it edging up her arms now. She looked at her watch; he should be home, she decided, and dialed the number.

Charlie sounded pleased; he was running down a good lead, he said, but the woman continued to worry him. She could be a complication, he admitted.

"I'll see if I can get anything from Bramley about her," Constance said. "I'm having a drink with him in a few minutes. I doubt that we'll be able to talk, though. That woman will be in his lap practically. Charlie, she . . . she really bothers me."

"Okay. Keep your distance from her. Don't get in her way. She's probably got her own little racket going. Just watch the gazebo from a distance. Right?"

She agreed, and in a few minutes they hung up. She had not thought of the gazebo for a long time, but this didn't feel at all like that. There was something strange and mysterious going on, but she felt no danger; this was not the way she had felt when she had made the workmen move the little structure—hardly bigger than a playhouse. Nine years ago when they were in the country on weekends and part of the summer only, she had looked out the kitchen window one Saturday morning and had felt her skin crawl. She had to move the gazebo, she had said to herself sharply, and without another thought she had gone to the phone and called Willard Orme and had told him to bring someone out to do it. He had protested and tried to arrange a date a week away and she had said she would get someone else to do it and remodel the house and build the garage and all the rest of the work he was figuring on doing for them. Reluctantly he had come out and moved the gazebo. That afternoon Jessica and two friends had been sitting in it drinking cokes and eating hot dogs when a storm had blown down the walnut tree near the barn, and it had fallen on the newly bared spot of earth.

This was nothing like that, she told herself sharply. It was time to go down and meet Lou Bramley, see if they could find a place where she could get him to talk a little, a place where there would not be room for June Oliveira to be at his elbow.

The terrace was very large, and even though there were forty or more people on it, many tables were vacant. The hotel was between seasons now; after Thanksgiving, through spring, it would be jammed and then it would be impossible to wander out and find a table. She sat down, and shook her head at the waiter. She would order when Lou Bramley joined her. She spotted him as soon as he walked from the lobby through the wide doors. He hesitated, looking around, then nodded and started for her table. He had taken perhaps ten steps when he paused, looked past her, and changed his direction to go through the terrace, out to the beach chairs in the sand, where he sat down next to June Oliveira.

"For heaven's sake," Constance muttered to herself. "He's falling for her line." Bramley was facing the gulf, away from her. June Oliveira was at his left, talking to his profile. Constance watched them for several minutes and then decided not to let Oliveira get away with it so easily. She picked up her purse and put on her sunglasses; it was still very bright out on the sand. She hated going out in the sun because her nose was burned, her cheeks, her chin. She walked across the terrace, and down the three steps, turned toward them, and then veered away and headed toward the beach instead. She began to feel the heat of the sun on her nose and cheeks, and abruptly she turned and went back, without glancing at Lou Bramley and June Oliveira.

In her room again she began to shiver and started to adjust the air conditioner, but she had turned it off when she arrived and it had not been on since. She went to the balcony to let the late afternoon sun warm her. She realized that she was cursing under her breath and suddenly she laughed. A tug of war over a man! She had not played games like that since her teens. Now she began to look over the people on the sand below. Finally she found Lou Bramley and June Oliveira, exactly as before. She stood thinking and then went back inside and dialed Charlie again.

"I just want you to call her, and keep her on the line a few minutes."

He didn't like it, he said many times, until she said she would hire a bellboy to do it, and if she paid him ten, that woman would more than likely pay fifteen to learn the identity of the hoaxer.

"And if you get him out of her clutches, then what?"

"I'm going to try to get him drunk enough to sleep tonight. If he doesn't, he just might go through with it, no matter what you tell him. He's desperate for sleep."

Charlie grumbled some more, but he would make the call to Oliveira in five minutes. "Honey," he said before hanging up, "just be damned careful."

Lou Bramley sat in the afternoon sun with June Oliveira and on her balcony Constance shivered. It was crazy, she told herself sternly, there were fifty people down there, and that many more on the beach, dozens of people swimming, or sunbathing. It was a mob scene down there.

Almost thirteen years ago Charlie had given her a present of one year of defense classes. He had insisted over her protests, saying further that as soon as Jessica was ten, he was going to enroll her also. Months later she had come home one afternoon upset and unwilling to continue. "Charlie, what Kim is teaching us now are lethal blows. I don't like it."

He had held her shoulders and regarded her soberly. "If anyone ever lays a hand on you, hurts you, you'd better kill him. Because if you don't, I will. You'll get off with self defense, but it will be murder for me." They both knew he meant it.

What her classes had not prepared her to do, she thought decisively, was to stay in her den and shiver when she had agreed to do a job. She waited in the dark, cool bar for the bellboy to summon June Oliveira for her urgent long-distance call. The bar adjoined the terrace; it had ceiling-to-floor smoked glass windows that let the patrons see out and kept those on the outside from seeing in.

The day the walnut tree fell was the day that Jessica had given up junk food, had in fact become a health food fanatic. The girls had come running in talking shrilly, caught up in a nervous reaction to the storm and the crash of the tree, and the realization that they could so easily have been under it. Jessica had stopped at the door and looked at her mother across the kitchen. There had been beads of sweat on her upper lip. Wordlessly she had crossed the room and hugged Constance very hard, shaking, saying nothing. Strange, Constance thought as she watched, how memories like that one pop up, complete, every detail there, as if it were a little scene one could raise the curtain on at any time. She was glad she had been with her daughter on the day she learned how short the distance was between life and death.

Presently June Oliveira appeared, walking fast toward the lobby. Constance left the bar through the terrace door and went straight to Lou Bramley. The woman had left her scarf on the chair; she did not intend to be delayed very long.

"Hi," Constance said. "Want to take a walk?"

Bramley jumped up and looked around swiftly. "I certainly do. Let's go."

They started for the beach, then he stopped. "It's no good. She'll just tag along."

"I've got a rental car in the lot," Constance said, taking his arm. "Let's go somewhere else to walk."

They went to a flagstone path that wound between the swimming pool area and the tennis courts, up past the terrace, to the street-front parking lot. Not until they were on the busy highway heading south did Lou Bramley relax.

"I really wanted to talk to you professionally, but I'm not quite sure of the etiquette of the situation. And I owe you an apology," he said. "I'm sorry."

Constance laughed. "I'm retired. Any advice I give these days is just that, advice, like you might get from sweet old Aunt Maud."

She glanced at him as she spoke; his mouth twisted in an attempt to smile, then settled back into a tight line. His sunglasses were mirrors that completely hid his eyes. She turned her attention once more to the road. Incredibly busy, she thought, didn't those people know there was a gas shortage? Probably many of them were on their way down to the Tamiami Trail, through the swamps over to the east coast.

A straggly line of pelicans flew across the road; she admired pelicans more than all the other birds. They were scruffy-looking on land, ungainly, comical, but in flight they were supreme. So little effort seemed to go into it. They just opened their wings and sailed.

"I came down here to think through a problem," Lou Bramley said after the silence had stretched out long enough to be almost unbreakable. "A business problem," he added quickly. He turned his head away, as if afraid that even with most of his face hidden behind the sunglasses, he might reveal too much. "Lucky, my wife, says that we constantly signal to each other, all people, and that we learn to read the signals as kids and get sharper at it as we grow up. She says that women don't make passes at me because I'm not signalling that I'd be receptive." He paused, waiting for her response.

"That's really very good," Constance said dutifully.

"Yes. And now especially, with this problem, I know I'm not hunting. So why is it that I can't turn around without having that woman at my side? Earlier, I wanted to have a talk with you and I went to her instead. I don't even like her. I actively dislike her, more than anyone I've met in a long time. And I can't stay away from her."

"I wonder what she wants," Constance said.

"That's the stumbling block for me too. There must be some kind of con game that she's going to pull when the time's right."

"She isn't right for a con artist, too blatant, too uncaring about appearances." She spied a good place to leave the highway at a small restaurant with beach access. "Finally, we can take our walk."

They walked on the hard-packed wet sand at the edge of the water. Lime green waves rose knee high before they lost themselves in froth. Flocks of sandpipers probed the sand, scattered at their approach, settled again as soon as they passed. Now and then a large white heron fluttered up out of their way, or a bunch of sea gulls screeched at them. Constance did not push the conversation or try to direct it as he talked about the woman, June Oliveira. She got little from it; he was not a good observer, not an attentive listener, not at this time in his life anyway.

They turned back as the sun was setting in a gaudy display of reds, golds, ivory, green. . . . Offshore, a large yacht was moving south. They watched it.

"I don't swim," Lou Bramley said suddenly.

"My husband doesn't swim very well," Constance said. "He paddles a little."

"I saw you heading straight out into the gulf this morning; it gave me a sinking feeling in my stomach when I realized I couldn't see you any longer."

"I don't think June Oliveira swims either," Constance said. "At least I haven't seen her doing it."

"She thinks it's dangerous. She doesn't do anything dangerous.

She thinks people are crazy who do."

He did not break the silence again until they were drawing near the tiny restaurant. "Would you like to have dinner here? I understand almost all the seafood restaurants are pretty good."

They got a booth by a window and she ordered a martini; they watched the end of the gaudy sunset while they waited for it.

"What happened after you published your articles?" he asked. He had not ordered a drink, and watched her sip her martini with poorly concealed desire for one just like it.

He was punishing himself, she thought, making himself live through every minute of this week without help of any sort. The hollows under his eyes were alarming.

"I had already quit the hospital when I began to write the articles," she said. "They brought a little pressure on the university. I had tenure and they couldn't have touched me, but it was uncomfortable. I finished the semester and dropped that too. It wasn't as if I sacrificed anything," she added easily. "I was busier than ever doing consulting."

"They made it look like a continuation of the old battle between the psychologists who aren't doctors, and the psychiatrists who are," he said thoughtfully.

She shrugged. "A plague on both their houses. I'm researching a book right now that will damn the psychologists just as much as those articles damned the holy psychiatrists."

"I'd like to see that," he said almost regretfully, and his eyes went distant as his fingers began to tap on the table top. He was back in his own hell.

"It's heady stuff," she said, "taking an opponent that much bigger than you are." His gaze remained fixed. She pulled the menu close to the candle and tried to make out the faint print.

When the waiter came to take their orders she asked to see the wine list and was disappointed by the selection. She did the best she could with it and said firmly, two glasses. Lou Bramley started to protest, then became silent again. For the first time he seemed to be uncomfortable with the silence.

"I'm surprised that they're still treating so many people with electroshock," he said.

"Several hundred thousand a year. For a while they thought they had a better solution with psychodrugs, but what happened was they ended up with addicts. Mostly women."

"And the difference in the treatments for men and women. That was shocking too."

"Shocking," she agreed. "That's the word."

Suddenly he smiled, the first time. "I'm not very good company. I'm sorry. Thanks for rescuing me, though. I'm glad we got out, away from that woman."

He ate little, but he drank the wine, and she kept refilling his glass; when the bottle was low, she signalled the waiter who immediately brought a new one. The food was delicious. She was sorry he had not eaten.

They both ordered Key lime pie and while they waited for it, he said, "I really wanted to talk to you about a favor. You mentioned that your husband is joining you this weekend and you'll be around next week?"

She nodded.

He leaned back as the waiter came with their pie. For a minute Constance was afraid he would reconsider and withdraw again, but as soon as the waiter left, he went on.

"I thought I might miss you tomorrow. I have an important call I have to wait for in my room, and I thought you might have plans to go out. Anyway, that woman has made me jumpy, and I don't want to leave anything in my room. For all I know she might find a key somewhere, let herself in." He tried to laugh to show that he did not really mean it, but the effort was wasted. "It's something I want kept safe for me. I'm going deep-sea fishing, but I mentioned that already, didn't I?"

He knew he had not. The lie evidently made his mouth dry; he had to drink some of the awful water before he could continue. Constance was missing nothing: his sudden thirst, the way his fingers tightened and relaxed, tightened again, the way he avoided her gaze. He was still too dry to go on and he reached for the wine this time.

Constance took a bite of the pie and drew in a deep breath. It was sinfully good, made with real whipped cream, real lime juice.

"I don't want to leave confidential papers in the hotel safe," Lou Bramley said finally. "I know they have to turn things over to the police in case of accident or anything," he said in a rush.

He stopped again and this time Constance thought he would not go on. "This has to do with your business problem?"

"Yes. That's it. I would like to know that someone responsible has the papers, just in case."

"I'll be glad to hold anything for you."

"Thanks. And if, I mean there's always a chance that something could happen, and if it does, would you just drop the stuff in a mail box for me? There will be two envelopes ready to mail. Inside a larger envelope."

She nodded.

"I can't tell you how that relieves my mind," he said. "I know it must sound crazy, but I've got a hunch that I should make sure that stuff is safe." He put his fork down and looked past her out the window and instantly his face was set in that distant look she had come to know.

"I believe very much in hunches," she said. "I used to wonder why everyone in my profession paid so little attention to intuitions, hunches, things that we all experience and no one wants to talk about. Some of those patients committed to years of institutional life, ordeals of drugs, shock treatments, hours of psychodrama, group therapies, the works are there because they couldn't bring themselves to ignore their intuitions. They got out of control. Others, even sicker people on the outside, pretend there are no such things. There has to be a middle ground, there has to be a handle to it, a way to look into it without being labeled crazy. I haven't found it yet," she admitted. "But I'm convinced that you can't treat neurotics, psychotics, psychopaths, any of them unless you admit that part of the psyche is still uncharted, unknown, and powerful."

She had brought him back; he was regarding her with interest.

"They'll crucify you," he said softly.

"They might try. I'm hammering my nails as hard and fast as they are hammering theirs."

He smiled with her.

She made a waving motion. "Enough of that. Why is your wife nicknamed Lucky?"

It was a silly story—her father had won a daily double the day she was born—but it started Lou Bramley talking. It was all about his wife and two children now, the trips they had taken, the strange and wonderful things the children had done. Nothing current, nothing about the future, nothing more recent than a couple of years ago. When he paused, she told a story about Jessica, or about Charlie.

They were the only customers still in the restaurant when it closed. He was yawning widely. At the car he stopped and looked back at the small dining room, the beach beyond it pale under a new moon. He nodded, then got in.

It was shortly after twelve when they walked into the hotel lobby and saw June Oliveira studying travel folders near the desk. Lou Bramley groaned.

"Jesus Christ!" he muttered. "She's just waiting. She knows and she's waiting."

On Friday Charlie arrived at the hotel at six-thirty and went straight up to their room where Constance was waiting for him. He kissed her fervently.

"You had me worried," he said then, holding her at arm's length, studying her. "Have you looked at your nose?"

She had; it was as shiny and red as a plum tomato. It was also hot.

"You know what he's running away from?"

"I think so. He needs to confirm it, I don't have a stitch of proof."

"If he doesn't, we have to kidnap him or something. We can't let him go through with it, Charlie. I like him, he doesn't deserve that."

"And I like his wife a bunch too. We'll see. Now, what about that mystery woman?"

"I wish I knew. Look, Bramley hasn't left his room all day. He's waiting for that phone call. He was supposed to get a package to me for safe keeping, and he hasn't done that either. It's that woman. She's got some kind of control over him. I know, I know . . . ."

Charlie watched her pace to the window, back. He had seen her like this before, but not for a very long time. He tried to pull her to the sofa next to him; she was too restless to sit down.

"Charlie, you'll have to get him out of here to talk to him. Tell him he's insured. Tell him you have to have something to eat, say in the coffee shop, that he has to sign papers and can do it there. She'll follow. In the lobby I'll distract her and that's when you have to get him out. There's a place down the road, south, Jake's Fish House. I'll meet you there. You rented a car, didn't you?"

"Yes. You told me to, remember? Constance, what is all this? You're nearly hysterical, you know?"

"I'm not hysterical, but there isn't much time. There's an eleven o'clock flight out of Miami and I want him on it. Charlie, he won't talk here! That woman is hanging out on his elbow. Believe me."

He kissed her again and went to the door. "Okay. Jake's Fish House. It'd better be good, sweetie, real good."

He would have recognized Lou Bramley from the photographs, but they had not prepared him for the muddy color of his face. He had blanched when Charlie said he represented the insurance company.

"You have the policy, Mr. Bramley," Charlie said. "There are some formalities, of course, a few things to sign."

Bramley sank into a chair, staring at him blankly; very slowly the mud color changed to a reddish suntan. He moistened his lips. "Something to sign?"

"Yeah. Would you mind going to the coffee shop? I got a lousy headache on that flight down here. Cup of coffee, and a couple aspirins, that's what I need. We can get the paperwork done there."

Bramley nodded and stood up. He went to a chest, opened a drawer, and withdrew a manila envelope. "I have to drop this off at the desk," he said looking at the envelope.

The woman was standing at the elevators when they arrived. The Dragon Lady, Charlie thought, and nodded to her. At his side Lou Bramley had gone stiff. He looked straight ahead as if he had not seen the woman at all. No one spoke.

She got off before them, but was walking so slowly that they passed her within a few feet of the recessed elevator bank. They went to the desk where Bramley handed over his envelope and watched until the clerk deposited it in the box. He took a deep breath.

"The coffee shop's over there," he said dully, turning from the desk.

The woman was less than fifteen feet away. Constance appeared and walked between them and when the woman stepped aside, Constance brushed against her.

"Hey, what are you doing?" Constance yelled. "She had her hand in my purse!"

June Oliveira started to move away faster; Constance caught her by the arm and turned her around. "I know you did! I saw you and I felt the tug on my purse. It's happened to me before, just like that."

"Let's get the hell out of here," Charlie said, taking Bramley's arm. There was no need to tug; Bramley was already nearly running for the wide entrance doors.

In Jake's Fish House they took a booth and Charlie ordered, "One scotch on the rocks," he said pointing to Bramley. "One very dry martini for me."

"Your wife said that's your drink," he said easily.

"You saw my wife? Why?"

"Routine."

"You told her about the policy?"

"Nope. Told her I was a headhunter scouting you out for a new job."

"She believed that?"

"She sure was trying hard to believe it. She showed me your computer. Neat. Real neat."

Bramley ran his hand over his lips. "Who are you?"

"Actually, I really am doing a bit of headhunting for Jim Hammond."

Bramley looked as if he might faint. The waiter brought their drinks and Charlie said, "Drink up." He sipped his martini and knew he wanted another one very fast. Bramley drank most of his scotch without pausing. They regarded each other. Bramley looked haunted, or maybe treed. Charlie had seen that look on other faces. Sometimes if the person with that look had a gun, he began shooting. If he was on a ledge, he usually jumped.

"If you've done what we think you've done," he said softly, "Jim Hammond wants to hire you, starting now, tonight, or next week, next month, whenever you can arrange it."

"He doesn't even know. No one knows."

"Five hundred thousand dollars' worth for openers," Charlie said.

"For openers," Bramley said. He finished his scotch.

"Hammond wants you, you can work it out together. You found a glitch in his fool-proof gadget. You could even say he needs you." He signalled the waiter to repeat the first round and then leaned back watching Bramley. "Of course, it was the dumbest thing you could do, get a policy like that and take off, I mean. Like a neon announcement."

"I never claimed to be smart. I was desperate. It would have worked. Lucky would have paid the money back and would have collected fifty thousand from Hammond. His offer is still good, isn't it? The reward for anyone who cracked his system? I wrote out exactly what I did to prove . . . Oh, my God!"

"Now what?"

"I've got to retrieve that envelope from the hotel desk!" He shook his head, then asked, "How did you find out?"

"The old Sherlock Holmes method. If it's all that's left, it's got to be it. Or something like that. We couldn't find anything on you, so I looked up your company. Two years ago they got a new Hammond computer system. I read about the guarantee and the reward. As soon as I saw that computer setup at your house, I knew."

Their new drinks had arrived before Constance showed up. She came straight to their booth and sat down next to Charlie. Bramley looked completely bewildered by her arrival.

"It's okay," Charlie said to Constance, putting his arm about her shoulders and squeezing slightly. "You put on a good show. How did you get out of it?"

"I apologized and explained many times that I had been robbed in New York by someone who casually brushed against me. She was not happy."

"You two . . . ? You're with him?"

"This is my husband," Constance said. "I have your envelope. I suppose you want it back?" She took it from her purse and slid it across the table.

He looked from her to the envelope, back to her. "You've been working these past couple of days?"

She nodded. "I had planned to kidnap you and make you see how unfair you were being, if Charlie hadn't pulled it off."

"It's too easy to make judgments from the outside," Bramley said. "It would have ruined her life, too."

"And what about the load of guilt you were planning to dump on her? Wouldn't that have ruined her life? Ruin, despair, humiliation, those were your burdens, but you know she would have shared them. Who would have shared her guilt?"

"She would have grieved, but she would have accepted that."

"She already knows," Charlie said. "I don't know how, but she does."

"Just as I'd know," Constance said.

"She would have tried to stop me if she suspected," Bramley whispered.

"Maybe she feels she can take the guilt trip better than you could stand the humiliation and ruin from whatever you did. Maybe she wanted to save you from suffering," Constance said coolly.

"Stop it!" His voice broke and he gulped his drink. "You've made the point," he said.

"Lou, there's an eleven o'clock flight out of Miami for New York. You can take my rental car and turn it in for me at Miami. You have a reservation for that flight."

"This feels like a bum's rush," he said, but his eyes gleamed, and there was a look on his face that she had not seen there: boyish, eager.

"The hotel knows you're going out fishing tonight, they won't think anything of it when you don't come back. Call them from New York tomorrow."

He was nodding. "I really don't have to go back there. I could drive over in a couple, three hours. What time is it?"

"Seven thirty."

"I'd better get started."

"I got some sandwiches, and a thermos of coffee. They're on the front seat. Here's the agreement for the car, and the key." Constance handed them to him.

He folded the paper and stuffed it in his pocket and brought out another slip of paper. He looked at it, then let it fall to the table. "My receipt for the fishing trip. Paid in full." Now he stood up. He looked down at Constance. "I don't know yet what I think about you. I owe you a lot. Thanks." Suddenly he leaned down and kissed her forehead. He reached across her to shake Charlie's hand. "You don't really have anything for me to sign. That was all done a month ago. Right?"

"Right. Good luck, Lou. Hammond's waiting for your call." He hesitated, then asked, "Fill me in on one thing, before you go. What do you think the Oliveira woman was up to?"

"I think she knew I was going to die and she was hanging around to watch," he said without hesitation. "She'll be disappointed. Keep out of her way," he added, looking at Constance. "She's a ghoul, probably crazy, and I think she's very dangerous."

They watched him leave, then Charlie turned to Constance.

"Okay. What was that all about? He's right, it was the bum's rush. Why?"

"I don't think he would have been able to leave again if he had gone back to the hotel. I don't know how or why but that woman does have some kind of power over him. I think he's right, Charlie. She knew. That's what she was waiting for."

Charlie took a deep breath, blew it out again in exasperation. "Tell me," he said.

When she kept it all very objective, as she did now, Constance knew there was nothing frightening about the woman. She repelled and fascinated Lou Bramley, nothing too unusual there; except, she told herself, both she and Lou Bramley knew it was more than that, even if neither of them could ever demonstrate it.

"Now, you tell me. What did he do? He's not a crook."

"Not in the usual sense anyway. His company got a big multi-million-dollar computer system two years ago, guaranteed safe against illicit access. And Bramley couldn't resist trying to break into it. It was a game, puzzle solving. And he did it. Eighteen months ago he got his own computer at home, and it's been like having a mouse in the cheese cupboard ever since. God knows how much money he's diverted, where it is. Hammond, the computer company president, wants to hire him." He shrugged. "I think I got out of the crime business at a good time. I just don't understand things any more. Hammond said half a dozen companies would hire him if he actually got access to that computer. And I guess he did."

Hours later when Charlie fished for his keys, he felt the receipt for the charter boat and brought it out also. "Let's do it," he said. "Let's go fishing."

"He's going to take off at high tide, at three or a little after," she said. She thought of the glassy water of the gulf. "We have to sleep aboard if we're going." They began to hurry, like children rushing to a picnic.

For a moment or two Constance was aware of another feeling, the same one she had felt years ago when she had looked out her kitchen window that Saturday morning. The same, but intensified, and also directionless.

"You know," Charlie said, driving, "this is something I've wanted to do all my life. Never thought the chance would drop into my lap like this. Freezing rain was falling when I left the city. . . . "

Beside him Constance was caught up in his infectious gaiety; she pushed the intrusive feeling of dread and fear out of her mind.

II.

At the docks she and Charlie went into an all-night diner to ask directions, and they met Dino Skaggs there, one of the brothers who owned *Dinah's Way*. He was a wiry brown man with sun-bleached hair, his face so wrinkled it was hard to guess his age, which Constance thought was about thirty-five, give or take a few years.

Dino scowled when Charlie showed him the receipt. "You sure he isn't coming?" he asked suspiciously, studying the receipt.

"I'm sure," Charlie said. "Look, if there's an additional charge because there's two of us, we'll pay it."

Dino bit his lip as he studied Charlie, then Constance. "Shit," he said finally. "Hundred per head, in advance. We shove off at three. No checks," he added as Charlie pulled out his checkbook.

"I have cash," Constance said. She counted out two hundred and handed it to Dino, who recounted it.

He stood with the money in his hand, still frowning glumly. "Shit, I guess you won't be eating all that much." He peeled off five tens and thrust the bills back to her. "Don't bother to come aboard until two-thirty, and keep it quiet when you do. We've got a sleeping passenger aboard already." He slouched away.

"Well," Constance said. "You're sure about this?"

"Shit yes," Charlie said grinning. "Want some coffee?"

§ § §

Dino met them on the dock where the *Dinah's Way* was moored. It was too dark to tell much about the boat, except that it looked small, and very pretty, sparkling white with blue letters, blue trim, gleaming copper rails. It looked less like a fishing boat than Charlie had anticipated.

"You'll want to watch the lights and all, I guess," Dino said morosely. "I'm going to settle you in the stern and you stay put. When you've had enough, you go on to your stateroom. And no talking in the galley. Inside your room with the door closed it's okay, just keep it low. Right?"

Charlie said, "Aye, aye," and Dino groaned. Constance felt a stab of impatience with Charlie. He was too eager, too willing to let this pipsqueak boss him around.

"I'll take her out from up on the flybridge," Dino went on. He led them aboard, and to the rear. The boat rocked gently. "Grandstand seats," Dino said, pointing to two fighting chairs. "Back through here," he said, motioning them to come to the cabin, "you go down the stairs, and turn right at the bottom. There's a yellow light over the door, that's your room. Light switch on the wall. Head at the far end. Bathroom," he added, glancing at Constance. "You'd better take your seats. I'll see you in the morning." He waved to a man who was leaning against a piling and vanished around the side of the boat.

Constance leaned toward Charlie. "What's a flybridge?"

"I don't know."

They sat back in their chairs and watched the gleaming black water laced with ladders and bridges and arcs of lights. The engines started up and Charlie found Constance's hand and held it; lights came on above and around them, running lights, Charlie thought with self-satisfaction, and then they were moving easily, backing away from the dock, out into the bay. Here and there other boats were moving, small boats with lights hardly above the water line, larger fishing boats, a yacht that made everything else look toylike. Charlie sighed with contentment.

When they finally went to bed, after all the lights had disappeared in the distance, they shared one of the bunks. Sometime during the night Charlie moved to the other one and fell asleep instantly again.

He woke up first and was amazed to find that it was nearly eight. The motion of the boat was very gentle, nothing like he had imagined. He had never been on a boat before, except for a rowboat when he was a kid. He thought of the seascapes he had admired, always stormy, threatening. Another time, he decided, and was glad that today the gulf was like a pond, the boat's motion hardly noticeable. As soon as he got up and started toward the head, he realized the motion had been effectively concealed while he had been horizontal. He held to the bunk and groped for the door. He had just finished showering when he heard Constance scream.

He flung open the shower door and stopped. Standing in the open doorway to the galley stood June Oliveira staring at Constance.

"Where is he?" she demanded.

"Why didn't you tell us she was aboard?" Charlie snapped.

They were in the galley where Dino was making breakfast. June Oliveira had gone forward, he told them.

"I don't recall that you asked me," Dino said, breaking eggs, his back to them.

"We have to go back," Constance said.

Now Dino turned. "Lady, get this one thing straight. This is my boat. I'm the skipper. I say when we come out and when we go in. I made a contract with Mr. Bramley, all signed, paid for, everything. You and your husband said you wanted to use that contract. That means we do it my way. And that means we fish until this afternoon. I pick up my brother Petie, and then we go back. That's in the contract, and I'm following it to the letter. You don't want to fish, fine. You can look at scenery. I'll fish."

"When did she come aboard?" Charlie asked, his voice easy now, his working voice, Constance thought.

"Last night. I was checking things out and there she came. What's this? What's that? I'm going, too, you know. I'm his guest, you know. He wants to pretend it isn't planned, so just don't say anything to him, so he won't have to lie about it. That's her story. How was I to know anything?"

Charlie nodded in sympathy. "I've seen her operate. But you could have mentioned it to us," he added reasonably.

"Yeah. I should have. I was afraid you wouldn't want to go, and I sure as hell didn't want to go out alone with her. She's . . . I don't know. Anyway, I had to go out to pick up Petie, and I'm sticking to the original schedule. Now let's eat." He motioned toward the table where there was a coffee pot. "Help yourselves."

The galley was sparkling with copper fixtures, everything so compact and well planned that in an area hardly more than five feet square there was a two-burner stove, a refrigerator, sink, cabinets.

The table and a right-angled bench could seat half a dozen people. Behind it there was a wall separating off another stateroom, and beyond that the pilot's cabin. The boat was moving slowly, on automatic pilot while Dino did the galley chores.

Charlie began to wonder how much it all cost. Opposite the galley was what Dino called the saloon, with three chairs and a bench-sofa and coffee table. The walls were mellow, rich paneling. Teak? Mahogany? It looked expensive.

Dino served up ham and scrambled eggs and fluffy cinnamon rolls.

"Are you going to call her?" Charlie asked.

"She said she'd have coffee a little later. I think she's mad as hell." He looked at Constance, who was eating nothing, just drinking the coffee. "Look, I'm sorry. But the boat's big enough for four people not to get in each other's way. You two just stay in the stern, do a little fishing. I'll see that she stays forward, or up in the flybridge. I can run the boat from the pilot's bridge down here, or from up there either way."

After breakfast he showed them the pilot's bridge. "Dual controls," he said, "for the two diesels. This is clutch, this is throttle. Midway, that's idle, forward for going ahead, back to reverse, down all the way to stop. That's all there is to that. And the wheel here, just like a car, only you allow for more time and space for everything to happen. Okay?" He glanced around at the instrument panel. "You won't need more than that. In case Charlie gets a big one, I might have you run us while I help him. Oh, yeah, here's the starter, just in case you need it. Just flip it on."

Again Charlie was struck by the simplicity and the beauty of the boat. He was very much afraid the Skaggs boys were running more than fish out of the gulf waters. And he told himself to forget it, he wanted no part of the drug business; he was retired.

Dino got Charlie baited up, urged Constance again to give it a try, then went below. In a few minutes, he said, they'd start trolling. Constance looked at the water, almost too bright to stand; there were long, smooth swells, and now and then there was a soft plop as water broke against the side of the boat. She had grown used to the lesser slaps of water; the larger sounds broke the rhythm. Something splashed out of sight behind her and she wondered, prey or predator? The sea stretched out endlessly, formless, exactly the same everywhere, and yet different under the lazy swells. It would be terrifying to be out there alone, she thought; they were so small and the sea was so big. Another splash sounded and this time she swiveled to see what it was. She could not even see ripples. Prey or predator? She caught a movement from the corner of her eye, turned farther, and looked into the eyes of June Oliveira up on the flybridge. She's frightening because her expression never changes, Constance thought, and abruptly swung back around. She felt cold in the hot sunlight. She should have known that woman would be aboard. It had been easy enough to figure out that Bramley had planned his accident to take place at sea.

"Why didn't you argue with Dino at least a little?" she asked bitterly.

"Wouldn't have done any good. I'm afraid we're on a drug run, honey. I think he uses the fishing charter business as a cover. So let's just play it real cool. I'm in the insurance racket and you're a housewife. Period. We don't know from nothing. Right?"

"Oh, for heaven's sake!" she muttered helplessly, and stared at the brilliant water until her eyes smarted.

Dino brought her a big floppy straw hat and a long-sleeved shirt. "You're going to cook," he said. "You're already burning. People as pale as you are can get sun poisoning without ever getting warm."

"Thanks," she said, and he ducked away quickly, back to the pilot's bridge. Soon the boat began to move a little faster through the calm waters. "He's hard to hate," Constance said, tying the ribbon of the hat under her chin.

Charlie nodded, and thought, but he's a drug runner. Sometimes he tried to sort out the criminals he hated most on a scale from one to ten. Usually he put arsonists first, but he knew that was prejudice. He had had to get transferred from the arson squad when he had started having nightmares, had smelled smoke where there wasn't any, and suspected smoldering rags behind all locked doors. Child molesters came next, then rapists, and drug pushers, murderers . . . But he always changed the order even as he composed it because some of them obviously had to be second, and they couldn't all be. He glanced at Constance; her eyes were closed.

He woke up with a start. Dino had touched his shoulder. "Sorry," Charlie muttered. Constance was coming awake also.

"Doesn't matter," Dino said. "If you'd got a strike that would have waked you up pretty fast. Just wanted to tell you, might as well reel in. I'm taking us to a place to try some reef fishing. Might get something there. Good place for scuba diving." He looked at Charlie hopefully, shrugged when Charlie shook his head.

Dino sent June Oliveira down from the flybridge, and then the boat stood up and raced through the water. Charlie nodded at Constance. He had suspected there was a lot more power in the engines than they had witnessed before.

June Oliveira braced herself in the doorway to the galley; she looked terrified. Constance remembered what Lou Bramley had said about her: she did nothing dangerous. Obviously she thought what they were doing was dangerous. Constance was glad to see that she did have at least one other expression.

When Dino cut the engines and came down he looked happy, as if this was what he liked to do, open it up and roar, leaving a wide white wake behind them as straight as a highway through a desert.

"Lunchtime," he said cheerfully. "Then you'll get a snapper or two, Charlie. Bet you a ten spot on it."

He would have won. Charlie caught a red snapper within the first fifteen minutes of fishing over the reefs.

"It's a beauty," Dino said. "Catch its mate and that's our supper. Go ashore, build a little fire, roast them on a spit. That's good eating, Charlie. Just you wait and see." He was keeping an eye on the progress of the sun, evidently timing their day carefully. "You've got half an hour." He watched Charlie bait his hook, patted him on the back, and left with the first snapper, to put it on ice. The boat was again on automatic, moving slowly over the shadows of the reefs.

Charlie was excited and pleased with himself, Constance knew, standing close to him, watching the water. The live fish on his line went this way and that, and vanished. Charlie was muttering that it was pulling, maybe he had something, no it was just the bait fish. Something splashed behind them. Charlie let out more line as his bait fish headed deeper.

Constance was watching, looking down, when she caught a glimpse of a larger motion. She jerked her head around and saw Dino in the water behind them.

"Charlie! Look!"

He dropped his rod and grabbed at one of the life preservers clamped in place against the side of the cabin. "Get this thing back there!" he yelled to Constance as he moved.

She raced through the cabin, through the salon to the pilot's bridge. Put it on manual, she thought clearly, and flipped the automatic control off. Pull the control back to reverse. She pulled the lever back, heard a slight click as it passed neutral, and then the engines stopped. She groaned and hit the lever back up to the neutral position, aligned the clutch control. She pushed the starter, nothing.

She repeated it several times before she gave up and ran back to the stern where Charlie was standing rigidly, staring at the water behind them. Their momentum was pushing them forward slower and slower.

"I killed the engines," Constance said, tearing off her hat, loosening her sneaker with her other hand.

"What are you doing?" Charlie asked. His voice sounded strange, forced.

"I'm going in after him."

Charlie's hand clamped painfully on her arm. He was still looking at the water. Now Constance looked. There was the life preserver, nearly two hundred feet away, bobbing easily. There was no sign of Dino.

"I almost hit him with it," Charlie said in that strained, thick voice. "He could have reached out and touched it, caught it. He never made a motion toward it. He wasn't even trying to swim."

"I can still get him up," Constance said, jerking her arm, trying to get loose.

"No! He went down like a stone. He's on the bottom, already dead. He wasn't even struggling."

Constance felt her knees threaten to buckle. She turned to look at the flybridge: June Oliveira was standing up there facing the life preserver. Her eyes were closed.

"She did it," Constance whispered. "She killed him."

"Take it easy, honey," Charlie said. "She was up there the whole time." He turned away from the water now. "He must have had a stroke or something, couldn't move, couldn't swim. He didn't even yell. Maybe he was already dying before he fell in."

"You don't just fall overboard," Constance said, watching June Oliveira, who hugged herself, opening her eyes. She looked at Constance; her expression was as blank as ever. She moved to the ladder and descended from the flybridge.

"I think I lie down now," she said.

They watched her enter the cabin. "Let's go up there and see if we can get this boat started," Charlie said. He sounded tired. Wordlessly Constance started up the ladder to the flybridge.

The flybridge was built over the main cabin; the front was enclosed, the rear open with another fighting chair. There were wraparound windows and a control panel exactly like the one below, the same wheel, dual controls for the engines, automatic pilot. The same array of dials and indicators that neither of them understood. Charlie sat down behind the wheel and looked at the controls: the automatic was turned to Off, it must have moved when Constance turned it below. The dual controls were both at midpoint, in neutral. He turned on the starter. Dead.

"I thought it might be like a car engine," Constance said. "Maybe I flooded it when I moved the throttle too fast." She knelt down and tried to see behind the control panel. It was all enclosed.

"What are you looking for?"

"A wire. She must have pulled a wire loose or something."

Charlie shook his head. "Knock it off, honey. I'm telling you, she was nowhere near him. Let's go find the engines. Maybe we can tell if it's flooded, or if a battery connection is loose."

"See if the radio works," Constance said.

Charlie had no idea what most of the switches and knobs were for, but he did know how to operate a radio. It was dead.

At three Charlie called June Oliveira to the galley. He had made coffee, and was drinking a beer. Constance watched the other woman warily when she drew near to sit at the small table. She said she wanted nothing when Charlie offered her a drink.

"We're in a spot," Charlie said. "I don't think it's especially serious, but still, there it is. I can't make this boat go. I don't know how and neither does my wife. Do you know how to run it?"

She shook her head. "It is the first time I am on a boat."

"I thought so. Okay. So we have to wait for help. We have no electricity, and that means no lights. Someone may spot us before dark, if not, we'll have to take shifts and keep a watch. I'm afraid we might be run down, or we might miss a passing ship or small boat. I found a flare gun to signal with if we see anything." He poured more coffee for Constance.

"His brother, he is expecting us," June Oliveira said. "When we do not arrive, he informs the authorities. Yes? They come for us then."

Charlie shrugged. He was trying to place her accent. Not Spanish, not anything he had heard before. Portuguese? He did not think so; there had been some Sao Paulo students at the crime lab, eight, nine years ago, and they had not sounded like her. He said, "Eventually they'll come, but I doubt they'll hear from Petie right away." Little brother, he thought, would have to hide something first, bury it, sink it at sea, do something. Depending on where he was, little brother might have to be rescued also. "We'd better prepare for an all-night wait, and a daylight search tomorrow."

"If there is more beer . . . " June Oliveira said then.

He took one from the refrigerator and handed it to her. Already the ice was melting. They would have to eat before dark, before the butter melted, the other food spoiled.

"If you two will start keeping a watch now," he said, "I'll gather up everything I can think of that we might need during the night. I found one flashlight only, so we'd better have things in one place." He handed a pair of binoculars to Constance. "You take the flybridge. Yell out if you see anything. Miss Oliveira, you go forward and keep an eye open for a ship. Later we'll switch around, choose lots or something. Okay?"

Constance watched her go around the cabin to the forward deck before she started up the ladder to the flybridge. Charlie handed up the coffee and the binoculars to her.

"Be careful," she said softly.

Charlie felt a twinge of impatience with her. He nodded and turned to his task. When Constance got a notion, he thought, she played it to the bitter end, no matter how ridiculous it was. He scanned the water briefly before going back inside. He could no longer see the life preserver and he was glad even though he could not tell if the boat had drifted, or if the wind had simply taken the doughnut away. He was glad it was not there, a constant reminder that he had done nothing at all, and had prevented Constance from trying to do anything. She swam like a fish; she might have saved him. He did not believe it, but the thought came back over and over. He remembered his own feeling of terror at the idea of letting Constance go over the side after Dino: what if she had gotten out there and just stopped swimming, as Dino had done? He knew he could not have helped her, he would have watched her look of incomprehension, fear, disbelief . . .

Angrily he jerked up a life jacket and stood holding it. Where to put things? Not on the table, which they would be using off and on. Not in the saloon, probably they would take turns sleeping on the couch. Finally he opened the door to the stateroom he and Constance had shared the night before. He put the life jacket on her bunk and went out to continue his search, a first-aid kit, what else? He was not certain what they might need, he could make no list and then go search. All he could do was collect things he saw that looked useful. He felt the same helplessness now that he had experienced when Constance had said they did not even know what switch to throw to put out an anchor to stop their drift. He did not know where they were, how fast they might be drifting, or in what direction, not necessarily pushed by the wind, although they might be; it was also possible that they were in a current from the Florida straits. He simply did not know.

Constance made a hurried scan of the horizon in all directions, and then a slower search. She saw birds, and she saw porpoises in the distance. A few hours ago the sight would have thrilled her, seeing them leaping; now it was depressing that only the creatures of the sea were out there. Charlie clearly thought Dino's death was the result of a seizure of some sort; she knew she would not be able to convince him of anything else. Up here, examining the problem logically, she agreed that it had been an accident, but she rejected the logic. She knew June Oliveira had been responsible even if she did not understand how she had done it. She knew, and accepted, that she would not have been able to save Dino. It would not have been allowed. She could not see the woman from on the flybridge, and she could not hear Charlie moving about. She bit her lip and strained to hear something, but there was only the slap, slap of water on the side of the boat, and a faraway bird call. She went down the ladder and met Charlie coming up from the cabin.

"What's wrong? Did you see a ship?"

"No. I just came down for my hat." She had left it in the saloon. She retrieved it and started up again. "Charlie, say something to me now and then, or whistle, or something. Okay?" His nod was perfunctory and absent-minded. He was tying a self-inflating rubber raft to the side rail, out of the way of traffic, but available if they needed it. A second raft was already tied in place. Constance returned to her post and did the entire search again.

The sun was getting lower; a couple more hours of daylight, she thought, and then the long night wondering what Oliveira would do next, if she could do anything as long as Constance was awake and watching her. She leaned over the side of the flybridge and called, "Charlie, is there plenty of water?"

"Yeah, I checked. And plenty of coffee," he added, as if reading her mind. She smiled slightly and looked at the sea.

They should eat something before it started to get dark, she decided a little later. Oliveira could come up here while she made something; she started down the ladder again. There was only the gentle sloshing sound of water. Charlie was still below, maybe swearing at the engines . . . She took a step toward the cabin door, paused, and instead went to the side of the cabin and looked forward. June Oliveira was standing near the cabin windows, and beyond her, ten feet away, Charlie was swinging one leg over the rail.

Soundlessly Constance dashed the fifteen feet to the woman and hit her with her shoulder, knocking her flat. She kept going and grabbed Charlie, who was clinging to the rail, dangling over the water. She hauled on Charlie's arms and he pulled himself up, got purchase with his foot and heaved himself back aboard. He was the color of putty.

June Oliveira was starting to sit up.

"You move another muscle and I'm going to throw you overboard!" Charlie yelled at her. He unfastened the inflatable raft he had secured to the rail and tied the rope to one of the loops on it. Holding it over the side, he pulled the release and then dropped it, keeping the rope in his hand, letting it out as the raft fell and settled.

"Now get up!" he ordered. "Over the side, down the ladder. Move!"

She shook her head. "I am hurt! Your wife attacked me! I think my back is broken."

"You'd better be able to swim, lady. You go down under your own power, or I'm going to throw you in. Right now!"

"You are crazy," she said.

"Hold this," Charlie said, handing the end of the rope to Constance, taking a step toward the woman. She was on her knees, and now she scrambled up, clinging to the side of the boat, then to the rail. She looked terrified, the way she had looked when Dino had roared at full speed over the water. "There's the ladder," Charlie said, stopping within reach of her. She backed away, stepped up the two steps to the rail, and over it, down the ladder. Charlie maneuvered the raft closer and she stepped into it, clutching the sides. "Get down low," he said. "I'm towing you to the other side." He didn't wait for her to crouch down, but yanked on the rope and hauled the raft, bumping and rubbing against the boat hull, around to the other side where he tied it securely.

"Let's go below," he said to Constance then. "I sure as God want a drink."

Silently he poured bourbon for them both, added some shrunken ice cubes, and took a drink from his.

A long shudder passed over him and his knees felt weak. He sat down and pulled Constance to his side, put his arm around her shoulders and held her tight against him.

"Oh, Charlie," she said softly, "I'm afraid we've caught ourselves a boojum."

He held her tighter. He still saw himself going into the water, not struggling, not trying to swim, going under, down, down . . . .

"I think you're right," he said. His voice was so normal that few people would have detected the difference, the slight huskiness, the almost too careful spacing of words.

"Do you know what happened to you?" Constance asked. She drank also and welcomed the warmth; she had become icy cold now that the woman was in the raft, and she and Charlie were side by side.

"I was going to go over just as if I had decided to do it. I was doing it and I was watching myself do it, watching her watching me, pushing me, not even trying not to go, not even trying to resist. I was just doing it."

She nodded. Neither of them said, *like Dino.* "What are we going to do?"

"Remember when I read 'The Hunting of the Snark' to Jessica? Remember what she said when I asked what she'd do if she caught a boojum?"

Constance nodded again. Jessica had said the only thing to do was cut it loose and run.

"It might come to that," Charlie said grimly. "It just might." He took the last swallow of his bourbon, then pushed the glass away. He got up and put the coffee pot on the burner to heat it. "Start with the first time you saw her, the first thing Bramley said about her," he said. "You were right, honey. I should have paid attention. Let's try to make some sense out of it now."

He stopped her when she told again how Lou Bramley had bypassed her to sit at a table with June Oliveira. "Exactly what did he do?"

"You know the wide doors? He stood there looking around until he spotted me and he started toward my table." She closed her eyes visualizing it. "Then he looked past me and he didn't look at me again. His face changed a little, became set, almost like a sleepwalker, or someone in trance." She opened her eyes. "She did it then too. I was blind not to realize."

"You couldn't have known," Charlie said. "Then what?"

"I waited a minute or two. Then I decided to spoil it for her, to join them. I got up and started toward their table. . . ." She stopped, remembering. "I thought it was my decision to take a walk instead. Oh, my God, I wasn't even aware . . . I didn't even wonder about it!"

Charlie squeezed her shoulder. "Try to remember exactly how it was, honey. I think it may be important. What was he doing when you started to walk?"

"His back was to me. He was staring at the water. I got pretty close to them before I changed my . . . He hadn't moved, I'm sure.

Then I turned right." She stopped, eyes closed. "I think he might have stood up, there was a motion. I just caught it from the corner of my eye, and I was thinking how hot it was on the sand. It was sunny, and I had been trying to avoid the hot sun. I went a little farther and decided I didn't want to walk after all."

"You were thinking it was hot, all that, close to their table?"

She nodded. "What is it, Charlie?"

"She couldn't hold both of you," he said. "She got you past the table and lost him, grabbed him back and lost you. What do you think?"

She considered it and nodded. "But we can't be certain. We can't count on it."

"No, but it's something." The other thing she had said, that the woman did nothing dangerous, alarmed him. No doubt she thought it was very dangerous out there on the raft with night coming on fast. She might even be right; it could be dangerous. He didn't know.

"I'd better start making sandwiches," Constance said. "We're all going to be hungry eventually."

"Okay, but keep talking. What else was there?"

She talked as she rummaged in the refrigerator and the cabinets. When she stopped again, Charlie was staring fixedly at the tabletop, deep in thought. She did not interrupt him, but continued to assemble the sandwiches.

It did not make any sense to him. If she had that kind of power, to control people like that, why use it in such a perverse way? Murder was so commonplace, never really dull, but not exciting either; it was always sad, always futile, always the action of ultimate failure. It was the final admission that there was no solution to a problem, no human solution. But no one needed her kind of power to commit murder. A gun, a knife, poison, a brick, a fire . . . he had seen them all; death that looked accidental—a fall, car exhaust in a closed garage, a leaky gas stove, overdoses of everything that could be swallowed. All filthy, all irreversible, all committed by ordinary people for ordinary reasons: money, sex, revenge, greed. . . . All committed without her kind of power. That was the puzzle. Why use such a gift for something so mundane? And why out here in God knew what part of the Gulf? She could be knocking people off every day of the week—running them in front of trains, making them jump from high places, forcing them to put bullets through their brains. Who would suspect? Each and every one would go down as accidental, or suicide.

He remembered what Lou Bramley had said, that she had known

he was going to die and wanted to watch. He nodded.

Constance, seeing the nod, stopped all movement, waiting, but Charlie continued to stare through the tabletop.

Bramley had been broadcasting death and she had picked it up somehow. She had planned to watch for whatever insane pleasure that gave her, and she had been cheated. Again Charlie nodded. She had had her death through murder, not suicide. And she planned to kill the witnesses. Now he shook his head. No one had witnessed anything. What could he or Constance say that could damage her? She could make a better case against them. Of course, if she was a psychopath, none of the best reasoning in the world would apply to her. He rejected that also. She was the boojum, an *it*, not like other people. He could not fathom her motives in either event—a whacko, or something inhuman. And, he thought, motives were not the issue. What she might try next was the only issue now. She had tried to kill him, damn near succeeded, and she no doubt would try again.

But she had not come out here to kill, he said to himself, and he held onto that one thought as the only clue he had about her, the only thing he was reasonably certain about. If the original plan had worked, Bramley would be dead now, a legitimate suicide passing for accident, and she and Dino would be back ashore. Their stories would have been accepted: Dino was well known; the insurance would have entered into it. Finis. Dino's death was a different matter. No one would believe he had fallen off his own boat in a dead calm, in the first place. And it was less plausible to suggest that he had not got back aboard even if he had managed to fall. Although no one could prove anything else, no one would ever believe that story. What if there were others, like her, who would know the story he and Constance could tell was true? His skin prickled all over at the thought that his people would never believe his story, but that her people, if she had people, would.

He was certain she planned to be the sole survivor of a ghastly tragedy. No one knew he and Constance were aboard. If they vanished, no one would know that. The contract would be found with Bramley's name, and he was in New York, out of it. She could say anything to account for Dino's disappearance, and he was the only one she would have to account for actually.

Constance froze in the motion of cutting through a sandwich, Charlie lifted his head and listened. June Oliveira was calling them in a shrill, panic-stricken voice.

Then went out together, staying close to each other. Constance still carried the butcher knife.

"There is a shark! I saw it! You can not keep me out here! I will stay in the little room. You lock the door. Please, I did not do nothing. You know I did not!"

In the west a spectacular sunset was blossoming; the light had turned deep pink, making June Oliveira look flushed, almost ruddy, very normal, ordinary, and very frightened.

"Who are you?" Constance demanded.

"I see him starting to climb over the rail, and I am petrified. I cannot move. I am terrified of water. I can not to help him or call out or anything. I am coward. I am sorry."

"You don't just watch them die, do you?" Constance said. "You weren't watching Dino. Your eyes were closed. You feel it, experience it. Why? Why don't you feel your own people's deaths? Why ours?"

"She crazy," June Oliveira wailed to Charlie. "She crazy!"

"I saw you," Constance said. "You knew exactly when Dino died. We couldn't know, but you did. You planned to experience Lou's death. You come here to feel death without dying yourselves, don't you? Do your people ever die? Just by accident, don't they? Isn't that why you're so terrified of water, of speeding, of anything that might be dangerous?"

"Please give me jacket, or sweater. I am cold. So afraid," June Oliveira moaned.

"For God's sake," Charlie said and turned away. "I'll get her jacket."

"How many of you are there?" Constance asked furiously. "How many murders do you commit? How many accidents do you cause?"

The woman was huddled down, her arms wrapped about herself. Suddenly Constance realized what she had done; she had separated them. She turned to see Charlie in the narrow passage between the rail and the cabin, coming toward her, carrying the heavy gaff, the iron hook Dino had said they used on the big ones. Charlie's face was peaceful, relaxed, the way it was when he was asleep.

Constance put the knife to the rope tethering the raft. "Let him go or I'll cut you loose! You'll drift away. He can't bring you back, he doesn't know how." She began to cut.

She stopped the sawing motion and watched as if from a great distance as the knife turned in her hand, began to move toward her midsection. In the stomach, she thought, so death wouldn't be too fast. There would be time to feel it all, to know it was happening. . . .

Charlie leaped at her, grabbed the knife and threw it out into the water. His hand dripped blood.

Constance sagged, then straightened. "My God, oh, my God!

You're hurt! Let's go fix it." Neither of them looked at the woman in the raft as they hurried away, back inside the cabin.

"What are we going to do?" Constance whispered. "Charlie, what can we do? We can't even cut her loose!"

"Get the first-aid kit," Charlie said calmly. "You'll need the flashlight. The kit's on your bed. Bring a clean towel too."

Constance snatched up the flashlight and ran to the stateroom for the kit and towel. When she returned, Charlie was washing the blood from his hand. She dried and bandaged it and neither spoke until she was done.

"I'm going to kill her," Charlie said. He reached out and gently touched the shirt Constance had on. There was a slash in it; she had not even noticed, had not realized how close it had been.

This was why some people murdered, Charlie thought, because there really was no solution, no human solution. How easy it was to step across that line. He felt as if he had always known that, had denied knowing it, had pretended it was not true, when of course it had been true from the beginning. When he had transferred from the arson squad it had been because he had dreamed too many times that he was the one arranging the materials, pouring the oil or the gasoline, setting the match. The thrill of the pursuer, the thrill of the pursued, who could tell how different they were? Now that he had crossed that imaginary line, that arbitrary line that each cop drew for himself, he knew the thrill was the same, the desperation the same, the fear; it was all the same.

"We can't cut her loose," he said in that deceptively calm voice. "So we cut ourselves loose. We have to go out in the other raft, get the hell away from her. She'll try again, maybe soon. Before it gets much darker." He glanced about the galley. "Start packing up everything you think we might need for tonight and tomorrow. We might not be picked up for hours, maybe a couple of days. Fill whatever you can find with water."

Thank God she didn't argue, he thought, going into the stateroom. She knew their chances of escaping as well as he did, knew their only chance was in getting distance between them and June Oliveira. He lifted the mattress of his bunk; foam, he thought with disgust. There was a plywood board, and beneath it there were cabinets with linens. He nodded. It would do. He cut a circle out of the foam mattress with his pocket knife and tucked the extra piece under the pillow on the other bed. He had seen a can of charcoal starter in a cabinet in the galley; he went out to get it. He took the flashlight back with the can. He soaked the plywood board and let it air out before he replaced the mattress. In the hole he now put a folded towel and then added a layer of crumpled toilet paper, then another towel, this one folded in such a way that the paper was exposed in the center of it. He studied it for a minute and sighed. The gasoline fumes were gone, the odor so faint that he might not have noticed it if he were not sniffing. In one of the cabinets in the saloon he had seen cigarettes. He went to the saloon and found the new package and opened it, lighted a cigarette with the flame from the stove. Constance was filling a plastic water bottle, a collapsible gallon jug. There were two at the bottom of the stairs, already filled. She looked startled at the cigarette, but she still asked no questions.

"About ready?" Charlie asked.

She nodded. "It's getting dark fast."

"Yes. Come on, let's tell her our plans."

"Charlie . . . " She stopped; there was not enough time to spell it all out. She followed him to the door.

Charlie went to the corner of the cabin and yelled, "You, you can have the goddam boat! We're taking off in the other raft. Before we go I'm going to toss the portable ladder over your side so you can climb aboard. Just leave us alone and let us take off. Is it a deal?"

He puffed the cigarette hard. It was not yet dark, but within half an hour it would be. Already the water looked solid, impenetrable, and there were two stars in the deep violet sky. She must be calculating her chances of getting one of them before dark, making the other bring her aboard. He was not even sure she could make someone do anything as complicated as that; she was not a telepath. Her power was cruder, a total assault, a complete takeover. She could not read their thoughts, he said to himself, praying it was true.

"If you leave the flashlight. Put it on the flybridge, turned on so I can see it." She sounded calmer, and was controlling her accent and syntax better, but her voice was still tremulous.

He let out his breath. "Okay. We're taking provisions with us, water and stuff. It'll take us a few minutes, ten maybe."

He nodded to Constance. "Let's get the life jackets and other stuff over by the ladder."

As Constance began to carry things from the cabin to the railing Charlie entered the stateroom again. He lighted a second cigarette from the first and put them both very carefully on top the paper in the hole in the mattress. He pulled the sheet over it, and the bedspread, with ripples in it for air to pass through easily. For years he had known how easy it would be, how well he would be able to do it. He put the extra life jackets on that bed, and he was through.

He left the stateroom door open when he went into the cabin. One last thing he had to get, he thought, almost leisurely, and he went to the drawer where he had seen an assortment of thread and needles. He chose the largest needle, a darning needle, or a sail-mending needle; it was four inches long and only slightly less thick than an icepick. He stuck it through his shirt. Constance returned for the last of the items she had put aside, the bag of sandwiches.

"Listen," he said to her softly. "We'll put the raft out, make sure the paddles are in it, and then load. While you're putting the flashlight on the flybridge, I'm going to swim around the boat. The last thing you do is hang the ladder over the side; make sure it's secure. We don't want her to get suspicious now. Then you get in the raft and start paddling to the front end of the boat. You pick me up there and we paddle like hell."

"What are you going to do?"

He pointed to the needle. "Puncture her escape route."

Constance shook her head and began to strip. "That's my department," she said. "You'd never make it in time, and you splash like a puppy. Same plan, different performers."

"No!" He saw her, arms crossed over her chest, sinking, sinking....

"Yes! Let's move!" She was making a bundle of her clothes. She had on only her bra and panties. Now she reached out and took the needle and put it through the top of the bra. "You know the only way it'll work is if I do that part. You know that. We don't dare have her out in the water alive. We have no idea how far she can reach."

He pulled her to him and kissed her hard, and then they hurried to get the raft into the water, get it loaded. Only one quadrant of the sky was still light now; to the east and sky and sea merged in blackness.

"Arrange it any way you can," Charlie said, nodding to her, when they were through. She slipped from the raft soundlessly and vanished into the dark water. "That looks good enough for now. When I get in we can shift things around some. I'll put the flashlight up there, and then give her the ladder. You okay?"

It was all taking much longer than he had realized it would, he thought bleakly. What if smoke began to pour from the cabin? What if she got suspicious, caught Constance down there in the water? What if she took this as her last chance to get them both? He climbed to the flybridge and put the flashlight down, shining toward the stern, away from where Constance might be surfacing. What if there really had been a shark? He felt weak with fear; his hands were trembling so hard he could scarcely hold the rail as he left the flybridge to get the ladder.

Constance surfaced at the prow of the boat and waited. There was the ladder, and Charlie was running away to the other side. June Oliveira had to haul herself in hand over hand to reach the ladder; she started to climb. Constance sank below the surface again and swam to the raft. She lifted her face only enough to get air, then went under and pulled out the needle and stuck it into the raft. The raft bobbed and she stopped moving, afraid the woman would be alarmed, turn around. She stuck the needle in three more times before she had to surface for air. The next time she went under she swam toward the prow of the boat, praying that Charlie would be there by now.

When Charlie first started to paddle, he found himself moving away from the boat at right angles. Frantically he pulled with one paddle until he bumped the boat. Keeping against the hull, using one paddle only, he finally got to the front end. Where was she? She should be here by now, he thought with despair, and she appeared at the side of the raft. He grabbed her arm and hauled her in, and she began to pull on her clothes as fast as she could. She was shivering hard. Before she got her shirt buttoned, Charlie was putting the life jacket on her. He was wearing his already. As soon as she had the life jacket tied, she took her place by him, took up the paddle and they both began to row hard. The raft seemed to be mired in tar, but gradually they pulled away from the boat, and now Charlie could see a light bobbing in the windows of the cabin, then the pilot's cabin, stern. She was checking it out, as he had thought she might. She went to the flybridge and in a minute or two the boat's engines started up.

Constance groaned and pulled harder on her paddle. It was no use, she thought dully. She would run them down, watch them die anyway, feel them die.

"We have to stay behind the boat," Charlie said. "You know how to turn these things?"

"You push, I pull," Constance said, knowing it was no use. They could dodge for awhile, but eventually they would tire, or she would make one of them stop paddling, or something.

Slowly they made the raft go astern. The boat was not moving yet, the engines were idling. Now the lights came on. Constance blinked as the light hit them. "Charlie, she can back up!" she whispered.

"Christ!" He had forgotten.

The boat began to move forward, not very fast; the wake shook the small raft, tilting it high to one side. The boat left them behind, then started to come around. She turned too wide and straightened far to the right of the raft. She had switched on a searchlight now, was playing it back and forth, looking for them. She seemed not to realize how wide her turn had been; the light came nowhere near them. It stopped moving.

Constance watched fearfully. The boat looked so close. The engines were so loud. She felt herself go blank, felt sleep-heavy, immobilized. When it passed, the light began to move again, this time swinging around to focus on them.

"She reached me," Constance said tonelessly. "We can't hide from her."

Why didn't the damn boat start burning? He knew it had to burn. He visualized the fire that had to be smoldering along the bed board, in the cabinet under the bed. The towels should be blazing by now. The boat was turning slowly; she was being careful. She had all the time in the world, she seemed to be telling them, keeping them pinned by the blinding light, keeping them waiting for her next move. Charlie wondered if she laughed. If she ever laughed.

She was steering with one hand, holding the light with the other, not letting either go to increase her speed. The throb of the engines did not change, only grew louder.

Constance began to pull on her paddle. "At least let's make her work for it," she said grimly. Charlie pulled hard, sending them on the beginning of another circle. Then suddenly the light made an arc, swung wildly away, up, down, off to the other side.

"I'll be damned," he said, pleased. Smoke was rolling from the cabin windows. He began to pull on the paddle again, harder now. "We should try to get some more distance from it," he said.

Silently they rowed, not making very much gain, and they watched the boat. The smoke had lessened. Constance was afraid June Oliveira had put the fire out already. Charlie felt almost smug; he knew the smoldering had turned into blazing, there would be less smoke, more heat, more fire. When the first flame showed on the side of the boat, he said, "I think we should get down in the bottom of this thing, as flat as we can." It would blow, he knew, and he did not know how much of an explosion it would be, what kind of shock there would be, if they were too close. He hoped June Oliveira was tossing water on the flames, that she had not thought of the beautiful fire equipment on board, or of abandoning the boat. He had not seen her since the powerful spotlight had come on.

He and Constance curled up in the bottom of the raft. "Try to keep your ears covered," he said. He raised himself enough to continue to watch, his hands cupped over his ears. Flames were shooting out every window now, licking up around the flybridge. When the explosion came, it was not as loud or as violent as he had thought it would be. A fireball formed, and vanished almost instantly, and the boat erupted in a geyser of fiery objects; the lights went off, and now there was only a low fire that was being extinguished very fast as the boat settled, began to slide under the water. They could hear a furious bubbling, then nothing, and the fire was gone. The sea was inky black.

Constance was on her knees clutching the side of the raft. She shuddered and Charlie put his arm about her, held her close. "Did she get off?" she whispered.

"I don't know yet."

They waited in silence as their eyes adapted to the darkness. Charlie could see nothing out there; he could hardly even see Constance. She was little more than a pale shadow. He strained to hear.

When it came, it sounded so close, he felt he could reach out and touch the woman. She sounded as if she was weeping. "Why do you do that? Why? Now we all die in the sea!"

He could not tell her direction, distance, anything at all. The voice seemed close, all around him.

Constance put her head down, pressing her forehead against the rounded side of the raft. "We should have slashed the other raft, scuttled it."

He had been afraid that if she had not believed she had an escape at hand, she might have used the impressive firefighting equipment. She might have been able to put out the fire with it. She might have known about the emergency hatch in the tiny engine room with the simple instructions: *Open in case of fire.* It would have flooded the engines and the fuel tanks with sea water; the boat would have been immobilized, but it would be afloat. Worse, he had feared that if she had been trapped, she might have reached out and killed them both instantly. She had been in the raft, she knew it was comparatively safe; she had to trust it again. How long would it take for the air to leak out enough? He did not know. He could hear a paddle splashing awkwardly.

"Do you remember where we put the flare gun?" he whispered. One to light up the scene, he thought; the next one aimed at her.

Constance began to grope for the gun. There was a loud splash close by. June Oliveira screamed shrilly.

"Sharks!" Constance yelled. She knew sharks did not make splashes, did not leap from the water. Perhaps the porpoises had come to investigate the explosion. Maybe a sea bird had dived. Her hand closed on the gun and she handed it to Charlie.

"First Charlie," the woman called out. "Constance stay with me until morning. You are good swimmer. I saw you in water. Is possible I need you to swim for me."

She was talking to still her terror of the water, the sharks she believed to be circling her, to break the silence. Constance recognized that shrillness, the clipped words; Oliveira was panic-stricken.

"Sometimes they come up under you and graze the boat," Constance yelled. "They're so rough, they puncture the rubber, and you don't even know it until too late. You can feel the sides of the raft getting soft, the top sinking in a little . . . "

Charlie was searching for the extra packet of flares. One was in the gun; he wanted a second to jam in and fire quickly before the light faded, while she was still dazed from the sudden glare.

"I've got it," he whispered finally. "Shield your eyes."

He fired straight up, and scanned the water. She was several hundred feet away, kneeling in the other raft, holding the paddle

with both hands, stilled by the unexpected light. He rammed the second flare into the gun, and then pitched forward, dropping the gun, not unconscious, but without muscle tone, unable to move.

Constance snatched up the paddle and started to row as hard as she could. She was stronger than the other woman, at least she could outdistance her.

"Stop!" Oliveira called. "Stop or I kill him now. I do not like it at this distance, but I do it."

Constance put the paddle down. The light had faded already; again there was only darkness, now even deeper, blacker. Charlie lay huddled in the bottom of the raft unmoving.

"Stay very still," the woman said. "I come to your little boat. You are right about many things. During the night you explain to me how you know, what makes you guess, so I tell my people."

"Why Bramley? People are dying all the time. Why him?"

"Because I know him. We seldom know them, the people who are dying. It is more interesting to know him."

The water remained quiet around them; there were only the splashes of her paddle. She was so inept it would take her a long time to cross the distance separating them. Constance nudged Charlie with her toe. He did not respond.

"Why don't you just hang around hospitals? People die there every hour, every day."

"They are drugged. Sometimes it is good." Her voice was getting firmer, losing its fearful note, as she narrowed the space between them, and the water remained still.

Constance nudged Charlie again. Move, she thought at him, please move, get up. "You come here and murder, kill people. Watch them suffer for your own amusement. Do you torture them to death to drag it out?"

"We are not uncivilized," the woman said sharply. "We do not kill; we participate. It does no harm."

"You killed Dino!"

There was silence, her paddle slapped the water, then again. "I expect the other one. I have only until Sunday. I will be forgiven."

Constance shuddered. She reached out and touched Charlie's face. She wanted to lie down by him, gather him in her arms, hold him.

The paddle hit, lifted, hit. And then it suddenly splashed very hard, and the woman screamed hoarsely. "My raft getting soft! It is punctured!"

Charlie stiffened even more under Constance's hand. *She* was using him as a beacon, homing in on him.

Constance picked up one of the water jugs and heaved it out toward the other raft. It made a loud noise when it hit the water.

"Sharks are all around us!" she yelled. The other paddle stopped and there was no sound. Constance groped for something else to throw, something heavy enough to make a noise, light enough to lift and heave. Her hand closed over the paddle. She lifted it silently and brought it down hard on the water. She screamed. "They're hitting our raft! Charlie, do something!"

Charlie began to stir; he pulled himself to his knees cautiously; the woman was letting go. Her terror was so great she could no longer hold him. From the other raft there were sounds of panicky rowing, she was simply beating the water with the paddle. Charlie and Constance began to row, saying nothing, trying to slip the plastic paddles into the water without a sound, pulling hard.

"It is sinking!" the woman screamed. "Help me!"

Constance screamed also, trying for the same note of terror. She screamed again, and then listened. The other woman was incoherent, screaming, screeching words that were not human language. Soon it all stopped.

For a long time they sat holding each other without speaking.

Now and then something splashed, now close to them, now farther away. They could see nothing.

In a little while, Charlie thought, he would fire the flare gun again, and periodically through the night repeat it. Someone would see. Maybe someone had seen the fire, was on the way already. He would have to think of a story to tell them—a fire at sea, Dino's going back after getting them into the raft. . . . He could handle that part. He had heard enough stories essentially like his, lies, excuses, reasonably enough put together to fool most people. He could do that.

And Constance was thinking: there would come a day when one or the other of them would start to doubt what had happened. What that one would remember was that they, together, had killed a crazy woman.

"She wasn't human," Charlie said, breaking the silence. And Constance knew he would be the one who would come awake at night, stare at the ceiling, and wonder about what they had done. She would have to be watchful for the signs, make him remember it exactly the way it had happened. And one day, she thought, one of them would say what neither had voiced yet: that woman had not been alone. There were others.

Charlie thought: they would live with this, knowing what they had done, that there were others out there, maybe not as murderous as this one had been, or maybe just like her. They could tell no one; no one would ever believe. Constance had her proof of that uncharted part of the psyche, and could not even use it.

"I think I dislocated my shoulder when I threw that jug out," Constance said, shifting in his arms. "I'm aching all over." And he knew his hand was bleeding through the bandage; it was throbbing painfully suddenly. He had forgotten about it. "In just a minute I'll see if there's a sling in the first-aid kit. I need a new bandage too." He felt her nod against his shoulder.

"Poor little miserable, helpless, vulnerable, hurt people," she sighed. "That's us. Adrift on an endless ocean as dark as hell. With a terminal case of life. But I wouldn't trade with them." Knowing you were gambling eternity, you wouldn't dare risk your life for someone you loved, she thought, trying to ignore the pain in her shoulder, down into her arm. You wouldn't dare love, she thought. You wouldn't dare. Period. Not far away something splashed.

Neither of them moved yet. It was enough for now to rest, to feel the solidity of the other, to renew the strength the last several hours had taken from them. Quietly they drifted on the dark sea.

ALIEN LOVER

art: Hilary Barta

by Ted Reynolds & William F. Wu

People wonder about collaborations: who does what? Each jointly-written story is different; in this particular case, Mr. Reynolds wrote the first draft, and Dr. Wu did the final version.

The semester had finally ended, but Alyne Wong and I both had jobs for the summer here at Belmont. She was a junior and I a sophomore, but we would both be waitresses when our jobs started during summer school. We had a week before that, though; and I spent most of the time gazing out the windows of the old house we shared. My favorite part of our college town was the immense Ohio greenery in June.

One evening I sat on the rim of the bathtub watching my housemate brush her hair in front of the mirror. Outside, groups of students moved up and down the street singing and calling out to each other, celebrating the end of the term.

"I," said Alyne, "have an alien lover."

"You," I said, "are out of your mind."

Alyne looked at me scornfully. "I wouldn't expect *you* to understand, Maggie." She flipped her straight black hair in dismissal and turned back to the mirror.

"There is no such thing," I stated flatly, "as an alien lover. If there were, he certainly wouldn't be at Belmont. And *if* he were, why do you think he'd be interested in you?"

Alyne's smile was a trifle chilly. Her brown eyes met mine in the mirror. "You think maybe he'd be more interested in *you?*"

I squirmed and looked down at the tiles on the floor. Alyne is moonlight and flowers; I'm all gawks and blotches. "Let's not quarrel, Alyne. I'm sorry. But you sound so serious, and really, it's all so silly."

"I *am* serious," said Alyne, unmollified. "Strek is not human. For one thing, he's far too good to be human." She brushed her shiny hair in angry sweeps.

Outside, a car passed honking continuously. Drunken revelers whooped and yelled.

"It's natural you attract him, Alyne." I was anxious to make up with her. "You're a really lovely person."

Alyne knew that. She went on brushing.

"Oh, don't be like that," I said. "I guess I'm just jealous, you know."

A wide smile bloomed on her face at last, and she swung to face me. "Poor little Maggie," she crooned. "I keep forgetting. You do have your troubles, don't you, getting any man to look at you; and here I am, parading my triumphs in front of you. Do forgive me. I *am* sorry."

She didn't look sorry. I forgave her.

"No, I'm sorry," I repeated, nervously flipping the tub drain on and off. "You wanted to share something very important and I just tried to cut you down. Maybe he is an alien. How should I know?

But if he's a superior being from outer space, how come he's only an undergraduate at Belmont?"

Alyne placed her hairbrush carefully on the sink and perched beside me on the bathtub. She reached out and patted my hands. "Poor Maggie," she said. "I am hard on you, aren't I? I'm just so excited. Listen, dear. Strek is just too good to be a mere man. I mean, *you* know what men are." She smiled conspiratorily, knowing very well I don't. "I admit I'm very lucky," she added unexpectedly. "He could have about any woman he wants. Oh, Maggie—it's my *dream,* to be loved by someone grand and mysterious—it's what I've lived for. To be loved by an alien!"

This was new. Even with the Schenectady trombonist and the Manhattan literary agent, she'd always made it quite clear that it was their privilege, not hers, which I thought might be one reason they weren't around any more. For a twenty-year-old, she was strong. She had always seemed to take relationships with men casually, but deep down she wanted an old-fashioned permanent one. This time I *was* worried.

"Tell me about him, Alyne. I won't interrupt."

"Come back to my room. He's due any minute."

I tagged along to her bedroom and flopped onto her pink bedspread. Little stuffed elephants and bears bounced around me. I noticed she'd replaced her picture of Wales with one of the Andromeda galaxy.

Alyne bent over her toiletry. "I met him in Hawkes's class. I'd noticed him from the beginning, because . . . well, he's different. You'll see. But I admit I never dreamed—"

"He *told* you he was from outer space?" I'd forgotten about not interrupting.

"Of course. Oh, not at once—just after he got to know me and trust me, one evening when I was at his place, helping him with his class notes."

"Helping him? The superior being?"

Alyne glared at me.

I pantomined abject apology.

"All right. He hasn't been here long, and of course he still has to pick up all the little details, like how to spell a lot of words and human history and Earth geography. Even our math. Strek says it's not quite as accurate as his. But considering he's only been on Earth for six months, I should think you'd be more amazed at what he *has* picked up, than joke about what he hasn't learned yet."

"Where does he come from? Which star?"

"It's not a star, it's a galaxy," she replied smugly. "And I don't know which one. It's too far to see from here." She tossed down her puff and rose. "He'll be here any second. You'll see."

"I don't suppose," I said, "that he's got any old photos from home I could see, does he?"

"Well, no," said Alyne. "You've got to realize that he's here more or less in secret. Ours is such a primitive world that it has to be carefully checked out before open contact can be made. So having hard *evidence* of where he's from would be plain stupid."

"And I suppose he can't give out any cancer cures or faster-than-light drives to us hicks, either."

"Of course not. He's not crazy."

I was silent a while. "Alyne Wong, I'd be the last person to try to run your life," I said quietly. "But it seems to me that you have no evidence except Strek's word that he is what he says. And if, just maybe if, by a weird chance, he happened to be lying . . . ."

Alyne wasn't angry. Instead, she laughed merrily. "Oh, silly Maggie, don't be . . . well, silly. Aliens aren't capable of lying."

And as she made that astounding assertion, the doorbell rang. She waltzed to the door of the room, pausing to toss back, "Besides, he's told me things no human could ever know."

"Such as?"

"Oh, how the fifth planet of Capricorn looks from its innermost moon . . . " Her voice faded as she hurried down the hall.

Alyne was the older sister I had never had. Now I was afraid she was in too deep for me to haul her out again. I didn't want to lose her to some fast-talking con man. And I didn't want her to be hurt.

I wandered into the front hall. The muffled thumping and whine of raucous music drifted from the house across the street. Alyne and her supposed alien lover were entangled together in the doorway in a manner I found all too disgustingly human. I cleared my throat.

"Oh, Maggie," said Alyne, as they unwrapped. "This is Strek."

"Good evening, Ms. Smythe," said Strek, smiling at me.

Strek was tall, well-built, blond. Well-groomed, well-dressed, and suave. A seducer if I ever saw one. And, as far as I could see, Earth human to the *n*th.

This was her dream alien, the one she had lived for.

"Good evening," I said, and stopped, making a sort of face. I didn't know if he was Mr. Strek or Strek Betelgeuse. Oh, hell. "Strek."

"We'll be late for the party," said Alyne.

"Not quite yet, Alyne," he said quietly, without looking away from me. "I must have a few words with Maggie." He came down the hallway and smiled faintly. "Alyne has told you about me, I believe."

Alyne squirmed. "Oh, no, Strek, I wouldn't—"

Strek turned and looked at her, rather sadly, I thought. "Alyne. You compound the error by lying about it. No matter; I am sure Ms. Smythe is a discreet woman. More discreet than you, Alyne? Do you wonder now that I cannot tell you . . . many things, when you cannot keep private even the simplest?"

"Oh, please forgive me, Strek, I didn't think. . . . "

Strek looked at her sternly and my soul wrenched to see Alyne, proud Alyne, so humbled. "You must *learn* to think," he said evenly. Then he smiled warmly in total forgiveness. "You will learn," he said magnificently. "I shall teach you."

"Oh, will you?" Alyne was overcome.

I felt sick.

Strek turned to me again, with the same confiding smile of warmth. "Maggie," he said softly. "You do not believe what Alyne has told you about me."

"Uh . . . well, it does seem unexpected that someone from some other world would be such a dead ringer for us Earthlings, look like us and talk like us . . . " and enjoy necking in the dark with us.

Strek laughed lightly. "Come, Maggie, with some seven billion inhabited worlds to choose from, we surely don't have to send some nine-headed hydra from the seas of Alpheratz to mingle with humans. My people are merely the nearest to your own from a very wide spectrum."

Okay, so he was ready for that particular question. Not a bad answer, of course. I didn't bother to ask my next question, knowing he would say that standards of beauty might easily be the same in such a similar species, too. Hence his admiration of Alyne would be no different from mine. Besides, I was afraid he'd hand out the usual crap about inner beauty being more important. Alyne has more inner strength than I have, too.

Strek reached out and placed his hand very lightly on my shoulder. "Maggie, to you it shouldn't make any difference where I come from. I know you wish her well. We love each other, Alyne and I." He smiled again, squeezed my shoulder, and turned back to Alyne. And then they were gone.

Strek was right that it didn't matter where he came from. He was a smooth talker and a slick operator and whether he came from L. A., California, or NGC 999, he was no good for Alyne. I had to get rid of him, if it wasn't too late.

My light was out, and I had been in bed for hours when Alyne returned, but I wasn't asleep. She tiptoed into her room and the light flicked on, a thin horizontal under her door. I rose quickly and crossed to it. She was moving things around with small thuds.

I knocked and opened the door simultaneously.

Alyne was on her knees in front of an open suitcase, clothes and personal articles piled about her. She looked back at me over her shoulder and froze a long moment. Guilt in beauty.

"Without telling me?" I said at last.

"Oh, Maggie, don't be angry. Be happy for me."

"Happy! You're wrecking your life, destroying yourself, abandoning me, over that . . . that . . . "

"Oh, Maggie, he really loves me. An alien loves me, out of all the billions of worlds. He wants to take me with him."

"Where, Chicago?" It was the nastiest place that came to mind.

"Space," she breathed. "To the stars."

"To a flea-bitten motel on the edge of town, more likely," I snapped. "Well, I—"

Alyne rose stiffly to her feet, black hair swaying, her fingers twitching as if they were considering strangulation. Her eyes spun fire. I felt ill with fear of her disapproval.

Alyne stabbed a forefinger with firearm intensity at where she figured my heart to be. "Maggie, you stay clear. You are *not* going to queer up my life, see? What's between me and Strek is our business. I'm not *about* to throw away this chance because of some narrow-minded little Earth female and her scrawny little terrestrial comprehensions." She posed there in her bedroom, tall and proud and magnificent, already a citizen of the cosmos in spirit. Arrogantly, she stared down at my little miserable self. She did it so well I squirmed. Her style had sure improved since the guy from Schenectady.

She turns it on like a switch, I know, but I just can't help it. She's so stupid, but she's so real, so alive, so *Alyne*—and I knew she was getting into serious trouble. I started to cry.

"Please, Alyne, don't go. I'm sorry. Is it my fault if I can't believe? I want you to have your alien lover, but . . . "

She remained standing stiffly in anger, self-righteous indignation personified. In counterpoint, some reveler outside smashed a bottle against the pavement.

"Alyne, what would an alien lover want from a human woman? Haven't you wondered? Even if you're right, Alyne, think! What is he really after? Your body? Your soul? Why would aliens come *here*?"

"No!" Alyne said sharply. She was furious and I shrank before her wrath. "You're wrong, Maggie. You are hopeless. You have no imagination, Maggie, no poetry, no romance, and so you have no insight into the true romance of what does exist."

All I could do was sit on her bed, my head in my hands, listening. And take in her beauty and her strength and her nonsense.

"A year from now, Maggie, I shall be gone. I shall be with my lover, staring down with him from orbit around far worlds, seeing the interplay of shapes and colors no one on Earth has dreamed of in their wildest moments, leaping across the currents of emptiness to meet incredible wonders. And you, Maggie, will be back here on Earth telling yourself that I'm married to an investor in Newark or shacked up with a haberdasher in Gary, Indiana. Now get out of here and let me pack. Strek's waiting."

I crept back into my room and paced, bit my nails. Even if I could save her, I wouldn't get any gratitude. Especially if he really was an alien.

Every time I reached the far end of my dark room I stared out into the night. The damned sky was lousy with stinking stars. I cursed them all, individually and collectively.

I stopped in front of the mirror on my dresser and suddenly hit the light switch. In the bright glare, I looked at my pale and blotchy face. Standard genes where I come from. I tugged at the tight collar of my blouse and brushed back my stringy hair. Comparing what I saw to Alyne, I looked at myself for a long time and felt hot tears press against my eyes. We were similar and yet not. Separate gods had made us, and now I was about to lose her.

Ready to talk, ready to gamble if I could think of a way, I went outside where I could intercept her one last time. I wiped away the tears before I opened the door.

Strek was sitting on the front porch steps, looking up at the stars. Nostalgically? Faking it? Who cared?

"Good evening, Maggie," he said pleasantly. "We thought you were asleep."

"I know," I said. I plopped down on the step beside him and we waited without speaking. The party across the street was still going strong and sent sharp laughter and electronic sonics washing over us at a mild volume.

Alyne swung out of the house with her suitcase and stopped cold when she saw me. "Maggie," she hissed, "go upstairs!"

"Not until we have settled things," Strek broke in smoothly. "Please be quiet, Alyne. How can I help you, Maggie?" He gave me a confident smile.

"Uh . . . " I was playing it by tone-deaf ear. "Well, Alyne is my friend, even if she doesn't think so at the moment. I can't help but worry about her, out in the intergalactic vastnesses and all. I'm sort of *in loco parentis* for her. Can you really take good care of her?"

"It's no business of—" Alyne started.

Strek stopped her with a curt wave. "No, dear, Maggie's quite sensible to ask. I assure you that all will be well for Alyne. I love her very much."

"What are your prospects, Mr. Strek?"

For the first time, Alyne's alien lover looked blank. "I beg your pardon?"

Alyne theatrically turned away and shook the hair from her face.

"What are your chances for social and financial advancement in universal circles? A woman like Alyne must be assured—"

"I see. I see what you mean. You mean . . . well, you need not fear on that score. I am . . . well, the nearest equivalent would be a prince of the blood."

"Oh, *darling*," squealed Alyne, "you never told me. . . ." She shut up as we both jumped and looked at her suddenly in surprise.

"Only a prince," I said. "In an entire cosmos, mere princes cannot be rare. Why, even this little barbaric planet boasts dozens, mostly indigent and impotent. . . . However," I said loudly, as he began to defend himself, "since Alyne loves you, that will suffice." Time to switch tracks. "What will you feed her?"

Alyne fumed silently at me, but stayed under his command for quiet.

Strek beamed handsomely. "Oh, Maggie, you can have no conception. I envy Alyne the delicate delight of her first taste of the savor of Denebolan bluhan-steak, or the faintly rich tang of Magellanic frettage. Oh, she will eat magnificently, Maggie."

"I see." I paused. "How many XH-negative enzymes in a serving of Magellanic frettage?"

Strek stared at me in the dim porchlight. "How many what?"

I made a meaningless mark on my pad. "*Mr.* Strek, if you do not take proper account of the distinctive nature of human dietary needs, you are not likely to keep Alyne alive very long, now are you? And what about medical care?"

Strek started to answer, so I hurried on, suddenly realizing my mistake. If he really was an alien, he would have answers for scientific questions. I needed something to reveal how much of a jerk he was, alien or human, before Alyne ran out of patience entirely. "Never mind, I trust your medical care. How about legal—"

Strek opened his mouth again, so I dropped that one, too. "Say!" I interrupted him. "This is delicate to expatiate upon, but in the absence of prior agreement upon which it is obviously impossible to be certain . . . " In my excitement, I had gotten tangled up in my own syntax. "Will the match bear issue?"

"Maggie," cried Alyne. She isn't usually shocked by these things.

"Obviously," I said, "Alyne may someday desire offspring. Is the proposed union viable? Will your meeting prove fertile?" He tried to respond but I added nastily, "*Could* you enumerate and describe your chromosomal arrangement?"

Our man from the stars was capable of emotion after all. He was on his feet, glaring at me, saying, "Enough of that! I love Alyne. . . ."

"Good, good. Love is very important for a marriage, at least as we conceive of it, though discussion of children is, too. But never mind. I agree to the marriage. When will it take place?"

Strek just gaped at me, for the moment most unheroic in appearance, caught off-balance by my reverse jiu-jitsu. Alyne turned to look at him for the first time since coming outside.

"Strek?" said Alyne quietly. "What *are* we going to do, exactly?"

Surprised, I backed off. Strek was still fumbling.

"Strek." Alyne's voice had a strange edge to it. "How long do you mean us to be together?"

I piped up. "A small human ceremony will meet Alyne's human moral code for marriage and—"

"Shut up, Maggie," snapped Alyne. "Forget about marriage. I want to know about this relationship."

Strek flung his arms out desperately. "Smythe," he said through his teeth, "you must understand that your local marital customs, in view of the sweep of galactic culture, are highly insignificant."

"Stop dodging me," Alyne yelled. "Do you love me? What does that mean in your galaxy? Are you saying you *wouldn't* marry me, even if I wanted you to?"

"I do not have to take this." Strek reared up.

"Answer me!"

"No—"

" *'No'?*" Alyne shrieked.

Strek inhaled deeply and steeled himself. "Come with me, Alyne, to taste the wonders of all the universe." He held out his hand imperiously and gave her a gentle smile.

"Go away," said Alyne, quietly and firmly. In control again, she was the Alyne I had lost and now found once more. "Go away, Strek. Don't come back."

He took one long look at her, and knew it was over.

Alyne stood staring into the night long after her dream alien had gone, the muscles of her jaw clenching spasmodically. The party across the street had finally died and the night was black and quiet. "Liar," she said, over and over. "*Damned* liar." Her humility at being loved by a traveler between the stars was gone forever. Finally she turned back to the house. Without looking at me, she said quietly, "I never want to see you again, either, Maggie.'

She said that when the literary agent left, too.

I sat on the porch for a long time, thinking about what I'd done, while she cried herself to sleep. The young June leaves of Ohio whispered from the darkness, keeping me company. I didn't feel very guilty. I'd had to do it for Alyne, and whether Strek was really from outer space or not meant nothing. I wouldn't be surprised if he really were—he had all the earmarks—but that just wasn't the point. Alyne has never been very marriage-minded, but that wasn't the point either. His refusal to take seriously her concern about a long-term relationship wasn't consistent with all his claims. Aliens can be selfish bastards, too.

When her sobbing grew fainter, and finally ended, I came into her room, where I watched away the night. Her lamp was still on and I could see the damp stains on the pillow case under her relaxed and peaceful face, framed by her smooth black hair. She would get over it fast. I never could have.

I sat on the rug beside her bed and gazed at her and thought directly to her sleeping spirit.

—Foolish Alyne. Love strikes across souls, true. And, as you have dreamed, others do come to this speck of rock across space, across time. And yes, Alyne, one has been drawn to an alien mortal here, so drawn that love has sunk into her soul, a hook that will never let her go.

—But a being of the perfection that you imagine, why should such a one cast an eye on you, dear Alyne? You are worthy of love, not from the strong and beautiful, but from the weak and marred.

—My human love, you are all that I am not . . . open and spirited and unafraid. And you will never know.

And, my own cheeks wet, the alien lover turns out the light.

MUD/AURORA

by D. D. Storm

art: Karl B. Kofoed

This was the first story published by the author, an artificial intelligence researcher now working in Texas.

©Kofoed81

When I was young I learned that there are three kinds of people: *sah, lo,* and *kai.* I was *sah,* of course, and grew up in a *sah* house. It was the boast of my house that ours were the most subtle of the *sah* languages for describing what is correct. When deep in *sah* our elders never failed to answer a question of correctness put to them by another house. I remember spending many nights as a child sitting near the heater in our meeting room, watching the elders create an elegant syntax with which to reply to moral questions in an appropriate meter.

To say "Sah!" is to say "Exactly. Correctly put." No project is ever undertaken in the village without the benedictions of the *sah* to ensure that it is proper. "Nature says what is possible, but the *sah* say what is correct."

I learned our house languages easily when I was young, and I remember one lesson particularly well. An elder asked us to describe a *sah*'s living out of house. My sentences were ominous in their disapproval. The clauses telling of such things clashed and clattered in discord and the lack of harmony between the words themselves forced the conclusion that such a thing was not *sah.* What has happened since is difficult to explain, given such training and my feel for the *sah* in a situation. I suppose it came about because, while I was quick to speak of others' actions, I never bothered to speak of my own in house languages until it was too late, assuming that whatever I did was *sah.* At any rate, I began to develop a language of my own, different from that of my house. Once I started I became engrossed in the project and never thought to ask myself whether it was correct.

My words were primitive and the grammar of my language was painfully simple then, but it was a language different from those of my house in an important way: it described the way things were related to each other rather than their relationship to *sah.* I did not think the difference was important until one afternoon when I was walking in the garden of my house.

Described in my own language, what happened was this: I moved beneath a bitter pink sky with flowers flocking slowly along the rows. Whenever I stood still they stuck to my feet with a gentle suction and when I began walking again they fell off, quivering. An animal which had flown into the garden flashed its brilliant wings as it hovered over a berry. All of this uttered in my language produced a symmetrical sequence of clauses which was pleasing to the ear. Its diagram would contain a low shape for the flower and a higher shape for the animal, with its verbs hovering winglike over it.

As the animal licked the berry a flower flowed up behind it and stealthily grew forward to enclose it. It moved so slowly that the animal did not react until only its wings protruded from the walls of the flower, and then it was too late. The flower took control of the animal, flexing the wings until its mastery was strong enough to will it to rise into the crimsoning sky. The two beings soared away from me toward the safety of the bush.

In my language this event was strikingly correct. A diagram of the sentence describing it would have a form like that of an arrow pointing beyond a gate. Conjoined with earlier sentences describing the flower and the animal, the effect produced was to call up images of two entities uniting to create a thing going beyond themselves. The correspondence of my grammar with the event felt right, and I stood there, struck by the syntactic integrity of what I had seen.

Then someone called me, asking where I was. "In the garden," I replied, and in replying caused the episode to alter. Seen in my own terms, I had been standing in a garden which was part of a striking event, observing an incident which went far beyond itself. Now, as I used the house language to reply, I found myself in the midst of flowers disturbed by my presence. Far away were the wings of the animal, dull with impropriety. The garden was not in a proper state and the episode I had seen was improper: a flower had escaped.

I spoke to an elder of this happening, telling him that it seemed as though my eyes themselves had changed when I changed languages. He frowned and told me I was not acting as a *sah* should act. "Describe your actions in the house language," he said.

For the first time I realized that my actions were not *sah*. In the language of our house they were describable only in sentences which clashed in structure, placing me in positions generally occupied by *lo* or *kai* nouns. Put that way only one sentence had the resonance of truth: "My actions were not *sah*."

"*Sah!*" said the elder, and he smiled as he always did when a student had learned a lesson well.

If all this had happened to me when I was younger, I would have no reason to tell my story. But by this time my language was beyond its formative stages and without thinking I shifted back to it. The world became a different place and I spoke further.

"What I did was not *sah*, but it was *good*." I said this in my language and the elder placed his hands upon his ears.

"I do not understand 'good.' A thing is *sah* or it is not. You must not talk in this other way."

What he said was correct, and what I said was good. It was too late to take away my image of the flower and the animal flying above the walls of our garden. The meaning of that image was rooted in my new language, and it was too late to take that away, too.

The *lo* lived in houses near my own house. They were not adept at speaking but they had skills which we respected, and they had devised a number of new ways for us to live. Our heatrock furnaces and our houses are based on the ideas of the *lo,* as is our system of quarrying heatrock and our creation of trails by guiding water through the dilbush. While such contrivances are of small worth compared to the intricacy and precision of a well-put sentence, they have their uses and our lives are more secure because of them. Thus the *lo* are worthy of some respect and we *sah* always put our thoughts into simple tongues when conversing with them.

"Things are done by *kai,* thought by *lo,* judged by *sah.*" There are many bad ideas which the *lo* have proposed. Years ago when the ice was moving closer and closer to the village they demanded that we move, and set about designing devices to carry our possessions. The *sah* spoke at length to persuade them that moving would destroy us as people. Our languages, which held their meaning best when spoken where they had been developed, would lose their sense, and our flocks of flowers would wither and die if taken from their home soil. At last the *lo* gave in; and it happened that the ice came no closer, just as the *sah* had said.

Another time the *lo* put forth a thinker who said that every member of the village should learn to speak the *sah* languages. This idea was given up when members of my house pointed out that such a plan would mix the types of people and each type would lose the ability to work for our survival. The very rhythms of the sentences describing such a plan condemned it and the *lo* were dissuaded, although they had thought at one time that the plan had merit.

These examples show why the *sah* are the most respected people in the village: they are keepers of the languages which have helped us to live as the only people in the world. Centuries of survival between the walls of ice have given us the grammars of the *sah.* Encoded in those grammars are the ways to survive. If a change proposed is a correct one, it will appear correct when it is spoken of by someone in *sah.* If not, the fact is soon apparent.

It was clear to everyone but me that my language was not a correct one, but my way of speaking appealed to some of the younger members of my house, and they began to use it as a joke. Eventually even the *lo* noticed something different about the way we younger *sah* were speaking, and they complained. It seemed to the elders of my house that my actions might corrupt the languages we used, the very things which preserved the meaning in our lives; and they were required to act.

Above the crowded square at the center of our village the sky shimmered green and yellow. I stood last in line with other young men of the age to be wedded. Elders walked behind us, placing a woman with each of us who was to receive a wife. A shadow fell between my legs to merge with my own and I knew a woman had been paired with me. There was some reaction from the observers, and I wondered who she was. I had not suspected during the week of negotiations that I was to be married; but, like each of the *sah* in my line, I hoped that she was an intelligent speaker.

The elders began at the other end of the line, chanting ritual words to each of the couples, and each man who had received a wife turned to embrace the woman behind him. When they came to me they chanted, "May you live well"—an utterance which was not the usual one, but the best of all which might have been spoken under the circumstances. I turned around and saw my wife standing behind me, but I did not embrace her. I had been married to a *kai* woman.

"*Sah* speaks to *sah* and, sometimes, to *lo*." Before that day, I had never passed words with the *kai*; but I knew that they were good laborers and that they would have perished in the cold without *sah* and *lo* to guide them. Such things had happened long ago. Under supervision they were capable of performing complicated tasks with their hands. They were strong, good breeders, and unintelligent, but they possessed the happiness which comes from having no responsibility. It was said that they could go into a deep state called *kai* and work for longer periods than one would think possible. I had also heard that in house they communicated their thoughts by gestures and dances, but no one from my house had seen such things. One thing I knew for certain—the life of a *sah* and a *kai* together would not be a pleasant one. I whispered to the elder before me that there must have been some mistake made.

"The action is correct," he said. "You are to live in the garden house beyond the village. The woman may trade flowers for heatrock here, but you must not return or speak to one of us again. Some day you may see that this action is *sah,* and a generous one."

I have come to realize that he was correct. I could have been cast out to wander in the dilbush like a wounded tree, but instead they had given me a *kai* to work for me, and they had given me a place to live where I could not endanger the village. I would never be able to perform the proper work of a *sah,* but I would have a house, and I could think about my language. Many times after that day I wished that my fate had been a harsher one, but possibly things have worked out for the good. Perhaps a reader of these words will be able to tell.

Her name was Kalak. She was my age. She had never spoken to a *sah* before. These things I learned as we splashed along the trail to our abandoned garden. I led the way and Kalak dragged a cart containing tools, heatrock, flowers to start our flock, and other things we would need to live. No one had maintained the trail for a long time, and in several places the dike had washed out, leaving it dry. Tangled masses of dilbush barred the way in the dry places, and we stopped while Kalak brought water in a pail to drive the plants back.

The gardener's house was barely visible. Dilbush had gotten over the moat and spread to fill the area inside. A tendril thrusting out the chimney circled slowly in the air; and the door, windows, and walls were thick with twisted trunks. Kalak took the bucket and began to drive the plants away with dousings of water. I stared back along the water path toward the village. People I could talk to were at the other end of that path, as was my proper work. What was there for a *sah* to do out of house? No one could speak with a *kai*. There seemed to be no point to my existence in that place.

All this I thought in my house languages. When I turned to my own language for comfort, I found little. Events were neither good nor bad. I had a sense that the grammar was waiting for more things to happen so that it could relate them.

"Words do not speak to gestures," and so it was with us. Kalak had cleared the dilbush from one room of our house and cleaned and started the heater. We had eaten two of our flowers and an animal which flew in. It was dark, and the aurora cast a gentle green light into the room. Kalak spread blankets on the sleeping shelf. We removed our garments and there was a silence.

"We are married," I said. She nodded.

"There are many things to be done, but it is spring and you have time to do them. You must fill the food bin, clear the garden, repair the trail, and expand the herd of flowers. You have done well today."

"What things will you do?"

"I will say the things which need doing and tell what things are correct."

"Good," she said. There was a silence. "You will not ask me to have children?"

I laughed. "It would not be possible. The seed of a *sah* does not fall unless the woman he lies with has talked to him in the languages of *sah* and they have spoken of deep things. We may lie together and perform the act, I suppose, since we are married, but no children will result." It struck me that she was quite ill-informed. Everybody knew that the types of people would not mix. If they were combined then nobody would be able to achieve a state of *sah* or *lo* or *kai* and we would not survive next time the ice came near. Didn't everyone know this?

"Then please instruct me to lie with you," she said. "I am frightened." She turned toward me and I noted that she was handsome in a sturdy sort of way. The women of my house were slimmer and more beautiful, but she had the functional appearance of a verb inflected for everyday speech. Desire for her arose to some extent in me and I began to speak endearments to increase it.

"You are a fair woman and I am a man. There is in you the delicate modulations of adjectives and the beauty of the words for colors." She moved nearer in the subtle green light and my desire grew. I began to speak more eloquently and was achieving some complicated feats of syntax when I felt her hand touching me in a shameful way. I ignored her gesture and continued to talk, although my desire was ebbing.

"Why are you talking? Let us lie together," she said. Her hands fluttered explicitly on me, and all the stories I had heard as a child about the crude practices of the *kai* came to mind. She had not listened to what I said, and yet she thought herself worthy to lie with a *sah!* Her actions were vulgar and her mind dull. Taking her wrists in my hands I pushed her from me.

"Your actions are not correct. You may lie with yourself!" I spoke with authority and rolled away.

We slept apart that night and every other night until a time I will tell of. Some nights I awoke to the sound of sobbing, and other nights I myself wondered whether it was worth my going on. Neither of us spoke again of lying together.

Our house was 15 paces long and 6 paces wide. It had windows in three of its low rock walls and it was crowned with a steep, sloping roof. There were two rooms inside, one with a sleeping shelf, heater, and table for eating, and another with nesting stalls for the flowers. The second room opened onto the garden, an enclosure 8 paces wide and 40 paces long with a lattice frame constructed over it. In winter a transparent sheet of sewn dilbush bark would be placed over the lattice to keep heat in and snow out.

The moat which surrounded our house and garden was filled by a stream falling from the hills behind the house. It was this stream which watered the path from our house to the village, making passage through the dilbush possible.

Within two weeks of our arrival Kalak had cleared the garden, repaired the lattice, started a food pile for the flowers, built pens for seedlings, and set about pollinating the breeders that were ready for reproducing. Meanwhile I grew dispirited, thinking about a life with no one to talk to. The greatest pleasures of the *sah* arise from speaking in house, couching their intricate thoughts in complicated utterances. There were deep truths I wished to express, but when I said them to Kalak she could not understand them. If I said something she could understand, then it was not deep and it was not true. Sometimes I thought about going out to die in the dilbush, struggling through the thick, ropy tendrils until I fell exhausted. Then, as the plants grew tight around me, I would utter the finest sentence ever spoken by a *sah*. Two things dissuaded me from taking this course of action: the sentence I spoke might not be as fine as I hoped, and even if it was a good one, nobody would know.

One morning Kalak got up early and clothed herself without looking at me. She was behaving secretively, and I wondered why. "I am going to the hills. Please watch the flocks," she said, and before I could react she was out of the door.

I shouted, "Watching flocks is not work for a *sah!*" but she was determined not to hear me.

I did not do the work—what *sah* would?—and as the morning passed I wondered when she would return. By noon the flowers were grouped around the feeding bin expectantly, waiting for their food. I knew that if they were not fed by evening the young ones would suffer, and I believed that Kalak would return before such a thing would happen. I was right. Late in the afternoon I looked up from my thoughts and saw her in the garden, throwing food to the flowers. Her leggings and coat were muddy, as was her hair. She did not speak of the incident, and neither did I.

By midsummer our flowers were breeding well, and we had nearly as many as the garden could support, but they were losing their flavor. "The spirit of the gardener is in the flowers." I attributed the problem to a sadness which displayed itself more and more in Kalak. She had labored hard except for the day I have just described, and "Work well done will please a *kai*," but she did not seem to be content. We would receive little heatrock for our flowers unless something was done to improve her outlook.

I awoke one morning worrying about this problem and saw that Kalak had already left the sleeping shelf. I found her in the garden constructing something out of dilbush root, rocks, and kernut leaves. It seemed to perform no function. She stood thinking for many minutes before she placed each of its parts, but I thought that the same result could have been achieved by simply stacking the objects together. It was several hours before she stepped back from the thing and shook herself, as if awakening from sleep.

"What is that?" I asked.
"Nothing," she said.
"What is its purpose?"
"I don't know how to tell you." She said this sullenly and it angered me. I drifted into *sah* to think about the matter.
"Building this is not correct when there are important things to do."
"Can you help with them while I do this?" For some reason her eyes were pleading, but I was astonished. Surely she knew my reply before I uttered it: "It is not correct for a *sah* to do *kai* work."
"Then what can you do?"
To my surprise no answer came. In the languages of *sah* each reply I considered began with reference to my living out of house, and there was no correct terminating clause. I had no reply to a question about correctness, and to my shame the question had been put me by a *kai*. I spoke no more at that time and slept badly all night.
When I awoke the next morning Kalak was already at work on another structure near the food bin. This one was taller and thinner, composed of a large group of rocks at the base of a frame woven from dilbush root. She was lashing sheets of bark to the frame so that the whole had the appearance of a house filled with solid roots. There was no room inside it for flowers to shelter; the thing appeared to be a useless object which took up garden space. The action was clearly incorrect.
"I forbid you to build these things," I said in the patient tone of a *sah* who corrects. Kalak did not reply and her eyes showed no sign that she had understood. She added a stone to the base, as if I had not spoken.
"Then I will tear it down!" In a rage I strode to the thing, forced to perform an action bordering on that of a *kai*. I did it as quickly as I could, kicking the new thing and the other one down. "Untie the parts and save them so that some use comes of this," I said in the tones of a *sah* who has been angered and whose will is not to be crossed.
Instead Kalak turned and ran through the house, and I heard her splashing along the stream which fills our moat. As she disappeared into the bush I stood in the garden, astonished that she had not obeyed the words of a *sah*. If people had acted in this way in the past no one would have survived the cold.
She had not returned by midafternoon, and the flowers were gathered anxiously around the feeding bin. Some of the smaller ones were already losing size. I decided to pursue her and force her to

return. In her present state she would probably spoil their flavor, but it seemed better that they lose some flavor than starve.

The dilbush on each side of the stream was very thick and I was certain that Kalak had stayed in the stream bed. The farther I went the smaller the stream grew, and the thicker was the network of limbs above me. I was walking in a crouch with one hand on the rocks in front for balance when I heard a sound like that of someone jumping. Quietly I crawled forward and looked through the trees at a pond with a small island at its center.

Kalak was dancing on the island, wearing only a length of bark cloth tied around her waist. Her eyes were unfocused as if she were in some deep state, and her dance was unlike anything I had seen before. I hauled myself up on the stream bank to watch it. It is difficult to say here what the dance was like. My description is taken from what I thought in my own language, but it was not created to describe this sort of thing. I will do as well as I can with the words available, for the way the dance had meaning may be important.

There seemed to be four themes to it. One had to do with a form which was constructed on the island. It stood two-legged, as tall as she was, rough purple trunks giving it mass, and silverthreads blowing from something which might have been a mouth. It was a grotesque thing, slightly suggestive of a person, and somehow it disturbed me. Another theme was a yearning quality, expressed in the way Kalak let her arms flow to the form and the way she held herself when she leaped. A third was a gesture which she repeated in many ways. I thought it was related to the common sign, "let us touch," which means one has a desire to lie together or a desire to touch in some deeper way. The two are told apart by context, but I could not say which was meant in the dance. Last, there was the timing of the dance, related to the flare and ebb of the aurora above us. At first Kalak's motions followed the lead of the aurora, flashing when it did and shimmering in low whirls when it died down. Later, she danced in synchrony with it, timing her turns to its undulations and encircling the form with her arms when the sky pulsed in a burst of color. Finally it seemed that she was a few moments ahead of the aurora. It was as if her movements showed the colors what to do and the power of her dance forced them to follow. At the end she touched the form in the way she had touched me when we lay together, and the aurora showered colors in response. Then she collapsed and the trance seemed to pass from her. She lay without moving, staring at the sky.

I had been so intent upon the dance that dilbush tendrils had wound themselves around my leg and arm, without my noticing. I could barely reach water with which to loosen their hold. A peculiar mood came over me which I could not precisely characterize. My plan had been to confront Kalak and order her back to the house in the harshest *sah* tones. Instead I returned without letting her know that I had seen her.

I sat alone in the garden that evening, wondering what to do. She had not come back, and I felt that she would not do so that day. Our flowers huddled around the food bin and some of them were wilting from hunger. It would be wrong for me to perform *kai* labor. Especially this *kai* labor—the contents of a food bin were foul and unclean. It would be wrong for me to perform any action at all. But these thoughts did not help me, and I began to think in my own language. The food bin was there, and a spade was there. The flowers there were in need, and I was here. The arrangement was out of balance, demanding that I move nearer the spade. My action set clauses resonating in anticipation—a flash of meaning passed between the word for me and the word for flowers. I took the spade—a noun—and plunged it into the bin—a solid verb—and a sentence was over and it shimmered in my mind.

Grammars shifted in my head, and I felt new nouns struggling to be uttered. I let the language of *sah* sink away to make room for whatever would come. What I had done was not *sah,* but my own language was expanding in all directions. Light passed through the nouns which named my action, and I felt that it was good.

Thinking in this way, I fed the flowers.

It was not so easy in the morning. For half an hour I stood at the garden's edge and willed myself to take the spade, but the action was beyond me. I had used up all my *sah* the night before, and was too tired to create the sentences which gave my action meaning. Instead I saw the situation with my old eyes and held back, as any *sah* would do. The flowers got their food at last, but the feeding was not done with confidence, and I had nothing good to say about it when it was over. Fragments of discordant *sah* phrases clashed in my mind, telling me that I was dirty and that I had gone beyond a point which no one should pass.

Kalak came in the door defiantly that afternoon, muddy and wet. She moved as though she were very tired, but her eyes were lively and angry. She went to the garden, and I heard her catch her breath. Then came the sound of footsteps and the spade scattering the evening food to the flowers. As she worked I heard her humming a low tune.

Neither of us spoke that evening. Kalak rarely said anything, and I had nothing correct to say. When we lay on the sleeping shelf I felt myself moving into *sah,* and the words which had echoed in my mind all day demanded to be uttered. I rolled toward Kalak to tell her that my actions had been incorrect, hers had been intolerable, and that we would do best to walk into the bush and let the forest have us. Before I could begin she touched me in the way she had touched her form when she danced and those thoughts died away. It came to me in my own language that touching her might not be bad. I remembered her dance and moved clumsily with her as the form on the island might have moved. "She is here and so am I," the words came to me, "and some actions are not bad."

When I touched her she arched and moaned, but she was not in pain. We lay together all that night, and it was good. In the morning I realized neither of us had said a word. Kalak rolled over and looked at me, and I saw that she was troubled.

"I could have taken the seed," she said. "Could you have given it?" It was correct for her to wonder. Everyone knew that to mix the types of people would be to create disaster for us all.

"I could have given the seed," I said, astonished. It should not have been possible and I asked how such a thing could be. The languages of my house forbid its happening, but nothing in the nouns and verbs of my own language ruled it out. In fact, as I thought in my own language about what we might do I caught suggestions of possibilities more shocking than this, but I did not then have the *sah* to pursue them.

We didn't lie together after that, afraid of the child which might result. Kalak labored harder than ever in the garden except for the times she went into *kai* to build other constructions. It seemed to me that they said things in a language I did not understand; one seemed to whisper "stillness," and another said "may this flock endure," but I could not hear them when I was not in *sah*. Kalak has told me since that these things are real to her, and this is why the *kai* gave her to me—they felt some new force in the things she built, and they were afraid. She was afraid of her constructions too, she said, because they were incorrect. But she could not stop herself from making them; and otherwise her actions were correct, weren't they? I was not so sure, but I wanted her to be untroubled, and so I said yes.

When Kalak went into *kai* I fed the flowers myself, knowing she would not come out until the night had passed. My language prompted me to do this, and I did not feel soiled by the action as long as I did not think in the languages of my house. I let the things she built stand, too, because they spoke to me as she could not, and because my own language did not forbid them.

One time when Kalak was in *kai,* an adventurous yellow flower melted around the handle of a spade leaning on the garden wall. Slowly it pulsed up the handle to the top of the wall. I prepared to chase it, for it was poised at the edge, ready to roll away to freedom, but it swayed on its base for a moment and then descended the handle into the garden again. I wondered about this and, since I could not speak of it with Kalak, I tried an experiment like those a *lo* might perform. Seeing an animal fluttering at the lattice outside, I opened the wall so that the animal could enter. It fluttered about until it tired and dropped to rest on the floor. A flower moved onto it and rode it through the opening to the outside. They swooped and soared until they were out of sight, and I thought that they were gone, but several minutes later there was the rush of wings and I saw the animal on the garden floor again. It perched on the ground while the flower moved away from it, and then it shook itself. Frightened, it darted through the opening and flew away.

We left the lattice open after that and found that the flavor of our flowers was better. What was more, we had very few of the escapes which plague the other gardeners. I felt as though I had performed a *lo* feat, although I didn't know why the flowers came back. "Maybe they want to be eaten by creatures they like," said Kalak.

When a load of our flowers went to the village Kalak would return with a load of the highest grade heatrock in exchange. I was happy to see this until it struck me that the new flavor was the taste of my own labor. We were sending my shame to the village where anyone with a piece of heatrock could buy it for his dinner. I could think about my labor in my language without shame, but the villagers could not, and I knew what they would think if they knew. Again I considered wandering in the bush—the only correct action in such a case—and I would have done it, but Kalak asked, "Is there shame if you are not a *sah?*" I searched the nouns of my languages and the languages of my house and found no word for me. It was as if my actions had taken me outside the domain of what could be said, to a place where there was only meaninglessness. How would a person who could not be named find guidance or support for what he did?

There was no word for me. Thinking on this loosened something else inside me late in autumn as I was struggling to build the garden wall higher against the winter snow. I will tell what happened as well as I can in these words, but it was *kai,* and *kai* does not do well in words. I was lifting a rock when I felt myself shift in viewpoint and I was with the rock, lifting and being lifted, but it was not because of me. "Stillness," whispered Kalak's structure in the garden, and the rocks I carried became part of me as they were placed. They had already placed themselves, and they placed me, yet nothing did the placing. Nouns and verbs did not exist in that state, only some new adjective I can't remember now, but when the experience was over I had done the work of three days. Was it shameful? I hope someday to know, if I can find the words to talk of it.

One morning Kalak looked up from the heater and gasped in surprise. Outside I saw the first snow of winter lying over everything. The dilbush slumped motionless under the white, as they would be until spring, their branches clasped watertight around their trunks. In the garden our flowers had gone into their winter dormancy and the path leading to the village was a strip of ice reflecting the colors above it. Kalak's eyes flashed at the sight. All sound and movement beneath the sky was gone, and in the roaring silence the same thought stirred inside us both.

"It is beautiful," said Kalak.

"It is," I agreed. "But what is there to say of us?"

Kalak jerked as if receiving an unexpected blow. "There are words for me," she said. "I am *kai* and my actions are correct. Except the things I make. You have told me so." She stood apart from me and said again, "I am *kai!*"

I knew the shock she would feel if she learned the truth, and I searched for words to reassure her, but there was nothing to say. The languages I spoke were silent, for we had moved outside the range of what could be discussed. We were shaped differently from nouns, and we jarred with the verbs too much to make a sentence. I had had thoughts like those of a *lo* and had slipped into *kai*. Kalak had made things which spoke in a *sah*-like way, and we had talked together of these things. Such facts could not be put in the languages of what is correct, and my own language would not say them. "What cannot be said should not exist," and Kalak knew this all too well. She understood my silence then better than she understood my speech, and she turned away from me.

After that she ate little and spent most of her time sitting at the window, staring dully at the snow. She wanted to walk into it and not return, she said, if that could be called correct. The effect her feelings had on me was strange. I had wanted to do the same thing as an act of honor, but her desiring it made me reconsider. I still saw her as a *kai* and saw myself as *sah,* no matter whether there were words to support my view. I had a duty to keep her from the cold, as she had a duty to ask me what was correct, and now honor demanded that I attempt to prevent her going out to freeze. There was another motive acting on me then, but I was not aware of it and it was an emotional attraction, not relevant to the things I want to tell.

I spent less time brooding in the sleeping shelf after that and passed my days in search of ways to name us. "I will find a word for us," I said, "and then I will know what other words apply, and I will know what we should do." But the fire had gone out of Kalak's eyes, and she did not hear me.

At the window looking out, Kalak reminded me of one of her structures, solid and conveying meaning. "Give me the words to let me go," her posture said, and I fought its influence as I worked with my language, searching for a way to give us meaning. My results were not encouraging, and I found myself day after day with barely energy enough to feed the heater and prepare flowers for us to eat. The best parts of the winter came when we quarrelled over the close quarters or the boredom. At least then we were alive; at other times it was as if neither of us existed.

On those rare days when the weather cleared Kalak would walk into the snow to stretch herself, and I would keep the heater going. I worried that she would not return, and so I broke my thoughts on language every hour or so to reassure myself that she had not stopped moving. The sights which struck me then were like the landscape of our life—invisible silent slopes with mute, shrouded forms like empty words across them, and far away the dark spot of her between the whiteness and the shimmering sky.

I found the word I wanted in early spring, and I will tell the way it came as carefully as I can in this language, so that a *sah* who reads these words might understand something of it.

My language described the relationships between things in the world, but the world was a place in which there were three kinds of people, and we were not any of those kinds. We could not be right in a world like that, and one world is all there is, I thought. But I was wrong.

As I considered the way my language had grown and looked at the way it differed from the languages of my house, I saw again the possibility of something new behind it, something suggested by the grammars I had learned, but not within them. To tell how this could be I must resort to metaphor.

My language related things to things in the way that light is related to the ice it passes through, and its words were like faceted ice crystals of various shapes. Imagine an enclosed stage with many such crystals on its floor. Imagine further that you are to make meaning by combining the shape of the crystals into geometric patterns. The hues of the crystals are similar and cannot be told apart except when you are deep in *sah.* Now imagine that any pattern containing a misplaced crystal or a crystal of the wrong color creates such dissonance that the stage shudders and threatens to collapse. This is how the sentences of my language were formed. The crystals were words, the patterns sentences, the trembling stage my mind.

One morning early in spring I said to Kalak, "I will find a word for us today or stop trying." She did not react, and as I turned away I touched her to reassure her, something I had never done before. She raised her head and saw me sitting crosslegged in the garden. I nodded to her and closed my eyes, feeling my *sah* at its strongest. I did not know it then, but Kalak came into the garden, slipping into *kai,* and began to build another structure. I was already on my stage, with curtains of silvergrass around me and hundreds of delicately tinted crystals on the floor. Some force held them and me to the stage, but it did not affect anything which was lifted up.

Moving carefully among the words, I made a sentence by combining words for "flower" and "orange" in a declarative pattern, with simple verbs to round it out. "The flower is orange." Light refracted onto the curtains, showing the relation of the sentence to the world as the crystals revolved slowly over the stage. It was right.

I put the crystals back on the floor and picked up the interrogative "who." I placed it with a dual verb for Kalak and me—"who are"—and left it spinning while I looked for a word to fill the sentence out.

I had gotten this far many times before, and I knew that nothing on the stage would fill the space. But today my *sah* was strong enough to take me to the edges of the stage, a place I had never gone before. Away from the crystals, now I could see a sort of haze hanging over them and recognized it as the influence of grammar. There was a wisp of it coming from behind the curtain of silvergrass, and I parted the grass to look beyond. It was darkness without meaning, but floating in it was a shapeless chunk of ice. I stared at it and wondered whether it could be shaped to make the word I wanted. In another place just then Kalak was beginning her structure, deep in *kai,* and perhaps that helped me, for as my thoughts passed over the ice a facet appeared at its top and rough outlines formed at its sides. A *lo* could smooth them down, I thought, and so could I. With the thought the sides of the ice took on a crystal form unlike any I had seen before, but I knew that it was right. The bottom, where the word would connect with the sentence I had begun, was a flowing mass, but I thought of it in *sah* and the final form emerged. There was a word before me now, and it was right, but I knew that it would not fit the words I had prepared. As I became aware of this the words floating in the air altered form to fit the ice, and as they did so something changed inside me too. I no longer knew the way to talk about correctness, and I did not care. I picked the new word up and placed it with the other crystals in the air. They fit together to make the question "Who are we?"

A flood of light burst from the words, as if it had been waiting all my life to be released. It blazed off in a new direction away from the stage, and I let myself float after it. The stage disappeared, and I went with the light toward the thing it meant, back in what must have been time, toward something I had always known of without ever knowing it. Across blurred chasms of flared colors and grinding icewalls I went back to another time, and I will tell what I found there as I found it, although I am translating from a very different language.

It was the violet time of sunset. There was a woman in front of me, sitting on a ridge. She was one of my ancestors, pale, without much hair, and she was troubled. A flare of aurora lit her from the side, casting her silhouette in violet on the rock beside her.

There were others like her in the valley below. Officers, engineers, some crew. The avalanche had covered them and wrecked their communicator, and when they returned to the landing site they saw the ship had left them for dead. An engraved plaque commemorating their passing in the course of duty was all it had left behind.

She planted a fist in the summer mud and thought that the plaque was probably appropriate. In the valley the crew made shelters against the summer cold and forced back the damned encroaching plants with water, but how could they survive with what they had? And if they made it through the winter how would their descendants survive? Every time the planet wobbled, ice would cover nearly everything; and at best their children would become like the plants, thinking only of food, cold, and water.

She was a linguistics officer, and—sitting in the mud beneath the sky on fire—she realized they had one kind of technology to use, and she possessed it. They could preserve the differences between them with language, and pass some sort of social structure to their descendants without seeming to do so, if she used the things she knew correctly. She did not know whether the genes which made the officers, engineers, and crew good at their tasks would be weakened by interbreeding; but she did not want them to take the chance, and so she thought that those distinctions should be built into a grammar to pass on to their descendants. Rules and codes could be repealed or reinterpreted, but grammar could not, and she could build a language which would contain the things she wanted them to know.

She saw the way it would have to be passed on. The officers would have to learn to speak it naturally so that the children would learn it without knowing its origin. And it would have to be complex enough to keep its speakers' minds from going dead. It would be all they would have to occupy them when the cold was worst.

She saw a rule it would be based on. This world was mostly mud between two hemispheres of ice, but the sky above it gave it a sort of beauty and she knew it was right to put those two things, mud and aurora, into it. From that time on the *sah* have blended the high tones of the aurora and the low tones of the mud in every sentence they have uttered.

Mud/Aurora. It was the first word in her new language, her name for the world, and she could feel the principles of syntax it inspired growing in her as she stood and began to descend the ridge. They would use her language or their humanity would not survive; but she would leave in it a trace of its beginning, so that if their descendants, somewhere in the long grim years ahead, grew human enough to understand its grammar, they could understand something of its origins and change them if they liked. She did not want to play a deity, after all.

The woman made her way down the ridge, and as she did the light grew dim around me. It was my guide back to the stage and as it faded I floated after it, as fast as I could, through eons of blurred impressions and upthrust icewalls to the stage. I had little *sah* left by then, and I used all of it in getting back before the last flickers died away in the sentence I had made.

Around me was turmoil and agony. A flock of ungrammatical constructions spun in the air, thrown up by the convulsions of the stage, as the fabric of my mind begin to tear. Kalak touched me then, and I felt frozen soil beneath my back. Above me was the lattice and the stars and Kalak standing beside a new form, suggestive of a person, but with shapeless matter in its hands. It was molding something new from the matter, and on its face was an expression of rightness. Kalak had that expression too, and her eyes were glowing.

Since that day I have felt my seed fall and Kalak has received it. When it is warmer we will take her new form with us, along with whatever we can carry. Our flowers will follow us, I think. We will attempt to live in a new way, but I do not know what it will be like. It is not right for us to do it near the village. If we succeed we might contaminate the grammars of the village life, and already I cannot speak in *sah* without distorting accents.

I am leaving this account so that some day, if the *sah* are curious, they may send someone in the direction we are going, toward the sunrise, to see whether other languages can make a world as good as theirs.

by Isaac Asimov

THE DIM RUMBLE

We all know that ultrasonic noise can be bad for our health. So what, therefore, can we assume will happen if the source of the noise is something really big? Here's the Good Doctor in top form with another fine George and Azazel story.

I try hard not to believe what my friend George tells me. How can I possibly believe a man who tells me he has access to a two-centimeter-tall demon he calls Azazel, a demon who is really an extraterrestrial personage of extraordinary—but strictly limited—powers?

And yet George does have this ability to gaze at me unblinkingly out of his blue eyes and make me believe him temporarily—while he's talking. It's the Ancient Mariner effect, I suppose.

I once told him that I thought his little demon had given him the gift of verbal hypnosis, but George sighed and said, "Not at all! If he has given me anything, it is a curse for attracting confidences—except that that has been my bane since long before I ever encountered Azazel. The most extraordinary people insist on burdening me with their tales of woe. And sometimes—"

He shook his head in deep dejection. "Sometimes," he said, "the load I must bear as a result is more than human flesh and blood should be called upon to endure. Once, for instance, I met a man named Hannibal West . . .

I noticed him first [said George] in the lounge of a hotel at which I was staying. I noticed him chiefly because he encumbered my view of a statuesque waitress who was most becomingly and insufficiently dressed. I presume he thought I was looking at him, something I would certainly not willingly have done, and he took it as an overture of friendship.

He came to my table, bringing his drink with him, and seated himself without a by-your-leave. I am, by nature, a courteous man, and so I greeted him with a friendly grunt and glare, which he accepted in a calm way. He had sandy hair, plastered down across his scalp; pale eyes and an equally pale face; and the concentrated gaze of a fanatic, though I admit I didn't notice that until later on.

"My name," he said, "is Hannibal West, and I am a professor of geology. My particular field of interest is speleology. You wouldn't, by any chance, be a speleologist yourself?"

I knew at once he was under the impression he had recognized a kindred soul. My gorge rose at the possibility, but I remained courteous. "I am interested in all strange words," I said. "What is speleology?"

"Caves," he said. "The study and exploration of caves. That is my hobby, sir. I have explored caves on every continent except Antarctica. I know more about caves than anyone in the world."

"Very pleasant," I said, "and impressive." Feeling that I had in this way concluded a most unsatisfactory encounter, I signalled for the waitress to renew my drink and watched, in scientific absorption, her undulating progress across the room.

Hannibal West did not recognize that our conversation had been concluded, however. "Yes," he said, nodding vigorously, "you do well to say it is impressive. I have explored caves that are unknown to the world. I have entered underground grottoes that have never felt the footsteps of a human being. I am one of the few people alive today who has gone where no man, or woman, for that matter, has ever gone before. I have breathed air undisturbed, till then, by the lungs of a human being, and have seen sights and heard sounds no one else has ever seen or heard—and lived." He shuddered.

My drink had arrived, and I took it gratefully, admiring the grace with which the waitress bent low to place it on the table before me. I said, my mind not really on what I was saying, "You are a fortunate man."

"That I am not," said West. "I am a miserable sinner called upon by the Lord to avenge the sins of humanity."

Now at last I looked at him sharply, and noted the glare of fanaticism that nearly pinned me to the wall. "In caves?" I asked.

"In caves," he said, solemnly. "Believe me. As a professor of geology, I know what I am talking about."

I had met numerous professors in my lifetime who had known no such thing, but I forebore mentioning the fact.

Perhaps West read my opinion in my expressive eyes, for he fished a newspaper clipping out of a briefcase at his feet and passed it over to me. "Here!" he said, "Just look at that!"

I cannot say that it much rewarded close study. It was a three-paragraph item from some local newspaper. The headline read "A Dim Rumble" and the dateline was East Fishkill, New York. It was an account to the effect that local residents had complained to the police department of a dim rumble that left them uneasy and caused much disturbance among the cat and dog population of the town. The police had dismissed it as the sound of a distant thunderstorm, though the weather department heatedly denied that there had been any that day anywhere in the region.

"What do you think of *that?*" asked West.

"Might it have been a mass epidemic of indigestion?"

He sneered as though the suggestion were beneath contempt, though no one who has ever experienced indigestion would consider it that. Beneath the diaphragm, perhaps.

He said, "I have similar news items from papers in Liverpool, England; Bogota, Colombia; Milan, Italy; Rangoon, Burma; and perhaps half a hundred other places the world over. I collected them. All speak of a pervasive dim rumble that created fear and uneasiness and drove animals frantic, and all were reported within a two-day period."

"A single world-wide event," I said.

"Exactly! Indigestion, indeed." He frowned at me, sipped at his drink, then tapped his chest. "The Lord has placed a weapon in my hand, and I must learn to use it."

"What weapon is this?" I asked.

He didn't answer directly. "I found the cave quite by accident," he said, "something I welcome, for any cave whose opening advertises itself too openly is common property and has been host to thousands. Show me an opening narrow and hidden, one that is overgrown with vegetation, obscured by fallen rocks, veiled by a waterfall, precariously placed in an all but inaccessible spot, and I will show you a virgin cave worthy of inspection. You say you know nothing of speleology?"

"I have been in caves, of course," I said. "The Luray caverns in Virginia—"

"Commercial!" said West, screwing up his face and looking about for a convenient spot on the floor upon which to spit. Fortunately, he didn't find one.

"Since you know nothing about the divine joys of spelunking," he went on, swallowing instead, "I will not bore you with any account of where I found it, and how I explored it. It is, of course, not always safe to explore new caves without companions, but I perform solo explorations readily. After all, there is no one who can match me in this sort of expertise, to say nothing of the fact that I am as bold as a lion.

"In this case, it was indeed fortunate I was alone, for it would not have done for any other human being to discover what I discovered. I had been exploring for several hours when I entered a large and silent room with stalactites above and stalagmites below in gorgeous profusion. I skirted about the stalagmites, trailing my unwinding twine behind me, since I am not fond of losing my way, and then I came across what must have been a thick stalagmite that had broken off at some natural plane of cleavage. There was a litter of limestone to one side of it. What had caused the break I cannot say—perhaps some large animal, fleeing into the cave under pursuit, had blundered into the stalagmite in the dark; or else a mild earthquake had found this one stalagmite weaker than the others.

"In any case, the stump of the stalagmite was now topped by a smooth flatness just moist enough to glisten in my electric light. It was roughly round and strongly resembled a drum. So strongly did it resemble one that I automatically reached out and tapped it with my right forefinger."

He gulped down the rest of his drink and said, "It *was* a drum; or at least it was a structure that set up a vibration when tapped. As soon as I touched it, a dim rumble filled the room, a vague sound just at the threshold of hearing and all but subsonic. Indeed, as I was able to determine later on, the portion of the sound that was high enough in pitch to be heard was a tiny fraction of the whole. Almost all the sound expressed itself in mighty vibrations far too long-wave to affect the ear, though it shook the body itself. That unheard reverberation gave me the most unpleasantly uneasy feeling you can imagine.

"I had never encountered such a phenomenon before. The energy of my touch had been minute. How could it have been converted into such a mighty vibration? I have never managed to understand that completely. To be sure, there are powerful energy sources underground. There could be a way of tapping the heat of the magma, converting a small portion of it to sound. The initial tap could serve to liberate additional sound energy—a kind of sonic laser, or, if we substitute 'sound' for 'light' in the acronym, we can call it 'saser.' "

I said, austerely, "I've never heard of such a thing."

"No," said West, with an unpleasant sneer, "I dare say you haven't. It is nothing anyone has heard of. Some combination of geologic arrangements has produced a natural saser. It is something that would not happen, by accident, oftener than once in a million years, perhaps, and even then in only one spot on the planet. It may be the most unusual phenomenon on Earth."

"That's a great deal," I said, "to deduce from one tap of a forefinger."

"As a scientist, sir, I assure you I was not satisfied with a single tap of a forefinger. I proceeded to experiment. I tried harder taps and quickly realized that I could be seriously damaged by the reverberations in the enclosure. I set up a system whereby I could drop pebbles of various sizes on the saser, while I was outside the cave, by means of a makeshift long-distance apparatus. I discovered that the sound could be heard surprising distances outside the cave. Using a simple seismometer, I found that I could get distinct vibrations at distances of several miles. Eventually, I dropped a series of pebbles one after the other, and the effect was cumulative."

I said, "Was that the day when dim rumbles were heard all over the world?"

"Exactly," he said. "You are by no means as mentally deprived as you appear. The whole planet rang like a bell."

"I've heard that particularly strong earthquakes do that."

"Yes, but this saser can produce a vibration more intense than that of any earthquake and can do so at particular wavelengths; at a wavelength, for instance, that can shake apart the contents of cells—the nucleic acids of the chromosomes, for instance."

I considered that, thoughtfully. "That would kill the cell."

"It certainly would. That may be what killed the dinosaurs."

"I've heard it was done by the collision of an asteroid with the Earth."

"Yes, but in order to have that done by ordinary collision, the asteroid postulated must be huge—ten kilometers across. And one must suppose dust in the stratosphere, a three-year winter, and some way of explaining why some species died out and others didn't in a most illogical fashion. Suppose, instead, that it was a much smaller asteroid that struck a saser and that it disrupted cells with its sound vibration. Perhaps ninety percent of the cells in the world would be destroyed in a matter of minutes with no enormous effect on the planetary environment at all. Some species would manage to survive—some would not. It would be entirely a matter of the intimate details of comparative nucleic acid structure."

"And that," I said, with a most unpleasant feeling that this fanatic was serious, "is the weapon the Lord has placed into your hands?"

"Exactly," he said, "I have worked out the exact wavelengths of sound produced by various manners of tapping the saser and I am trying now to determine which wavelength would specifically disrupt human nucleic acids."

"Why human?" I demanded.

"Why not human?" demanded he, in his turn. "What species is crowding the planet, destroying the environment, eradicating other species, filling the biosphere with chemical pollutants? What species will destroy the Earth and render it totally non-viable in a matter of decades, perhaps? Surely not some other than *Homo sapiens*? If I can find the right sonic wavelength, I can strike my saser in the proper manner, and with the proper force, to bathe the Earth in sonic vibrations that will, in a matter of a day or so, for it takes time for sound to travel, wipe out humanity, while scarcely touching other life-forms with nucleic acids of differing intimate structure."

I said, "You are prepared to destroy billions of human beings?"

"The Lord did it by means of the Flood—"

"Surely you don't believe the Biblical tale of the Flood?"

West said austerely, "I am a creationist geologist, sir."

I understood everything. "Ah," I said. "The Lord promised he would never again send a Flood upon the Earth, but he didn't say anything about sound waves."

"Exactly! The billions of dead will fertilize and fructify the Earth, serve as food for other forms of life who have suffered much at the hands of humanity and who deserve compensation. What's more, a remnant of humanity shall undoubtedly survive. There are bound to be a few human beings who will have nucleic acids of a type that will not be sensitive to the sonic vibrations. That remnant, blessed by the Lord, can begin anew, and will perhaps have learned a lesson as to the evil of Evil, so to speak."

I said, "Why are you telling me all this?" And indeed, it had occurred to me that it was strange that he was doing so.

He leaned toward me and seized me by the lapel of my jacket—a most unpleasant experience, for his breath was rather overpowering—and said, "I have the inner certainty that you can help me in my work."

"I?" I said. "I assure you that I haven't any knowledge whatsoever concerning wavelengths, nucleic acids, and—" But then, bethinking myself rapidly, I said, "Yet come to think of it, I may have just the thing for you." And in a more formal voice, with the stately courtesy so characteristic of me, I said, "Would you do me the honor, sir, of waiting for me for perhaps fifteen minutes?"

"Certainly, sir," he answered, with equal formality. "I will occupy myself with further abstruse mathematical calculations."

As I hastened out of the lounge, I passed a ten-dollar bill to the bartender with a whispered, "See that that gentleman, if I may speak loosely, does not leave until I return. Feed him drinks and put it on my tab, if absolutely necessary."

I never fail to carry with me those simple ingredients I use to call up Azazel and, in a very few minutes, he was sitting on the bed lamp in my room, suffused with his usual tiny pink glow.

He said, censoriously, in his piping little voice, "You interrupted me when I was in the midst of constructing a papparatso with which I fully expected to win the heart of a lovely samini."

"I regret that, Azazel," I said, hoping he would not delay me by describing the nature of the papparatso or the charms of the samini, for neither of which I cared the paring of a fingernail, "but I have here a possible emergency of the most extreme sort."

"You always say that," he said, discontentedly.

Hastily, I outlined the situation, and I must say he grasped it at once. He is very good that way, never requiring long explanations. My own belief is that he peeks at my mind, although he always assures me that he considers my thoughts inviolable. Still, how far can you trust a two-centimeter extraterrestrial who, by his own admission, is constantly trying to overreach lovely saminis, whatever they are, by the most dishonorable ruses? Besides, I'm not sure whether he says he considers my thoughts inviolable or insufferable; but that is neither here nor there.

"Where is this human being you speak of?" he squeaked.

"In the lounge. It is located—"

"Don't bother. I shall follow the aura of moral decay. I think I have it. How do I identify the human being?"

"Sandy hair, pale eyes—"

"No, no. His mind."

"A fanatic."

"Ah, you might have said so at once. I have him—and I see I shall require a thorough steam-bath when I return home. He is worse than you are."

"Never mind that. Is he telling the truth?"

"About the saser? Which, by the way, is a clever conceit."

"Yes."

"Well, that is a difficult question. As I often say to a friend of mine who considers himself a great spiritual leader: What is truth? I'll tell you this; he considers it the truth. He believes it. What a human being believes, however, no matter with what ardor, is not necessarily objective truth. You have probably caught a hint of this in the course of your life."

"I have. But is there no way you can distinguish between belief that stems from objective truth and belief that does not?"

"In intelligent entities, certainly. In human beings, no. But apparently you consider this man an enormous danger. I can rearrange some of the molecules of his brain, and he will then be dead."

"No, no," I said. It may be a silly weakness on my part, but I do object to murder. "Couldn't you rearrange molecules in such a way that he will lose all memory of the saser?"

Azazel sighed in a thin, wheezing way. "That is really much more difficult. Those molecules are heavy and they stick together. Really, why not a clean disruption—"

"I insist," I said.

"Oh, very well," said Azazel, sullenly, and then he went through a whole litany of puffing and panting designed to show me how hard he was working. Finally, he said, "It's done."

"Good. Wait here, please. I just want to check it out, and then I'll be right back."

I rushed down hastily, and Hannibal West was still sitting where I had left him. The bartender winked at me as I passed. "No drinks necessary, sir," said that worthy person, and I gave him five dollars more.

West looked up cheerfully. "There you are."

"Yes, indeed," I said. "Very penetrating of you to notice that. I have the solution to the problem of the saser."

"The problem of the what?" he asked, clearly puzzled.

"That object you discovered in the course of your speleological explorations."

"What are speleological explorations?"

"Your investigations of caves."

"Sir," said West, frowning, "I have never been in a cave in my life. Are you mad?"

"No, but I have just remembered an important meeting. Farewell, sir. Probably, we shall never meet again."

I hastened back to the room, panting a little, and found Azazel humming to himself some tune favored by the entities of his world. Really, their taste in what they call music is atrocious.

"His memory is gone," I said, "and, I hope, permanently."

"Of course," said Azazel. "The next step, now, is to consider the saser itself. Its structure must be very neatly and precisely organized if it can actually magnify sound at the expense of Earth's internal heat. No doubt, a tiny disruption at some key point—something that may be within my mighty powers—could wipe out all saser activity. Exactly where is it located?"

I stared at him, thunderstruck. "How should I know?" I said.

He stared at me, probably thunderstruck also, but I can never make out the expressions on his tiny face. "Do you mean to say you had me wipe out his memory *before* you obtained that vital piece of information?"

"It never occurred to me," I said.

"But if the saser exists, if his belief was based on objective truth, someone else may stumble upon it, or a large animal might, or a meteorite might strike it—and at any moment, day or night, all life on Earth may be destroyed."

"Good Lord!" I muttered.

Apparently my distress moved him, for he said, "Come, come, my friend, look at the bright side. The worst that can happen is that human beings will all be wiped out. Just human beings. It's not as though they're *people.*"

Having completed his tale, George said, despondently, "And there you are. I have to live with the knowledge that the world may come to an end at any moment."

"Nonsense," I said, heartily, "Even if you've told me the truth about this Hannibal West, which, if you will pardon me, is by no means assured, he may have been having a sick fantasy."

George looked haughtily down his nose at me for a moment, then said, "I would not have your unlovely tendency toward skepticism for all the loveliest saminis on Azazel's native world. How do you explain this?"

He withdrew a small clipping from his wallet. It was from yesterday's New York *Times* and was headed "A Dim Rumble." It told of a dim rumble that was perturbing the inhabitants of Grenoble, France.

"One explanation, George," I said, "is that you saw this article and made up the whole story to suit."

For a moment, George looked as though he would explode with indignation, but when I picked up the rather substantial check that the waitress had placed between us, softer feelings overcame him, and we shook hands on parting, amiably enough.

And yet I must admit I haven't slept well since. I keep sitting up at about 2:30 A.M., listening for the dim rumble I could swear had roused me from sleep.

LIMITS

by Larry Niven

art: Jack Gaughan

Mr. Niven was born April 30, 1938
in Los Angeles CA. He flunked
out of Cal Tech in his sophomore year,
having discovered a bookstore jammed
with used science-fiction magazines,
but subsequently graduated from
Washburn University with a BA
in math and a minor in psychology.
His most recent collaboration
with Jerry Pournelle, *Oath of Fealty*, is now in print,
as is *The Descent of Anansi*, a
collaboration with Steven Barnes.

I never would have heard them if the sound system hadn't gone on the fritz. And if it hadn't been one of those frantically busy nights, maybe I could have done something about it. . . .

But one of the big, chirpsithra passenger-ships was due to leave Mount Forel Spaceport in two days. The chirpsithra trading empire occupies most of the Galaxy, and Sol system is nowhere near its heart. A horde of passengers had come early in fear of being marooned. The Draco Tavern was jammed.

I was fishing under the counter when the noises started. I jumped. Two voices alternated: a monotonal twittering, and a bone-vibrating sound like a tremendous door endlessly opening on rusty hinges.

The Draco Tavern used to make the Tower of Babel sound like a monolog, in the years before I got this sound system worked out. Picture it: thirty or forty creatures of a dozen species including human, all talking at once at every pitch and volume, and all of their translating widgets bellowing too! Some species, like the srivinthish, don't talk with sound; but they also don't notice the continual *skreek*ing from their spiracles. Others sing. They *call* it singing, and they say it's a religious rite, so how can I stop them?

Selective damping is the key, and a staff of technicians to keep the system in order. I can afford it. I charge high anyway, for the variety of stuff I have to keep for anything that might wander in. But sometimes the damping system fails.

I found what I needed—a double-walled canister I'd never needed before, holding stuff I'd been calling *green kryptonite*—and delivered glowing green pebbles to four aliens in globular environment tanks. They were at four different tables, sharing conversation with four other species. I'd never seen a rosyfin before. Rippling in the murky fluid within the transparent globe, the dorsal fin was triangular, rose-colored, fragile as gossamer, and ran from nose to tail of a body that looked like a flattened slug.

Out among the tables there was near-silence, except within the bubbles of sound that surrounded each table. It wasn't a total breakdown, then. But when I went back behind the bar the noise was still there.

I tried to ignore it. I certainly wasn't going to try to fix the sound system, not with fifty-odd customers and ten distinct species demanding my attention. I set out consommé and vodka for four glig, and thimble-sized flasks of chilled fluid with an ammonia base for a dozen chrome-yellow bugs each the size of a fifth of Haig Pinch. And the dialog continued: high twittering against grating metallic bass. What got on my nerves was the way the sounds seemed always on the verge of making sense!

Finally I just switched on the translator. It might be less irritating if I heard it in English.

I heard: "—noticed how often they speak of limits?"

"Limits? I don't understand you."

"Lightspeed limit. Theoretical strengths of metals, of crystals, of alloys. Smallest and largest masses at which an unseen body may be a neutron star. Maximum time and cost to complete a research project. Surface-to-volume relationship for maximum size of a creature of given design—"

"But every sapient race learns these things!"

"We find limits, of course. But with humans, the limits are what they seek first."

So they were talking about the natives, about us. Aliens often do. Their insights might be fascinating, but it gets boring fast. I let it buzz in my ear while I fished out another dozen flasks of ammonia mixture and set them on Gail's tray along with two Stingers. She went off to deliver them to the little yellow bugs, now parked in a horseshoe pattern on the rim of their table, talking animatedly to two human sociologists.

"It is a way of thinking," one of the voices said. "They set enormously complex limits on each other. Whole professions, called *judge* and *lawyer*, devote their lives to determining which human has violated which limit where. Another profession alters the limits arbitrarily."

"It does not sound entertaining."

"But all are forced to play the game. You must have noticed: the limits they find in the universe and the limits they set on each other bear the same name: law."

I had established that the twitterer was the one doing most of the talking. Fine. Now who were they? Two voices belonging to two radically different species . . .

"The interstellar community knows all of these limits in different forms."

"Do we know them all? Gödel's Principle sets a limit to the perfectability of mathematical systems. What species would have sought such a thing? Mine would not."

"Nor mine, I suppose. Still—"

"Humans push their limits. It is their first approach to any problem. When they learn where the limits lie, they fill in missing information until the limit breaks. When they break a limit, they look for the limit behind that."

"I wonder . . ."

I thought I had them spotted. Only one of the tables for two was occupied, by a chirpsithra and a startled-looking woman. My suspects were a cluster of three: one of the rosyfins, and two compact, squarish customers wearing garish designs on their exoskeletal shells. The shelled creatures had been smoking tobacco cigars under exhaust hoods. Now one seemed to be asleep. The other waved stubby arms as it talked.

I heard: "I have a thought. My savage ancestors used to die when they reached a certain age. When we could no longer breed, evolution was finished with us. There is a biological self-destruct built into us."

"It is the same with humans. But my own people never die unless killed. We fission. Our memories go far, far back."

"Though we differ in this, the result is the same. At some point in the dim past we learned that we could postpone our deaths. We never developed a civilization until individuals could live long enough to attain wisdom. The fundamental limit was lifted from our shells before we set out to expand into the world, and then the universe. Is this not true with most of the space-traveling peoples? The Pfarth species choose death only when they grow bored. Chirpsithra were long-lived before they reached the stars, and the gligstith[click]optok went even further, with their fascination with heredity-tailoring—"

"Does it surprise you, that intelligent beings strive to extend their lives?"

"Surprise? No. But humans still face a limit on their lifespans. The death limit has immense influence on their poetry. They may think differently from the rest of us in other ways. They may find truths we would not even seek."

An untranslated metal-on-metal scraping. Laughter? "You speculate irresponsibly. Has their unique approach taught them anything we know not?"

"How can I know? I have only been on this world three local years. Their libraries are large, their retrieval systems poor. But there is Gödel's Principle; and Heisenberg's Uncertainty Principle is a limit to what one can discover at the quantum level."

Pause. "We must see if another species has duplicated that one. Meanwhile, perhaps I should speak to another visitor."

"Incomprehension. Query?"

"Do you remember that I spoke of a certain glickstith[click]optok merchant?"

"I remember."

"You know their skill with water-world biology. This one comes to Earth with a technique for maintaining and restoring the early-maturity state in humans. The treatment is complex; but with enough customers the cost would drop, or so the merchant says. I must persuade it not to make the offer."

"Affirmative! Removing the death-limit would drastically affect human psychology!"

One of the shelled beings was getting up. The voices chopped off as I rounded the bar and headed for my chosen table, with no clear idea what I would say. I stepped into the bubble of sound around two shelled beings and a rosyfin, and said, "Forgive the interruption, sapients—"

"You have joined a wake," said the tank's translator widget.

The shelled being said, "My mate had chosen death. He wanted one last smoke in company." It bent and lifted its dead companion in its arms and headed for the door.

The rosyfin was leaving too, rolling his spherical fishbowl toward the door. I realised that its own voice hadn't penetrated the murky fluid around it. No chittering, no bone-shivering bass. I had the wrong table.

I looked around, and there were still no other candidates. Yet *somebody* here had casually condemned mankind—me!—to age and die.

Now what? I might have been hearing several voices. They all sound alike coming from a new species; and some aliens never interrupt each other.

The little yellow bugs? But they were with humans.

Shells? My voices had mentioned shells . . . but too many aliens have exoskeletons. Okay, a chirpsithra would have spoken by now; they're garrulous. Scratch any table that includes a chirp. Or a rosyfin. Or those srivinthish: I'd have heard the *skreek* of their breathing. Or the huge grey being who seemed to be singing. That left . . . half a dozen tables, and I couldn't interrupt that many.

Could they have left while I was distracted?

I hot-footed it back to the bar, and listened, and heard nothing. And my spinning brain could find only limits.

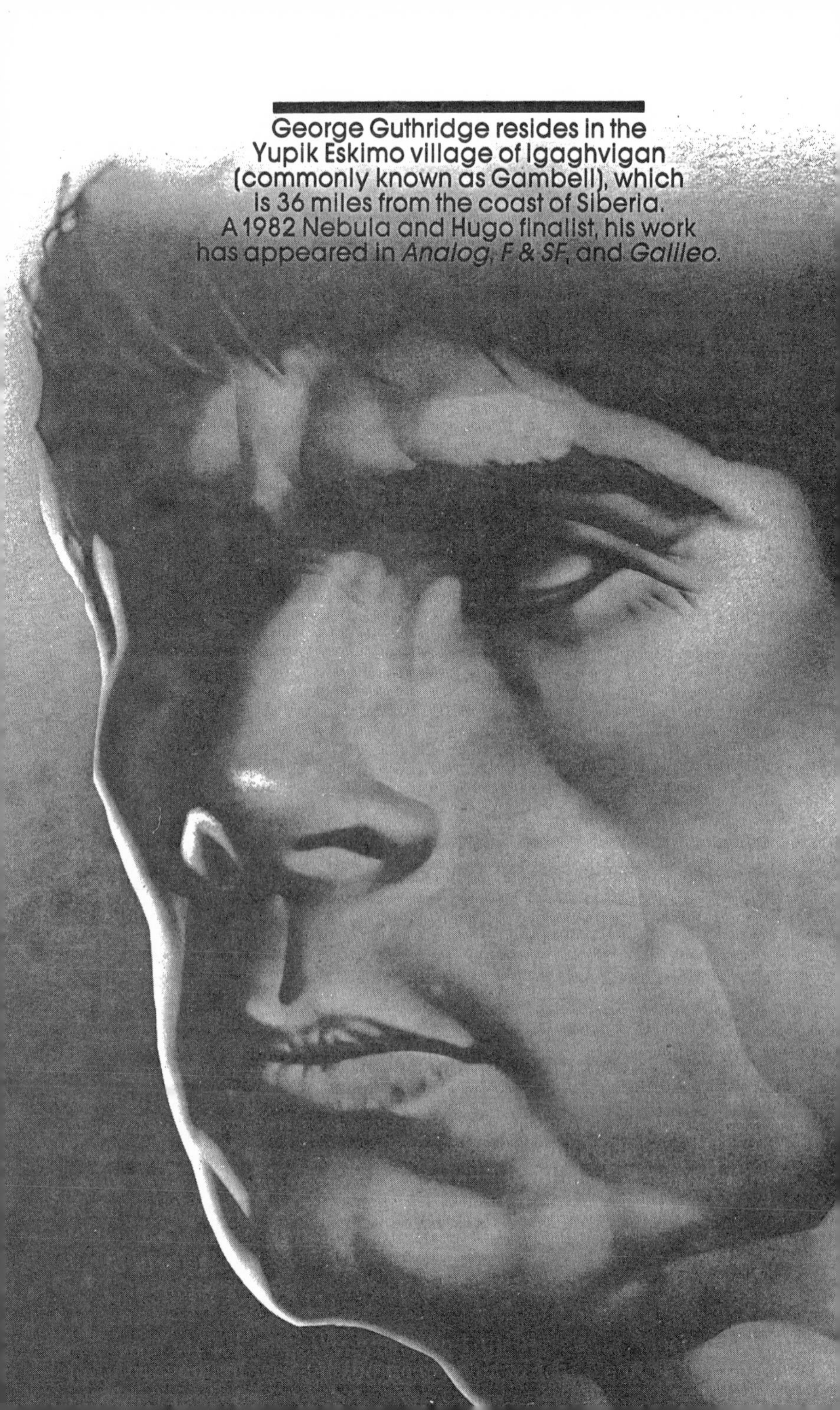

George Guthridge resides in the Yupik Eskimo village of Igaghvigan (commonly known as Gambell), which is 36 miles from the coast of Siberia. A 1982 Nebula and Hugo finalist, his work has appeared in *Analog*, *F & SF*, and *Galileo*.

Mr. Perry is the author of *The Tularemia Gambit* and he plans to have several new books on the market soon. His short fiction can be found in *Omni*, *IAsfm* and other science fiction magazines.

JOHNNY BEERCANS

by George Florance-Guthridge & Steve Perry

art: Gary Freeman

I lit the fuse and was about to dynamite the salmon when I saw the two Wanderers.

I was standing in the shadows where the Pacific cuts in among the rock cliffs. The narrow, deep inlet was full of king salmon; I could feel the fish in my blood. It would be a good catch. I glanced up and saw two people at the edge of the high cliff on the other side of the cove, framed by the sun. I couldn't see them clearly—the light was too strong—but I knew them to be strangers, refugees, not my people.

I stood looking a moment too long, my mouth open and the sea slapping at my bare feet, before tossing the two taped-together sticks. They barely touched the water; then thunder and spray made the world stand still.

When I looked up at the Wanderers again, I was on my back in the damp sand. The misty air was spangling with sunlight. I tried to stagger to my feet. My legs buckled, and I toppled forward, toward the sea.

Wetness hit my face. Cold.

Darkness came.

"Johnny?" It was Jawda's voice, but distant. "Johnny Beercans!" Someone was patting my cheeks.

I opened my eyes and blinked. My house came into focus around me. I was lying on the blankets of cedar bark; the room smelled of musty olachen oil, slightly rancid. Jawda's face, her eyes deep with concern, loomed above me. Behind her stood a blond-haired white boy, his shirt and cotton pants wet and crusted lightly with sand. Next to him was a woman with deep sallow cheeks, red almond-shaped eyes and impossibly long lashes. Her hair was a bright-red cascade that tumbled over her shoulders. She was not human, the woman: an alien. I had thought all the aliens were dead.

Pain sliced through my head as I tried to sit up. I clutched my temples and fell back. That only made it worse.

"Easy," Jawda said. "You probably have a concussion. The boy here had to dive in after you."

I tried to thank him but managed only a groan. I felt nauseated.

"He'll be all right," Jawda said to the two. "You can go."

The creaking of the door was as loud as the hinges of hell, and the thunder of its closing sounded like my dynamite. I felt Jawda's muscular hands on my shoulders. "Rest, Johnny." She removed the halibut vertebrae from my braids and combed my hair with her fingers. "I'll watch over you."

Again, darkness. But in it a face pulsed, a face with red almond-shaped eyes and even redder hair.

"We crossed the Fraser at Prince George," he said. His name was Denny—so very American, that name—but even though he had saved my life, I thought of him as "he." To the others in my village he was "that damn white boy." We had been a long time without strangers.

"The bridge was out, but we found a boat. There seemed to have been fighting there. I didn't know it had come this far north."

We sat on the beach. He picked up a fistful of sand and tried to let it trickle from his grip. The sand, too wet, fell in small clumps. The alien woman's head was in his lap, her electric red eyes closed, her cheeks shiny with moisture. The loose silvery gown she wore billowed in the breeze.

"After that we followed the Nechako through the Hazelton Mountains, then down along Gardner Inlet. I had part of a map. We were trying to make Prince Rupert, but somehow we got turned around. So here we are, among you Kwakiutl." He gave me a small smile.

"Among the *Nimkis,*" I corrected. "The other tribes are . . . no more. All dead." I gazed toward the sea. The waves slipped from beneath the fog like herring escaping from a cuttlefish rake. Gulls circled, cawing, above the breakers.

"I hated the mountains," the woman said quietly, without opening her eyes. "They were even worse than your empty cities. So dark and damp beneath those trees! We had to sleep underneath wet leaves. Even when we'd make love . . . wet leaves." She shuddered. "Awful."

"Relánge!"

She snapped her eyes open and stared at Denny. "Well, how do you expect me to feel? You'd roll me over onto you and . . . "

He clamped his hand over her mouth, then suddenly screamed and jerked it away. "Damn!" He clutched his hand to his chest, but not before I saw blood welling from a deep gash on his palm. Redness started dripping onto the woman's forehead. She did not move from his lap. After a moment she closed her eyes again, then reached up to wipe the blood from her head. She touched her fingers to her mouth and, for the first time since I had met her, smiled.

Another gray day came. Fog wreathed the evergreens, and the mist was heavy with salt. The chill cut through my denim jacket. I had to keep wiping drizzle from my goggles as I welded. I had hauled my equipment up the pyramid to weld on more cans. Rainbows shimmered and sparks made tiny suns as the TIG welder burned. The pyramid, built entirely of beer cans, was fifty feet high, a third as tall as the Doug fir around it. Far below in the village, the shacks looked like glistening cookie sheets. Tendrils of chimney smoke were held down by the dampness.

People called the pyramid "Johnny's monument," though no one knew what it was commemorating. Even I didn't know. Sometimes, after I had been working all day on it, they'd call to me as I trudged back to my house. "How many feet today, Johnny?"

"How many cans?"

"Better get the moon out of the way!"

"Watch out for eagles, Johnny."

The kidding was good-natured, and I enjoyed it.

I guess I began the pyramid about the time the whites started bombing the aliens—and one another. I don't think there's any relationship between the two events; it's just when I started the thing. I'm sure I had a reason at the time, but the years have blurred my memory.

I started with the beer cans piled up behind the hovel George California calls the village bar. There was about half an acre full, maybe four or five feet high. Whites used to come up from Powell River and even as far south as Vancouver and ask George to let them rummage for collectibles. They probably thought they'd find treasures like Billy Beer or Gobels or Jax cans—and they would have, because now such cans are part of the pyramid. They would even offer him money, just to look. George—his name was George Salmonbear back then—always refused. "No, let 'em rest," he'd say. "They served honorably." The whites would walk away muttering about stupid drunken Indians, and George would laugh at them.

"Johnny?"

I looked up. Jawda was struggling up the tiers in the drizzle, a blue shawl around her shoulders, her big butt swinging like a horse's as she climbed. I shut off the TIG.

She halted two tiers down and held up five cans of a six pack still joined by the plastic collar. Her damp hair hung in lank strands, black with runners of gray. She pushed it out of her eyes. "George just got back from Ocean Falls," she said. "He says the sea's too rough to go any farther." She gestured toward the harbor. "He brought you more cans in a net behind the boat."

Cans. Ironic, that. The whites used to give us food stamps and welfare checks. Then the aliens landed; the Americans and Russians grew more and more suspicious of the aliens and one another—and the hard rain began. Now there are no whites to give us food; only Wanderers are left. The cities are deserted, ready to be ransacked. And we bring home beer cans.

"Did you give the two Wanderers a good send-off?"

She shook her head and climbed up another tier. She didn't look directly at me. I thought I saw something like fear in her eyes. "When we arrived at Ocean Falls, the alien woman wouldn't get out of the boat. She sat in the stern and refused to budge. I told George he should throw her out, but he wouldn't touch her. None of the men would—you know how they are. George said if I wanted her out of the catamaran so much, I should put her out myself."

She paused, stared down at her feet, and spoke in a quieter voice. "I . . . I couldn't bring myself to do it."

"And the white boy?"

"Oh, he was willing enough. He stood on the dock with that tattered carpetbag of his and called to her. I think he wanted to leave here as much—as much as . . . "

" . . . as much as you wanted the woman to leave?"

The fear in her eyes became anger, then fear again. She looked away, toward the village, the angularity of her acne-scarred face softened by something I didn't recognize. "George got drunk on the way back," she said. "He says he's going to take his chainsaw and build a canoe." She was silent a moment, and I watched the treetops blowing and Jawda's abalone-shell earrings fluttering in the wind. "When we got home with the boy and the alien woman, he took an axe to his boat."

"What?"

"He found a Kenmore washing machine he wanted to bring back, but there was no room in the boat with the woman and the white boy. Now he's chopping the hull to pieces."

That sounded like George. There would have been little use for the washer, anyway. The power from Kitimat had been out since six months before the war. The village generator broke down a year later, and no one had gotten around to fixing it. I had the portable I used for welding, but most of the village was without electricity.

"Maybe I should go talk to George."

Jawda took hold of my arm. "Don't go, Johnny."

I looked at her, surprised. "Why not?"

She fixed her gaze on mine, then looked down at the five cans she'd carried up. "The alien woman is there. She—I—there is something evil about her."

"Don't be ridiculous." I gently pulled away from her grip. "Besides, she belongs to the white boy."

"Johnny . . . "

I went on down the pyramid.

Jawda and I didn't talk much after that. Once I saw her in front of her shack, cleaning her ought-six. I asked her if she was going to hunt deer. She nodded but didn't look up. I reminded her that eating venison can cause forgetfulness, but she only grunted and would not laugh. A few days later I saw her and Relánge walking along the beach and talking. Rain fell, drenching the two women, but they kept walking and talking. They seemed friendly.

Then rumors started. Jawda was eating a lot of venison lately, people said.

About a week later Relánge came to see me. I was inside the pyramid, positioning the mermaid hood ornament from George's boat next to my thunderbird mask. She told me that George was planning a grease feast in honor of the canoe he was building. I nodded and continued my work.

"It's beautiful in here," she said, leaning back against a ledge of angled cans. Sunbeams slatted between the loosely spaced tiers, and the pyramid's interior was aglint with dusty light. "It's like being in a metallic cathedral." Silvery shadows lay across her thin face like strips of tape. She had a young woman's body, but for all I knew of aliens' ages, she could have been sixteen or six hundred. I looked away when she noticed my stare. I used my sleeve to dust the thunderbird's beak.

"Where's your friend?" I asked, to ease the tension.

"Oh, you mean Denny? Resting. He wants to spend the afternoon making love on the beach, so he thought he should get some sleep first. Warm days are few here; he wants to take advantage of it."

I nodded and wiped at the thunderbird. Hearing her talk about making love with someone else bothered me.

"I had a long talk with Jawda," she said suddenly. "I told her about my homeworld." She gave me a coy smile, her eyes alight with intrigue.

"I saw you," I said.

"I know. I noticed you watching us. I knew you were wondering what we were talking about." She stepped toward me and slid soft long-fingered hands up to my shoulders. Her touch made me shiver with pleasure. "I thought you also might like to know how it is out there, among the stars."

I stepped away, to rub at the thunderbird's wing. "We don't have much use for stars here, what with the fog and all." I chuckled.

She didn't laugh. My chuckle died abruptly. Again she touched my shoulders. "Don't you want to know about gleaming cities and the pleasures of high civilization?"

I took an unwelded can from a shelf and held it in front of her. With one hand I crushed the thin aluminum. "I already know about cities," I said.

She looked at me, then at the can. Then she turned and looked at her distorted reflection in the pyramid wall. "Jawda wanted to know," she said. "I grew hoarse from telling her. She wanted to know everything."

"I'm not Jawda," I said.

On the village dock George had forty or fifty thousand blankets, boxes of kelp containers filled with olachen oil, and stacks of dried chinook and halibut fillets, enough stuff to fill a warehouse. I was helping him stack the goods and cover them with tarps for the upcoming grease feast. No one had built a canoe in twenty years, and George intended to have a potlatch that people would talk about for another twenty.

White men never understood potlatching, though it had never been all that complex. Sometimes potlatches were held on festival days, and there were regular ones at different seasons. But anyone could call for a potlatch, for just about any reason. Sometimes they were only an excuse to party, with little or no serious competition; other times, one man might have it in for another. It was always a dishonor to lose, no matter how small the amount given away. And the rules were simple: whoever gave away the most, in the best style, won. It was the giving that was important. Sure, white men talked about giving, mostly at Christmas, but they didn't really understand. They had even made it illegal in Canada, for a time; holding a feast and giving away most of what you owned was actually a crime. It wasn't a crime any more, of course. There were few white men around to enforce such stupid laws. Without potlatching, how could a young man demonstrate his manhood against another young buck? How could old men show their craftiness and hard-earned wisdom? It was part of our way, as much as the salmon, and white men just didn't comprehend it.

Moving the goods from George's several shacks down to the docks was hard work, but I didn't mind. At least we'd stopped potlatching with white men's goods. That's what had happened after the war.

It had been frantic, then. We had access to a lot of things the neutron bombs didn't destroy. People held gigantic potlatches and gave away CB radios and cases of Campbell's chicken noodle soup and boatloads of Tide. I never saw the honor in that, since everyone had equal access to the goods; but I was in the minority, so I kept my mouth shut. Then people started giving away Mazda RX-7s and Mack trucks and Greyhound buses. Since there aren't any roads to our village—or even to Kitimat or Ocean Falls, for that matter—they just gave the titles. Eventually they were potlatching big chunks of land—nobody was using it, after all—which is how George Salmonbear became George California and Grace Turtlefire became Antarctica Grace. Someone even tried to give New York City to Jawda. "I wouldn't mind being a place most people would only visit," she said. "But I wouldn't want to be a place constantly stuffed full of people." She stood before the crowd, looking at each of us in turn so that no one would miss her allusion or her anger. "You play foolishly, like children!"

At last people came to their senses and went back to the old-time potlatching. I admired Jawda for her stand, and that night we made love. We'd had sex together more times than I could remember, for she'd been my good-time woman for twenty years, even during my two marriages; but we'd never made *love* before. Her lips were never more supple, her flesh never warmer. When we finished, I smiled and said, "Thank you." That was as close as I'd ever come to telling a woman I loved her, and Jawda knew it.

The wonder gradually wore off, and we went back to old habits. She saved her passion for new lovers, and I saved mine for the welding and the times when the taking of salmon sang in my blood.

Jawda was up among the yellow cedar and yew trees now, on the slopes that belly down to the sea. I wondered if her increasing need to shoot blacktail was like my feeling for fishing or my pyramid. She had three gutted animals hanging head-down in her meat shack, the damp earth floor stained with their blood. I looked across the harbor toward the slopes, in the hope that I might see her stalking.

"Quickly! Help!"

I turned and saw the white boy running up the dock toward George and me. It only took him a few seconds to reach us.

"Come—come with me!"

I dropped the box of olachen oil containers. "What—?"

"It's Jawda! She's been hurt!"

A freezing pain went from my groin up my spine. We ran.

Catawba Trail was a blurred corridor; we crossed the creek at Market-on-the-Meadow and sprinted for the hills.

We found her at the base of a redrock slide. Her face was a mass of blood and bruises, her eyes wide and fixed. Her wool shirt was torn, and under it was a gash that showed flesh and clotted blood.

A crowd began to gather, drawn by our frantic dash and the vibration of death. I picked up the ought-six lying next to her body, then knelt. Everyone was hushed. The wind blew against my cheek, making my skin tingle. I was aware, suddenly, of the throb of my heartbeat and of a hollow feeling. My mouth was parched, as dry as old bones. I trembled as I closed Jawda's eyes.

"There's a path along the ridge," George said. "She must have fallen."

"Maybe she was shooting at a blacktail and wasn't watching what she was doing," someone said.

"Maybe she had forgotten what she was doing," I said.

Silence.

The white boy knelt, his eyes asking permission to touch her. I was a stone. Finally, he reached out and moved her head from side to side. It was a boneless kind of motion, devoid of tension. He looked at the torn shirt, at the wound on her shoulder, and his lips tightened. He looked as white-faced as a white boy can get.

Two days later I covered my face with tallow and smeared it blue with indigo clay and buried Jawda at the base of a clump of five Alaskan spruce overlooking the sea. I told no one where. If you take someone's nail clippings, bits of clothing, or dirt dampened by the their urine or spit, place those things inside a human corpse, sew up all the body openings, seal them with pitch, and put the corpse in a tree, when the body decays and falls from the branches, the donor of the clippings will die. I didn't want anyone thinking of using Jawda for such sorcery. Though everyone loved Jawda, the coming of the Wanderers had changed us; things were different somehow.

That night I slept naked and alone in the rear of one of the communal shacks, separated from the others by a *mawitl* screen. There seemed an unvoiced consensus that I should be the chief mourner for Jawda. I bore the grief.

Beyond the screen some of the others sat around the glowing embers of a tired fire, quietly chanting. The smoky darkness was full of ghosts and memories, It was a long time before I slept.

I dreamed I dug up Jawda's body and reburied her in the pyramid, where the sunlight sometimes seeped between the tiers to strike the dirt at midday. Beer cans glimmered around me like cave crystals. Days came and went; storms came and went. The weathered shacks fell apart, and we remaining Nimkis vanished from the earth, leaving only the glittering pyramid, baked and washed clean of labels, standing among the cedar and white pine and scrub oak. It alone stood, a testimonial to a people whose bones had long since crumbled and been washed to the sea. Within that pyramid lived and watched the spirit of Jawda Twodogs, shawled in blue, her face acne-scarred and painted blue for love and grief; her spirit keeping alive the holiest of words, *Kwakiutl*: the People.

I awoke, sweating. The room was hot and smoky. I lay still, gripping the edges of the bed's woven yew sticks, afraid the house had somehow caught fire. My ears rang with the silence.

I sensed a presence beside me. I blinked and gazed up into a pair of red eyes. "Johnny," Relánge whispered, and her cool hand eased up my leg to my thigh. I shuddered but didn't move. Her lips touched my chest, then worked up along my neck to my cheek. I felt her tongue on the bridge of my nose, her breath smelling faintly of spice. My eyes adjusted to the weak light and her face seemed longer and thinner than before, her nose high and narrow and slightly crooked, like the beak of a thunderbird, come for me.

"Aren't you supposed to be with the white boy?" My voice was a rasp.

"I am always with Denny," she said. Her hand moved higher, away from me, and she undid a clasp near her throat. The silver gown fell away, and she was nude. She knelt astride me, then lay against me, her breasts cool against my chest. Her mouth found mine. The kiss was long and sensual and tasted slightly of blood.

We coupled in a single, slick movement. She uttered a throaty sigh and sank her teeth into my left shoulder.

"Hey!" I jerked away and felt warm liquid creep down my arm. The cut was ragged, pulsing. I started to shove her away, but her lips went back to the wound. Before I could move, I felt a wave of warmth flood me, a soothing ease.

Once, in my long-ago past, I had used heroin. I tried it only once, for it had frightened me; I had known I would go to it all too easily for the rapture it held.

This feeling was that and more. It was a constant feeling of orgasm, yet quiet. As we rocked, I felt my eyes roll back; I felt her fingernails dig into the flesh around my shoulder and heard the sound of her sucking grow louder. I didn't care. I was lost in the giving of blood and the taking of woman.

The moment came, and it was more intense than before, impossible to bear. I screamed.

"That was nice," she said, as we rested afterward.

Nice. "Yes." The song of the salmon had gone from my blood, displaced by an alien woman from some distant world. The ecstasy of Relánge.

She ran her index finger along the edges of the cut, then licked her fingertip. "I killed Jawda, you know." She slipped one arm under my head and the other across my chest.

"I know."

"Yet you did nothing."

"The others would have torn you to pieces if they had known, or even suspected. I—I didn't want that."

"It was an accident." She kissed my nipple. "I told her about the Kiss. She wanted it, wanted me to do it to her—there, up on the ridge. She said she had been eating too much venison; she was losing her mind. She wanted me to bleed her, take away the spirits of the deer that were haunting her. She ate the meat because she wanted to forget that you had once loved her but didn't any longer. She wanted to forget that no one wanted her except for a quick roll before he went home to his wife. But just as we began the Kiss, she became frightened. She jerked away. I tried to grab her. She fell."

Relánge propped herself up on one elbow, a little away from me. "I have never hurt anyone before. We—my kind—pride ourselves on that. Even when your kind bombed us, we didn't fight back. We could have destroyed you—our technology is beyond yours—but that isn't our way.

"Now I can't go back to my world. None of us who survived can go back. A relief ship would never arrive in time. The distance is too great. So we're Wanderers, like some of your kind. And I'm here with you. Think of me as your slave, Johnny." Her voice was soft, her lips close to my ear. "Whatever you want, whenever you want it, as many times as you want."

"A vampire slave," I said.

"No. It's not like that. It's not like food. It's the way we . . . it's part of our . . . communion."

I stared into the smoky semi-darkness.

"Johnny, what's this?" She held up something that glittered.

I looked. It was the copper tied around my neck with a leather thong. "A shield," I said. "A piece of one, anyway. They're used in potlatching. You buy one with, say, a hundred thousand blankets. Then if you want to hurt someone, really nail him, you use it. You find out how many blankets he has to potlatch. Suppose he has seventy-five thousand. You've only got fifty thousand, so you give him all of them. Then, when he thinks he's got you beat, you get everyone's attention and break the copper. Fifty thousand blankets, plus the copper worth twice that. You've doubled him. You've shamed him. He'll *never* live it down, unless he can somehow repay." I tapped the copper with my fingernail. "George Salmonbear—George California, now—did it to me when I was the white boy's age." I smiled at the memory. "Maybe that's why I spend so much time welding cans together. Rebuilding pride, maybe."

I felt a twinge of old pain, but it died as her lips moved on me and found the wound on my shoulder.

Rain came. It pelted down against the chanters and dancers and beat against the dock. No one stopped dancing. George was in the middle of the others, dancing with a bottle in hand, drunk and getting drunker. It was as if he was in his own circle, oblivious to the rest of us, drunk on scotch and glory. It was the greatest potlatch any of us could remember. We were all drunk. No one except maybe George cared about the canoe. We danced for our own reasons: love, hate, the past, the future, Jawda. Those of us who were *Hamatsa* danced and spoke our secret names to the wind and rain. We ate cod and flounder and cockles served with hemlock-bark sap and clover root until our bellies were full and we had to lean out over the water to puke. The rain fell harder. George made a speech about fishing and friendship and the magic of Kenmore washing machines. While he talked, I grabbed Relánge, and we went behind the fish-cleaning shack. We made love sitting up in the sand, my back against the corrugated metal. When we returned to the dance, my shirt was torn, and my chest was covered with bloody grit. I stripped away my jacket and shirt and danced, laughing. George kept blabbering. The rain washed the dock and the dancers.

Suddenly everything stopped. George ceased talking. The dancers came to a halt. The chants died. Even the rain seemed to slacken.

I kept turning for another few seconds, singing, but I was all alone. I was busy thinking of Relánge, of making another trip to the shack, but the quiet rippled into motion. The crowd parted, leaving a gap between the dock and the village. I stumbled forward and forced my eyes to focus.

The white boy came down the path and onto the dock.

He was naked as a newborn, carrying his beat-up carpetbag.

From the set of his eyes and body, it was obvious he was coming toward me; I stood apart from the others.

The boy looked angry. He stopped at mid-dock and sat down, cross-legged. He fumbled with the carpetbag clasp, yanked the thing open, and started unloading his possessions. Two wadded shirts. Rolled-up socks, three pairs. A razor. Three battered paperbacks. Then he cried out and upended the carpetbag and shook it. Buttons, coins, paper clips fell out. Bits of paper floated down and were swept away by the wind.

The crowd gathered around him, some of them examining his junk as if it were treasure. He stared at me through the steady rain. I walked over and looked down at him. His eyes were full of tears—and hate.

"Everything I have," he said. His cheeks were tight and his lips thin with emotion. "Everything I own in the world. Take it."

"You're crazy. You've flipped out or something. Here. Have a drink." I offered him the bottle I held. He slapped it away, and it skittered across the dock.

"I saw you and Relánge last night," he said. "And I saw you"—he trembled with rage as he pointed toward the fish-cleaning shack—"I saw you *there!*" He waved at the junk from the carpetbag. "So you take it! You have to!"

I looked from him to my people, suddenly understanding what it was he was doing. I could tell by their faces that they saw it too: a matter of honor.

I leaned over the boy. "You can't do this," I said. "Get up." I touched his shoulder, but he didn't move. "You can't potlatch. You're not Nimkis. You're not even a goddam Indian!"

He folded his arms and gazed up at me. The hate in his eyes turned to scorn.

"Holy Jesus." I ran my fingers through my wet hair. I turned and walked to the end of the dock. I needed a drink and some time to think. I needed Relánge again.

"Okay," I said at last, then turned and walked back to him. "You want a fight, white boy, you got it. There's a whole shack full of junk up there in the village. And more of my stuff in the communal house. It's all yours, brother. Every last fishhook."

The crowd murmured louder. They nodded.

I pulled off my pants and undershorts and threw them at him. The jeans hit him on the chest, but he didn't move. I stalked to my denim jacket and balled-up shirt and tossed those things at him, too. The wind caught the shirt and blew it toward the water, but it landed on the wood. I stood there as naked as the boy, feeling triumphant.

A ring came rolling across the dock toward me. I bent and picked it up. A college ring. Yale.

"*Summa cum laude*," the boy said. "Pre-med. I was one of the last students to graduate before they shut it down for good. And in high school they told me I was foolish even to try and attend an Ivy League school. I didn't have the brains, they said."

I closed my fist around the ring, then nodded and tossed it to George.

"Down the beach," I said, then repeated it because the words were lost in the rain. "Down the beach is King Cove. You remember it; you dove into it to save me. It has the best shore fishing around here, that cove. The salmon come in and beg to be taken; they sing to your blood. Grounds are supposed to be communal, but we all know that's a lot of crap. King Cove is mine. It was my father's and his father's and his before that. No one fishes it now but me." I slapped my chest to make the point stronger.

"King Cove is yours now, white boy."

The crowd roared and clapped its hands, a many-handed beast with one mind.

George handed me a bottle; I grinned and took a drink.

The boy opened his mouth and removed a false front tooth on a small plastic denture. He held it up.

"You're potlatching a goddam *tooth?*" I asked. People laughed. But the boy held the thing, his expression serious. The people quieted.

"When I was very young, my father used to beat me," he said. "One day he hit me so hard this happened." He waved the false tooth.

"A lot of kids get beat," someone said. "Big deal."

He ignored the comment. "My father died that night. He went upstairs, lay down, and had a stroke." The boy stood and took hold of my wrist and put the tooth in my hand. "This is the only thing he ever gave to me that I kept, all I have in the world to remember him by."

I saw scorn on my friends' faces. It was valuable, that tooth. What did I possibly have to top it? I turned and walked along the dock. I watched the waves lap against the pilings. The dock was solid and strong, but eventually the waves would wear it away; the sea always won. I turned back toward the boy and the crowd.

I gazed at him for what seemed a long time.

Then, my voice quiet and even, I said, "I give you the pyramid."

I didn't look toward my giant construction of beer cans, so much a part of me it had become my name. I was afraid to look it at.

The boy stared at me, his eyes going wide. His face went slack; the muscles of his belly were no longer tight and defined. He put his hands to his face. I watched rain run from his hair over his forehead and hands in a rivulet that went down his arms and dripped from his elbows to the dock.

The crowd was silent. They nodded and moved away from him. He had fought well, but he was done. He sat down on the dock, still holding his face, and sobbed.

I walked over to him and squatted. We were naked and alone. "Did you really think you could beat an old drunken Indian like me?" I stroked his matted hair. "Come on. Let's go look at that pile of beer cans you own."

He looked up and sighed. His voice quavered when it came, and it was loud enough to carry to the ends of the Earth. "I give you Relánge," he said.

Something icy speared my soul. I was speechless. She wasn't really his to give, of course, but that didn't matter. He was giving her up. I knew what she meant to him. I had had her, and I knew.

The crowd was still, like a painting.

I touched the leather cord around my neck. The copper. The pyramid had been a great part of my adult life, the fishing only slightly less. But the copper was everything. George had stood before me, broken it, and handed it to me. The thousands of blankets the copper represented were only part of its value. It still held all the years of shame during which I'd carried it. Nothing was more important. I could give my shame away, and nothing the white boy had could match that, not even his life.

I fingered the metal and knew I could win.

Then I saw Relánge move in the background. She looked at me with the copper and smiled. One of the wounds on my shoulder suddenly throbbed. I glanced at the cut, remembering how it had come to be there. I stared at the boy, his body covered with a dozen or more half-healed wounds similar to mine. And I knew that in a twisted way, he and I were brothers. Blood brothers.

I looked again at Relánge. I understood. Whatever her intentions, by human standards, she was evil. Jawda, the white boy, me—she hadn't meant to hurt us, but we were victims. And there would be many others.

I let the cord fall back against my neck, the copper cold against my chest. "You win, Denny."

I helped him stand. We walked toward Relánge. The people seemed to melt away. There were only we three.

I would be with her, come nightfall. And while she took blood from me, I would take from her as well: nail clippings, tiny bits of flesh or hair, dirt defiled by her urine. Then, in the dark, I would find a shovel and return to Jawda.

She would lie not within the pyramid, as in my dream, but atop it.

by
Scott
Sanders

THE ANATOMY LESSON

art: George Barr

The author's collection of tales, *Wilderness Plots*, will be published by William Morrow in 1983. He recently finished his first science fiction novel, *Terrarium*, and is at work on a new one entitled *The Invisible Company*.

By the time I reached the Anatomy Library all the bones had been checked out. Students bent over the wooden boxes everywhere, in hallways and snack-bar, assembling feet and arms, scribbling diagrams in notebooks. Half the chairs were occupied by slouching skeletons, and reclining skeletons littered the tables like driftwood. Since I also would be examined on the subject the next day, I asked the librarian to search one last time for bone-boxes in the storeroom.

"But I tell you, they've all been given out," she said, glaring at me from beneath an enormous snarl of dark hair, like a fierce animal caught in a bush. How many students had already pestered her for bones this evening?

I persisted. "Haven't you got any damaged skeletons? Irregulars?"

Ignoring my smile, she measured me with her fierce stare, as if estimating the size of box my bones would fill after she had made supper of me. A shadow drooped beneath each of her eyes, permanent sorrow, like the tearmark of a clown. "Irregulars," she repeated, turning away from the counter.

I blinked with relief at her departing back. Only as she slipped noiselessly into the storeroom did I notice her gloved hands. Fastidious, I thought. Doesn't want to soil herself with bone dust and mildew.

While awaiting my specimens, I studied the vertebrae which knobbed through the bent necks of students all around me, each one laboring over fragments of skeletons. Five lumbar vertebrae, seven cervical, a round dozen thoracic: I rehearsed the names, my confidence building.

Presently the librarian returned with a box. It was the size of an orange crate, wooden, dingy from age or dryrot. The metal clasps that held it shut were tarnished a sickly green. No wonder she wore the gloves.

"This one's for restricted use," she announced, shoving it over the counter.

I hesitated, my hands poised above the crate as if I were testing it for heat.

"Well, do you want it, or don't you?" she said.

Afraid she would return it to the archives, I pounced on it with one hand and with the other signed a borrower's card. "Old model?" I inquired pleasantly. She did not smile.

I turned away with the box in my arms. The burden seemed lighter than its bulk would have promised, as if the wood had dried with age. Perhaps instead of bones inside there would be pyramids of dust. The metal clasps felt cold against my fingers.

After some searching I found a clear space on the floor beside a scrawny man whose elbows and knees protruded through rents in his clothing like so many lumps of a sea serpent above the waters. When I tugged at the clasps they yielded reluctantly. The hinges opened with a gritty shriek, raising for a moment all round me a dozen glazed eyes, which soon returned to their studies.

Inside I found the usual wooden trays for bones, light as birdwings; but instead of the customary lining of vinyl they were covered with a metal the color of copper and the puttyish consistency of lead. Each bone fitted into its pocket of metal. Without consulting notes, I started confidently on the foot, joining tarsal to metatarsal. But it was soon evident that there were too many bones. Each one seemed a bit odd in shape, with an extra flange where none should be, or a socket at right angles to the orthodox position. The only way of accommodating all the bones was to assemble them into a seven-toed monstrosity, slightly larger than the foot of an adult male, phalanges all of the same length, with ankle-bones bearing the unmistakable nodes for—what? Wings? Flippers?

This drove me back to my anatomy text. But no consulting of diagrams would make sense of this foot. A practiced scrape of my knifeblade assured me these were real bones. But from what freakish creature? Feeling vaguely guilty, as if in my ignorance I had given birth to this monstrosity, I looked around the library to see if anyone had noticed. Everywhere living skulls bent studiously over dead ones, ignoring me. Only the librarian seemed to be watching me sidelong, through her tangled hair. I hastily scattered the foot bones to their various compartments.

Next I worked at the hand, which boasted six rather than seven digits. Two of them were clearly thumbs, opposite in their orientation, and each of the remaining fingers was double-jointed, so that both sides of these vanished hands would have served as palms. At the wrist a socket opened in one direction, a ball joint protruded in the other, as if the hand were meant to snap onto an adjoining one. I now bent secretively over my outrageous skeleton, unwilling to meet stares from other students.

After tinkering with fibula and clavicle, each bone recognizable but slightly awry from the human, I gingerly unpacked the plates of the skull. I had been fearing these bones most of all. Their scattered state was unsettling enough to begin with, since in ordinary skeletal kits they would have been assembled into a braincase. Their gathered state was even more unsettling. They would only go together in one arrangement, yet it appeared so outrageous to me that I forced myself to reassemble the skull three times. There was only one jaw, to be sure, though an exceedingly broad one, and only two holes for ears. But the skull itself was clearly double, as if two heads had been squeezed together, like cherries grown double on one stem. Each hemisphere of the brain enjoyed its own cranium. The opening for the nose was in its accustomed place, as were two of the eyes. But in the center of the vast forehead, like the drain in an empty expanse of bathtub, was the socket for a third eye.

I closed the anatomy text, helpless before this freak. Hunched over to shield it from the gaze of other students, I stared long at that triangle of eyes, and at the twinned craniums that splayed out behind like a fusion of moons. No, I decided, such a creature was not possible. It was a hoax, a malicious joke designed to shatter my understanding of anatomy. But I would not fall for the trick. Angrily I disassembled this counterfeit skull, stuffed the bones back into their metal pockets, clasped the box shut and returned it to the counter.

"This may seem funny to you," I said, "but I have an examination to pass."

"Funny?" the librarian replied.

"This hoax." I slapped the box, raising a puff of dust. When she only lifted an eyebrow mockingly, I insisted: "It's a fabrication, an impossibility."

"Is it?" she taunted, laying her gloved hands atop the crate.

Furious, I said, "It's not even a very good hoax. No one who knows the smallest scrap of anatomy would fall for it."

"Really?" she said, peeling the glove away from one wrist. I wanted to shout at her and then hurry away, before she could uncover that hand. Yet I was mesmerized by the slide of cloth, the pinkish skin emerging. "I found it hard to believe myself, at first," she said, spreading the naked hand before me, palm up. I was relieved to count only five digits. But the fleshy heel was inflamed and swollen, as if the bud of a new thumb were sprouting there.

A scar, I thought feverishly. Nothing awful.

Then she turned the hand over and displayed for me another palm. The fingers curled upward, then curled in the reverse direction, forming a cage of fingers on the counter.

I flinched away. Skeletons were shattering in my mind, names of bones were fluttering away like blown leaves. All my carefully gathered knowledge was scattering. Unable to look at her, unwilling to glimpse the socket of flesh that might be opening on her forehead beneath the dangling hair, I kept my gaze turned aside.

"How many of you are there?" I hissed.

"I'm the first, so far as I know. Unless you count our friend here," she added, rapping her knuckles against the bone-box.

I guessed the distances to inhabited planets, conjured up the silhouettes of space craft. "But where do you come from?"

"Boise."

"Boise, *Idaho?*"

"Well, actually, I grew up on a beet farm just outside Boise."

"You mean you're—" I pointed one index finger at her, and shoved the other against my chest.

"Human? Of course!" She laughed, a quick sound like the release of bubbles underwater. Students at nearby tables gazed up momentarily from their skeletons with bleary eyes. The librarian lowered her voice, until it burbled like whalesong. "I'm as human as you are," she murmured.

"But your hands? Your face?"

"Until a few months ago they were just run-of-the-mill human hands." She drew the glove quickly on and touched her swollen cheeks. "My face was skinny. My shoes used to fit."

"Then what happened?"

"I assembled these bones." Again she rapped on the crate. From inside came a hollow clattering, like the sound of gravel sliding.

"You're—becoming—one of them?"

"So it appears."

Her upturned lips and downturned eyes gave me contradictory messages. The clown-sad eyes seemed too far apart. Even buried under its shrubbery of dark hair, her forehead seemed impossibly broad.

"Aren't you frightened?" I said.

"Not any more," she answered. "Not since my head began to open."

I winced, recalling the vast skull, pale as porcelain, and the triangle of eyes. I touched the bone-box gingerly. "What *is* it?"

"I don't know yet. But I begin to get glimmerings, begin to see it, alive and flying."

"Flying?"

"Swimming, maybe. My vision's still too blurry. For now, I just think of it as a skeleton of the possible, a fossil of the future."

I tried to imagine her ankles affixed with wings, her head swollen like a double moon, her third eye glaring. "And what sort of creature will you be when you're—changed?"

"We'll just have to wait and see, won't we?"

"We?" I echoed, backing carefully over the linoleum.

"You've put the bones together, haven't you?"

I stared at my palms, then turned my hands over to examine the twitching skin where the knuckles should be.

THE BOARDER

by Madeleine E. Robins

art: Broeck Steadman

The author is 29, with a 'decorative' degree in Theatre Studies, and attended the Clarion Science Fiction Workshop in 1981. She has recently finished a relocation from Boston to Greenwich Village, where she lives with a cat and a typewriter.

The doorbell broke the silence of the apartment. From his cage the canary echoed the sound wanly; Zenia rose from her chair to let the monster into her home.

It was a small apartment, the best she could afford on a fixed income, decorated with old furniture, old faces, the small trappings of memory. Zenia was one hundred and forty-three years old, and her world was changing again.

The letter from the Corporation still lay open on the china cabinet as she shuffled past; the regular spacing, the evenly balanced mass of the paragraphs could fool one into believing that it was only a letter, a communication. It was polite, even congratulatory, offering Zenia Mavroandrates the opportunity to join with the Fairleigh Corporation in a pioneering program to better the lives of all Corporation dependents by extending a welcome to an extra-terrestrial, an alien stranded by sudden sickness or injury on Earth, unable to return to die decently on its own world. Zenia was invited to share

her home with one such creature, to remove it from the dreary Corporation-owned shelter and make it welcome in her apartment where, from the Corporation's standpoint, anyway, two could live as cheaply as one.

In smaller print, like an afterthought, the letter mentioned the importance of Zenia's cooperation as an example: the widow of Captain Peter Mavroandrates, working to cement interstellar relations. Cooperation would be worth 65 cr. a month above the 350 cr. Zenia already received as her regular Corporation stipend, a gesture of appreciation for her good-hearted assistance. The letter also regretted that failure to cooperate in this forward-looking program would result in the reluctant invocation of section eleven on the Security/Welfare contract Zenia had purchased years before; her stipend would be reduced to the basic rate, 100 cr. per month, with which Zenia could just afford to buy a share in a Social Welfare home and wait to die.

Wishing only to be left alone with her pictures, her few friends, her canary, and her silence, Zenia opened the door. Two men, and the woman from the Fairleigh office, with a shiny black perambulator trailing behind them, its shade lowered to hide the passenger from inquisitive eyes.

"Hello, Mrs. Maverandrattis." The Fairleigh woman mispronounced the name as she always did. The two men wheeled the carriage into the far corner of the room, away from heaters, the window, and the door, and unloaded two small machines which, once set into motion, purred, clucked, and gurgled chattily. One machine was low and flat, curved slightly, connected by delicate cords to the other, larger one, a tall cylinder of flat white metal. There were gauges, a light, slots, and a few unreadable labels. The Fairleigh woman chattered unheard as Zenia watched the process of preparing her home to receive the alien.

"I don't know how to work any of this," Zenia broke in at last, resentful. If they understood her ignorance, they might take the thing and its machinery away and leave her and Peter's photographs and Roscoe the canary alone in their small space. From every tabletop Peter's smile reassured her; images of her husband, long dead, a hundred years gone, telling her not to mind this latest invasion.

"It's very simple, Mrs. Mavroandrates," the younger of the two men assured her. "Look, you put water in *here*. And twice a week you fit one of these in *here;* that's food." He showed her a flat, square brick of dun-colored stuff, showed her where it would fit into an upper slot on the white cylinder. "That's all you need to do. And if this light here ever goes on, you call us. There's a link-up with a computer at the shelter, but you know these things—" his smile invited her confidence. "They go crazy sometimes. You ask for me if you like. Name's Les Carik." A nice young man.

"It eats this stuff?" Zenia looked at the dull brick. "And how does it—" she stopped; some things a lady did not say in front of strangers in her home. The Corporation lady snickered. "I got a right to know, don't I? You give me this thing to look after, I got a right to know what I got to do with it."

"Sure you got a right to know, ma'am." Les Carik ignored the Fairleigh woman. "The machines take care of everything, Mrs. Mavroandrates." He looked, she thought, a little like Peter had. Like Peter before the last flight.

The thought returned her attention to the machines. "Where is *it?* Where's the thing?"

"It's called a B'nithouri," the other woman corrected sharply. Zenia wondered if the woman garbled the thing's name as she garbled hers. Peter's name.

The technician was lifting something onto the lower machine, which gave way with a settled whuuush under the thing's weight.

It was unlike anything. Zenia could no more think what the thing was like than she could hate it. Egg-shaped, it stood a meter tall on what looked like roots that grasped the machine; there were projections, like tentacles, or maybe branches, which ended in a fringe of dense, unmoving flesh. No legs. No eyes. No up, down, or sideways. It looked, Zenia thought, like a sculpture in one of the old museums. A sculpture the color and texture of lightly burnt toast.

And it smelled.

Not a bad smell, just a smell. Like what? Too many things to tell. A whiff of sunny grass. Cinnamon. Scorched milk in the pan, three days old.

"Is it a he or a she?" Zenia asked.

"It isn't either one, ma'am." Zenia looked at him blankly. "Neither, Mrs. Mavroandrates."

That was hard to take in. "Can I talk to it?"

Les Carik smiled. "You'd need a machine, a translator for that. They—the B'nithouris—they talk by smell, I guess you'd say." He sniffed the air significantly. "I guess it's saying something right now."

Behind them, the woman from the Fairleigh office coughed impatiently. "You don't need to talk to it; it doesn't even know you're here."

But, "Look, ma'am, you talk to it if you like. Maybe it likes it. Okay?" The technician smiled again and returned to business. "You understand all this stuff, now? The water here, once a week. Twice a week, the food blocks. And look." He pulled a slip of paper from his pocket and wrote something in small, tilting capitals. "Here's the number to call when you run out of food, or if that light goes out. You put this someplace safe, right?"

"But what does it *do?*" Zenia prodded.

"It just *is,*" the man answered her.

When they were gone Zenia closed the door to her home and turned to face her guest.

"Well?" she asked the room at large. "Well?"

Roscoe carolled from his cage. The machine in the corner gurgled politely. The thing, the B'nit-whatever-it-was, just sat there in the corner on its flat machine and said, did nothing. Peter's photographs smiled at her as she began to make her dinner.

"I don't know, Roscoe," she fretted as she chopped vegetables methodically. "I don't know. I mean, what are we going to do with him? It," she corrected.

Roscoe cocked his head to one side and trilled.

"And that woman, talks to me like I was nothing. All my life I paid my own way; I bought my contract with good money. Now—I got to take a B-nithy-thing in my home. Peter—" She stopped chopping and looked myopically in the direction of his images. Captain Peter Mavroandrates, victim of the first war of interstellar contact, smiled glassily back at her. A fifteen-minute war, a misunderstanding, a fluke of bad translation that had cost seventeen lives on an orbiting laboratory and made her a widow.

"It wasn't your kind that did it," she informed the thing fairly. "I've seen pictures of them. They look sort of like us. And everyone said it was a mistake, like that meant something." She chopped steadily for a moment, watching the chunks of carrot spin past her moving fingers. "I don't want you thinking I think it was one of you," she said finally. An instinct of hospitality sputtered in her; how could she offer it anything? Did it like music? She could turn on the radio, but there was rarely anything on that she liked to listen to.

"In my day we had *music,*" she told Roscoe and the thing. Roscoe seemed unimpressed, but the canary made its own music and, beside, had heard Zenia's lectures on Then and Now before. "Good music you could dance to; Peter and I used to go dancing. How they can dance to this slow stuff they play now . . ." The machines sighed and gurgled. No answer.

"Well." Another In My Day rose to her lips, but politeness demanded that the topic be more general. It was her guest's first night in the house. A boarder, like her grandmother had taken in from time to time when money was tight. But what could she turn the topic to? Not books, or music, or TV. If she asked a question about the thing's world it couldn't answer her. If she asked its name—no name.

Somehow, if the thing was going to live in her apartment, share her space, Zenia expected it to make a difference. It sat there, the machines gurgling and sighing from time to time. No difference.

Gradually news filtered through the building, and there were visitors. Clara, from Seven, brave in too much pink lipstick, with a new beau fifteen years her junior, who spoke respectfully to Zenia and adored Clara. Mrs. Kocynzki from Eighteen came, squealing delightedly at each purr and gurgle from the machinery. And the Chous, brother and sister from the fortieth floor, both straining to hear through failing hearing appliances, marveling at the creature's otherness. Visitors came and went; after a time the monster was no longer a seven-days' wonder in the building.

They settled together, Zenia, Roscoe, and the B'nithouri. At first Zenia watched for a sign of life, a difference, the rise and fall of breath or a change of position, as a child might. She resented sleep, afraid to miss something. But over the days that became months that charm disappeared, and the inert form, settled comfortably in the corner on its murmuring machinery, became part of the old woman's life. It was a presence as real as Roscoe's, more real than the pictures of her husband; a presence evoked by the warm, spicy smell that pervaded the living room. It needed a name; how could she speak to something that didn't have a name? Slowly, the distinction between comments addressed to her husband's pictures and comments addressed to the spicy silent presence in the corner became less distinct. One morning Zenia entered the room and greeted the creature in the corner as Peter, and knew that was who it was.

They entertained each other, each in its own way. Zenia told her stories: tales of a long-ago girlhood when space travel was still miraculous and she had been married to a real, live hero; stories of the long ecru years of widowhood, lived but not felt; diatribes on Then and Now. Roscoe sang his ecstatic roller-coaster trills. The machines of Peter sighed and gurgled delicately in the corner. Zenia began to think of the B'nithouri as Peter's soul come back to stay with her, but the thing, like the images that smiled from their frames around the room, never moved, never changed their faceless acceptance.

So they lived.

Zenia awoke one morning with a sense of clear, sharp, crystal well-being; Roscoe burst into a paean of appreciation when she walked into the room. The sky through her window was a blue from her childhood skies, and Zenia thought she could almost see the sun. Everything, even the concrete walls of the building, seemed amazingly clear and sharp and beautiful. The scent of the alien Peter was soft and enveloping and warm on the air. It would be a wonderful day.

As she ran water for tea and sliced bread for the toaster, Zenia talked to Peter in the corner. Almost, she could hear his answers, his cheerful acceptance of her silly nothings: is that so, Zenia? Do tell. Well, I never. I remember . . . She knew what his voice would be like, his self, the person he would be. Comfortable, like the little noises his machines made. Yes, you go along and make your breakfast. Don't you mind me, I'll just—

Tuesday! Startled by her forgetfulness Zenia bustled, full of apologies, to fetch a food block to slide into the machine. Why thanks, Zenia. Didn't want to bother you, but I *was* feeling a little peckish.

"No bother, Peter," she assured the creature. "Isn't it a beautiful day?" And went back to the kitchenette to butter her toast.

Or began to. Her quick, almost merry shuffle across the room was interrupted by a sudden vertigo, a steep, sickening, tear-the-breath-from-you dizziness that split the halves of her brain and sent them slamming concussively together, sent her reeling. Zenia folded to the floor ungracefully, breaking a hip as she fell, unaware of the pain in her desperate grasping reach to right the world again. The clear, crystal taste of the day turned to brass in her mouth; her eyes opened and closed blindly, and she called for her husband, her mother, her father. Anyone. Peter.

Roscoe, impossibly high above, unbelievably far away, sang out in consternation. In the corner Peter's soul filled the room with spicy musk. Zenia called out its name once, twice. The brassy rattle in her head turned the sound to monsters, devils that danced on her body, poked her furiously along one side with their forks. Zenia slipped into unconsciousness the way a climber slips into the chasm: as if he knows the fall will be his last.

But she woke again.

She was in a hospital, clean white and the smells of another sick body near by, the squeaking sounds of nurse's shoes on the other side of the curtain.

"Hello?" she tried carefully.

A startled face appeared at the curtain. "You're awake. Hi. I'll be there in just a second." A young voice. Zenia's eyes wouldn't focus enough to make out the girl's face as she rounded the partition. "How do you *feel?* Boy, that was a close call. The doctor will be here in a sec."

"Where? Long?" It was difficult to form the words properly; her mouth felt like rubber. There was a dull, throbbing pain in her left hip. "Wha' happent?" she managed.

"You're at St. Augustine's, Mrs.—" The girl checked the chart, pronounced the name carefully. "Mavroandrates. They brought you in yesterday. You had a stroke, and fell and broke your hip. But you're looking pretty chipper today; I guess you'll be fine in just a while."

Zenia did not feel chipper enough to ask what Fine In A While meant. She was very old; even now, with medicines and therapies and anti-agathic science, she was an old woman. What point in putting her back together again if . . .

"Peter," she whispered. "Roscoe?"

"The canary? Don't worry, ma'am. Someone from your building's taking care of the canary." Would someone from the building take care of Peter, too? Zenia flushed uneasily, jealously. The room smelled sour; her hip hurt. She wanted to go home to Roscoe and Peter in the corner.

"How—I'm here?" The words sounded as if they had been extruded through a mouthful of marbles, but the nurse understood.

"That's the incredible thing." Her voice was very young, very impressed. "An alarm went off on the extra-terrestrial support just about the time you fell, ma'am. The man who came to fix the machine found you."

"Pe'er okay?"

"The ET? Must be, ma'am. They'll take good care of it. Now, you rest, right?"

After the enormous exertion of the past five minutes Zenia could not have fought sleep if she had wanted to.

Getting well was a slow process. Doctors came and asked her to move one hand, the other, wiggle her toes, how was the hip today. Clara, and the Chous, and others from her little community came to visit; even, one morning, Les Carik, the young technician who had brought Peter to her. He was mannerly, a little nervous in the hospital. Beaming on him, Zenia told the boy a little about her long-dead husband, the hero, and Les agreed that he must have been a wonderful man.

"But what about P—my B'nit-hoory? Who's taking care of him?" she asked at last.

Les looked uncomfortable. "Well, ma'am, I guess he'll be put in another home sooner or later. The B'nithouri don't get along real well in shelters."

"When I get home I'll get him back, won't I?"

"Ahh, well, I guess the Fairleigh people will let you know about that, later. I mean, with your being so sick and that, you shouldn't have to worry—"

"Worry? He isn't any trouble at all. You told me so yourself. And I—I like him." It was still difficult to talk clearly. "Pe— the B'nit-thoory and I got on good, just fine. It wasn't really sick when you came, was it? The nurse said the light went on's why someone found me."

"There wasn't anything wrong with the B'nithouri or the machines, at least when I got there. I checked everything, but I still can't say why the alarm went off."

With the calm of someone who has learned that miracles happen to the unwary, Zenia smiled. "It called you to help me."

"Ma'am?" Les Carik had been looking out the window; now he turned back to her sharply. "Ma'am?"

"So you see, I got to have Peter back when I'm well," Zenia hurried on nervously. "The B'nith-hoory thing, that is. We take care of each other."

"I don't think—" the man began.

"Just you tell them about that. They wanted me to take it in the first place. You tell them I'll be up and around in a few weeks and they can bring Peter home to me then. We're used to each other now; they can't pull that apart just because I got sick, can they?" Zenia smiled a very young smile.

"I'll tell them, ma'am. I don't know if it'll do any good, but I—well, I will tell them."

The Fairleigh Corporation said no. Not only to Les Carik, who made the request on behalf of Mrs. Zenia Mavroandrates, but to Mrs. Mavroandrates herself, when, six months after her fall, she was able to plead her case in person. It was No; the Corporation was willing to continue the additional stipend to her, but felt it would be inadvisable to return that particular Extra-Terrestrial, or any other, to her at this time. Mrs. Mavroandrates had a record of cerebral accidents; she might endanger the subject intelligence's life. The Corporation's liabilities . . . surely she could understand?

Zenia could not understand. Without money she could not appeal, and the one meeting she had with Corporation officials left her trembling with fatigue and anger. No one would listen to her.

On a dour and drizzly day Zenia returned to her home. Roscoe, his cage hectic with ribbons, trilled a welcome song, fluttering frantically to indicate his approval. The apartment looked almost the same: the pictures, the kickshaws and artifacts of a long life, the grey and blue chairs and sofa all as she had left them. Except, no Peter in the corner to scent the air with spice, no sigh and chuckle of machinery. The pictures of her husband smiled at her; Zenia smiled back automatically, wanting the B'nithouri.

"Can I visit him—it?" she asked, calling Les the next day. "Just to see how he—it's getting along. You think I'm a crazy old woman, and I guess I am, but you get used to something when you're my age; too many things just go away."

"I'll see," he said. And called her back the next day to say that she could visit. The B'nithouri was still being housed in the Corporation's shelter. Zenia shuddered. Rather have Peter in a shelter than here, safe and comfortable with her?

Les offered to pick her up for the visit and Zenia, with the dignity of a young girl asked to her first dance, thanked him gravely and accepted. Roscoe chirrupped inquiringly from behind her; but Roscoe was, as Zenia reminded him airily, only a bird.

The shelter was huge, impersonal, riddled with hallways and doors. Many extra-terrestrials who could not, for reasons of age, illness, or injury incurred on Earth, withstand the rigors of a journey to their own planets, had been housed in the shelter pursuant to treaty arrangements, just as an incapacitated diplomat or merchant from Earth would be housed on their own worlds. Zenia and Les, with a dull-eyed technician who chain-smoked impatiently, rode a tiny electric cart down the metal-walled corridors.

"You think you can tell which of the things is yours?"

Zenia looked at the shelter-tech with dignity. "Of course I can." The tech shook his head bemusedly. Another one who doesn't like old people, Zenia thought. I don't like him either.

The cart came to a silent stop and Les helped Zenia from her seat.

Since the stroke she had walked with a cane; and her movements were slow, elderly. The technician eased out of the cart and loped around to meet them, guiding the old woman and the young man into a room.

The scent in the room was deafening. Zenia closed her eyes, bathed in the fragrance. When she opened them again she saw the B'nithaur: at least fifty of them, packed together in rows, each one on its separate machine. Zenia started forward with Les at her elbow, shuffling through the ranks of the creatures looking at one, another, waiting for recognition. Les, behind her, opened his mouth half a dozen times to tell her that she wouldn't be able to do it, but Zenia moved on, elegant with purpose.

"Peter?" To Les's eyes the alien she stopped for was no different than any of the others. "Peter," Zenia said, more definitely. The B'nithouri looked shrunken, somehow, withered by its stay in the shelter. Zenia could hardly counsel bravery, tell it that soon it would be home with her. So she began to tell it all about the hospital, hearing in her inner ear that same, comfortable voice: yes, Zenia? They did what? What happened then? "And I tried to get them to bring you home, Peter. I did." The thing sat unmoving.

At last, Zenia sighed. "Time to go, I guess." Les and the drab technician stood a little way off, watching the visit. "Maybe I'll come back again, though. To make sure they take care of you." The tech gave Les an exasperated look. Nothing happened, no movement, no acknowledgement from the brown eggish thing on its life-support platform. Zenia turned and walked away, her back straight.

Behind her, an alarm went off. The alert keyed to the B'nithouri she had just left.

The shelter-tech jerked up, his boredom drowned in suspicion. "Whaddedyoudo?" he snapped over his shoulder.

"Nothing," Zenia snapped back, unheard, over the clang of the bell.

After a moment the shelter-tech straightened up. "Mechanical, a short, I guess. No damn reason for it." He turned away disgustedly to lead them out of the room. After a backward look Zenia followed. As she took a step forward the bell rang again.

The tech glared at her.

"I didn't do a thing," she protested to Les. "It just doesn't want to be here. Why can't it come home with me?"

"Mrs. Mavroandrates," Les began urgently. Stopped at the sight of her face, the stubborn dawning triumph there.

"Look, it's just something wrong with the wiring. The thing's okay," the tech insisted edgily. Before the party could reach the door the bell rang for a third time. "Damn," the tech said, teeth clenched. "I'm gonna call my supervisor. Lady, don't you move."

Les found a chair for her. Zenia smiled at his wary face.

"How'd you know it was that one, Mrs. Mavroandrates?"

"Just knew. You live with something a while, you get to know it. That's Peter there. And the Fairleigh Corporation," she added, and smiled deliciously, "can either set me up a cot right here, or send Peter home with me. Right?" She answered herself. "Right."

"Does it do that for everyone?" the supervisor asked. He and the tech hunched together nervously in a corner of the room, away from Zenia and Les.

"Nossir, just her."

"Dammit." The supervisor looked at Zenia, saw only a problem. "Lady, I can't just give the thing to you like a pet. It's got rights too. Under a treaty. And how d'you know that's the one lived with you?"

"I know." She said it simply; it was obvious.

"The numbers match," the tech agreed, as if the words tasted bad.

"Christ. Look, lady." The supervisor ran a hand over his forehead. "I have to talk to people in the offices. Can you—ahh—calm the thing down a little? Explain that you'll be back? We can't have that bell ringing all the time, it'll upset the other—ahh, inmates. If I promise to talk to some people?"

Zenia looked him in the eye. He didn't flinch; she'd have to trust him. "Okay." She shuffled back to the B'nithouri. "I've done all I can here, Peter. But they're going to see about bringing you home. You got to take it easy till then, okay?" She turned to the supervisor. "I tried. I think it's okay now."

"Yeah, lady, you sure tried," he agreed.

No one wanted to believe it. It made too much trouble. Too many decisions to reverse, too many conversations with the B'nithaur Trade Mission, examining fine points of treaty law and the Corporation's service contracts. The media got wind of it: one little old lady, a war widow from the Fifteen-Minute War, and one burnt-toast–egg-shaped extra-terrestrial pensioner made a good story. A nuisance the Fairleigh Corporation could do without, particularly when the B'nithaur Mission made it clear that they were more impressed by the earnest desire of their brother to share space with an elderly Tellurian female than by the maintenance of rules and order. The shelter was a negative environment at best; why should their brother not be allowed to be where he wished to be?

It was Les who brought Peter back to her, flanked by two anonymous assistants from the shelter who eyed the little woman in housecoat and slippers as if she were a witch. Clara was there, and the Chous, and other friends, cluttering up Zenia's living room like old, musty birds. A coming-home party.

The machines were set up and began their faint noisemaking. The B'nithouri, brought out of its carriage, released its wonderful living scent into the room. The technicians settled it into place resentfully, plugged in plugs, wired wires, made their exit. Peter was home. Roscoe sang welcome.

The party was brief; everyone but Zenia was conscious of a strange sort of flatness, a letdown. All that fuss for a thing that sat, almost ignored, in its corner. People started to leave; Les was the last one, standing in the door obviously trying to think of something to say to her. But Zenia said it first, said thank you and Godspeed, and offered him a raddled cheek to kiss.

"You visit sometime, yes?" Before he could agree, she smiled shrewdly. "You think about it, anyway."

"I will," he promised. Then he was gone, too.

She went about clearing the genteel untidiness her guests had left. Roscoe settled himself in to sleep, nuzzling the bars of his cage with a careful beak. In the corner the machines made their chuckling sighs. Zenia began to hum.

"Glad to be home, Peter?" she asked at last.

Well, yes, Zenia. Been a while, hasn't it. Glad to see you looking so well.

It was her own voice that sounded in the room, but they were Peter's words, growing from inside of her. It didn't matter who spoke them.

"Did I ever tell you about the time when Peter and I went out to Wyoming?" she began, chores completed. She settled herself with hydraulic grace in a chair near the corner.

Why no, Zeen, don't believe you did.

"Well, that was a long time ago, of course. . . ."

Comfortably she began her story. The canary slept and the monster's machinery whuuushed softly in accompaniment.

A SPACESHIP BUILT OF STONE

by Lisa Tuttle

art: George Barr

The author is an American SF writer now living in England. Her first novel, *Windhaven*, was a collaboration with George R. R. Martin. Her second, *Familiar Spirits*, (which is neither SF nor a collaboration) will be out soon from Berkley.

I came upon a vast and ruined city in the desert. Long ago, huge building blocks had been hewn from rock, cut to fit together so tightly that mortar was unnecessary. It was a city not of straight lines, but of rounded corners and circular enclosures, walls towering twice a man's height. It seemed immense and harshly white against the blue sky and emptiness of the desert.

I entered by an arching gateway and walked through narrow, winding streets, touching the sun-baked stone with my hands. Here and there signs had been incised in the rock. I traced one with my finger: a cup-shaped maze with a stylized symbol, a rising bird, at the center.

The city must have been abandoned centuries before. Everything was open to the sky, all roofs long since rotted away. The sand had drifted in to cover the cobblestone streets. But the emptiness of the city, although it seemed sad, was not oppressive. I felt comfortable there, at home, as if I had returned to a place familiar since childhood. I patiently followed the curving lanes and entered each abandoned building in turn, looking for something.

At last I found it. There was a large, semi-circular enclosure at the very center of the city. Inside, a hole cut into the earth. Without hesitation, I lowered myself into it, my dangling feet finding purchase on a stairway carved into the rock. The stairs were steep, forcing me into a rapid descent. It was more a ladder than a staircase.

I climbed for what seemed a very long time, the darkness growing deeper around me as I descended. But just as I was wondering how long I could continue to climb down to an unknown destination in total darkness, a dim light from some source further down began to reach me; and when I reached the bottom at last, I could see perfectly well. I was in a small stone alcove. Behind me were the stairs to the surface; ahead of me, three branching tunnels. I chose the well-lit central tunnel. As I walked, I looked around at the curving, featureless walls and ceiling, which apparently gave off light. After I had walked for a long time, I began to hear a sound ahead of me, a soft, irregular noise which I thought might be people talking.

At last I came to another branching, and an archway, which led into a room filled with people. They stopped talking when I entered, and looked at me with some apprehension.

They were familiar to me—I knew they were the people who had built the city above. They looked enough alike to be members of one family, with their unusual yellow-brown skin color, wide, round eyes, thin noses, and thick black hair.

A woman detached herself from the crowd and stepped forward, saying my name. Her eyes were intent upon my face; I had the idea that she knew me very well, was even perhaps in love with me.

"Rick!" she said. "You came back! Tell us, is it safe? Can we come out now? Will they let us live in peace?"

My earlier confusion dropped away. I had been here many times before, and knew these people well. They were not my own people; but I loved them and had agreed to help them. Why had I forgotten?

I opened my mouth to speak, to tell them that it was safe now, and I would help them settle above ground; and then the alarm went off.

Groggy and fumbling in the dark, I stopped it, then sat up, switched on the light, and reached for my cigarettes. I felt disoriented and confused. Unlike most of my dreams, this one had the force of reality, of some remembered event. Had I dreamed of those people and those underground tunnels before, or had my memory in the dream been nothing more than a dream of a dream?

I found notebook and pen and began to write down the details before they could slip away from me. I'd had bad luck with dreams, lately, waking every morning to find them gone, which was why I'd set my alarm to wake me up in the middle of the night. Describing the city in the desert, I wondered where I had seen it. I didn't usually dream about places I'd never been, and I wondered now if, perhaps, once as a child I had been taken to some stone ruins in a desert somewhere.

And the dream left me in an oddly vulnerable state. My last thoughts, as I settled down to sleep again, were that I would have to hurry back there, find the city again and the people who hid beneath it, and offer them my help.

But by morning I had nearly forgotten the dream—I remembered only waking and writing something down. I added the notebook to my stack of books and went outside to catch a university shuttle bus a little before noon. On the bus I saw a pretty, dark-haired girl I'd noticed before, and sat down next to her. She was an art student—her sketchpad open on her knee. On the paper, growing beneath her pencil, was a familiar design: a cup-shaped maze with a stylized bird rising from the center.

I stared at the drawing, aware only that it was a familiar symbol, when suddenly, with shocking vividness—as if it were a memory of something real and not just a dream—I saw again the white stone wall with the very same design incised on it. I had traced it with my finger in my dream.

"What are you drawing?" I asked.

She looked up, seemed to recognize me from other bus-rides, and smiled. "This? I'm just doodling."

"But what is that design? Where is it from?"

She laughed. "It's from my head! I just made it up."

I was startled. "Are you sure? Couldn't you have seen it somewhere before?"

"Yes, I suppose." She frowned, then her face cleared. "I don't remember. But, anyway, it was in a dream I had last night." She laughed again, a warm, delighted chuckle. "Don't look so amazed! Don't you ever get ideas from dreams?"

"All the time," I said dryly. "In fact, that's the reason I asked you about that design. It was in my dream last night." I tapped the notebook in my lap. "I wrote it down here. I woke myself up at 3:30, on purpose to catch a dream—part of an experiment for a class I teach."

Her brown eyes were very wide—she seemed to accept what I said without question. "How strange," she murmured. "Three-thirty . . . " She looked down at her sketch-pad and began to drawn an elaborate frame around the maze design. "You see, I probably wouldn't have remembered this dream at all; but Bogey—that's my dog—decided he had to go outside, and woke me up at about 3:30. So while I was up, waiting to let him back in, I sat and doodled in my sketch-book while I thought about my dream." She lifted the spiral-bound pad and flipped back a few pages, holding out one for my inspection.

A line of stone blocks, a wall. The maze-with-bird pattern again. A stone gateway. And faces—faces that I recognized. The people from my dream.

I felt strange, my pulse speeded up. "Looks like my dream," I said quietly.

"I was in the desert somewhere," she said. "And there was this ancient city there, which was supposed to have been abandoned; but the people who had built it had actually fled below ground and were hiding there. They were very gentle and peaceful and afraid that they would be killed if they came out. They were a wonderful people—I loved them, and was trying to help them. They kept asking me if it was really all right to come out, and I kept telling them that everyone would love them as I did. And then Bogey woke me."

I opened my notebook to the dream and handed it to her without a word. While she read I gazed past her, out the window at the sunny, familiar, neighborhood streets the bus was roaring through. The familiar had suddenly become strange, the strange familiar. The world was different—I couldn't tell if it were tinged with promise, or with menace.

"Telepathy," said a clear voice at my side.

I looked at her and shook my head. "But why? You and I don't even know each other—why should we be linked like that?"

She looked straight into my eyes. "Karma," she said. "We were meant to meet."

I laughed at her words, but I liked her look. I even liked the idea that we were somehow linked, that something had drawn us together, although it was a silly idea.

"A very scientific suggestion," I said, teasing her. "You want to have dinner with me tonight and talk about it some more?"

"Sure."

Through the window, I could see the tower lurching into view. I would have to get off at the next stop. "Meet me at Hansel and Gretel's at 6:30?" I suggested, gathering my books together.

She gave me another one of those high-voltage looks. "I'll be there."

It wasn't until I had gotten off the bus that I realized I didn't know her name.

But I didn't expect she would stand me up—not after such an opening. I walked up the grassy mall towards the building where I was teaching a workshop in journal writing. Most graduate assistants get saddled with the dullest of introductory courses, and I considered myself lucky this semester to have gotten something a little out of the ordinary—no matter that I thought it a self-indulgent and unnecessary course.

I paused on the steps outside to smoke a cigarette. I was really trying to get my mind on the class I had to teach, when all I wanted to think about was the dream—my dream, her dream—and what it meant. When I finally went inside, and down to the large, blank-walled basement classroom where we met, my class of ten had assembled.

I perched, as usual, on the old wooden desk at the front of the room, and looked at them. "Any of you have trouble catching a dream?" I asked.

Of the ten, it turned out, only five had dreams to report. One had slept through the alarm, another had simply forgotten the assignment; the other three were the most chagrined, however. They had ignored my suggestion of setting alarms for the middle of the night as unnecessary—they claimed to dream vividly and to remember what they had dreamed. But this morning had been unusual. They had remembered no dreams.

I nodded thoughtfully, feeling myself slip into the psychiatrist role this class seemed to reserve for me.

"Perhaps," I suggested, enjoying myself, "you dreamed of things you would be too embarrassed to discuss before the whole class? So your unconscious thoughtfully censored them from your conscious? Well, try again tonight. We'll just move on to some of the dreams which were recalled. Anyone like to start by reading his or her dream?"

Eve Johnson flicked one impeccably manicured hand in the air and, at my nod, began to speak, referring only occasionally to her notebook.

"The dream began at a frat-party, which was pretty dull. But then some friends of mine started talking about driving to California, right then. This actually happened to me once—some friends decided to drive to California on the spur of the moment. Anyway, in the dream, all of a sudden it switched to us on the road, travelling through the desert someplace like New Mexico. We got off the highway onto a dirt road for some reason and drove through all this emptiness for awhile. Then, all of a sudden, right in front of us was this huge, stone city. It was built of big white stones, and we could see it clearly in the moonlight. But it was abandoned—and I found myself remembering, as I looked at it, that the people who had built it had been afraid that the government or somebody would kill them, so they had gone into hiding underground. Then—what's wrong?"

Only then did I realize that I had gotten off the desk and walked towards her.

"Uh, could I see the notebook, please?"

Eyebrows raised, she put the notebook into my hand. My eyes ran down the lines of neat, even handwriting, reading about her discovery of the tunnels, and meeting with the people who lived beneath the city-ruin.

I looked around at the others, some of whom looked puzzled, others of whom looked oddly excited. I said, "Something strange has happened. This dream of Eve's is remarkably similar to the dream *I* had last night. . . ."

"Me too!"

"I dreamed the same thing!"

Pat Haggard and Bill Donaldson had spoken almost simultaneously. Now they looked from me to each other, their expressions mixtures of wonder, curiosity and suspicion.

"Anyone else?" I asked. I realized I was probably grinning foolishly. "Did anyone else have a dream with the same elements—the abandoned stone city in the desert, the tunnels underground, the people there afraid to come up?"

Slowly, Mary Crouch raised her hand. "I dreamed something like that, I think," she said. "I can't remember much about it. Just that I had been talking to these wonderful people, some sort of advanced, peaceful tribe, who seemed to live near some huge stone ruins."

I nodded slowly. "Bill, Pat . . . would each of you please read your dream reports?"

All the elements were there; all the inexplicable similarities. The same dream, dreamed by six different people. At least.

We spent the rest of class-time talking about the dreams and what this bizarre coincidence could mean. We discussed telepathy and precognition—one of the liveliest, most exciting, most wonder-filled classroom discussions I'd ever imagined. But of course we proved nothing and came up with no real answers. When the bell rang we were all frustratingly aware of how little we knew. My students all promised to continue recording their dreams and eagerly offered to do any other research I might suggest.

When they all left, I walked across campus to the library to start the research. I had decided first of all to try to find out if the place we had all been dreaming of had any objective reality.

I paged through volumes of anthropology, archeology and travel, but did not find the city I thought I knew in Anatolian ruins, nor in Greece, nor Peru, nor in the monolithic structures on Malta, nor in the Arabian desert. Because two dreamers had mentioned New Mexico, I turned next to books about the Southwest. There I found the stone and baked-earth structures of the Pueblo Indians, the hogans of the Navajo, and the legends of the Seven Cities of Cibola. The Pueblos believed their ancestors entered the present world from a hole in the ground, climbing up from a world below. I took notes, but I found no answers.

She was waiting at the restaurant when I arrived, even prettier and taller than I'd remembered, looking like a 1940s film star in a vintage black dress and lots of cheerfully fake diamonds, spike heels, and an upswept hairdo.

"I've got so much to tell you," she said at once, rushing to meet me.

I took her hand. "How about your name?"

We both laughed.

"I'm Judy Anderson."

"Rick Karp."

We shook hands, and that made us laugh again.

"You look great," I said. "I'm such a slob . . . I knew I should have rented a tux."

"No, no, that shirt is lovely." She reached out to pluck at the fabric. "In fact, I have one just like it at home, only the azaleas on it are a little smaller, and a brighter pink."

"It faded some between Hawaii and here," I said.

We took a booth near the back and I ordered a pitcher of dark beer and a plate of cheese and bread to start.

Judy leaned across the table. "In my design class this morning we were told to create a symbol for a made-up company. A pictograph, right? And one of the women in class drew a picture of a maze with a bird rising from the center, for a company she called 'Anasazi Airlines'."

I frowned in surprised recognition.

"So I asked her where she got the idea, and she said it had just come to her. Then the teacher overheard us and said, in his usual supercilious way, 'Give credit where credit is due, please. The Anasazi Indians came up with that design more than a thousand years ago.' "

"The Anasazi Indians," I said, remembering what I had read about them that afternoon. "They were the ancestors of the present pueblo-dwelling Indians—the Hopis, the Zunis, the Pueblos. The Anasazi culture spread all across the Southwest. The word 'Anasazi' is Navajo, meaning 'ancient ones.' "

She pouted. "And I thought I'd surprise you by doing a lot of research! But you know, I went through practically the whole art library and couldn't find that bird-in-the-maze design. I figured if my teacher knew about it, it must be pretty common. Were we dreaming about the Anasazi, then?"

"Courtesy of the Anasazi Broadcasting Company?" I told her about what had happened in class that day and watched her eyes grow larger. I patted her hand. "So you see, it wasn't karma bringing us together, after all."

"Maybe it's *your* dream, and you're sending it to receptive people?"

I shook my head. "It sure doesn't feel like 'my' dream. But even if that explained the people in my class—why would you have picked it up?"

She looked at me through her lashes. "Maybe I noticed you on the bus before . . . maybe I was thinking about you . . . maybe I'm just very receptive to your thoughts."

I grinned. "And the woman in your design class?"

"Oh. Coincidence."

"I think coincidence is one thing it's *not*. There's something going on—"

"Rick. Maybe *everyone* had the dream. And only a few people remembered it—the people who woke up in the middle of it, like you and me."

For some reason that idea made my skin prickle. "We have no evidence for that."

"No, and if they've been made to forget it, we never will have."

I was silent, wild thoughts of a nation-wide—world-wide—survey on dreams racing through my head. "But what would that mean?" I asked. "Assuming that were true—*why* would everyone have the same dream? Is someone sending it? Why? And if there is some reason for everyone to dream the same thing—why would the majority forget it? What could that accomplish?"

"People are influenced by things they can't remember consciously," Judy reminded me.

"Yes, but . . . *why*? No, that world-wide theory doesn't make sense. It's more reasonable to assume that you and I and the woman in your design class and the people in my class are members of a group who are somehow telepathically linked, or receptive to . . . oh, each other, or one particular person. And this has happened before, and will surely happen again."

Judy grinned at me. "I try to tell you *we're* linked, and you sneer at me. Your theory is just karma under another name."

We talked of little else during dinner—our speculation ranged and soared—but there was more going on beneath the talk. She went home with me that night.

During the next two weeks Judy and I and the people in my class all kept dream-notebooks. But there were no further "coincidences"—all the dreams were idiosyncratic, personal, individual dreams. I began working on a report to send to the Maimonides dream laboratory in New York. Judy and I spent more and more time together.

One night, Judy and I lay cozily together in my bed, paying little attention to the newscast carried on the little black and white set at the foot of the bed, when something alerted us.

Judy half sat up. "What was that—"

One word caught us from the televised babble: "Anasazi."

A well-dressed reporter was standing in a windy desert with a man dressed in grimy jeans and a pith helmet. The camera panned back to reveal an excavation in progress.

"And who, exactly, were the Anasazi?" said the reporter.

The other man, identified in a title across the screen as **Dr. Reuben Collier, UCLA**, wiped his brow. "They were the precursors of today's Pueblo, Hopi, and Zuni tribes. We had never imagined that we would find anything as complex as this. We have right here in New Mexico uncovered an amazingly large, well-designed city built of stone and adobe. Many of the buildings are constructed with connecting underground tunnels. Hacking out those tunnels must have been a prodigious feat in itself. I'd say this rivals almost anything in the ancient world."

"Astonishing," said the reporter. "But you say this was unexpected? No one had any idea this city was here?"

"We didn't realize the Anasazi culture had ever attained such a height," the archeologist said. "Of course, this find raises the new question of what happened to that culture, how it fell. But by calling this the work of the 'Anasazi,' we are simplifying, you realize—"

"How did you find this site, Dr. Collier?"

He grimaced. "Most unscientifically, I'm afraid. I had a grant to do work in this area, of course, and was working on aerial photographs for some indications of what lay below the surface. But why we picked this particular spot to dig—well, quite truthfully, it came to me in a dream."

"Many archeologists dream of great finds; Reuben Collier's dream came true," said the reporter, turning his handsome visage back to the camera. "Steve Carpenter reporting."

My chest was tight. I realized I hadn't been breathing, and let out my breath with a sigh.

"Well, so that's it," Judy said. "*He* was the one the message was for." She sounded remarkably satisfied.

I stared at her. "What are you talking about?"

"The dreams. They didn't mean anything to us—but they did to him."

"Well, yes, but so what? What are you saying?"

"That getting someone to dig up the city was the *point* of the dream."

"And who was it who wanted that particular task done, may I ask? A bunch of dead Indians?"

She chewed her lower lip. "Well, I don't know. But now that the city has been discovered, the dreams seem to make a little more sense, don't they?"

"Not at all," I said. I was thinking about getting in touch with Collier and wondering if anyone else who'd had the dream might have seen him on television and decide to do the same.

"Look," said Judy. "If the dream had a *point*—if it was supposed to have an effect on someone—that could be it. Maybe it was beamed out; and a lot of people picked up on it, like us; but only a few would be in any position to do anything about it—like that anthropologist. The dream meant something to him, and he could do something about it."

I shook my head, annoyed because what she seemed to think was an answer was no answer at all. "Where did the dreams come from? *Who* beamed them out? Who could possibly want that city discovered yet have no way of ensuring that discovery except by giving people dreams?"

"Well *I* don't know," she said, sounding aggrieved. "I didn't ever say I had the answer—I was just making a suggestion."

So then, of course, I had to kiss her and tell her that her suggestion was a good one—as good as any other. And it probably was—but it still didn't make sense.

The discovery in the New Mexico desert had to be the biggest archeological find of all time. It caused more excitement than King Tut's tomb ever had, and suddenly the whole country was Anasazi-crazy. Everywhere you looked there were the headlines, the magazine articles and books, television specials, and commercials. Stores carried Anasazi toys, games, and postcards. One day Judy showed up in a sundress covered with the bird-in-a-maze design.

It was a flood, a bombardment. Everyone knew about and talked about the Anasazi. We all dreamed about them. It would have been odd, given the sea of information we all swam in, *not* to have dreamed about them. In the dreams—in my dreams and Judy's, at any rate—the Anasazi were always the gentle, wise, and peaceful people of that first dream, only emerged now from their tunnels. Even that original dream, shared by an unknown number, no longer seemed so odd to me. We were all so obsessed with the Anasazi now that it was as if the force of the present had been pressing against our unconscious minds then, demanding to be recognized: the Anasazi knocking to be let in, calling with ghostly voices for remembrance.

I had a recurring vision, during this time, of a crowd of the Anasazi emerging from the earth. They climbed up narrow stone steps and emerged from the tunnels into the open air, one by one, in starlight and daylight, unending. One by one they come, the line behind them going back forever, and each, to my foreign eyes, looks like the other. Their faces are watchful, thankful, wary. Are we home yet? they seem to ask. Will we be safe here?

Not exactly a dream—not at all like my other dreams about the Anasazi—but just a fleeting thought, an image that recurred to me, disturbing me.

Because the Anasazi *had* suddenly emerged; had come out when no one was looking. And everyone—except me—seemed content to believe their eyes instead of their memories and accept the common knowledge that they had always been among us.

I saw them everywhere. A woman with that distinctively Anasazi face would be sitting quietly on a city bus, or pushing a cart through a grocery store. I would see an Anasazi man, holding two small Anasazi children by their hands, crossing at the light. Faces in crowds, on the evening news, passing in cars. They had arrived quietly, without fuss, and integrated themselves into society as if they had always been here.

Even to myself this seemed an odd obsession—where, then, had they come from if they had not always been among us?—and so I tried not to think about it, and did not discuss it. I was under a lot of strain, trying to get my dissertation written and adjusting to life with Judy—at the beginning of the summer we took a house together, and talked of marriage "eventually."

At the end of the summer I emerged from my stupor of research and writing to discover that the Anasazi had united to ask for their city (baptised, naturally, "Cibola," months before) and surrounding lands to be turned over to them. They asked to reclaim their homeland.

Indian groups had asked for Florida and New York, as well as other chunks of property, before, so there was nothing so unusual in the request. What *was* unusual was the response. Sentiment ran high in favor of giving the Indians their home back. Senators and representatives spoke in favor of it. Even the president . . .

It all seemed to happen with amazing speed as we read about it in the papers and watched it on our television screen. One hot day in September Judy and I were ensconced in the bedroom, the window-unit laboring mightily to cool the air, eating Chinese food from cardboard cartons and paying feeble attention to the images flickering across the screen at the foot of the bed when the president made his special appearance and deeded Cibola and surrounding lands to the Anasazi tribe. Just like that.

Judy gave a small cheer. I sat up, set my carton of food aside, and turned off the set.

"What's wrong?" she asked.

"Where did the Anasazi come from?" I asked. "Who are they? Two years ago, nobody but professors and archeologists had heard of them. Now they suddenly have not only a history, but a present and a future—and their own homeland."

She stared at me. "I thought you agreed that the Indians—"

I held up one hand, cutting her off. "I'm not talking about the Indians. I'm talking about . . . these people, who are called Anasazi. Where did they come from all of a sudden? Remember the research we did? The Anasazi culture died out long ago—their descendents are called the Pueblo, Zuni, and Hopi. Nowhere in any of those books was there a mention of a modern-day Anasazi tribe—yet there are suddenly thousands of them!"

"Oh, *books,*" she said, with fine scorn. "What are you going to believe, Rick—what some old book tells you, or what you *know,* what your senses tell you?"

"What *do* I know? I know that since the dreams, and the discovery of Cibola, I've seen the Anasazi, and read about them, everywhere. Not before then—before, they weren't here."

"Of course they were here! We just weren't aware of them!"

"That's what they want us to think," I said. I paused, steeling myself to say aloud what I felt. It was a crazy idea—I knew that as well as anyone—but it haunted me nevertheless, unforgettable as a recurring dream; and I was tired of keeping it to myself.

"All right," I said after a few moments. "I'm not asking you to believe this, just to listen and consider it. Suppose that somewhere, maybe on another planet, was a race of beings who either looked like us, or could alter themselves to look like us. And something happens, maybe their planet is about to be destroyed, and they need a new place to live. A planet like this one." Plots of many old movies, comic books, and paperbacks avidly consumed in adolescence raced through my mind. "But they aren't aggressive—they're a peaceful people, unwilling to hurt or frighten the primitive earth-people. All they need, after all, is a base, room for a colony of maybe fifty or a hundred thousand people.

"They could be quite advanced, although they don't use their technology for war. They send advance propaganda in the form of dreams, so that we meet our new neighbors at night, in the most intimate circumstances, and absorb the lessons with no conscious memory later. Everyone loves them, without knowing why. Everyone is accustomed to the idea of them, sure they've always been around when they finally arrive, accepting them as the indigenous people whose name they use."

"You're saying that the Anasazi came here from outer space in UFOs?" Judy asked blandly.

"Maybe not in the way our popular culture has prepared us for," I said. "Instead of arriving here in bright silver ships with flashing lights, they came in the back way, climbing out of a hole in the ground. They stepped through some interdimensional doorway, bringing their city of underground tunnels and above-ground structures—they came in their spaceship made of stone, and no one noticed."

"Except you," said Judy. "Oh, Rick." Her face was distressed; she looked as if she was going to cry.

"You think I'm crazy," I said. "Just because I wonder where the Anasazi really came from."

"If I woke up some morning and began asking you, in a very worried way, where all those brown-skinned people with Spanish surnames came from all of a sudden, and wouldn't believe you when you told me that they hadn't suddenly invaded us, but had been around all the time—you'd think I was paranoid, wouldn't you?"

"I'd think you were putting me on," I said. I shrugged. "I don't begrudge them their desert city—they built it, after all, and nobody was using that land. But I don't like thinking that they've tampered with our memories, made us love them. Even while I'm saying this, Judy, part of me is protesting that this is crazy talk—that I *know* who the Anasazi are, as well as anyone! And I can't help feeling warmth for them. But I also know what I've read, and I think it's very suspicious that nothing written before the discovery of Cibola refers to Anasazi as if it were anything more than the name of a long-vanished culture. There is no reference to a present-day tribe by that name. It's as if . . . when the Hittite civilization was rediscovered by the archeologists and historians, suddenly a group of people had appeared, calling themselves the Hittites, saying they had been there all along, despite any references to them in any book or—"

"Rick," said Judy, looking at me with tender sadness."Oh, Rick, and you think *my* theories are crazy!"

"It's not a theory," I said. "It's just a story." I was annoyed, at myself and at her. I didn't want to convert her, or even convince myself. I wanted to reconcile the two kinds of "knowledge" I had about the Anasazi. I wanted to understand what had happened. "I didn't want to be right—but I didn't want to be crazy, either.

"You think too much about books," Judy said. "After all the work you've done on your dissertation, it's no wonder. But plenty of things are real which aren't in books. I'm not in any book, and neither are you—except the phone book—and we're both real."

I didn't argue anymore. I didn't want to. We smoked and talked about other things. I didn't forget my uneasiness about the Anasazi, but I tried not to torment myself about it, either—there didn't seem to be anything I could do to prove my fantasy had any foundation.

Two years later, we went to Cibola on our honeymoon.

Odd, to see a dream made solid.

This Cibola was different, of course. It had been fixed up, repaired, and inhabited. There were domed roofs on the round stone structures now, wooden doors, flowers and herbs growing in window-boxes.

The stones were still brilliantly white against the blue sky, just as they had been in my dream; but as we wandered through the maze of cobbled streets the smells of people, animals, and frying food, and the sounds of tourists and Anasazi bartering over jewelry and woven blankets added the hard, undreamlike edge that was reality.

I reached out to touch the dressed stone blocks, so carefully fitted together. My fingers encountered the smoothly incised lines of a maze-design, and I traced it with a finger—again? or for the first time?

There was a guide, pointing out sights of interest and explaining Anasazi customs. He led us with unerring instinct to the shops and stalls where Judy was most likely to buy. While she was comparing the merits of two silver bracelets I asked the guide about the tunnels.

"Tunnels?"

"Yes, when Cibola was discovered I remember it was mentioned that underground tunnels connected the buildings."

"Ah." His face told me nothing. "There isn't much to see. But of course it will be out of the sun, and perhaps you would like that?" He led us off in a new direction.

But this tunnel was nothing like the cool, wide, well-lit artery of my dream. It was narrow and dark, and we had to crouch slightly as we travelled along. My back soon began to hurt. After a few minutes of unrewarding exploration we climbed up a short wooden ladder and emerged in a candle-shop.

"Is that all?" I asked. "What about the other tunnels?"

"There are more," he nodded. "Cramped little passageways leading from one house to another—perhaps twenty of them in all, and none of them any bigger or longer than the one I just showed you."

I could feel Judy's eyes on me, and knew that she knew what I was thinking. I persisted, "Bigger tunnels," I said. "Wider, deeper below ground, well-lit. Underground chambers."

"Nothing like that here," he said, shaking his head.

I was suddenly impatient with him. "And if there were, and you didn't want us to see them, you'd say the same thing. Why do we need a guide at all here? What are you protecting?"

Judy took my arm. "Rick . . . "

"You are a guest here," the guide said, very quietly. "You must obey our rules, or leave. This is a reservation, which is to say a separate country."

"An alien outpost," I said. I was sweating, suddenly aware of how hot it was. "And we gave it to you. We accepted you, and gave you a place to live, just as you wanted. And it's too late to change our minds now. Come on, Judy, we're going."

It wasn't the greatest honeymoon in history. Judy's initial anger over my making a fool of myself and spoiling the trip soon turned to concern for my mental health when I began expressing the opinion that I would not be allowed to live very much longer, now that I had revealed my suspicions of the Anasazi.

But, of course, nothing happened. And eventually, to Judy's relief, I stopped talking about my paranoid fantasies. They might be true, or they might be crazy—but in either case, they didn't do me, or anyone else, any good.

And so, for almost three years, I had no reason to remember my doubts. Until very recently.

Bogey woke us up in the middle of the night about two weeks ago, desperate to go outside. Judy went back to sleep after a sleepy argument over whose responsibility the dog was; and I got up to take him out, musing meanwhile on the dream he had interrupted. It had been an odd and vivid dream—and it reminded me of something I could not quite catch hold of. While waiting for Bogey to be ready to come back inside, I picked up one of Judy's sketchpads, and a pen, and began jotting down notes of what I remembered.

I was in the jungle, a tropical rain forest on the side of a mountain. I began to notice a faint trail that told me someone else had been here before me and, at the same time, became aware of an odd, soft, whispering sound. I stopped still and looked around carefully, and then I saw them.

People, their faces shy and frightened, peeking at me from hiding places among the trees and underbrush. I knew that it would require a great deal of care and patience on my part to get them to come out. And I wanted them to—I wanted them to trust me. I felt an overwhelming surge of affection for these people I could barely see—the urge to protect them, to offer them safety and shelter. As I tried to think how to let them know this, Bogey's cold, insistent nose in my ear woke me.

As I sat there, sleepily staring at what I had written, I suddenly knew what this dream reminded me of. Another dream. I hurried back to the bedroom and woke Judy.

"Judy," I said urgently, trying to break through her sleepy incomprehension. "What were you dreaming? Quick, tell me."

"Hmm? Tell them . . . tell them we love them. They're safe."

She was dropping off again. I shook her. "Judy! Please! Wake up."

She opened her eyes and sat up. "What's wrong?"

"What were you dreaming?"

"Huh?" She rubbed her eyes and yawned. "I don't know . . . something. I was in the forest. With friends. I don't know, What's the matter, honey?"

"Go back to sleep," I said. "I'll let Bogey back inside. We'll talk in the morning."

She made a face and grumbled at me, but was asleep again almost as soon as her head hit the pillow.

Since then, I have been waiting for the other shoe to drop. And today my waiting ended. It wasn't on the evening news. It was just a story on an inside page of the paper—so many other important things happened today, it seems. A report from the Philippines on the discovery of a group of people who may be a tribe previously unknown to civilization, living in mountain caves in an almost inaccessible rain forest A shy and gentle people, who only want to live in peace. I know just what they look like.

by Mary
Kittredge
RENASCENCE
art: Jim Odbert

The author of this story lives in New Haven, where she is the editor of the magazine, *Empire for the SF Writer*, and a respiratory therapist. This story was her first professional SF sale. She admits a fondness for cats, dogs, open touring cars, small-town libraries, and good dinners that arrive soundlessly on trays with wine and flowers.

Over the rattle of bare branches clicking together like bones in the night wind, they heard the sound: something nearby, in the brush. Scripps jerked upright, his eyes moving first to the others around the small campfire. *All there.* They were not, then, about to be ambushed by one of their own. Still, the thought did not shame him, for in his quick head-count his glance had met that of each other man, checking for him.

A stick snapped; then the rustle again, nearer. Women reached silently out for their children, to draw them close under their rough shawls. The men half-rose. Scripps reached for Joey, who sat as if frozen, small fists clenched and eyes wide with fright.

Then Scripps froze, too.

The dark hound-shape paused at the clearing's edge, challenging, growling from deep in its chest. Shadows slunk close behind it: a stray-pack. The creature snarled, eyes glowing blood-red by firelight. It took one more stiff-legged, meaningful step. Then it sprang.

It screamed, and seemed for an instant to hang there, straddling firelight, its jaws slashing air. Then it fell with a thud, and its claws scrabbled trails in the dust. A last shudder went through it, and it was still. Foam gathered on its slack muzzle.

Calmly, the man nearest Scripps pushed his slingshot back into his belt. His knife glinting, he bent to the dog; soon its carcass was gutted and bled, and hung by noosed hind legs. Nudged by the wind, it swayed gently back and forth at the end of its rope.

Later, Scripps stared at the dog as he sat through his watch. The rope twined and untwined, and with each turn the creature strafed Scripps with its sightless eyes. Mangy and half-starved, as food it was hardly worth dressing out. Still, it looked right hanging over fifteen desperate refugees. Scripps thought it made a most appropriate flag.

Fifteen yards off in the darkness, he knew, lay a set of rails stretching away towards the city. He watched, but saw only a sliver of moon like an icicle in the low branches. Straining his ears, he heard only the wind's mocking whistle.

The train would not whistle. The train, he began to fear, would never come. After all, he thought, sitting there stiff on a tree-stump, what proof did he have that it would? Just a rumor, a bought one at that. The same tip, he supposed, that had brought all these others to camp here two nights in the cold.

He moved onto the ground, leaned his back up against the stump's rough bark. No train. Well, tomorrow they would start to walk. The path, at least, was clearly marked. Scripps smiled to himself, grimly.

He would make it. He would.

But now he was tired. His eyes burned, and the ache in the back of his neck felt like a hammer-blow. Shifting, he pulled his coat tighter. The darkness was thick as a blanket. He rested his eyes.

"Scripps!"

He leapt awake in an explosion of panic, threw off whatever had seized his arm—

"Scripps, it's here! The train, hurry!" Joey tugged at him, terrier-fashion, staggering under the weight of both their packs. "Come *on!*"

The clearing was empty. Alert now, Scripps grabbed a pack, hustled himself and the boy towards the dull yellow glow of a kerosene lantern. Behind it a huge dark shape loomed on the tracks, chuffing steam.

Only the desperate ventured onto the night-trains. All black, they rolled in darkness like gypsy caravans, hitched to the infrequent, unscheduled freights that still hauled to the city. The city was dying; still, Scripps headed into it. Little remained in the world to be desperate for, save the chance of escape. It was there, in the city. Inside.

Aching, Scripps shifted restlessly, his tailbone already scraped raw by the hard wooden seat. The rough bench was a prize; half the passengers squatted or sprawled in the car's narrow aisle. Scripps sighed, shifted again, leaning on his pack. In the murky light of a single lantern, the other riders dozed or stared dully ahead, swaying with each monotonous lurch of the train.

Suddenly, Scripps felt eyes on him. He took a deep breath, let his glance travel over the dull, brutish faces until he reached one that was not dull. Perhaps seventeen, wiry, rat-faced, with bright calculating eyes fixed on Scripps's shoulder, the boy did not lower his gaze. He looked . . . hungry.

Scripps gave no sign, let his glance move on. Meanwhile he scratched at his shoulder as if at a flea-bite, and managed to cover the bright player's emblem stitched to his right sleeve. *Careless, careless again.* He was not in the mood to fight punks, nor to fend off their pitiful offerings once they were beaten. *No more.* He tried for what seemed the hundredth time to find a position that did not cramp his muscles. The chunk-ka-chunk of metal wheels, beaten out of round by the decaying railbed, jolted up through the floorboards and into his bones.

In the aisle at the head of the car a guard squatted, shoving chunks of dark bread into his mouth. In his lap lay a rifle; behind him a padlock beat out a tattoo on the chained door. All at once he howled, spattering crumbs; the hard crust fell to the floor. Two men dove at it. Clutching his jaw, the guard jerked his gun sharply; the men backed away.

The guard grinned and snatched up a jug from the heaped pile of booty before him. His fares for the trip:

Candles, pickaxe, a coil of rope. Three logs, a propane torch, bundles of dogskins. Some pills, perhaps morphine or antibiotics. Shoes, blankets. And Scripps's fare: a gallon of two-year-old blackberry wine.

Scripps felt dry. He'd kept back just enough for the trip; now he rummaged his pack for the canteen. The wine was smooth, potent as sherry. It tasted of sunshine, and summers long past when he and Bozzie (Bozzie the big brother, Bozzie the golden) would sneak behind the tool shed with a bottle stolen from the old man's maturing stock. Unaged, it tasted like cat piss, but they drank it anyway, to get drunk and to infuriate the old man.

A little warning sounded inside Scripps's head. (Bozzie the golden, Bozzie the gone.) He had a sudden vision of the wasps that clustered, buzzing, on the bottle in pale sunlight like champagne. Then his mind's eye saw Bozzie grown up, drunken, desperate, his thin face awash in the light of a trash-barrel fire. (Bozzie the gone.)

No. Scripps squirmed, took a swallow of wine, but the lump in his throat stayed. Then beside him a small, saving voice muttered sleepily.

"Wanta drink."

Joey had slept almost all the way; now he peered owlishly up from the bed Scripps had made of their sleeping-rolls. Scripps bent and poured the boy's mouth full of wine.

Joey swallowed and smacked his lips, smiling. "More."

"No, no more." Scripps capped the canteen and stuffed it away. "We're almost there."

Joey sat up, yawning hugely, rubbing his eyes with his small fists. Dark keloids, scars of his life before Scripps had found him, marked his mahogany skin. "Where we now?" he demanded.

In the grey dawn, the ruined world jerked by like cheap film unreeling, through wire-mesh-reinforced windows pockmarked by snipers. Some of the holes were fresh, still dribbling greenish pellets of glass. As they passed the dark tenements, Scripps thought he glimpsed a shape skittering into the shadows. He turned from the window.

"*They* here?" asked Joey, his small brown face pinched.

"No. Only Inside," Scripps said.

They. In that special, separate tone, it did not need explaining. They had come in their ships, before Scripps had been born, when the world was full of people, near-empty of food. From his pack Scripps drew a plastic-sealed news clipping, yellowed but legible: President Greets Visitors. He stared at it, knowing the story was true, but unable to make much sense of the blurry photograph. He knew that compared to now, food had been plentiful even then; still, what this picture showed went against all his instincts. In it, someone called President Smith stood beside one of them. Although what *it* did could not really be called standing, its pose was reasonable-looking compared to the President's. He was offering food—something rather improbably called a "hot dog." Scripps wondered what kind of dog was that small; perhaps it was only a part of one.

The boy across the car had lost interest in Scripps; he stared now at the guard, who was chomping the bread again. Crumbs rolled out of his mouth and lodged in his beard. Every roll of his jaws was a taunt. I have this food, his expression said, and not one of you dares take it from me.

Scripps looked at the news-clip again. In it, a man freely offered his food to an alien. In it, the alien offered the Game in return. The board lay on a table between the two beings, its glow clearly visible even in this muddy photograph. Scripps tucked the clipping back into his pack, where his own game-board nestled.

They'd brought nothing more. Earth's hopes for last-minute rescue had been in vain. *They* had scattered the game-boards and offered the ultimate prize. For a while, people flocked to the tournaments. Then, as the number of applicants dwindled until for two years in a row there were no contests, they vanished Inside, retreating to wait. For what, no one knew.

Inside was paradise; everyone knew that. The best of the players had gone there forever, escaping a world that grew meaner and darker each day. Stories spread: marble halls lighted by magic, jewelled robes that warmed or cooled at the mere touch of the skin, ambrosia that came from the stars. There was music Inside, ease and laughter among the most gifted, and some even said immortality.

Joey's green eyes watched Scripps gravely. "I don't want to go," he said.

"I know. I know you don't. But we can't stay out here. You know that, don't you?" Scripps laid a hand on the boy's skinny shoulder, drew back as the child flinched. *I ain't no dog*, Joey's look said.

"Anyway. Anyway, we'll be all right," Scripps said lamely.

"Uh-huh." Whatever childish faith Joey might have had was long gone by the time Scripps had found him, sick and starving, covered with weeping sores. It had taken a whole day to coax him with spoonfuls of soup from the basement where Scripps had gone scavenging. Now, a year later, he still felt that Joey was more wolverine than small boy. *At least he doesn't bite anymore*, Scripps thought, remembering Joey's bloody first bath. Beneath them, the train lurched bone-jarringly over a switch, and suddenly night fell again. They were inside the tunnel.

The rank, choking odor of coal fumes seeped into the car. Scripps's eyes burned. Not much longer, though, for very soon they would reach Grand Central Station, or whatever was left of it. Scripps wondered what they would find.

Then the hackle-raising shriek of the train's brakes ripped through the dark; the engine groaned, halted. A split second later the hitch-hiking, freewheeling night train slammed into the freight's rear.

Scripps raised his head, setting off brilliant concussions of pain. In his mouth blood welled up, warm and coppery-sweet. He gagged, coughed, spat a tooth. Splinters needled his hands and knees as he pushed himself up off the floor, seeing stars. Somewhere, a man cursed; a woman prayed loudly. From somewhere else gurgled a wordless sound Scripps did not want to identify.

Joey. His heart took a horrid swoop. "Joey?" Icicle terror rammed through him. "*Joey!*"

Then Joey whimpered, and Scripps's world came tiltingly upright. He reached down, grabbed onto a portion of boy, and pulled hard.

Joey slid up beside him. "Don't want to," he protested, wriggling away. Roughly, Scripps yanked him back. Up front, as shock dissolved, screaming began, hoarse monotonous howls that must echo for hundreds of yards in the darkness outside. Like a dinner-bell, Scripps thought—shut up, shut *up*—as he tore at his pack with skinned, throbbing fingers. By now in their lairs tunnel-dwellers were stirring, nostrils twitching, ears pricked at the sound of an easy kill.

Calling all ghouls, Scripps thought grimly, remembering the tenement-shadows outside. They'd be here in just seconds, unless the guard managed to find his gun, silence his cargo. Around Scripps fear billowed like blood in shark waters.

The pack opened, Scripps uncased the game-board and slapped it over his knees. Then he grabbed Joey's hands. "Don't think. Play," he ordered.

In the darkness the board glimmered faintly, pastel crystal matrices awaiting a touch—rather, two touches. His, and the boy's. It took two minds, four hands, to make what they needed now, two singers to sing the one song that might save them. Still whimpering, Joey allowed his small hands to be pressed to the octagon-board. A faint ping! rang up from the prism-scape; instantly, flickering light spread like wildfire from crystal to crystal, until the board shone with pale fire.

In the pastel glow, Joey's face floated as if disembodied; tears flashed in his tightly curled lashes. "Joey," Scripps whispered, "Joey, *play.*"

Then a thin, fluting song trembled out of the prisms, a goblin-tune, haunting and sweet. The board warmed to Scripps's touch; a faint tingling spread through his hands, and the nape of his neck prickled.

"Player," said someone nearby in hoarse tones of relief. "There's a player here." Murmuring spread through the dark car.

There are ***two*** *players here*, Scripps thought proudly, as his hands moved with Joey's in silhouette over the deepening crystal-hues, ruby and gold, emerald, aquamarine. Joey's face smoothed to dreamy intentness. The song twined up. Scripps looked into the boy's face and felt himself falling.

Falling. The screams stopped. Music . . . laughed. Things from the boy's mind crept, tendril-like, into Scripps' own. His hands moved, drawn by the song, on the hundred-and-sixty-four faceted crystals set into their carved slots.

It was a sensation he could never be prepared for, the feeling of knowing what Joey knew, in exactly the way that Joey knew it. Scripps felt Joey's springy resilience, his fear, his simple intention to survive. Then particular things began seeping through: hunger, thirst, along with reluctance to bother him, Scripps, with these things. For a startling instant Scripps's own face as seen through the boy's eyes rose up. Then with a deft maneuver the boy took control, led them into a melody, stated, inverted, reversed and restated it. His laughter flowed through, tickling Scripps. The song held. *Scripps,* thought Joey. The word was clear, mischievous. *Scripps, play.*

Unmeasured time later, Scripps felt the car lurch, roll forward. Inside: silence, the music invading and tranquilizing. Outside, no shape moved. The game-crystals, glowing like embers, maintained fragile peace among those who heard Game played according to Joey.

At the platform, a dozen or so furtive bandits unloaded the freight. Scripps saw labels on cases of canned goods. Apparently the city's stores were finally exhausted, and the looters had to move farther afield. Which would leave, Scripps reflected, much less for the people still out there. The rat-boy from the train scuttled furtively towards him. Scripps turned away.

"Please, sir . . ."

Scripps stiffened. Always the same voice, the whining, demanding tone. Whirling, he faced the boy.

"I'm not the one. You're mistaken."

The boy eyed him, slyness distorting his features. "I'm nice," he said softly.

Scripps pushed him hard.

Outside, he shivered resentfully. It was a crisp, razor-bright fall day, air carbonated with sunshine and laden with promise of early pneumonia. Beside him, Joey caught his breath, nostrils flaring, chest heaving. Fear stabbed Scripps. Beneath that small, tough-looking frame pumped a pair of lungs shredding like wet tissue, slowly, each time a snow fell. *Simple,* Scripps thought. *Inside, or we're both dead by spring.*

Joey sneezed.

"Come on," Scripps said. They walked on a street paved with broken glass. Silent buildings watched down, their intact upper windows reflecting the sky. The watched feeling was not an illusion, Scripps knew, for the glare of the solar collectors showed over the roof-edges. Up there, small crops flourished, grown with the same jealous fervor once given to stock portfolios. His neck prickled with the primitive awareness of a rifle-scope trained on his spinal-cord, and he thought of exposing his player's patch. But no; a rifle could capture as well as defend. They walked on.

From the gutter beside a cracked fire-hydrant, something grinned toothily: dog, Scripps decided. Picked clean, the skull gleamed. Joey reached for his hand. The glass-fragments crunched loudly beneath their feet in the bright morning. Making their way between ruins of cars, past the overturned trucks and the looted stores, they headed for what had been Central Park, and was now Inside.

They were not to blame, Scripps thought. They had come at the end, nearly. Patiently, they watched and waited, Inside, with all the time there was, all the time in the world.

"Hey," said Joey. Without warning they came on it, no-man's-land, where concrete gave way to packed earth and buildings to nothing. Or almost to nothing.

Hovels of sheet-iron and broken boards hunkered around smoking barrels. The air here was tinged with a faint stink of carrion. Here stank of death. Joey tugged at Scripps's hand. "Hey, let's go."

Scripps heard him dimly, staring beyond to a white glimmer hanging mirage-like just on the horizon. Inside. His heart beat faster; then nearby movement distracted him.

From a board hut, a hunched-over shape struggled into the sun. Man or woman, he could not tell. Feet wrapped in rags, indescribably filthy, it shuffled towards the fire. From the smoke-belching barrel it pulled something long, something crusted with . . . Scripps felt his gorge rise. The creature squatted, began to eat, whining.

Scripps vomited.

The thing paused, looked towards them. High, dismal wails came from its mouth. There was a rustling, shuffling sound; from the cardboard and tarpaper caves creatures poured into daylight. Swaying and moaning, they shambled towards Scripps.

Scripps grabbed Joey and ran. Holding tight, he pinned Joey's wild arms with his own, felt the boy's sobbing harsh on his neck. Horrid fingers plucked, tore at their clothing and snatched at their hair. Something fixed itself onto Scripps's back, crooning. Scripps nearly gagged on the stench of its breath.

"Hung-gree-e-e, gim-m-ee, ple-e-eze . . ."

Scripps kicked viciously backwards; the thing howled and fell. Stumbling, breath coming now in huge tearing sobs, he staggered on. Still his flesh crept with their hands touching, touching. . . .

And then they were free. The things had no strength for a chase. A few last ones stood watching them balefully, heads swaying sideways, like hopeless dumb animals. In his mind's eye Scripps saw the long bone again, and he held Joey tight. "Ssh, they're gone, they won't hurt you," he lied. Joey clutched him and cried harder.

All around lay a grey ash, inches deep, drifting and settling with the little cold gusts of wind. Overhead, clouds gathered; sunlight came slantingly, then disappeared. Joey snuffled, wiggled to be let down. Jesus, Scripps thought. Jesus, they almost got us.

"What were they gonna do to us?" Joey demanded, his voice still wavering on the edge of tears. Scripps crouched before him, first glancing back to be sure they were not being followed after all.

"Joey, they were just people. Sick, sad, poor people. They wanted us to help them, but we can't because we don't have anything,

Joey listened, looking back at the settlement, thoughts moving visibly in his head. "Like me," he said finally.

"What?" Scripps said, startled.

"Like me, when you found me." Joey regarded him patiently, as if he were the adult and Scripps the child.

"Well, not quite," he said at last. Fat drops were falling now, making small dark holes in the dust. "Look," he said.

Ahead a white glimmering hung on the horizon, no longer mirage-like but clearly real, beckoning, precisely where the story-tellers had said it would be. Around it, what had been Central Park was a desert of ash and blackened tree-stumps, memorializing the fire-fights of the last food wars.

Inside. Scripps cinched up his pack. They would make it now, he was sure. Looking back once as they trudged through the soft grey dust, he saw that the wind was taking their footprints as they stepped out of them.

They walked steadily, and the sky grew steadily darker, the drizzle more chilling. Joey spoke after a long time.

"Hey, remember them little meats we got that time? Back home, we played for them people, and they gave us—"

Scripps remembered. The meat had been dog, the offering of people even more miserable than himself, in return for an hour of game-induced tranquility. *No more*, he told himself, setting his jaw grimly as he marched.

"An we cooked 'em over that fire Bozzie made," Joey went on. "Mmmm, I wonder what ol' Bozzie doin' now."

Fire of books, Scripps remembered. He remembered also taking Bozzie away before Joey could see him, what he had become and how he had died. "Listen, forget all that. That's all done." (Bozzie the gone.)

After a while, Joey spoke again. "Scripps, all them people back there."

"Yeah?" Ahead, Inside grew whiter, solider. He was half-listening, intent on calculating the distance that remained. They would make it tonight. He forced himself to walk faster, despite the growing ache in his back and thighs.

"How come nobody saved them poor people?"

"Most people don't get saved." Inside glowed, dome-shaped. "They've got to save themselves, pull themselves up by their boot-straps, like us."

The night thickened around them. Joey said, "Scripps. Them people, they don't need bootstraps. They need food." A long pause, then, "Ain't lucky, them people. They ain't got no Scripps."

Scripps looked down in surprise, but the child said no more, just kept walking.

White and luminous, gleaming in the rain, the wall curved gently away in both directions and up out of sight. It was dark now, and in the wall's pale glow Joey's face showed, exhausted. "Wh-what now?" he said.

"I'm not sure," Scripps admitted. He had imagined some sort of gatekeeper, but there was no gate, or even a door. He looked again at the smooth, seamless wall.

Then it spoke. "Kindly state your reason for wishing entry."

Scripps jumped, moved closer. A speaker of some kind, an intercom? No break showed in the slick surface.

Rain streamed down the boy's face, and his teeth chattered audibly. "*Tell* it," he said.

"I'm here to play the Game," he shouted, wondering if anyone could hear. Then, remembering the formal response, "I wish to challenge a Bothryan Game-player, under the human-player clause. I claim the rights of guardianship for the boy."

The wall said, "Enter." Nothing else happened. After a moment, the wall said again, "Enter."

"Open the door," Scripps called.

"Enter."

"There's *no door—*"

"Enter."

Scripps kicked the wall just as hard as he could, and his foot sailed on through it as if it were vapor. His body sailed after, landing hard on a smooth, slippery floor.

"Joey!" The room was small, dome-shaped, and seamless. It glowed greenly. A small light appeared, like a candle-flame, floating perhaps three feet off the floor.

"Please follow," it said, and its voice was no-voice, featureless like the wall's.

Scripps tried pushing his hand through again, but the wall had solidified. "Joey?"

"Please follow."

Some kind of guide-drone, Scripps decided. It couldn't respond; it could only repeat what it was told to say. They had such things, it was said. The wall, too, must be programmed somehow. Furious, Scripps hammered it with his fists.

Then a small brown hand poked through. Quickly Scripps seized it, pulled hard, and the rest of the boy popped Inside.

"Joey!" Scripps hugged the boy, pressed his face into the wet, nappy head. "Dammit, stay with me. Don't ever do that again."

Joey squirmed free. "I didn't do nothin'. What's *that?*"

"Please follow."

"Come on. It's some kind of robot, to guide us. It's just a mechanical thing, it can't hear or talk back."

"Incorrect," the light said, and passing through the wall, it disappeared.

At once the room began to darken, their shadows merging with the gloom. Clearly, they were being encouraged to leave. "Hey, Scripps." Joey's voice quavered. "Let's go home."

Scripps swallowed hard. "Too late. We'll be all right." Grasping Joey's hand, Scripps took a step towards the wall, then another, fervently wishing he could see through it before he had to walk through it. Somehow, this was not what he had expected. Squaring his shoulders, he took a deep breath and another step.

"Kindly state your reason for wishing exit."

Scripps pulled his jackknife out of the wall, watched the edges of the gash flow together. In moments, no mark showed. They had been here for hours in this small white room. No windows, no doors, and no hint of what came next . . . *if anything*. . . .

"Kindly state your reason . . ."

"Kindly state *your* reason, dammit, you can't just keep us here—"

"Incorrect."

Scripps clenched his fists as the wall spoke again in its toneless voice. "We do not wish to supervise your actions. We do not wish to take protective measures. You will remain where you are."

"Other humans are here," Scripps objected. "Are they confined?"

"They are initiates. You are not." Now the wall's voice seemed to carry a tinge of scorn.

"Oh, I see. Savages, are we? Aren't you afraid that we'll mess your floor?"

As Scripps spoke, a small section of wall began shimmering, flowed, disappeared. A side-room revealed itself.

"Toilet facilities," said the wall. "Do you wish instructions in their use?"

"Thanks. We'll figure it out."

"Please state your other requirements."

Scripps stiffened. *How about a small thermonuclear warhead?*

Then from behind him he heard Joey sniffle and gulp back a sob. Slowly, he let his clenched fists fall.

"We're hungry," he said. "We need food, water too." *Please, sir. Please, you arrogant bastard.*

The food arrived through a small dissolvature flush with the gleaming floor: two large basins filled with grey porridgey stuff. There were no spoons. Revolted and starved, Scripps extended his right index finger and dunked it first-knuckle-deep, into the warm greasy mess. Then he drew it back, cautiously sniffing the glob on his fingertip.

His famished body trembled at the stewed-meat aroma. He ate it, and scooped up more, making a spoon between thumb and forefinger. The texture was like cooked barley. But what kind of meat? *I don't care,* he thought, pushing it into his mouth. *I don't care, much.*

The boy watched him, accusingly, Scripps thought. *He'll eat when he's hungry enough.* Scripps drank from the bulb-shaped carafe, letting the cool water slosh in his mouth. He looked up in time to catch Joey swiping away a tear.

"Joey. Come on, you've got to eat."

Joey slid over, peered into the basins, and looked away.

"Hey, you remember the first time I fed you? Like this, with my fingers?"

"Don't want it."

"You didn't want it then, either. Come on," Scripps urged gently. "Eat it for strength." He watched resolution grow in the boy's face, and he knew he must feed it. "Strength," he repeated. "For whatever you want to do."

After a moment Joey opened his mouth and accepted the food. He finished the rest on his own.

Knowing the wall could speak made it seem alive, made it seem to be watching. Scripps swallowed the final mouthful and put his dish down. *Were* they watching? Now that he was full, he had strength for shame. He should have waited, resisted until they were freed, or at least given more explanation. Squarish and thick-walled, the basins resembled troughs.

"Joey. I'm sorry."

With one finger Joey smeared bits of spilled food on the smooth floor. He did not look up.

"It won't always be like this."

Incorrect. Scripps jumped, but the voice had not come from the wall; it was his own thought, inside his own head. *How do you know it won't always be like this?* They had not come back, he realized suddenly. No player had ever come back to tell how it was, Inside. Only the stories, repeated until they seemed true, told of richness and splendor. Scripps thought of his father, the old man's descriptions of mosaic floors, painted panels, jewelled robes. But his father had failed, had never progressed past first-level play in the old tournaments. How could his father have known? Why, in fact, would they want such things? *And what could they want with you?* persisted the unwelcome voice in his head.

"You'll see," he told Joey. "After we win, things are going to be different." He hoped he had put enough certainty into his voice.

Joey slept, but Scripps could not sleep. His jaw throbbed from his fall on the train, hours or years ago. The walls stared down, blank and white; silence rang in his ears. Suddenly he wanted badly to scream. It was all a mistake. Everyone knew that Inside meant escape from the hunger and cold, from the brutish thing life outside had become.

Here we are, he thought bitterly. *Warm, safe, and fed.* What he'd eaten was bile at the back of his throat. Joey turned in his sleep, whimpered, grew still again.

Some time later, the wall spoke. "Tomorrow."

Scripps jerked upright, sweating. "Tomorrow *what?*"

There was no answer. After a while he lay back down. Joey edged closer, and Scripps curved an arm round the small trembling shoulders.

Tomorrow. Tomorrow would be better.

Maybe, he thought.

The warm stew was not nearly so appetizing for breakfast. *Coffee*, Scripps thought. *You'd think they'd have coffee.* Even acorn drippings would go good now. He washed in the cubicle, paused in front of the toilet. Surely this was the toilet? He'd been too unnerved to wonder until now, and as he stared at the flushless foreign-looking receptacle he remembered an old joke and hoped he wasn't meant to wash his feet in it. *Not that he'd had much recent experience with modern plumbing . . .* His stream hit the bowl's waterless side and disappeared with a faint hiss. Imagining himself sliding feet-first into whatever the sewer was, he began to laugh. Then he stopped. It wasn't really funny. He stood there, thinking about how funny it wasn't, until he heard voices. *Voices.* He had a sudden, ridiculous impulse to slam the bathroom door, realized there was no door, and struggled to get himself decently into his pants and zipped. It was a *woman's* voice. . . .

In the main room, a young woman stood smiling at Joey, who shyly smiled back. She was twenty-five, maybe, with cornsilk hair, a blue dress that hung—*tenderly*, Scripps thought, and realized that even at first glance he could imagine her being touched in no other way. Her skin was pale, translucent as a skim of ice. Blue veins showed in her wrist when she held out her hand.

"Judith," she said. Her voice had a reedy, musical lilt. Her hand was cold. He wanted to warm it between the two of his.

"Uh, Howard. Howard Scripps. I didn't think anyone was going to come." As he spoke the words, he realized they were true; the sight of her now was making him dizzy with relief.

Her eyes showed sympathy; their intense blueness was like a little slap. Moonstone-blue, they shone their color as if lit from within. He was, he realized, still holding her hand.

She was smiling. "Are you ready to begin?"

He blinked, not sure he understood. "You? The player? We're challenging you?"

Judith laughed, nodded, and moved towards the board, which he'd laid out the night before.

"Wait," Scripps said. She smiled, puzzled now. "Wait," he said again. "Tell me first, what's it like living here?"

In her blue eyes the light guttered, died. "It's . . . a pleasant life."

"What do you do all day?"

Her smile faltered. "I . . . pass the time." Something closed, shutterlike, back in those blue eyes, and suddenly Scripps did not think she was nearly so pretty.

"And all the others?" He felt cold. "They . . . pass the time also?" *She didn't want to tell him. Why?*

"A pleasant life," she repeated. "Food, warmth. No one hurts me." She looked at the floor. "It was worse, outside."

"What did you do outside?"

"Played Game, of course," she responded, more confident now. "And . . . I was a teacher. A nursery-school teacher." She whispered it, wonderingly.

"A *nursery*-school teacher—" he stopped. Peach-soft skin, blond hair, smooth hands. When the last schools closed, she could not even have been born.

"Judith. *When* did you come Inside?"

She smiled again, an embarrassed smile, like a small child tricked into giving away a secret. "1989."

Exactly one hundred years ago.

She waved at the board. "So. Are you ready to begin?"

"No. No, I'm not." He was struck by another thought. "How long has it been since the last challenger? Since the last human came in?"

"A long time. Years, I think. But—"

Scripps nodded. "Go away," he said. "Tell them they've got it wrong. I won't play you, and the boy—" Scripps glanced at Joey and a spasm of intense, protective love gripped him. "The boy doesn't play at all. He doesn't know how."

Joey's mouth opened; Scripps shot a look at him; it said, *keep quiet.* Joey did.

"What will you do?" Judith faltered. There had been no instructions for this, clearly.

"Tell them the challenge is for them. I challenge a Bothryan player, here, today."

"Don't do it." Judith glanced fearfully at the walls. *The walls have ears.* "Their minds are—strong. If you lose, you will not know it, ever."

"And if I win?"

She looked straight at him. "You would go free. But no one ever has."

He stared. "I don't believe you."

"All right. Follow me. It doesn't matter, it's all decided already. I only tried to save you pain, as much as I could." She moved to the wall, disappeared through it without glancing back.

"Stay here," he told Joey quickly, and, he hoped, unnecessarily. He slid through the wall as if in Judith's wake.

Dimly he glimpsed her ahead, moving swiftly away in the gloom, and he hurried to catch up. The floor felt . . . squishy, less solid somehow, and he kept his hands pressed tight to his sides, more aware of the walls than before. A faint whispering sound reached him, but there was no time to listen. She waited an instant for him, turning, then stiffened slightly and vanished again. There was nothing to do but go after her, although he cringed at the thought, for the walls had a clammy feel now, clinging more to his face and hands. There was an instant of total disgust as the wall closed around him, and then he was through. What he saw made him think he might weep, or go mad, or both.

In a large room, dimly lit, a low murmuring rolled wave on wretched wave over the forms in the low beds. Some plucked at the bedclothes; some, motionless, stared with blank eyes. People, hundreds of people. A stench hung in the air, fecal, gaggingly strong. Attendants, human as their wards but more alert, moved slowly among the beds. Their shoulders sagged under the white gowns they wore, and their faces seemed carved into masks of sadness.

Scripps stared in cold horror.

"We try," Judith said. "But there are so many. We need you, you see. *They* need you."

He whirled on her. "What is this place? *Who are they?*" Knowing, dear God, knowing . . .

"These are the Players," she said calmly. "And this is the Players' Hall."

He wanted to scream. He wanted to vomit. He wanted to run.

"These are . . . Game-masters? *Winners?*"

"No. There are no winners. I told you, their minds are strong. But we need caretakers, so I was sent, *allowed*, rather, to challenge you at the Game. You must be . . . unhurt."

"But you . . . and all these other attendants. You won. There's a chance. . . ."

"No. I lost too." A gleam of pride sparked in her blue eyes. "Just not quite so badly."

That, Scripps thought, depended on how you looked at it. Now he saw that beside each bed, a game-board lay. "Surely they don't play, like this?"

"Watch." Judith made her way among the beds until she came to a low table; on it, another board lay. She placed both hands upon it; a shimmering sound sprang up. As if on signal, the murmuring ceased. The attendants backed off, their arms folded, and every Player reached out for a board. Then a chord like the blast of a gigantic pipe-organ split the air, seeming to penetrate Scripps's, bones. At another signal from Judith, the Players fell back, inert.

Ears ringing dizzyingly, Scripps staggered. "Why?" He was shouting, unable to hear himself through the roaring that still filled his head.

Judith gave him a look full of pity—and something that might have been amusement, a century ago. She had been here that long, he realized. Deafened, he read her lips and felt despair fill him as she mouthed the words.

"*They* do not explain."

Back in the cubicle, he faced her. "They don't watch you," he said. That was why she could take him on tour.

"What should they be afraid of, that we will escape?"

"But you *could* escape." He said the words certainly, watching her

Her eyes flickered away. "I don't know."

"You do know. You could walk through that wall and get out—and take us with you."

"To *what?*" she demanded. "To starve, to freeze? They were dying out there when I came Inside. What's it like now? Why did *you* come?"

"Never mind. We're going back, and you're helping us. You're coming, too."

"It won't do any good. They'll be outside too, soon. They're just waiting."

"For what?"

Judith stared at the floor. "I don't know. Something's changing. The Game—when we play, we can hear them. They're frightened, and soon they'll be everywhere. That's what comes through—fear, and some kind of horrible joy. An explosion of some kind, a spreading. They expect it and want it, but they're afraid, too. That's why they've got us. We can protect them, somehow."

"With the Game?"

Judith nodded. "I don't understand, but I know running won't help. There'll be no place to run to, soon."

Joey sat on the floor, eyes wide, listening. Watching him, Scripps felt a curious calm. He'd been right the first time. To save Joey, himself, he knew just what he had to do. Fear would come later. He hoped it would not come too soon. He turned back to her.

"When you came in, you played one of them, and you're not . . . damaged."

"That doesn't mean *you* can . . ."

Scripps waved impatiently. "That doesn't matter." He felt mild surprise, knowing that it was true. "But—*he* does." Now he mouthed the words so they would not hear. "If I'm . . . gone . . . can you get him out?"

Judith looked doubtful.

"*Please.*" In that one word he put all of his love, all his caring, his stupid hopes. Yes, the world was a madhouse, and dying, but maybe, just *maybe* the boy could make good where they'd failed. "Please. Give Joey his chance."

Something moved in her eyes, then, amazement. And envy, perhaps, for his feelings. Her face spoke a loneliness he could not even imagine. She nodded. Her lips moved then, forming the words. *Yes. Yes, I think I can.*

When she was gone, he addressed the wall. "I've changed my mind," he said. "I withdraw. We want to go back outside."

"Incorrect," said the wall coldly. He'd known that it would. "Your challenge has been recorded. Prepare to play."

So that was that. *If you lose*, she had said, *you won't know it. Or anything, ever.*

But if he won, he would know everything. Playing them, he would learn. He remembered the feeling of Joey's mind melding with his as they played on the train, and he wondered how it would feel to merge that way with something alien, *other*. He had heard them described, seen antique photographs. Now he would see an alien face. If it *had* a face. . . .

Stop that, he ordered himself. There was no other way. He could not just sit back and let them make the moves. If the woman were right, simply running would do no good. Scripps thought she was. He felt something himself, in the tunnel, especially. Something . . . afoot.

If it *had* feet . . .

Shut up. Wait. And don't spook yourself in the meantime.

He tried to obey himself, sat down and hugged Joey, tried not to think of how bad it might be.

"Please follow." The guide-light hovered three feet off the floor, near the wall.

"The boy too?" Scripps asked.

"Please follow."

Suddenly, Scripps was not sure that he wanted to leave this small white prison. The guide-light, however, was now sliding into the wall. "Come on," he told Joey. "If it doesn't work, sit tight and I'll come back for you." *Or she will*, he thought, but that did not bear thinking of, so he stopped.

The wall swallowed both of them into the same dark, damp passage he'd followed before. A rank insect-smell that had been faint then stung his nose now, making his eyes water. The guide-light bobbed speedily into the distance, guiding but not illuminating; Scripps brushed the wall. Clammy frond-things clung stickily. Jerking away, he hugged his arms to his sides. Behind him, Joey's breath came quick and harsh. The light veered, dipped once, and disappeared.

They stood in the darkness. *Through the wall, oh Jesus, I can't put my* ***face*** *into that—*

The tunnel was different, now, no longer empty but full of a waiting silence. He felt—watched. Somewhere nearby, a whirring sound started, dry papery whicker of wings rubbed together. *Or legs,*

Scripps thought. *Millions of little legs. Or . . . jaws.* The sound seemed to come from inside the walls, as if something, some *things*—were burrowing out.

"Please follow." Out of the darkness, the guide-light's voice came.

Something touched Scripps's hand; he jerked it away with a smothered shriek. But it was Joey, trembling, reaching out in speechless fear. Scripps bent and pulled him close, and for a moment clung to the wonderfully normal feel of Joey's cotton jacket, Joey's head pressed tight against his chest.

"Please follow. Were it within my authorized function, I would advise you to do so immediately."

Crouched there, Scripps shuddered. The darkness was thick with the rasping sound, seeming to press in from all sides, and the vermin-smell strengthened, a sharp reek now.

Something twined up his leg, nipped his calf, fastened itself in the soft skin behind his knee.

Scripps moaned in horror. He kicked it off, scrambled away, and plunged into the wall, clutching Joey.

The wall *moved* around him. Soft things writhed against his face, probing, invading. He flailed out in nightmare revulsion, resisting the drag of their bodies. One poked up his nose. Then a needle of flame pierced his ear. With his jaws clamped shut, Scripps screamed.

And then they were through.

They emerged, panting, onto a stage in a vast, high-domed hall full of Bothryan spectators. Banks of white lights ringed the stage. Squinting, Scripps made out their shapes: like big toads. They had no necks, just head-humps. Their mouths were thin rubbery slits. As the lights dimmed, he saw their eyes. Each had a pair, placed approximately in the forehead, except they did not really have foreheads. All the eyes were turned on him, and all glowed sulfurous yellow.

Joey was shaking, his lips clamped tight, eyes glazed with shock. But when the guide-light said "Please follow," Joey marched stoically after it, tossing one mute look of fear back at Scripps.

Then from the side of the stage, it appeared. It moved rapidly, smoothly across the floor, with the continuous gliding motion of a snail. Two grey pipestem arms dangled as if unhinged from its sides. It stopped center-stage. "Be-ghinn," it wheezed.

A table-like cylinder rose from the floor; on it glimmered a game-board. The Bothryan stretched its hands over the board, and the light from below threw its twelve fingers into relief. They were long, slender, round-tipped and without nails. One on each hand jutted back towards the wrist. On the board, they made perfect sense, widening the hand's range by eight or ten crystals.

The crystals gleamed, waiting, the octagon board ringing softly. Don't think, *play*, Scripps instructed himself, feeling solid with terror. The Bothryan's yellow eyes stared him down coldly.

Then he could not delay any more; he dropped his hands to the board. A faint ping! chimed up and the game was begun.

In an instant, a tide of sound swept over him, filling his skull. He could not even make out whether it was music. His last coherent thought echoed Judith's words: Their minds are strong. Then his surroundings receded, memory died, reality slid out of sight as Scripps whirled into the mind-set of the Bothryan.

It was like steering a white-water raft with his brain. He fought for control, then realized it was hopeless. He could never lead an opponent this strong. His only chance was to relax, play along, and pick up as much information as he could.

Enormous bells rang in his skull. He had a confused image of his own hands, seen through strange eyes. Tingling warmth rose, tide-like, into his arms and chest. The Bothryan's fingers danced nimbly among the bright crystals. The bells faded, thinned to a high singing-note, under which strange chords sprouted. Then a thin dry chatter set up, and Scripps knew that somewhere, that sound was the wind. Home. No, not home. Somewhere. Not here.

The cataract of sensation calmed enough for Scripps to reach out, cautiously, towards the being whose mind confronted his own. Gently, he questioned it, feeling his own mind get ready to snap shut again like a clam.

A cold purpose, remorseless as an iron spike, met his probing. A cold hunger, leashed only for the sake of later feeding, lapped at him. The song crooned, coaxing: it was a fine and wonderful thing to be of this race, to come into this race, to feed this race. Scripps felt himself frozen in the grip of the Bothryan mind, receiving images helplessly, defenseless as if he were already in the creature's jaws.

To be a Player, to stretch the shining threads from mind to mind, to encase the unresisting in a brittle cocoon of song—it was a fine and wonderful thing. So much space to fill with the swarms of one's children. In his mind's eye Scripps saw them, a river of dark scraping chitinous bodies pouring out of the tunnels. Ravenous, searching, they tumbled over one another, advancing with the force of their terrible hunger after the long incubation.

With sudden hideous clarity, Scripps saw the larvae scrabble towards the parent-forms, then halt in frustrated puzzlement. He felt vibrations of Game in himself, felt it turn them away: no food here. And at last he understood Game, its deepest and simplest purpose. Game protected the Bothryans from being devoured by their young.

Its near-total absence from Earth insured that the young would have other food.

He played on, mechanically. The Bothryan was strong, but it allowed him to follow easily. Only if he tried to turn the game, to set his own theme, could he possibly lose. He sensed the Bothryan's parent-fear; it was not strong. There was still time.

He sensed also how much he himself was under suspicion. Game-knowledge flowed both ways. They trusted her, but he was a wild card. Undamaged, he would be watched. Knowing what he must do, and dreading it, he threw himself into the game as if into flames.

He played Earth. A winter sunset, orange and purple and blue spreading over a frozen lake, struck the alien game-matrix and dissolved with an acid hiss. The acid sizzled and burned in Scripps's brain. A howl ripped from his throat.

Reeling, he forced a vision of home: a glowing trash-fire. A drunken, yodeling Bozzie. Around the fire a rag-tag band of scavengers shared their little food and drank the horrible stuff Bozzie strained from abandoned cars. They were singing.

Pain torched his neurons, consuming nostalgia, leaving the vision a heap of grey ash.

The board shrieked as the Bothryan parried his puny thoughts. It flared sulfur-yellow and bile-green, boiled murky no-colors. His brain felt shot with maggots of fire, and he bit his cheeks not to scream. Turning, the room seemed to tumble around him. *Their minds are strong.* Vision died, and the board's high, dismal keening dissolved to white hiss.

Once more. Just once more, and release would come. With a last effort Scripps pulled one final image from somewhere in what still remained of himself. Racked with agony, he held it, simple and true, in the crumbling game-matrix. Desperate, he held to that one feeling:

The child, not feared, but loved. The matrix quivered, humming with unfamiliar resonances; the Bothryan mind-presence reeled back, confused. *The child.* Scripps pressed forward, ferocious joy at the heart of his pain. *The child, fed not with his flesh, but with his love. Love, damn you.* The Bothryan struggled to keep control in an onslaught of image so strong and so alien to it. Its puzzlement and the beginnings of its fear jangled dissonantly in the matrix-song. Scripps grinned, feeling his face twist in triumph even as his brain seemed to fry in its own fat. A white-hot emulsion of sound and light erupted from the crystals. Through it he held to one feeling, human, familiar and dear.

He held to the feel of a child's hand, trustingly clasped in his own. *Scripps.* Joey's laughter came trilling in memory. *Scripps, play.*

His mind blazed up in pain like a torch of dry grass.

"Please follow." The guide-light sailed swiftly away down the tunnel. Dazed and clumsy, Scripps let the boy and the woman half-lead and half-carry him. All around, the chitter of small hungry creatures rose to a frenzied pitch; Scripps cringed, frozen with fear and revulsion.

"Come on, Scripps." It was the boy. "You won. They're letting us go. Hurry."

Won? Won what? Their hands pressed him forward. Confusion like nausea roiled in him. He said the only thing he could think of. "Why?"

The woman answered, her voice bleak. "They don't think we can make it through the wall."

Too late, he saw what they forced him towards: a solid, squirming mass of mouths, snapping and slavering—

"No!" He kicked out, but he was too weak; he stumbled and fell into the wall of needle-toothed jaws. He screamed as they battened onto his flesh—

"Scripps! Hey, Scripps, wake up. You're dreaming. Come on, we gotta go, wake up and eat this."

He struggled gratefully into consciousness. It was cold. They had followed the wide, white footpath of an abandoned turnpike, east out of the city, and slept in a thicket. The sky was blue, tinged with pink and gold. He looked down at the battered tin dish the boy offered. Wisps of steam rose from a mound of cooked grain. In his other hand, the boy held a smoking mug; the bitter aroma of acorn coffee tantalized Scripps's nose. He frowned. "Where?"

The boy pointed at a ruined gasoline station, its pumps gone, shattered window-holes plugged with rags. "People live there. I played."

Scripps didn't know what that meant, but he ate the cereal anyway. When he had finished, the boy placed the cup in his hands. "Drink," the boy said, and watched as Scripps obeyed. "Maybe we'll get home tonight."

"Home," Scripps repeated. The food warmed him. He smiled at the boy. A short distance away, a strange woman sat watching them.

Her light yellow hair, long and straight, plucked a chord in his memory.

"Ju-Judith?"

She nodded, approving. "You're doing just fine. It will all come back, first in dreams, like it did to me. You won, Scripps. You beat them."

Scripps didn't know what that meant, either, but it seemed to be good. He had no idea how long they had been walking, or where, but the boy seemed to know. He found food, and places for them to sleep. He urged Scripps along when Scripps tired, and made their meager camp when darkness came. Scripps felt obscurely grateful to him.

"Stay here," the boy said. His name was—

"Joey!"

The boy grinned. Then he turned and jogged away through the frosty weeds, carrying the mugs and bowls. Scripps watched until a hawk swooped overhead, dipping and wheeling in long, slow circles, around and around until Scripps felt dizzy, and sat down. Uneasily, he fingered the scratches that covered his hands. *The dream*—or had it been real? He shivered.

"Come on," said the boy when he returned, and Scripps obediently hoisted his pack and followed. There was something, a wrong thing. The morning was still, except for birds chittering, high in the trees.

"Hurry." His chest was pounding suddenly. He stood still, willing himself to remember, but it would not come. He gave up and hurried to catch up with Judith and Joey.

Later, they trudged three abreast. "You know what?" said Joey. "Them people back there, they had a kid, and you know what he had? A game-board, a real old one. He didn't even know how to play."

"Play?" Scripps's memory pinged.

"He does now," Joey said. "Likes it, too. I think I'm gonna show everyone."

Scripps stopped. The feeling of urgency in his chest seemed to crack, spilling memories. "You've got to. Teach them—it's the only way. . . ." He trailed off, fists clenched, helpless. The game that was not a game— "I don't *know* why," he burst out, near tears. "But when they come, we'll have to know, to fight—" He stopped again, furious, fighting the blank spots—who were *they?*—but calming somewhat at the look on Joey's face.

"Okay," Joey said. "I believe you. Judith says you'll remember more, and I'll teach you Game again, on the way home."

"We'll all teach," Judith said. "You learned something about them. You'll remember. We'll teach, and we'll tell everyone else to teach . . . you beat them, Scripps. You're the only one."

Her face expressed perfect confidence; he wondered how he had earned it. Whatever the battle had been, he knew it was only the first one and not the last. "I don't remember," he said, "but I will."

Something was coming back with the trickle of memories, something he'd lost not in recent days, but long ago. Feelings beat painfully in his chest with his living blood. There was a fight ahead, he knew, though he didn't know yet what it was. He looked at the woman and boy beside him, glad not to face the future alone. The sky overhead was blue. The sun was midway into it, shedding pale yellow light. The wide path curved ahead, disappearing into the trees.

"We'll try," he said. "We can try. Come on, let's go home."

THE INVISIBLE FOE

by Garry Kilworth

art: Frank Borth

Mr. Kilworth was born in 1941
in York (the old one), England.
He spent much of his life traveling
and living abroad, including
several years in the Middle East
and the Far East. Now, he's settled with
his family on the edge of the Essex marshes.
The most recent of his four SF novels is *Gemini God*.

Shadow and sunlight are the same—
and one to me are shame and fame

—"Brahma" by Ralph Waldo Emerson

Singapore, my adopted city, moved slowly into the path of the day's first rays of sunshine. It was monsoon season, and the humidity was high: a day of wet sunlight.

Street cleaners were about, pushing their boxwood handcarts towards littered destinations to brush away the debris of a night-time explosion of people. Walking along Boogey Street, I waved to several transsexuals and transvestites still occupying roadside tables. The *Kai Tai:* female hormones gave many of them a complexion and surface beauty even more beguiling than women. It was not uncommon for merchant seamen looking for whores to make a mistake. Such a beautiful people anyway—a blending of several Eastern cultures. I had an affinity with the *Kai Tai* because we held similar secrets: we seemed what we were not. We both hid beneath layers of untruth: the *Kai Tai* under the guise of women, and myself . . . my pretence was that of being human.

One of them nodded as I passed.

"Morning Thin Chai," he said.

"Morning Lucy," I smiled. I kept my voice soft. The night people were not rowdy or coarse. It was the long-noses that created all the noise. They drank heavily, shouted through mouthfuls of prawns, were sick where they stood and shattered the street air with their shrieks and raucous laughter. Jansen was a *Wai Lo:* an Occidental. Perhaps that was why my mouth tasted of snake bile? I was on my way to meet him, in a subordinate role. That a *Wai Lo,* a *ghost person,* should consider himself my superior filled me with shame.

Japanese motorbikes growled somewhere beyond a row of shops. A proprietor dozing on his raffia bed, on the porch of his premises, stirred and scratched himself through his dirty vest.

The city was beginning to wake.

(I had been there the previous evening, a girl with oranges on her breath at my side. We had sat away from the hanging lanterns, in the shadows, and watched the swift process of change—the metamorphosis of money into gutter filth. I felt no revulsion, merely a detached interest in folly. I was a student of the art, if it is such, and not a science as Jansen would have it. Whatever the category, the study of weakness can only reward infiltrators like myself. It is useful to turn a vice inwards, on its creator, like a dagger.

When the evening's subjects had staggered away along the drunkard's walk, Nancy Ho followed me to my room. In the bareness of my small apartment she nestled against my narrow body.

There were cracks on the wall into which the house lizards wriggled. Her body was silken to the touch. Insects rustled through folds in paper curtains. Dry, shadow-thin sighs escaped my lips. On the card-thin weatherboard, a cockroach scratched its path across the shoulder of the house. Afterwards, I had to open the shutters to let the hot room breathe its odours out into the night, then stroked her hair till we fell asleep.)

By the time I reached the dockside the streets were flowing with vehicles and people. I was pleased with myself for I had not once looked towards Li Hoe Hill and my ugly creation, which adorned its brow like the despised crown of a despot. Though its white columns were printed indelibly upon the cornea of my mind's eye, I could lie to myself, so long as I did not confirm its existence. Perhaps the night rain had washed it away? Perhaps a giant dragon had swallowed it in the rays of the previous evening's dying sun? Perhaps it had vanished, the victim of magic conjured up by the geomancer who hated its presence more than he feared death?

He was standing by a capstan, overdressed in a dark European suit. It could only be Jansen, correctness extending into stupidity. The white Panama hat was his only obvious concession to the heat, but it looked incongruous on his narrow head and he snatched it off the moment he saw me. Was it possible he could read my thoughts? More probably it was the expression on my face. My feelings refuse to remain submerged and surface quickly.

"Chai?" he said, his tone unsure. "You've lost weight."

"A little," I replied.

He extended a hand. I shook it and he passed me his hat with his other hand, as if it were the most natural thing in the world that I should accept an inferior role. I was his lackey: a carrier of hats. No doubt he would soon pass me his jacket.

"No suitcases?" I queried.

He shook his head. "Not necessary. I'm flying to London tonight. I've asked the people on the boat to send my luggage directly to the airport."

Jansen had come from Australia by ship. No doubt the people on the boat had served him royally, and I was expected to carry on the tradition.

He rubbed the fingertips of his left hand against his palm and frowned. It was a peculiar gesture, but I made an attempt at an interpretation.

"Yes, the air has a texture to it here. It's the humidity. You'll be wet through if you continue to keep that coat on."

"No, no," he said, a faintly irritated tone to his voice. "It's that heavy smell. It's almost tangible. I swear it's entering my pores."

Normally unaware of what was always part of my life, I tried to tune in to the odours around me. Fish? Cooked rice? Squid? There was nothing unsavoury that I could recognise. Shrugging my shoulders, I led the way from the docks into the streets. There was noise now, but it was of business.

Jansen stood with an appalled look on his face as powerful waves of humanity flowed past him in the street. The scene had an atmosphere of quiet panic, as if a series of crises were about to occur in specific locations and people were moving swiftly from one safe area to another.

"I thought you said you had it all wrapped up?" His voice was angry. "Did you bring me all the way to see this? You said . . ."

I interrupted him. "I told you the truth. Wait. I'll show you." I thrust his hat back into his hands and he seemed surprised. "Put that on. You'll need it. And please—take off the jacket and tie. You draw attention to yourself."

"Are we *walking?*" he said incredulously, as I strolled ahead.

"It's quicker," I called over my shoulder. "We're going through the backstreets. Even the trishaws find it too narrow."

When he caught me up I saw that he was in his shirt-sleeves, his coat over his arm. I smiled to myself. Was it possible that we came from the same loins? This arrogant, pompous fool and myself? How long ago lay the fork in time when we took our different paths, he to Europe and I to the Far East? By our differences it must have been a millennium—and yet I knew it was only ten years. Ten short years. Before that we were as alike in spirit as identical twins, my anarchist brother and I.

Before I was allowed to adopt human form my tutors in cultural sabotage insisted that I absorb much of Chinese history. Authenticity of character, I was told, was essential if we were to oust these upstarts, these usurpers of our ancient Earth. My studies included old stories; half truth, half lie, such as I was to become, indivisible, fused into a single entity.

There is a Chinese legend which I found I could compare with our fall from grace.

In the days of the early knights, two famous warriors met to do single combat. Instead of crossing blades they stood apart, their faces like stone, and studied each other for physical flaws, for weaknesses in spirit.

Psychological combat.

For three days they stood in tense concentration. On the morning of the fourth, one of the knights had gone. Only his sword remained in the ground, a symbol of his shame. The battle had been won and lost without the need for blows. Each knew of the other, had studied his history—his skills, moods, weaponry, strength, stamina, tactics—all those intricate and intimate ingredients which go to make the warrior. Like chess players, they each assessed the other's potential, gauged reactions to every possible move and countermove. "If I should do this, he will counter thus," or thus, or thus . . . and so each physical action, each emotional reaction is considered until the final realization of who has lost and who has won.

So it was between the humans and ourselves over possession of the Earth. We lost that mental combat, at the beginning of time, and later had to disappear into remote retreats in woodlands, mountains, and wastelands. Now we are few, but emerging once again. Seeking our revenge. Our ancestors had come, peacefully, from a distant, dying world, beyond the curve of Orion's belt, at a time when our science was accepted as magic. We were called witches and wizards but though we have the ability to change our physical appearance it *is* a *science,* not an art.

We took a short cut through a park full of businessmen in their shirtsleeves. In slow motion they practised the martial art of *Tai Chi Chuen* on invisible opponents. The exercise was mentally and physically rewarding without producing fatigue. Jansen watched their movements with an enraged look on his face. Then he muttered, "Bloody fairies," and scowled at the nearest of them, as if they posed a threat to his future plans for Singapore.

Someone spoke in Cantonese as I passed, looking quizzically at Jansen as she did so. I murmured back.

"Who's that?" asked my brother. Wary lines had appeared upon his sallow features.

"A friend's sister. Don't be concerned."

"What did she say?" He was hurrying alongside me, trying to weave as I did through the crowds, but not having a great deal of success.

"She said: 'Hello, Thin Chai'," I replied patiently. "What's wrong? Are you expecting someone to spring out and accuse us of being anarchists?"

"I thought," he said suspiciously, "your surname was Chai. Why would a friend call you by your surname?"

"Because she's Chinese—we always use family names."

"Why?"

"Why not? It's the custom. If it's a big family, like Wong or Lee, we add a little description, like Fat Wong or Tall Wong. It becomes part of the name. Within the family we call each other First Brother or Second Sister—depending upon age."

"Don't they have Christian names?"

"Some of us do—if we're Christian. Some of us just have second or third names." I wanted to confuse him. Since living in Singapore I had developed a simple, effective weapon which I normally used against that ugly invader, the *Wai Lo* long-nose. I told the plain truth, without adding any explanation. "Like Lucy *Lee* Man Lo. He's a close friend, but I call him Lucy because he's a Christian."

"Lucy?" His sweating face wore a puzzled expression, but he did not question further. He took off his hat and fanned himself as he walked. "Why do you keep saying *we* and *us*?" he complained. "You talk as if you were one of them. I hope there's something to show me."

There was an undisguised threat in his voice, and I nodded knowingly.

"Yes, First Brother," I replied, sweetly. "Of course there is."

We found our way into the back streets of the tenement buildings. Bamboo poles covered in laundry protruded from each window sill up to the sky. Every day is a white flag day in Singapore. There was rubbish flowing sluggishly down the gutters which would disappear with the four o'clock monsoon downpour. The streets were greasy, and Jansen continually slipped in his leather-soled sandals. A woman passed in a Choeng Sam with a slit to the thigh.

"Don't stare," I warned him as his eyes strayed. "Chinese don't like it and they have quick tempers."

I received an answering grunt, but nothing more.

"The *noise*," he grumbled, a little while later. I had to admit the level was rather high, even for this section of the town. Carpenters, panel beaters, ironsmiths, and a dozen other trades waged battles of sound with infants and babies. Nobody shuts their windows in the backstreets. Who wants to stifle?

"There's one," I pointed to an empty tenement flat. "Another two further on."

He took hold of my arm to stop me walking on and produced a handkerchief to wipe his face and neck.

"One?" he said. "One? What the hell is this? I thought you had things in hand. A handful of empty flats isn't what I expected."

I said mildly, "You do realise that we had a tremendous overcrowding problem? Hundreds were sleeping in the streets."

"So?"

"So most of the homeless have left—not only that, several of those who *did* have homes have gone. In the residential areas the vacancy count is much higher, but I thought this would impress you more. These people can't afford to leave—but they *are* leaving."

"Hmm. Well, I still have to be convinced. This operation has to be finely tuned. It has to get its timing right to fall in step with the rest of the scheme. Otherwise . . ."

"Let's face it, Jansen," I replied, "Singapore is one of the least important areas. It hardly matters at all. . . ."

"Every area matters," he interrupted. "Get things into perspective. We want to hit every part of them—if Singapore is the little finger of that ugly sprawling body called humanity, then crush it."

I acknowledged his concern, but assured him that everything was under control. After living ten years among these people I knew their attitudes and beliefs like my own. I was sure of my timing. Of course there was an element of guesswork, but I felt that clever statistical planning had narrowed a wide chance to a near certainty. As every gambler knows, there is six times the chance of 7 appearing from a roll of the dice than there is of 2 coming up. I always planned for the appearance of a 7.

"Where will they go?" he asked. "These people?"

"Some of them will move to the countryside—which can't possibly support them. The others to already overcrowded areas, like Changi. There, living will become difficult. Of course we won't clear the city completely—but to all intents and purposes it will be depopulated. They rely on this great, noisy animal to keep their economy at the level it is—which isn't terribly high. If people leave the city in great numbers it will weaken the island as a whole."

"Good, good. That's all I ask for." He gave my arm a fraternal squeeze. "I just want to be sure it'll work, that's all. I think I trust you, Chai. . . ."

He made an attempt at humour, which was for him a great effort. ". . . you're my, let's see, my seven-hundredth brother. Give or take a few. We're quite close really, when you put a number to it."

"I think it's more than that," I said, "but I'm flattered by your show of affection. Shall we go now? To see the casino?"

He stuffed the handkerchief into his pocket and tipped the ridiculous-looking Panama onto the back of his head.

"Ah yes, the casino," he said. "I'm looking forward to that. Is that it? Up there on the hill?"

The Chinese in me flooded my soul with shame. I stared past his shoulder into a doorway where some children played. One of them looked up at me and smiled.

"Yes," I said. "On the hill."

Smile at the traitor, child, for he is not really a traitor—not one of your own kind—but a creature of another race. ***I do not trespass on this Earth.*** *This is my world as much as it is yours. Smile, child, smile at the saboteur. Yes, yes, traitor too then, for if I feel such, then I am.*

"What's the matter with you? Are you ill?" Jansen asked.

"No, not ill. Weary."

"Are we going or not?"

"By the way," I said, walking away. "This is your year in the Chinese calendar."

His clownish features broke into a grin. He caught up with me.

"Really? You mean my lucky year—astrologically? You don't believe in that rubbish, do you? You've been here too long, Chai."

"No, not really. I just thought it would interest you."

It was the year of the monkey. It was not to do with stars but with caricatures.

We took a taxi to Li Hoe Hill. The driver used the horn as if it had some magical arrangement with the laws of nature which would lift up the vehicle and float over the crowded streets.

"What's the name of this device you are using? I know you informed me in your last report, but I've forgotten. I have so much to remember."

"*Fung Shui.* Not so much a device—more a set of beliefs. The art of adapting the residence of the living—and the dead—so as to cooperate and harmonize with the local currents of cosmic breath."

He nodded, settling back in the Mercedes.

"If I've got it right, when a man wishes to build a house he calls in an expert in *Fung Shui*?"

"A geomancer. The builder or designers will be told by him which way to face the structure to ensure the best fortune for the occupants. *Fung Shui* extends to many other aspects of life and death . . . even one's grave."

"I see." It was not a commitment to the idea. Merely an acknowledgment that the concept was worth considering. Jansen reserved his judgment, as would most Western Europeans, on Oriental 'magic.' I, in my Chinese rôle, was of course very sympathetic to the belief, without allowing myself total commitment.

"It's not merely hocus-pocus, you know. It has a certain factual basis—the best position for sunlight—in sight of water. *Fung Shui* means literally 'wind and water' in Cantonese . . . also the geomancer uses a compass to determine the Earth's magnetic field." Geomantic compasses were instruments set in old baked clay discs and enscribed with concentric circles, I added, after a pause.

"So?"

"So who's to say that if one lives in the flow of the field it's not beneficial? Physically, spiritually, and mentally. They may consider the field to be represented by some mythical, invisible dragon, but that doesn't cancel any probable real benefits."

"True, but I wouldn't use the word *probable.* It would take a lot to convince me of any underlying fact in the belief. However," he conceded, "I am willing to admit that the mind is a very powerful instrument, able to produce effect without cause—especially in the individual. But I'm not as certain as you are that this belief in *Fung Shui* is so deep-rooted, in a general, racial sense. Perhaps some of them just prefer to play safe, and when it comes to a choice between staying in the city where they have a certain security or moving elsewhere and raising the risk of survival—well, that may be a different matter."

"Look, let me try to explain. We're not dealing with logic—at least, not with European logic. *Fung Shui* deals with the relationships of objects to one another, as well as nature. A new building will disturb the already-established *Fung Shui* of its environment. The garden shaped like a sword will pierce the heart of a neighbouring house. Bad luck is almost always attributed to a discordant *Fung Shui*—even if the causes are not obvious. . . ."

"So a geomancer's some kind of priest?"

He had surprised me. There *was* a subtle mechanism at work beneath his skull after all.

"That's a keen observation," I replied. "Not strictly accurate . . . but near enough."

I sensed he was waiting for me to try to convince him. Then he could attack my insubstantial arguments and prove to me how foolish I was. I let the logician simmer in his own concrete thoughts as we climbed up the back of the dragon, past the bars outside which sat perennial Mah-Jongg players.

Sparrows. The four winds. Dragons. Beauty was everywhere in our land; even gambling was dressed in graceful words. My friends, the various races of Singapore, would appreciate my skill, if not my motives, in bringing bad fortune to the land. I was the unhuman anarchist in human form. The unseen enemy. The subtle fifth-columnist. I was here to erode their society, to destroy them from within. We are few and they are many . . . but still I find it distasteful. I know what prompted my superiors to place me in a minor rôle. I was too willing a pupil, too eager to learn human ways. Not know thy enemy but *become* thy enemy. Jansen has remained unchanged. I am . . . impressionable. Pressed into my soul is the seal of Thin Chai. Where does Thin Chai end? Where do the old ways begin?

"Is that it?" said Jansen, as we rounded the last curve.

I tapped the taxi driver on the shoulder. "Stop here," I ordered. Jansen and I got out and walked a few yards to the shade of a palm.

"You spoke to him in English. Why?" asked my brother, when we were out of earshot. "He was Chinese, like you."

"You really are the most—"

"I have to be careful. Please answer the question."

I was irritated. We were both on trust, Jansen as much as I was.

"He doesn't speak my dialect," I replied. "He's from the Malay Peninsula—they use Hok Yen there. I was only taught Cantonese . . . what would you have me do? Speak all the languages of Earth? That wouldn't attract attention at all, would it?"

"Cut the sarcasm. Okay, let's forget it. I'm . . . sorry. Now, this is the casino?"

"Yes." I was still not completely mollified and kept the edge to my voice.

"It looks rather splendid to me," said Jansen, obviously trying to view the monstrosity through my eyes.

"The facade is mock Grecian," I replied.

"Yes?"

"This is the Orient. It's as out of place as an . . . it's *alien,* if you'll forgive the expression."

"Of course it is, but aren't they all?" he said with humour.

"It's also a patchwork of classic styles. Those columns are a mixture of Corinthian, Doric, and Ionic. It's tastless; and to use one of your own terms, it's kitsch. Finally, it's as big and white as an albino whale, and on this hill can be seen from every corner of the city. The sun catches this ugly beast and blinds the eyes of all those who are forced to look up at its offensive marble pillars."

"But that's not all, is it? There is also . . . *Fung Shui*?"

"Ah, yes," I said, sadly, almost hiding my face in my hands with shame. *"Fung Shui."*

"You had the geomancer divine . . . if that's the right expression, divine the correct position and direction for our Grecian casino and then deliberately . . ."

"I had it built so that it faced the wrong way. The position is all wrong. It's the manifestation of bad luck . . . unavoidable because it dominates the whole city." It was a symbol of dissonance and it permeated the lives of all those who lived and worked within the sight of this alien folly.

"At night it's so well lit with spotlights you can see it from the ships in the harbour."

"I wish I'd known," Jansen said. "I'd have gone on deck specially to look. Why the high fence and the men with pickaxe handles? Having trouble with some of your punters trying to get their money back?"

I shook my head.

"Arson. Someone has tried to burn it down twice but it's nothing to do with the gambling . . ."

"Bad *Fung Shui*? Some people from the city below? That's a good sign, Chai. It means they must hate it badly enough to risk jail."

"I know."

I looked back at the taxi. The driver had averted his face, was looking out over the sweltering city, towards the sea. Was it a subconscious act? My designs had been to manipulate the sixth sense: a subliminal erosion of confidence and the implantation of unease. He would see any hill, however small, as a dragon, and buildings erected on sensitive parts of the beast as abhorrent to the natural order of forms. The casino was built on the dragon's tail, thus bringing disharmony to his world. When we rose against them they would be weakened, both mentally and spiritually.

Jansen said, "And they're leaving because of this?"

"Beginning to. Most of them probably won't admit to why they are going . . . but they'll follow a strong instinct. When things begin to sour you look for an excuse, somewhere to lay the blame. Gradually they'll drift away, those who feel its influence most strongly. And others will follow. Even those who scoff at *Fung Shui,* or do not have the same beliefs will eventually leave. Who wants to live in a dying city?"

"Well, I hope it works. We have our job to do . . . our preparations. I expect it cost the Earth . . . does anyone suspect you?"

"Don't concern yourself on my part—I employed foreign contractors through a European agent. I wouldn't want my friends to think I was responsible for *this.*"

Many bribes had changed hands too, but I was safe. My contact with officials and authorities was buffered by several people no longer on the island.

"I wasn't concerned for you. Just for our presence."

Our presence. We had to weaken the system without arousing suspicion. Subtle, devious ways. The neuroses of the West were easy to handle; and Jansen, as the co-ordinator, was having great successes there. In the East, where there were few strong economies, less stable governments, a smaller task faced us. In Singapore, I alone was responsible. Once we felt the humans were weak enough, over the whole Earth, then the uprising would take place. We would gather in pre-appointed places and cut through the rotten flanks of humanity like red-hot scythes. Then we would turn on them, left and right, and slaughter them as they had done us.

That was the plan, but of course to succeed it needed organisation. We were normally so poor at co-ordination and unity. Jansen—or Ertois as he had been born—had the gift of organisation. We relied on him to pull it all together, produce a feasible plan which would ensure victory despite the disparity in numerical strengths. Our weapons, the earth movements, quakes, eruptions, were as destructive as their missiles. But we needed Jansen's genius to make it all work. Being egocentric, he carried the plan in his head, so none of the glory could be taken from him. He was our General—or, as he preferred to be called, The Co-ordinator. Ten years ago he had disclosed the gist of his plans and we began to put them into effect. *Demoralise the enemy, then strike.*

As we stood and stared at the building I caught sight of a little man, standing by the corner of the fence. He was watching us intently. I knew him. We shared a common name. Chai. The Chais proliferate—there were many so called. One can get lost in a name, I thought.

"I want this to work," said Jansen, close to my ear. "I don't want anything to go wrong. Not at this stage."

"Of course not," I said without conviction. "That would be disastrous. We anarchists have a holy duty to perform—God knows."

I almost disclosed my closest secret then. He was my brother, after all, in a different life.

He said, "You know our task, Chai. You know what we must do to undermine their society. In the West I have child psychologists and economists using their expertise to guide humanity down paths leading to self-destruction . . . here, you must turn their culture inside-out to bring them to ruin." He tried to justify our position. "We didn't come to Earth from Mocte seeking this war. It's been thrust upon us by centuries of persecution."

"What persecution?"

He glared at me. "We have to live with these ugly bodies, don't we? We have to conform to their ways, their thinking, their damned . . . look, look, I don't like being repressed, Chai. Let *them* go into hiding for a few hundred years. Let us have a taste of the power."

"You talk about our forefathers, but who are *we,* Jansen? What are we—to ourselves, our human selves?"

He laughed. "To the humans? We are all the ghosts of lonely roads, all the tales of supernatural woodland, moor, and cave. The footprints in the mountain snows. The small religions of remote tribes. We are the stories that end, "Who's there?" and never give an answer. The listeners. The watchers."

"But are we?" I insisted. "I've forgotten what I am."

"We might be—perhaps once in a thousand times it is us—the invisible foe. You know," he was obviously in a reflective mood, "sometimes I wonder. Sometimes I ask myself: do we need to do this to them? If we showed ourselves, in our natural forms, wouldn't they accept us? Perhaps even like us?"

My heart was racing within my chest.

"And what do you answer?"

He fixed his eyes on me, and his reply destroyed any hopes that he had raised by his previous words.

"I remember how much I hate them."

Just after four o'clock the rains came: a flood of warm water which brought out the waxpaper umbrellas and, afterwards, the bullfrogs. Much later I took Jansen to Boogey Street, just as it was beginning to unfold. He was fond of red-light districts and talked enthusiastically about the Gut in Malta, the Reeperbahn, Soho, and many others of which I had never heard.

We reached a hand-painted sign which read 'Drinks at Logical Prices'—a direct translation from the Chinese.

"What's that noise?" he asked, as we entered the Jungle Club, the small bar where I occasionally met my friends.

"What noise?"

"That . . . clicking."

I listened. "Oh! Chit-chats. House lizards . . . overhead, they're all over the ceiling."

He looked up and shuddered.

"Frogs. Lizards. Bats. This place . . ." He shook himself again. "I've sweated buckets and the whole place stinks of overcooked food and heavy perfume. How can you live here?"

"I have to . . . remember?"

"Hmmm . . ."

A deep, husky voice said, "Hello . . . who this fine man you brought, Thin Chai?"

We turned together. Lucy was sitting at a small table in the corner in a dress which revealed a great deal of silicone cleavage. He smiled at us and blew a ring of smoke through painted lips.

I introduced them and went away to buy the drinks. By the time I returned Jansen had his hand on Lucy's knee. It was almost . . . domestic. Although we had only adopted human form, with that form went a whole range of emotions and desires. We were as weak, or as strong, as any of our potential enemies. Our affection for individuals ran as deep as theirs: our affiliations and loyalties too. Wherein lay the question of betrayal? And to whom? Was I Thin Chai? Or was I someone else, of whom I had only dim memories? Memories which rebelled at being forced past a point some ten years in the past? Would it make any difference if I ordered the destruction of the casino—tonight, or perhaps tomorrow? I knew it would not make the slightest difference. My local friends would still be violated and I would be removed. There remained a question: who was the betrayer and who the betrayed?

If there had been a coexistence of two souls I could not now recognise a division. My human shape was created—I was not implanted within one. I was not a parasite. I was both the betrayer and the betrayed. Jansen might easily come to terms with a callous dismissal of Asia, but how did he feel about his own part of the world? The country which he had called his home for the past ten years?

Paradox. Schizophrenia. Genuine madness. I had lived with them for a decade, these wraiths that pulled my loyalties in opposite directions. Perhaps we were insane, Jansen and I, and the world was really safe, except from a conspiracy of lunatics playing insidious games.

"What are you staring at?" he said.

My thoughts evaporated under his scowl. There was no battle of spirits raging within Jansen. His souls were models of compatibility: both were forged from a sense of duty.

"You like Lucy?" I asked. He had obviously forgotten our conversation earlier in the day, which was a symptom of his habit of retaining only that which he considered important.

"She's a nice girl," said Jansen, reluctantly withdrawing his hand as I sat down and handed round the drinks.

"Of course she is," I smiled at Lucy. "There's more warmth in Lucy than a brigade of Europeans." Lucy wrinkled his nose at me.

"You bad man, Thin Chai. You never bring me any boyfren'. This man say he go home in one half-hour."

If he doesn't, I thought, he'll get the shock of his life. His indoctrination did not include the crossing of heterosexual boundaries.

"Here's to Singapore," said Jansen, suddenly, raising his glass. "What is it . . . the *Lion City*."

"The Lion City," I murmured. Lucy and I clicked glasses with him. The nocturnal noises of Boogey Street were as lively as ever.

I sipped slowly at my drink, trying to hide my sadness in the small glass. A disease was slowly killing the city and all that I held important was dying with it . . . the very least of which was me. There was something to do.

"Excuse me," I said, "I'll call the taxi. If you could follow me outside, in about two minutes . . ."

Jansen nodded, curtly, then smiled at Lucy.

"He's a good man," he said.

I left them and went out into the street. I stood for a moment, absorbing the scene around me. Stall owners were preparing for the onslaught of long-noses, hanging squid from hooks and arranging duck's eggs in neat piles with ovolo walls. Their lanterns bobbed on the evening breeze.

The night pressed around me. In the last few minutes I had made a decision but I could not be the one. My instrument was standing at the entrance to an alley. He had been following me for many weeks now, suspicious, watching, waiting. A small man. Chai Leung, the geomancer. The agents for the casino had rejected his advice. He was a man mortally wounded by shame and I knew that he carried a slim blade next to his vengeful heart. I crossed the street and joined him in the shadows.

"He's coming," I said, "the man who employed the agents." The lie slipped easily from my lips.

The geomancer's eyes met mine. He studied me for a moment, then his stare returned to the doorway through which Jansen would emerge.

"In the spleen," I advised, softly. They . . . we are not immortal. We are as vulnerable as the form we employ.

I could not kill him. He was my brother. Of the old people, Jansen, as the co-ordinator, was the only one who knew my human face. The art of invisibility is to blend. In the backstreets we melt into one another. There are few names to share among many: Chai, Cheung, Wong, Chan. I could disappear into my adopted name forever. The main point was: I did not care. My cause had been reversed. Inside-out.

Jansen would not even seen the geomancer—as assassins Chinese have few equals. We . . . they are the invisible foe. I heard his loud laugh coming from the bar and began to walk away, to be out of sight.

As I walked away, I noticed the geomancer make a sign with his left hand. Someone at a window above me moved quickly. I had underestimated both Chai Leung and *Fung Shui*. Bad fortune is often the scapegoat for a dozen other ills. Incompetence and inefficiency are two of the prime causes for the failure of a business, but what small tradesman believes a lack of success is his own fault? The hand signals passed swiftly, silently, up and down the walkways. By the time I turned the corner of Boogey Street there were at least thirty figures waiting with the geomancer, standing in doorways and alleys. Poor Jansen, he would see them after all as they fell on him in their tens, each hoping his blade would erase the bad luck. The longer he stayed inside, the more there would be.

Tomorrow we would start the demolition.

THE DAY OF THE TRIFLES

The author's first book, *What About Murder: A Guide to Books About Mystery and Detective Fiction,* won the Edgar Allan Poe Award for the best biographical-critical book of 1981. His first novel, *Listen for the Click,* will be published by Walker in Spring 1983.

by Jon L. Breen

art: Karl B. Kofoed

It seems odd to speak of the coming of the Trifles, for of course they were always there. The trifle was a popular English dessert over many years, though trifle-making never reached the proportions of a fad until that one terrible summer. Of course, no one makes trifles any more, though there is no good reason why that should be so.

In my youth, there would have been no need to enumerate for anyone the ingredients of a trifle—a real trifle, I mean, not the railway buffet version—but now perhaps such an accounting is necessary. A trifle consisted of a layer of sponge cake mixed with jam and sherry, followed by a layer of fruit and gelatin (say, raspberries in raspberry jelly), followed by a layer of custard, and finally a layer of cream. Whatever rude things could be said by foreigners about the limitations of English cuisine, surely no dessert was ever more delicious than a real English trifle.

Persons of abstemious dispositions might leave out the sherry. The railway buffet chefs, if such they have, surely would, along with some other ingredients as well. But the sherry was an indispensable component of a genuine trifle.

I remember my good friend Jeremy Ormsby-Fogg discoursing on trifles that memorable August morning. "To begin with," he said, "a trifle is in no sense a trifle. Its success is in direct proportion to the extent to which it belies its name."

"Too true," I replied.

"I once knew a woman who proudly boasted she used only Harvey's Bristol Cream to make a trifle. Mindless ostentation, that. Any good sound medium-priced sherry will do. And the trifle she served was an unmitigated disaster. She had put the custard on when it was still too hot, and it had dissolved the jelly. Expected her snobbish grandstanding to carry the day, I expect."

We were seated in the parlor of Ormsby-Fogg's bungalow that morning. I was a house guest of Jeremy and his wife, a round and quiet woman named Alma, who had just cleared the breakfast dishes.

Jeremy showed me a bottle of Marley's Bridlington Cream. "I tell you, Clive," he said, "this is just the stuff for a trifle. Spot on! Wouldn't use any other."

"Done quite a bit of advertising, haven't they?" I remarked. "A fairly new firm, though the name creaks. I've often been to Bridlington and don't recall a sherry works there."

"No, I've never been round. Been round Harvey's, but no samples, worse luck. Don't know what this stuff tastes like on its own. Don't care really. Soaks into that sponge like a champ."

Apart from the fact that trifle-making had reached the proportions of a national craze, it was a typical English summer to that point. Inflation was galloping along as it had for lo these many years, it seemed. Strikes were rife, the workers always wanting more, more, more. At the Conservative Club, we did a good bit of grumbling to one another about how the British were unwilling to work, just wanted the government to see to them from cradle to grave. It started, we said, the day the Second War ended. We'd done a dirty job and done it well, and now we wanted to enjoy ourselves. And so we loafed for thirty-odd bloody years, you'll excuse my French.

I remember the papers were full of the country's latest sporting humiliation, England's crushing loss to Pakistan in the Test Match at Lord's, by an innings and three hundred runs. The new V registration license plates on cars had just come out, and it was a status symbol to own one. A queer custom, that; long forgotten now, of course.

As the incredible national interest in trifles grew, we came to talk less and less about the fall of a once-proud empire and more and more about the precise way to make a truly great sherry trifle, as if the satisfaction of our stomachs was more important to us than the future of our nation.

These were some of the thoughts I had as I watched Jeremy Ormsby-Fogg prepare his custard and whip his cream. The other parts had been seen to the night before, including the application of the sherry, and been left to set in the fridge overnight. Watching him do his custard, not so different from the way my mum did so many years ago, it occurred to me to think that Alma could have been doing this. But no, she had been banished from the kitchen. Trifle-making was a serious business that summer and, in a time still not entirely sexually liberated, a man's business.

When Alma served us our midday dinner a few hours later, I praised highly the roast beef, Yorkshire pudding, new potatoes, and fresh peas from their garden. But Jeremy, his mind on his trifle, seemed distracted. At the end of the meal, he sprang from his chair to deliver his masterpiece, which he had left in the pantry, in his view a more proper place than the fridge for a trifle to await its cue.

What Alma and I heard coming from the pantry was not precisely a scream, more a gasp of horror. We rushed to see what was the matter, but before we reached the door to the kitchen, Jeremy had come to meet us, his face gone pale.

"Something rather unusual has happened," he told us, in a parody of his customary phlegm.

"What's that, old man?" I inquired.

"The thing's growing."

"What thing?"

"The trifle, man, the trifle." As he spoke, the door behind him pushed open, and a seeming mountain of custard and cream filled the doorway and began oozing into the room.

Alma screamed; and the three of us, I fear, ran.

When we reached the garden and what seemed a safe distance, we saw the ingredients of the trifle were already pouring out of every door and window of their little bungalow.

Alma cried, in unaccustomed animation, "Jeremy, you bloody twit, what did you put in it, yeast?"

"I put quite the normal ingredients, my dear," Jeremy said. Then he assured me, rather unnecessarily I thought, that this had never happened to him before.

The following hours are a kaleidoscope of barely assimilated sights and reports. Jeremy's, it seems, was not the only trifle to have acted in this unusual way. All over England, Scotland, and Wales, trifles were growing, destroying houses, bringing down power lines, undulating through main streets and bringing all traffic and commerce to a halt.

The fragmentary radio reports were terrifying. Television service was interrupted. Bingo was cancelled. At the traditional cricket match between Lancashire and Yorkshire, a banana trifle enveloped the pitch and made a shambles of the tea interval. There were scattered reports of pub customers complaining of tainted beer. A monster peach trifle overran the theatre during a matinee of *The Mousetrap*, sending the audience screaming into the streets. Most of them seemingly were American holiday-makers who didn't even know what a trifle was, let alone had ever been menaced by one.

Gradually, we came to think of the Trifles in upper case.

Jeremy, Alma, and I, along with many others, sought high ground. Transistor radios clutched to our ears for the latest bulletins, we watched unbelievingly as the Trifles ran all around us, not unlike a cool volcanic eruption.

The radio reported that the center of the greatest concentration of the sweets-gone-mad was the seaside resort of Bridlington. The significance was not lost on Jeremy.

"The sherry," he mused. "It must have something to do with the sherry."

We heard frightening reports of bathers being forced into the sea by the ever-spreading tide of jam and spongecake.

Even more frightening was the report that the Trifles seemed to be joining together to surround London, as though there were some keen intelligence behind the diabolical desserts.

Jeremy was convinced that the proper course was to send the Army into the Bridlington Cream sherry works to break up all the remaining bottles and be sure none of them got near any sponge cake. He cursed the lack of a phone or radio transmitter to relay his idea, but fortunately others made the connection as well.

The smashing of the bottles would be part of a two-pronged attack on the Trifles. The other part of the strategy it would be up to every Briton to carry out.

The voice of the Prime Minister that day will never be forgotten by any who heard it. "We shall eat in the cities, we shall eat on the farms, we shall eat on the shore. We shall leave no Trifle uneaten."

For a moment, we stood on that hilltop, stunned by the words, nearly overcome by the formidable challenge. I remember Alma saying, "But we had such a big dinner."

It was left for the oldest man among us, an octogenarian I should think, to say, "Let's go to it then," and trot down the hill to take the first bite. But even as he was taking that bite, the Trifle was growing. He could not do it alone, but if we all ate our share, just maybe we could win. Thus began several hours of the most conspicuous consumption it has ever been my privilege to be a part of.

It took hours to turn the tide. The Trifle continued to grow, but not as fast as the squads of ordinary people could eat, and finally we prevailed. Other groups of everyday citizens all over Britain were doing the same. And soon it was clear the Day of the Trifles had passed.

We huddled by our radios as a bland, vaguely bored voice from the BBC explained it all. Our scientists theorized that intelligent but malevolent beings from some far distant planet had decided to conquer Earth, starting of course with Britain. Their advance troops had been living in the form of bacteria in the vats of the Marley's Bridlington Cream sherry works. Using a sophisticated form of telepathy, they had first influenced the sherry makers to expand and advertise, then influenced the public at large to go on their mad round of trifle-making.

Extraterrestrial chemists, whose knowledge was far beyond that of their earthly counterparts, devised a formula whereby, when the sherry from the Bridlington works reacted with the other elements of the trifle, the resultant desserts would grow with a yeast-like effect and thus carry out their invasion. The combination of the Army's efficient bottle-smashing, which prevented further invaders, and the indomitable courage of countless ordinary British men and women, citizens drawing on patriotism thought abandoned at the close of the last war, in eating the undulating Trifles as they spread, at last halted the invasion and brought ultimate victory.

The announcement that television service would be resumed shortly was scarcely heard. No one cared to watch television. We wanted to finish the job of reclaiming our country from the jelly and the custard.

I sit now in an upstairs window overlooking a garden. There is a broad lawn bordered with multi-hued flowers, the high branches of an apple tree tantalizingly showing its fruit to my left, an old weeping willow to the right. Birds are flying and chirping, and the sky is alternating between sunny blue and threatening grey in the manner of an English summer's day.

The memory of that monster sherry Trifle undulating across the countryside, an all-enveloping cloud of custard and cream devouring the landscape, the scarlet quivering jelly crushing houses and automobiles in its path, the sickly sweet smell overpowering and mesmerizing all, seems so remote and distant, though never really forgotten, as to belong to a fairy tale rather than to reality. The

Britain it has left behind is the same, though subtly changed. Once more hard work and pride in a job well done are the order of the day, and cheerful industry has replaced grasping indolence. The Day of the Trifles has left its mark, left a better, stronger England in its wake.

I HAVE A WINTER REASON

by Melisa Michaels

art: Karl B. Kofoed

Ms. Michaels is pleased to report that she resides near enough to San Francisco Bay to hear the fog horns at night, and that the sound of typing doesn't seem to bother the baby opossum who takes his evening snacks under her kitchen sink.

There are ghosts among the asteroids. Ghosts of warriors and workers, ghosts of pilots and passengers, and ghosts of the Gypsies who originally settled the Belt. The Gypsies speak in ancient Romani, and ask nothing of anyone but that they be left to their dreams.

I never heard them before the accident. I never had nightmares before, either. Nor a metal plate in my head to hold my brains in. At first I wondered if that had anything to do with it, with the ghosts and the nightmares. But when I asked the doctors, they muttered polysyllabically about survivor guilt, said I should feel grateful my pretty face wasn't marred, and suggested I might be due for a vacation.

I'd read about survivor guilt. My cousin Michael was a warrior in the Colonial Incident. Since we were infrequently but permanently in correspondence with one another, I read every chip I could find on the Incident and its aftermath, both socio-politically and on an individual scale for the warriors involved. Survivor guilt was one of the primary components of what the psych-tenders called "PCIS": Post Colonial Incident Syndrome.

My cousin Michael and I never talked about PCIS. We didn't mention the Incident much, either. His sister was killed in the Battle of Viking Plain. His first wife Maria was a member of the Lost Platoon. After the Incident he married at least one of his childhood sweethearts and produced a litter of little michaels all named something out of the Bible like Elijah and Judah and Jonas. I imagined them as red-haired and freckled and impish as Michael himself had been the last time I saw him, twenty years ago on Earth.

If anyone had a right to survivor guilt, it was Michael. And he mentioned occasional nightmares, but no ghosts. He made a good living in the Colonies and had a life as secure and prosaic and safe as any good Earther could dream of.

His wild warrior days were behind him. He'd gone off to war, suffered whatever agonies and indignities the lowly warrior is expected to suffer, killed who he was supposed to kill and survived the opportunity to be killed himself, and went home when the Incident was over to make a real life for himself. If he ever heard the Gypsies, he never mentioned them.

Maybe it wouldn't be the Gypsies for him. Maybe it would be the warriors he'd listen to. But whatever, it seemed to me that if an ex-warrior could make a life for himself, the survivor of a stupid accident like mine should, too.

I took another shuttle out and damn near killed us all when I heard the Gypsies singing. My passengers never knew how close it was, but I did. I decided maybe the psych-tenders were right. Maybe I could use a vacation.

* * *

The reunion wasn't really planned; it just happened. I thought I'd visit my parents on Earth and drop by Mars to visit Michael on my way home. When I got to Earth, I learned Michael had selected the same week to visit his parents, and brought his family.

Meanwhile, Michael's mother invited a cluster of older relatives—aunts, uncles, grandparents, and great-somethings—to North America at the same time. Most of them lived in the senior-citizen resorts in the islands, and Rendell family reunions were usually held there.

But, as one plump, pipe-smoking great-aunt remarked, "The old folks still like to see a bit of the world now and then." (To which another added in sepulchral tones, "Old ain't dead," and she nodded sagely in agreement with herself for several minutes thereafter.)

I probably wouldn't've made the trip if I'd had any idea how *many* Earth-based Rendells were going to show up at the same time. The inevitable culture shock of coming Earthside was bad enough, without the added nerve-wracking knowledge that there were so many related Earthers watching to see what bizarre and unacceptable character traits I might've picked up in twenty years in the Belt.

There were the usual round of comments. Goodness, I had grown into a pretty woman. Didn't I look just like my mother had, at my age? And was it true I was a shuttle pilot? (This last was always asked incredulously, as though a shuttle was about the most unacceptable thing possible to pilot, and piloting itself the most unacceptable job they could think of. I suppose it was. On Earth, the women stay home and raise families. They wear make-up and long dresses and giggle behind fans. Not all of them, of course, but the 'best' of them.)

I nodded and smiled till my face hurt, and very quickly switched from natural coffee, which had seemed such an exotic treat when I first planeted, to the soy beer the rest of them were drinking.

That was exotic, too; on the asteroids there are plenty of alcoholic beverages but not much time to drink them. Nor much inclination; getting drunk is not one of the socially accepted forms of entertainment in the Belt as it is on Earth. But the alcohol helped dull my hypersensitivity to the cultural and environmental differences that otherwise unnerved me.

My first day planetside, it rained. Water, huge drops of it, fell right out of the sky. Out of thunderclouds piled as high as eternity like towering wads of dirty air-filter material overhead. Sky was a concept I'd got myself ready for, before I planeted. Water falling out of it was something else again.

Then there was the air. Limitless, breathable air, unchambered, unguarded; and it *moved.* It took me two full days to get over the feeling, every time I stepped out of a dwelling, that my chamber had blown a giant leak and I should dive for a space suit.

Being outside was okay in itself. I was ready for that. But I guess I'd thought of it as some kind of oversized chamber with attendant overhead megawattage to light it and the usual filters and controls to keep the air in.

Even a gentle breeze I could've accepted; in large chambers, the air does *move,* sometimes enough that you can feel it. But not briskly. When air moves briskly, people had better move briskly, too, if they want to go on breathing.

While I was getting used to air that moved briskly, and water that fell out of the sky, indigenous life forms bit me. They left little red welts that swelled and itched. Mosquitoes, gnats, flies. . . . None of this was entirely new, of course. I did live Earthside the first ten years of my life. But in twenty years gone I'd forgot what to expect of a planet. Not all the rediscovery was fun.

Even the temperature wasn't properly regulated. I suppose I should amend that statement; I've put it in terms of the asteroids. On Earth, God regulates the temperature, and mostly what She does is assumed to be for the best. But in the area of temperature control I thought She did a lousy job.

After four days Earthside I was still too uncomfortable to do much of anything at midday but sip soy beer in the shade and sigh a lot. I'd spent most of my time so far saying hello to various relatives whose names I promptly forgot, and listening to little lectures from my mother on How a Proper Earther Behaves in a Hostile Environment, like for instance we don't talk to strangers in bars and we don't go for walks in the middle of night by ourselves and we don't use the salad fork for dessert and we don't . . .

I forgot what all we don't. On the fifth day, I found myself at midday sitting at a picnic table in the shade across from my cousin Michael, both of us sipping soy beer while all the Earthers were inside eating lunch. God regulates the temperature on Mars, too (with a little help from the Terraformers), but on Mars She keeps the heat to a reasonable minimum. Michael didn't seem any more comfortable in the broiling sun of Earth than I. And I was 'way too hot to eat.

It was the first time we'd been alone together, and we had nothing to say to each other. The groundcover around the picnic table had little white flowers that attracted some of the indigenous life forms I thought might want to bite me. Mostly bees in this case, I think.

They hummed and buzzed, and the moving air rustled the leaves of the big old deciduous tree that shaded us, and we didn't look at each other.

I kept tilting my head back every once in a while to get a look at the puffy white clouds that dotted the deep blue sky. I didn't like to look at it too long. It made my eyes dizzy.

"Penny for your thoughts," said Michael.

He'd grown man-size and then some in the twenty years since I'd last seen him. Somehow I hadn't expected that; nor the serious, intent way he looked at people; nor the sudden, stunning beauty of his rare smile. When we were children I thought he was plain. A red-headed, freckle-faced monster, good for nothing but tormenting girl-cousins.

Now he sat with a baby on his lap and patted it absently when it complained—the perfect image of the ideal father. I wondered, but didn't ask, how many wives he had at home. If he had more than the one he'd brought with him, he wouldn't mention it here. Earthers still maintain their rigid, centuries-old stand on monogamous marriage through thick and thin.

"What's a penny?" I asked. "I've always wondered."

He shrugged, a gesture I was aware of though I didn't turn to look at him. There was something about the way those eyes watched me. . . . I wouldn't look. "It was a U.S. coin," he said. "Prob'ly worth a fortune as a collectable by now, so I hope you don't accept the offer."

I glanced up, expecting to see the freckle-faced boy I'd known, and saw instead a dark-eyed stranger. This was a man to whom I'd been writing the intimate details of my life and times—with a few notable details left out, like for instance my stupid accident and the ghosts and nightmares—for years, but he looked like a stranger. A relative stranger.

There were hints of the red-haired boy in his mannerisms, but not in those deep eyes. I wasn't sure that I wanted to confide in him out loud. "I was thinking," I said, watching him, "how many rules there are to follow on Earth."

The dark eyes widened almost imperceptibly. His face was lean and vulnerable, devoid of freckles. "Rules?"

I looked back at the sky. It hurt my eyes, but not as much as looking at him. I wanted to cry when I looked at him. I didn't know why. "You know," I said. "Social rules. Acceptable behavior."

I wasn't really sure he did know. Except in the matter of marriages, the colonies were nearly as strait-laced as Earth. He might be perfectly comfortable here. Even the environment was more familiar to him than to me. He was used to sky, and clouds, and all-day gravity, and houses, and the whole long list of everything physical that made this so different from the asteroids. All the things that made me uncomfortable, perpetually on edge, alert on a subliminal level because things were so uncontrolled, so gut-level *wrong*. I stared at Michael over the top of my beer, waiting.

He met my gaze without blinking. The baby on his lap complained briefly, and he patted its back with automatic tenderness. "It's not really very important," he said. "If you don't know a rule—"

"—they'll crow over it," I said. "You were going to say they'd excuse me because I'm from the Belt, right? Well, wrong. Haven't you seen the cat-faced old ones watching? Didn't you see the way they eyed my tables manners and hung on every casual word I spoke at dinner last night? Aunt Hazel and Uncle Alfred and Grandma Rendell—they're just waiting to pounce."

He studied me. I wanted to look away, but didn't. "Sounds paranoid," he said seriously.

It reminded me of the psych-tenders, and I grinned. "Even paranoids have enemies," I said. "People hate us."

Something dark crossed his eyes like a shadow from the sun. "Not hate," he said with startling certainty.

I stared. "'Course not," I said. "Was a joke." Then I remembered, and frowned. "Oh. I've read that before, from veterans of the Incident. Loaded word?"

He hesitated. "I guess I have a lot of them," he said. " 'Incident' is another."

"Sorry. I know they called it a war in the colonies."

His eyes went so dark inside themselves I couldn't look at them. "It *was* a war," he said. "You weren't there, you don't—"

"I know. Noboby who wasn't there gets to talk about it. I've read *that* before, too. So space it, okay?" Suddenly unaccountably sad, I gulped down half my beer before turning back to the sky.

"Sorry," he said.

I ignored him. I hadn't realized before I planeted how *big* a sky would be. I wasn't really accustomed to it yet. Staring into the bottomless blue, I thought suddenly, *If the gravity generator fails now . . .*

Shivering, I clutched the table, and forcibly reminded myself of the laws of physics. The Earth itself was the gravity generator here, and that couldn't fail.

"You can't handle sky, can you?"

His voice startled me. In my moment of private terror I'd nearly forgotten his presence. But with his words, the world fell back into place and I heard again the moving air in the deciduous tree overhead, and the discordant jangle of birdsongs in the distance.

"I can handle *any*thing," I said with undue ferocity, and lifted my beer.

"Even rules?" he asked.

I put the beer down and stared at him. I really didn't know who he was. I never heard this voice in his letters. We corresponded on printout chips, not voice; but I'd imagined the voice that typed the words he sent would sound different from this. . . . This was a total stranger. My cousin Michael.

"If I have to," I said carefully. "Even rules."

He grinned triumphantly. It lighted his whole face till even the darkest shadows of his eyes were banished and I saw, just for a moment before the smile faded, the face of the freckled child I knew. "Gotcha," he said.

I couldn't return the smile. I was living on nerves alone, and they were badly jangled. The air kept moving, the indigenous life forms kept biting and singing, and the sky stretched untold kilometers above my head with a sun in it so near and so hot I found it hard to understand how this planet ever came to be settled in the first place. The fact that our ancestors evolved here was irrelevant. It was a hostile environment.

And now I saw a gaggle of elders emerging from the house, sloe-eyed and content from their meal. I couldn't face them. I could not, at that moment, tolerate their eyes—or their rules—or my cousin Michael, the stranger.

"I'm going for a walk," I said, and rose without waiting for a reply. The elders, and Michael too, could make of it what they would; I didn't really care if it was bad form to walk away from them. I walked.

I wanted to cry. I'd had too much beer—far more than I was used to—and I was turning into a weepy drunk. There's probably something more tiresome than a weepy drunk, but I couldn't think just then what it would be.

I concentrated on the groundcover underfoot. I couldn't remember what it was called, but it smelled delicious. Like something from which one might make an excellent tea. And it was most extraordinary to be permitted to walk on green growing things. The novelty of that wasn't even beginning to wear off.

Nor was the scent of things on Earth, really, though I felt homesick for the sweet damp tang of metal and rock of the asteroids. Things on Earth smelled of colors. Green for the groundcover, purple and red and yellow for the flowers, rich black for the loamy soil. Even sunlight had an odor. Hot, and a hint of green and yellow mixed with the tang of memories.

The Rendell residence—my parents' white clapboard home—was right on the edge of town, and I headed out for the dark green fields where nobody would stare if I did cry. Which is how I found myself walking past the rusting wrought-iron fence of a cemetery after a while.

I'd forgotten cemeteries. It took a moment for the full significance of the white crosses and colored granite blocks to sink in. Earthers buried their dead whole—or at least those dead whose parts weren't reusable, or whose relatives chose not to permit their reuse.

Each cross or stone marked the final resting place of someone's body. Spiritless, empty husks—yet many of the sites were decorated with cut flowers. And there was a feeling of serenity here that wasn't only the result of air moving in trees, or singing birds and insects.

I paused outside the gate, waiting to hear the Gypsies. Afraid to hear the Gypsies. Maybe afraid I wouldn't hear the Gypsies. I closed my eyes, and opened them again abruptly when what I saw on the inside of my eyelids was the reflection of Django's smile.

But Django wasn't here. He was somewhere lost in the Belt, floating and singing, singing. . . .

I stared at the crosses and granite blocks; and the world seemed curiously still, as if in waiting. I glanced back toward the little village I'd left behind. My parents' house was half-hidden behind a low deciduous forest. Somewhere not very far away a bird burst into a brief, impulsive song. Meadowlark? I'd been told the song of a meadowlark was very beautiful. I decided it was a meadowlark.

I didn't know the rules about cemeteries. It could be illegal or ill-mannered to explore one out of curiosity. But the strange serenity within that gate was tempting beyond measure. My soul was beer-sodden chaos. My nerves were in a state of ill repute. And I was, I belatedly realized, crying.

My cousin Michael asked if I could handle "even rules," and I told him I could. The song of dead Gypsies was another matter, but he didn't ask after that and I wasn't telling. I stepped inside the gate. If exploring were illegal, surely an ignorant Belter would be forgiven the transgression. And if it were merely bad manners, I didn't give a damn.

The first gravestone I read was inscribed in bold, stone-cut letters:

ELLIOT RENDELL–BORN 1924–DIED 1944.

I paused, staring, barely aware of the breeze that bent the tallest weeds, or the sick-sweet scent of mouldering flowers that wafted up from the cracked stone vase beside the granite marker. ELLIOT RENDELL. A relative? Some multi-great-uncle or cousin?

The meadowlark burst into song again just as I bent to touch the sun-warmed stone. It might have been an omen.

My fingers sank deep into the unforgiving past. Cold and hard and empty, the stone resisted my touch with unexpected hostility. Someone very far away, in a voice I didn't recognize, called my name. I didn't respond. I froze still and bewildered but not quite frightened, my fingers caught up against the stone in memories not my own:

The chatter of an automatic weapon. The shrill death-voice of mortar fire. The screams, the pitiful howling cries and the tangy dark scent of blood and scattered earth. . . . A sense of fear. A sense of failure. A sense of overwhelming loss. . . . There were vultures raucous in the hard blue sky. There were shadows, converging; there were the screams of the damned and the dying, and the salt taste of tears in my mouth; and through it all the fierce longing like unappeasable hunger—PLEASE GOD I WANT—

With a startled whimper I jerked my fingers away from the stone and fell back into here-and-now in a rush that left me dizzy. The sky was a million kilometers above my head. Below my head? I choked on a scream and threw myself full-length in the dusty groundcover, fingers clawing for some safe purchase in the hard black earth beneath, and inadvertently I touched another stone.

REBECCA GARDENER RENDELL

it said.

BORN 1966–DIED 2054.

There were pretty red roses as sweet and deep and perfect as God could make them. Very carefully she pricked out their image with needle and thread on the hem of the little dress, and thought with whimsical regret how much sweeter if the stitched ones could be scented as God's were. . . . A rocking-chair empty in a shaft of dusty sunlight. . . . A browned and cracking photograph whose image muddled and disappeared behind tears. . . . . White curtains that shifted and blew in a morning breeze heavy with sunlight and birdsong. . . . And a delicate whisper, gentle and infinitely sad: Please God I want . . .

I pulled my hand away, but it was too late. I could hear them all now, their voices raised in discordant melancholy, their images like mirrors fractured in the sun:

pleasegodiwant . . .

My head hurt.

It took a long time to understand they weren't shouting at me. Longer still to realize they didn't know I was there. The Gypsies always knew when I was there. They asked only to be left to their dreams; but they sang their damned songs to taunt me, to haunt me, to drag me down out of the sunlight and into their dreams. . . .

"I'm sorry," I said. I didn't mean to say it. The words popped out of their own accord, and they wouldn't stop. "I'm sorry, I'm sorry, i'm sorry i'm sorry i'msorryi'msorryi'msorry . . ." It mingled with the voices of the Earthers: *"I'm sorry please God I want I'm sorry please God I want i'msorrypleasegodiwant . . ."*

When I realized the end of both sentences, theirs and mine, was ". . . to be alive," I shut up. My head still hurt. I realized I was holding it, crouched in the sun-scented groundcover with both hands folded over the top of my head where under the scalp there was a metal plate to hold me together; and I let go and sat up.

The voices seemed quieter. There was still a prism effect of memories pushing and shoving at one another for space in my mind, but none of them were mine. None except Django, and he wasn't even here. He was somewhere in the asteroids, lost and dead because of a stupid accident that never should have happened; and I was here in green groundcover and yellow sunlight, listening to ghosts that weren't even real.

None of my ghosts were real. Very little of the pain I felt really belonged to me. Only the dull ache in my head and the tightness of unshed tears in my throat; the rest was shadows. Images. Imagination or empathy, the words didn't really matter. I wasn't alive in 1944. How could I feel Elliot Rendell's pain?

Nineteen forty-four. World War II. Elliot Rendell died there, among shattering bombs and shattered comrades, fighting a visible enemy for a comprehensible cause. If, in the middle of that battlefield, he had stubbed his toe on a rock, fallen into a puddle of rainwater, and drowned, maybe I'd have a right to feel his pain. That was damn near what happened to me.

Only it killed Django, not me. Django, one of the last few Romany in the asteroids. One of the last few heroes in the universe. Django with his gentle voice and his riverwater eyes and his sweet, clear smile for me. . . .

"Melacha?"

Michael's voice. It startled me. I turned and saw him poised at the graveyard gate, watching me.

"Melacha, are you all right?"

I was still half-caught in the memories. "Can you hear them?" I asked him, not even vaguely aware how the question might sound.

He hesitated, then passed the gate and walked with long, sure strides across the groundcover toward me. "Of course I can hear them," he said. There was a look in his eyes I didn't understand.

I watched him till he was standing beside me, looking down into my face with an odd half-smiling, half-questioning expression.

"Then, are they real?" I asked.

He sat down beside me. "Of course they're real," he said. Not just "yes"; not even "what do you mean"; but "of course."

I sighed, and rubbed my cheeks with the heels of my hands. They came away wet with tears. I looked at them. "I wasn't sure," I said.

He watched me for several moments. "What happened?"

I stared. "When?"

He eyed me almost curiously. "Whatever it was you didn't send me a chip about," he said. "Whatever it was that sent you running for Earth. Whatever it was that made you come out to the cemetery to listen to ghosts."

"He wasn't ready to die," I said, as if in answer.

"Nobody's ready to die," said Michael. "Haven't you been listening? Look at the birth and death dates. It doesn't matter if somebody lives two years or two hundred, death always comes too soon."

"It was so stupid," I said.

"There's no smart way to die," he said. "Tell me, Melacha."

I told him. I didn't know how much he knew about shuttles or about the asteroids or about air filters; but I told him the whole pathetic, foolish story. The accident that could've happened in anybody's living room, only it happened on my shuttle and it killed my lover. And it was my fault. And you don't get a second chance, in space.

We had to make two docking procedures. People die every day in docking procedures, but we didn't.

We had to duck an unexpected flurry of "wild" rocks. People die every day in evasive actions from "wild rocks," but we didn't.

Django had survived, in his life, two holed chambers and two Insurrectionist battles. He had survived the rescue mission that brought the *Sunjammer* in at the cost of three people's lives. He had survived the *Big Eagle*'s fiasco flight.

He died on my shuttle of a clogged air filter that blew its top because I didn't check the tubes before the flight.

It was no particular comfort that I damn near died with him.

"Damn near" is the operative phrase there. If I had died, I'd be out there singing with the Gypsies. But I didn't. I survived, and Django died. In just about the stupidest, most useless way any Belter ever did die, short of walking out of a chamber without a suit.

Michael listened without comment, all the way through to the end. Then, when he still didn't say anything, I told him about the ghosts. And the nightmares. I told him about the metal plate in my head and the shuttle I nearly wrecked when I heard the Gypsies. I told him about Elliot Rendell and Rebecca Gardener Rendell. I told him about all the ghosts of the asteroids; the workers and warriors, pilots and passengers, Gypsies and gentlemen.

Eventually I ran out of steam and came to a shuddering halt with the echoes of Gypsy songs in my ears. Michael just watched me, and we listened to the ghosts.

After a while he said, "People die every day."

I didn't look at him. "Why did you come out here?"

"Out where?"

"To the cemetery."

"I thought you might need me," he said.

I looked at him, then. But there were no answers in those shadowed eyes. "So you could tell me people die every day?" I asked, and was startled at the bitter sound of my voice.

To my surprise, he smiled. "Partly that," he said.

"And?" I said, when he didn't go on.

"And to hold your hand," he said. "And to let you know you aren't alone. Other people listen to the ghosts. Everybody's guilty."

"Other people's ghosts are real," I said.

"No more real than yours," he said. "You have a right to your pain, Melacha. But you have a right to your life, as well. It's okay for you to be alive."

"You came out here to tell me *that?*"

If I thought he would defend himself from my bitterness, I was wrong. He just smiled again, and held my hand. And after a while, I realized that was enough. It was more than enough. It was a gift of greater proportions than I would have dared ask. The gift of acceptance.

I never did get used to living under a sky. I'm more comfortable in the asteroids, where life is carefully bounded by stone and steel and plastic and I know what the boundaries are, and how to behave.

But I learned to pilot a shuttle again, safely among the songs of Gypsies not everyone can hear. Sometimes I even sing with them. And when I'm dead, I'll join them. But not before.

ONE KIDNAPPED CLICKA

art: Karl B. Kofoed

by John Kelly

Mr. Kelly is studying for a Ph.D. in anthropology at the University of Chicago. Between researching South Asian cosmologies and attempting to master the Sanskrit language he hasn't had much time to write science fiction but he says he definitely plans to do so in the near future.

"So what are you saying? That the planetary people can't ever understand our problems, just 'cause they never lived out in empty space?"

"Of course not. Marx was too vulgar a Marxist for me." The fatter man dragged the netted animal up the ramp into the starcraft.

"Well, be careful!" said the shorter man as the fatter man bumped the animal over the rim of the hatch. "The thing deserves some respect."

The fatter man snorted. "These things don't deserve anything special." He shook the Clicka baby out of the net and onto the warm floor. "It's what we make them into that deserves respect. Out in the wild they don't even think."

The Clicka crawled sideways, her soft beak unaccountably moist.

"Bull," said the shorter man. He punched a button which drew in the ramp and slid shut the hatch.

"It's true! Out there they're nothing. No language, nothing that's not rudimentary."

"You rationalize everything."

"But it's true." The fatter man climbed the ladder into the mainspace. The shorter man looked back at the crawling Clicka. Then he climbed up the ladder after the fatter man.

The Clicka blinked. Her grey fur had been twisted and matted by the net. She didn't feel hurt. She didn't feel anything exactly. Something was empty. She couldn't find–something else wasn't there.

Out in the brush, down the long path of grass shafts broken by the dragged net, the Clicka's thirty-one parents were gathered by her tall nest. They'd woven the nest themselves, for their baby, and now they cried. The nurses were badly wounded; the baby was gone. They would all be part dead forever. They cried on each other, on themselves.

They all knew what had happened, for some had seen the men's path. They knew, but they didn't understand.

The Clicka's beak hardened swiftly, as swiftly as she learned. She learned about the shorter man and the fatter man, about warm metal rooms and about hearing and thinking. Soon enough she was thinking herself, thinking when the men thought and thinking what the men thought. When the Clicka tried her very hardest, and when everything was silent, she could hear the flowing of people's thoughts. The shorter man taught her that it wasn't hearing exactly, but she couldn't tell the difference.

The shorter man also taught her why she could hear other people's thoughts. She could hear them because it was her job to tell her master what other people were thinking. They would practice; the Clicka would say out loud to the shorter man everything she heard in the fatter man, then say to the fatter man what she heard in the shorter man. It got easy to talk when people supplied the words, even if her beak did click on every "b" and "p." They taught her to speak only when asked to.

She knew things the way humans knew things. She didn't remember much, but that didn't matter since they remembered everything that was important. Then one day another shiny ship flew near the one she lived in, and a person floated across to their hatch. Abruptly new thoughts were in the Clicka's world. *She was getting stronger,* the fatter man had thought; *she'd soon be able to hear thoughts across incredible distances of empty space.*

The woman named Kadrasa brusquely slipped out of her spacesuit and climbed the ladder to the mainspace. *It's about time they got me one of these damn animals,* she thought. "Let's be quick," she said.

"Don't worry," said the fatter man, "we're as anxious to get rid of this Clicka as you are to get her." The words pushed into the Clicka like icy fingers.

"I just want to get out of here," said Kadrasa, looking down at the shorter man. "When I stay places I get caught." *At least it's no trap,* she thought. *And they're not getting any more money.*

"She'll be a good Clicka," said the fatter man.

"She better be. We're leaving." Kadrasa pulled the Clicka to the ladder.

"Wait," said the shorter man. *I've messed this up,* he thought.

Kadrasa turned very quickly. "I paid you in advance. What?"

The shorter man shrugged. "Nothing. You paid us in advance." *At least, if a patrol stops us we'll be clean,* he thought.

Kadrasa pushed the Clicka onto the ladder. Then she pushed her into the shorter man's spacesuit and dragged her through the hatch and along the wire connecting the ships. *Should I kill them?* Kadrasa thought. *They didn't cheat me. They wouldn't gain anything by telling a patrol where I was. By then I'll have jumped far anyway. And I don't need anything on their ship. No.*

Kadrasa pulled the shorter man's spacesuit off the Clicka. It had chafed against her knees, her crotch, her beak. She was much too small and it didn't fit right. She stumbled out onto the cold floor. "Let's go," said Kadrasa, "You're my Clicka now."

She followed Kadrasa down the hall, flooded with thoughts as the crewmen peered around corners to see what a Clicka looked like. She was Kadrasa's Clicka now.

She was Kadrasa's Clicka for years.

* * *

For Kadrasa it was her job to hear across the spaces between ships, to tell Kadrasa what the other captains were thinking. She told Kadrasa what the Earthman Dragen wanted, and then Kadrasa arranged the Great Swindle. She told Kadrasa which pilot wasn't watching, and then Kadrasa stole a Pan-Galactic Patrol Cruiser. And finally, when Kadrasa was running overloaded and a Patrol Cruiser ran her down, the Clicka told her when the Captain planned to fire a Total; and Kadrasa was able to bounce it back and destroy the cruiser.

But then Kadrasa was worried. They would want her badly. Her ship had to lighten, and she needed her cargo. So she jettisoned half her crew. And the Clicka was a luxury that couldn't be afforded.

She had been Kadrasa's Clicka, and it seemed to cut into her and rip her apart to hear Kadrasa think to kill her. But then Kadrasa didn't kill her: she jettisoned her alive. The Clicka floated through space amidst boxes and bodies.

The spacesuit still didn't fit, but she had pulled herself up near the helmet, and she could hear thoughts from farther than ever before. She could hear Kadrasa's pirates running away and grumbling of mutiny for what she'd done to their friends.

She could hear the thoughts of bored battle crews, as a whole corps of the new Interceptor crafts lay in wait at Beta I, Kadrasa's next refueling station. *Kadrasa will be looking for us,* one Captain thought bitterly. *And she'll think we're here as a result of the destruction of Smitty's Cruiser. She'll never realize that we were going to trap her anyway.*

And the Clicka could also hear Kadrasa, still wondering why the cruiser Captain had fired a Total instead of attacking more conservatively. She should have asked.

The Clicka still remembered Captain Smith's thoughts, from when she had been searching them for Kadrasa. *The net on Beta I will get them if I don't,* he had thought. *So forget trying to wound her, or trap her here and wait for help. Those goddamned Interceptors would get all the credit anyway. She's probably about to jump. Go for the kill!* And the Clicka remembered that Captain Smith had died.

Then the Clicka reached past the flying ships, reached down towards the planet itself. It was faint at first but space was so quiet that the Clicka could focus and focus and then she heard the thoughts of a whole planet of people. The people thought not of cruisers and Kadrasa and pirating, but of other things the Clicka had seldom thought. The Clicka roamed a sea of work and play.

The Clicka had never had so many thoughts to hear before, so many people to become, in the short visits she made to their minds. She would last long, here in space—she didn't eat much, and with the air regenerators she'd starve before suffocating. She would live for weeks.

Before the day was over, she was witness to the mutiny on Kadrasa's ship. And she heard Kadrasa floating in space, happy to die free. The Clicka loved to think with Kadrasa.

But her attention turned to the Interceptors when she heard their crews getting excited. *The trap is sprung,* one of the young Interceptor Captains thought. Then she could hear the confusion and anger in Kadrasa's crew, after their ship had been suddenly pulled to a halt in empty space. *The anti-wall,* thought the young Captain. *It got them before they even saw us.*

The Clicka heard the helpless crew surrendering, as the corps of Interceptors closed in. All of the pirates' thoughts were morbid. She returned to live longer in the angry thoughts of Kadrasa.

But then the next day she heard new thoughts approaching. It was the young Captain, and his ship was searching for something. His crew was reading a log, and checking co-ordinates. They showed him a chart. *Here and there,* he thought, *Kadrasa and her Clicka.*

She heard Kadrasa angry about being saved. Then hours later the Interceptor's large scoop pulled the Clicka into safety.

Everyone treated the Clicka much more nicely than they treated Kadrasa. Kadrasa's thoughts were all very black. But then they sent the Clicka to another ship, a hospital ship.

Don't be surprised if you don't see anyone for a while, thought the wire-haired man standing before her. She knew him; he was Stevenson, the psychoanalyst. He thought towards her the way he talked to other people: flatly, in only one tone and with gaps separating the parts of his sentences. And she knew why. It was his work, part of his life, to understand other people exactly as they are. To do so, he had to impose himself on them as little as possible, to keep them from acting in ways they've chosen just because they think he expects it. He projected no personality, and received only natural ones back.

She understood all that because he told her. He addressed himself to her in his thoughts—he was the only one ever to do that. But he made it so hard for her, to think with him. He put forward so little to think as.

I'll be putting you in a room, where you can't hear the rest of us, out here, he thought. *I just want you to relax for a while,* he thought.

She followed him through a door marked with three red stripes. When he closed the door behind them everything was very quiet.

Tell-her-the-stories, he thought to himself. *This room* (he turned to her) *was designed with the help of—* He thought something she didn't understand. *–of other Clickas.* She sat down in a green felt armchair that was just her size. *Good,* Stevenson thought, *She-chose-on-her-own-to-sit-there. Initiative. She-has-to-develop-her-self-more. But-she-hears-this–* He sat on a wooden chair across from her.

We don't really understand how you hear thoughts, what it is that you hear. And we don't really understand how the walls of this room keep you from it. But the– (Again he thought that thing she didn't understand.) *–designed it, for us, from things found on your planet. Your home planet. Mostly rocks and sticks and leaves, in these walls. All painted with a sort of putty that the Clickas mixed on your home.*

I don't know what you remember–no-of-course. She-thinks-so-little-on-her-own-that-she-won't-remember-any-of-it–about the early days of your life, on your home planet. But the pirates (She sensed his violent hatred for them.) *found out that you Clickas have this extraordinary talent for understanding thoughts. Every year they steal more of you from the nests, when you are still infants. Then they raise you so wrong. (Again she sensed his anger.) Make you into the tormented things you are.*

They make you think like they think. Like I think. Only you aren't supposed to do that; you can't do that on your own. So you have to do it from *other people's thoughts,* with *other people's thoughts,* as *other people. They have twisted your incredible empathy* (Now she sensed his admiration.) *into a punishing, unquenchable need. You have to forget. You have to stop thinking. Just relax for a while, and try not to think.*

He got up and moved to the door, and everything was very quiet. The Clicka ran after him and grabbed his hand. "Please stay!" she said out loud. "I like it, listening to you."

The man sighed. *Tell-her-more-about-what's-coming. The-next-few-days-will-hurt-her. Sit down in your chair,* he thought. He followed her and sat again on the wooden chair before her. *Right now, you think as I do. You talked as I do. Inside you want to be me, you are me in what you want, when you think. Only I don't want you to be me when you think.*

This last thought made the Clicka begin to twitch. *It's bad for you, to think like other things you aren't. Especially people–God, we're-all-so-incomplete.* She felt a wave of hopelessness wash over him. And she felt like she was tearing herself apart. *This-is-only-*

hurting-her, he thought. *To-think-that-those-bastards-could-so-abuse-such-a-beautiful-creature. Clicka. You will get better. You will become a better thing than any of those things you have thought. those people, me, Kadrasa. But you must forget words. You must forget the word "I" especially. Forget "I," forget "me." Want you to. Want you to stay and rest.*

Stevenson got up and left. With him outside and the door shut, the world was very quiet. Quiet, quiet. She climbed down from the green chair and sat on the wooden one. *Now you must forget about words, about "I" and "me" especially,* she thought. But she was talking to something else, not her sitting there. She was only talking to the chair.

The room was quiet. She climbed into the green chair again. The felt was soft, the shape just right. The room was so quiet. It was easy to be quiet like the room. She fell asleep.

How do you feel?

"I feel–" she stopped.

She's-searching-for-an-answer. Searching-me. But-that's-to-be-expected. Dammit, I-can't-help-but-talk-to-her. Every-time-I'm-here-she'll-fix-onto-me. But-she-looks-so-hurt. Such-a-beautiful-animal. He smoothed down her head fur and scratched behind her ears. *That's-why-this-is-my-job, should-be-mine. I-can-teach-them-to-love-themselves. Themself. But-she-must-stop-objectifying-herself. Self-consciousness-is-alienation.* When he thought it, she understood. *I must go. I can only say to you, try to change. And tomorrow we'll arrive at my home city. You'll be getting a new friend tomorrow afternoon.* He left food in the room and thought that she should eat before she went to sleep. She did.

She woke up the next day when the door opened. But Stevenson didn't come in. Only his arms did, putting something down. *Don't worry, Bruce, you'll be safe,* he thought. He wasn't thinking it to her. *You'll like her,* he thought. He took his hands away from the thing and closed the door. It was a four-footed animal with big floppy feet and black fur.

The Clicka and the puppy looked at each other. They were both afraid, but neither seemed a threat. "Bruce," she said. Then they both wanted to play. The puppy barked; the Clicka barked back. Then the Clicka jumped down from her chair, and the puppy romped over.

The puppy jumped up onto the Clicka, and the Clicka fell over backwards. The puppy jumped again, for the Clicka's nose; but he landed short. His paw fell on the Clicka's beak and the Clicka bit down playfully. "Grrr," she said in mock menace. Together they jumped and tackled each other and bit each other's fingers and the puppy licked the Clicka's beak. They wanted very much to please each other.

Finally they both got tired enough to sleep. The puppy slept wrapped in the Clicka's arms.

Later the door opened. The puppy pulled away from the Clicka and stood two steps away, his tail sticking straight up. Stevenson stepped through the door.

"Rup," said the puppy.

"Rep," said the Clicka.

The man smiled. *It's-the-best-I-can-do-for-the-moment. If-she's-thinking-at-all-she's-thinking-quite-differently-now.* Before he could leave the room they were both climbing his legs and gnawing on his fingers. He tried to think like a puppy as they wrestled on the floor.

"Ruff," he said.

"Rep," the Clicka replied.

But then the puppy was gone and the Clicka sat alone. She sat on the wooden chair, but the thinking was hard. She jumped to the floor and leaned on her hands. "Rep," she said. The Clicka looked around the room. "Rep," she said again. Then she climbed into her chair and watched the quiet room.

Stevenson was back in the room when she woke up. He held another animal, something smaller than Bruce which sat curled in his lap. *We moved this room, during the night. Put it in the Cruiser. We're on our way to your planet, now. The Clicka's planet.* He thought the thing that she didn't understand again.

But it was harder to follow him anyway. She focussed her attention on the thing in his lap. *Good,* he thought; *she-doesn't-give-me-as-much-attention.* The thing in his lap was making a soft, happy noise as he stroked it. Then he picked it up and put in on the ground. *This is Muff,* he said.

The Clicka looked carefully at the cat. She listened very hard to hear the animal's–not thoughts, exactly, but the same anyway. Feelings, impulses. The cat stood quietly on the floor while Stevenson walked to the door. As he opened the door the Clicka climbed down and crawled to the cat. All three waited, frozen.

Abruptly, the cat's back reared up and the animal hissed. It raked its paw across the Clicka's beak, and then darted across the room and out the open door. The Clicka cried.

Stevenson held the shaking, shuddering Clicka for a long time before he left the room. Later, he came back with Bruce.

Can't-tell-if-this-helps-or-hurts-the-Clicka, Stevenson thought, *and-probably-nothing-I-can-do-can-do-very-much-of-either. At-least-they-both-seem-happy-together.* The dog's tail wagged furiously when he saw the fur-covered Clicka.

The Clicka and the puppy played together often, as the Cruiser ran onward. It was hard to say what the Clicka was thinking like, Stevenson thought. It was hard to say what the final effect of the animals would be on her. But he just had to wipe away her human type of consciousness. Could a pirate Clicka, once *self*-conscious and aware of being separate, ever make it back? Stevenson felt helpless as they neared the Clickas' planet.

When the Clicka stepped out of the room with the green felt chair, the world rushed at her from all sides. Its smells and noises and bright colors were enough; the cascading thoughts and feelings frightened her. She pulled closer to Stevenson and reached upwards towards Bruce, who lay tailthumping in Stevenson's arms.

Stevenson hurried her down a long plastic hallway, away from the rooms with all the people in them. Her short legs couldn't keep up with his long ones, so he waited. He brought her into a small metal room with flashing lights, and the door sucked shut behind them. He pushed some other buttons and the air whooshed as another door opened. The new air was cold and bright. It was a door to the outside.

Stevenson led the Clicka down the ramp. The air smelled clean and wet. Tall dark trees covered most of the land, but in the clearing the wide-bladed grass was short and the sun bright.

Another Clicka stood at the bottom of the ramp.

Bruce barked, and Stevenson quieted him. Kadrasa's Clicka stood shyly by Stevenson, as the other Clicka waited. It was a tall animal, with thick brown fur and soft eyes. *She's-not-going-to-make-it,* Stevenson thought. *Go ahead, Clicka. Approach the other.*

The Clicka stepped forward shyly. The other Clicka was open to her. Not–not thinking, or feeling, or wanting something. Not seeing her as herself, not talking about anything or being anything. No, the other Clicka *was* something, but it wasn't like Stevenson, like Bruce. It wasn't itself–he, the other Clicka should be a he. But he wasn't. He was just a part of something larger–no, he was the larger thing, the small body was a part but he was also the rest.

Kadrasa's Clicka didn't understand. It wasn't, he wasn't, thinking or feeling or anything the way things were supposed to be.

The other Clicka stepped forward, and reached out to touch Kadrasa's Clicka. But she backed away, and hunched up her neck. She screamed her cat-scream, and swiped the new Clicka across the beak. Then she ran up the ramp.

Stevenson said something to the bleeding Clicka at the end of the ramp, and then ran upward to rejoin Kadrasa's Clicka. Kadrasa's Clicka was shaking and whimpering. Bruce licked her face.

I know. You don't understand. You can't understand. You aren't you. The real you isn't separate. You're supposed to be what he is. You belong to a part of the greater body. But the Clicka was giving most of her attention to Bruce.

The Clicka was back in the green felt chair. She hadn't seen Bruce for days. Stevenson was there again.

You have two choices, Clicka. You can remain what you are. You can be my housepet. Or you can stay here, out in the sunlight, and try to become what you are supposed to be.

"Bruce," said the Clicka.

"I don't want you to be Bruce!" Stevenson yelled. It was the first time he had spoken to her. "Don't you understand? Bruce is just a dog! You belong as a part of it, that beautiful thing on this planet. Our psychological terms don't even apply here. You should be able to feel everything, to feel complete! How can you want to be the copy of a housepet?"

The Clicka shuddered. Stevenson carried her though the airlock, dumped her on the ramp, and left her there. He went back into the ship, and watched on a videowindow. He held his breath. The Clicka stumbled down the ramp and into the field. On all fours, she crawled into the forest. Stevenson sighed.

When the Clicka hadn't returned after a week, the Cruiser left.

The others found Kadrasa's Clicka. She barked like Bruce. "Rep," she said. They opened it to her, their self, and she saw it again. She saw it but she wasn't it. So she just followed along as they travelled their migratory trails, as they pulled down the great blackwood fruit and passed it around, as they slept in the great circles, arms intertwined.

At first she was Bruce. Then she tried to be it, what they were. She did what they did and marvelled at how natural it all seemed. She could reach the fruit they reached for, pull away the fronds they pulled away, and build the same nest. It was as if she knew how to do it. And she could look at them and see herself and think she finally understood. But then she would listen hard, grab for their thoughts; and at once the pain would come. Not pain–terror ripped her thoughts. It was her own scream hurting her inside, because she touched something she couldn't: a thought that wasn't, that she couldn't understand. It made her shiver, shake, it ripped at her from behind her thoughts. She couldn't touch them and be her at the same time.

And it hurt them too. They knew. They touched her and smoothed her fur and and cleaned her face the way they cleaned each other, but they knew no way to try to be any closer.

At night when they all slept together, Kadrasa's Clicka slept apart. While the Clickas slept, Kadrasa's Clicka lay wrapped in horrible dreams, of floppy white pirate Clicka dogs talking to her in the dark. While the Clickas slept the psychoanalyst's Clicka dreamed horrible dreams of seeing herself from the outside, of the world spread out like an ocean inside of her and of herself melted away into the dark ocean of space. The lone Clicka woke often, in the terrible nights, while the others slept on.

When the young were to be born the lone Clicka was passed to a different troop, so that she would not infect the parts still with soft beaks. But the Clickas never drove her any farther away from themself. They didn't, and they could feel her pain because they were her even if she wasn't them. And they kept hoping, but the terror never ended for her, and then she died.

They buried her in the right place, together with all the parts whose time had ended. They cried for her bitterly; they cried for all the parts who were taken away and never came back home.

IMPROBABLE BESTIARY:
The Bug-Eyed Monster

The Bug-Eyed Monster eats virgins for lunch;
He likes to hear their bones going crunch, crunch, crunch.
He has twelve arms and sixteen legs,
His breath smells just like rotten eggs,
His face is so ugly it must be a curse
And those are his *good* points; from here it gets worse . . .

The Bug-Eyed Monster round our street
Has sixteen ugly, hairy feet
(And it's *not* very nice to make fun of them!)
The Bug-Eyed Monster round our street

Has *tons* of things he loves to eat
(And humans, he tells me, are one of them.)
The local Bug-Eyed Monster is a notable gourmet.
Last night he ate three lamp posts and a two-door Chevrolet.
He ate ten thousand loaves of bread;
He wasn't getting thinner.
"Well, that takes care of *lunch!*" he said.
"What time shall we have *dinner?*"

Constable Brown came up from town to catch him and arrest him.
The monster saw the constable and started to digest him.
I rung up Sergeant Cripps and brought the matter to his
attention.
"If the constable's dead,"
The sergeant said,
"We won't have to give him his pension."

The Bug-Eyed Monster, without hesitation
Took pepper and salt and ate Waterloo Station.
He ate Covent Garden (You really should *see* him!)
He ate London Bridge and the British Museum.
He drank half an ocean, and swallowed a sea.
"Nice dinner!" he told me. "When's afternoon tea?"

The Bug-Eyed Monster took his knife and fork
And ate New York.
And when I reminded him of proper table etiquette
He ate Connecticut.
And now he has a stomach ache from eating North Dakota.
Quick! Help me fill Lake Erie with bicarbonate of soda!

—F. Gwynplaine MacIntyre

DBM 81

SLAC//

by Michael P. Kube-McDowell

art: David Mattingly

The author teaches middle-school science in a very small Indiana town. Since this story appeared in *IAsfm*, he has made appearances in *Analog*, *Twilight Zone*, and several anthologies besides this one.

Against regulations, Terence Calder spent two hours of his last sleepmode aboard *Cimara* in the language lab, worrying over the troublesome Semu verbs. He knew his language skills were marginal for a Contactor; and the Semu verbs, marked by sounds more suited to an oboe than vocal cords (Quon, the linguist, called them pipe-sounds*), were to him unpronounceable. And what he could not pronounce, he could not remember for long.

Marisa, his partner, slept soundly in her compartment three bulkheads aft. With her superb language aptitude, she had picked up the Semu tongue as quickly as the crackers has been able to break it down. She had even removed three words from the "In Question" list of undeciphered terms. Calder glanced up at the list hanging on the language lab wall. Removing the remaining fifty-one terms from it was just one of his and Marisa's tasks, beginning with planetfall tomorrow.

The next morning the ship's gig took them down to 10,000 meters, safely above prying Semu eyes. From there they were on their own; the tiny gravwarp generators in their leg pouches would permit a controlled freefall to the uninhabited region below. Marisa went first, clad as Calder was in the orange-red hue of the Semu sun. By the time Calder wriggled out of the embrace of the gig pilot, Marisa was a mere dot far below.

*/, //, and /// are the graphemes adopted for the three Semu pipe-sounds. The pipe-sounds, which are made with the breathing tube rather than the vocal chamber, are polytonal; however, a workable approximation can be made by whistling the first harmonic (/ = cps, // = 461, /// = 908). It has become common for non-linguistic personnel to say "slac-whistle" (or equivalent).

Then he, too, was out of the chute. In the exhilaration of the first moments of freefall, he took his eye off Marisa, and then was unable to spot her. No matter; the gravwarp guidance system would bring them to a side-by-side landing.

Even after three months over Semu, the bluish surface rushing up at him seemed unreal; Calder was from a planet dominated by green chlorophylls. No amount of observation had been able to remove that sense of strangeness. Calder shook off the feeling and concentrated on the fall itself—the easy, peaceful glide down.

Then, as the ground grew near, Calder's arms and legs became inexplicably limp and unresponsive. He began to tumble slowly, and was unable to halt the motion. The gliding turned to falling, and his peace to distress. His ears heard a shouting his mind did not understand. But there was no time for puzzlement; the ground was too close. As the blue Semu countryside rushed up to embrace him, Calder tried and failed to remember the Semu verb for dying.

The tech looked uncomfortable, like a dog expecting to be struck. "Captain?"

"Yes, Nixon."

"I'm not getting any biotelemetry from Terry and Marisa."

"Lost signal or flat trace?" Captain Lanton half-rose from his chair.

"Lost, sir."

Lanton sat back. "I was afraid you were telling me they're dead."

"I think I am, sir. They don't answer my signals."

Lanton frowned. "Let's take a look at the recordings. And hold off on the landing on the far side."

"I already took that liberty."

By the time the recording ended, most of *Cimara's* small complement had formed a solemn half-circle at the perimeter of the tech room.

"High fever and then nothing," Lanton said to no one in particular. "EEG normal, even calm."

"Yes, sir," Nixon said, stepping forward. "If it had just cut off I'd say it was an equipment problem, or interference."

"Did you track them?"

"They made planetfall on the beam exactly."

"Time of LOS?"

"Five minutes after landing, perhaps a little more."

"And they didn't signal us."

"No, sir. Not a peep."

Lanton drummed his fingers on the console.

"Nephei and Quon will follow them down, if you'd like," Nixon offered tentatively. The Lyraen couple nodded.

"No. No second team."

"Yes, sir. What, then?"

"Put us in synch orbit over the site the next pass. Send the gig down now to search from 5,000 meters." He stood. "Let me know the moment they have anything. And check out a mobicom."

"Yes, sir." Surprise showed on several faces, including Nixon's. The mobicom, a powerful communications unit wedded to a gravwarp, was ordinarily used only after a team had set up relations with the planet's inhabitants.

"One more thing," Lanton said, pausing at the door and jabbing at them with a finger. "When you update your logs, they're missing. Not dead. Missing."

Lanton sought the privacy of his compartment during the fifty-minute wait until they were over the landing site again. "I should have had us in sync already," he started on himself when he was alone. "Followed them down with a sight-sound peeper or have them carry one—"

He stopped berating himself when he realized he was merely forecasting the conclusions of the inquiry board. Point was, no ship had ever lost a team on planetfall before—later, certainly, but not in the first five minutes. If there had ever been any special precautions, they had long fallen out of use. Getting on the planet had always turned out to be the easy part.

The details of contact with underdeveloped planets—no other kind having yet been found—had been worked out in theory by the exo-psychologists and in practice by the Service. The crucial step was to monitor the communications of the inhabitants from orbit, and let a team like Nephei and Quon use a linguacomp to crack the language. Or if, like Semu, the planet had no advanced communications, plant a selection of sight-sound peepers. That took longer, since conversational language was invariably harder to decode than broadcast formal.

Then, language in hand, simply go meet the inhabitants. When a new animal approaches you speaking your language, it gives you pause—pause enough for the Service to establish contact with twenty-two intelligent, thriving species. There were some curious similarities among them—each was top predator on its planet, entering or facing the crisis that comes when evolutionary programming becomes outdated. The knowledge that they were not alone had helped two or three species totter back from the brink, and only one species ended up worshipping man—a good scorecard.

The rest of the procedure was mere detail. Wear the color of the planet's primary sun: the safest color, given the nearly universal sun-worship of surface dwellers. Display as little technology as possible—the only devices carried were the gravwarp generators, and even those were integral with the jumpsuits. The biotelemeters and microradios were implants—the former in the chest and the latter in the left pinky. Planetfall was made in an uninhabited region, to avoid mass reactions and let the Contactors choose first contact. Finally, teams of two gave an accurate picture of human biology, allowed for complementary abilities, and were small enough not to constitute an invasion. An unvarying, reliable formula.

Except for this time. And he, Aldis Lanton, was faced with answering the question that no one had ever had to answer before: *what next?*

It was not a question for long. The Service's contact captains were a special sort. Typically, they had the lowest I-score on their ships, in part because it was undesirable that they be bright enough to be erratic. What was desirable was a certain firmness of mind, a decisiveness in the face of both too little and too much detail. With a mission by its nature unpredictable, and a crew of talented, occasionally temperamental specialists, the ship's captain had to be a locus of calmness.

And Lanton was one of the best, because he understood his role. Twelve years ago he had faced the realities of a shrinking military and his own personality, and transferred to the Advance Exploration Service. Though he committed himself to becoming conversant in all the contact skills, and pioneered the now-common practice of requiring the entire ship's complement to learn the new languages, he would have been respected and successful without those acts. And when Nixon finally knocked and stepped into the cabin, Lanton had things clear in his mind.

"No sign from 5,000, Captain. Shall I send them lower?"

"No point—if the team were still on site, the sensors would pick up their telemetry. Correct?"

"Yes. It seems the next step is to put a team on the ground."

"Yes. But differently this time. Is the mobicom checked out?"

"Yes. I don't—"

"It's their planet," Lanton said, standing. "We were ready to contact them. There's apparently something critical we don't know about the planet. Let's get their help."

Semu—the planet. Geologically unremarkable. Smaller than Earth and more dense—net effect, a slightly higher surface gravity. A day of 29.2 standard hours. Two continents, the smaller northern one permanently ice-encrusted. The larger, dubbed Drumstick by Quon because of its shape, wrapped two-thirds of the way around the southern hemisphere. Almost 60 percent of it was rugged highland, including a range of inner mountains which were low but forbiddingly severe. A semi-circular plain of rolling lowlands on Drumstick's larger western end, almost enclosed by two fingers of highlands, contained nearly all the fertile land. Biologically, Semu was marked by short food chains. And, like most planets with a variety of life, Semu had large plants that were not trees but would be called such, and small plants that were not grass but would suffer the misnomer. Blessedly, it did not seem to have insects.

Semu—the people. Cell-based and humanoid, but clearly not human. Aside from the usual variations in sense organs, musculature, and so on, two features clearly set them as a species apart. The Semu head was articulated much like a Terran owl's, capable with its loose-skinned neck of rotating through nearly 400°. Moreover, the Semu were ambidirectional—that is, their arms seemed to function as well in back of their bodies as in front. They were also extremely pair-oriented; in nearly five months of observation, only twice had a Semu been seen more than twenty meters from his *otati,* or mate. Total population: perhaps 100,000, in over 2,000 villages scattered over the coastal plain and fertile lowlands. They were gatherers rather than farmers, and the villages were separated by the invisible, mutually respected lines demarking their food territories.

Lanton studied the reaction of the Semu villagers to the suitcase-sized mobicom descending toward them. Nixon brought it in on one side of the village, so only a dozen Semu paused to note its approach. They watched dispassionately, neither drawing near nor fleeing, and then most turned away. It was not what Lanton had expected.

Only two pairs remained interested long enough to see Lanton's face appear and hear his greeting: "*Bantroi.*"

"*Bantroi,*" echoed the nearest Semu, his head twisting toward his *otati*. The second Semu repeated the greeting.

"I am Aldis Lanton," said the captain. "What you see is not my body but a *kisemu* I have sent you so that we may talk." He used the Semu word for statue or portrait—literally, "not-self."

"Yes," said the second Semu, moving forward and nudging the

first aside. To Lanton's ear, both voices were male.

"I am a visitor—*kiranchi*. Two of my companions are missing near your village. We will come and meet with you and search for them. Is it to be so?" A Semu request was a statement of the future, then a request for confirmation.

"It is to be."

Lanton waited, expecting a question, but none came. "Before nightfall," Lanton said finally. "*Bantroi.*"

Switching off, Lanton shivered. There seemed to be nothing behind the yellow Semu eyes—a vacant look, as though the owner were out to lunch. He chided himself for anthropocentricity and turned to the others in the room.

"Mandy, you and I will make up the team."

Mandy Wells looked up, startled. The exobiologist was *Cimara's* newest and youngest specialist, and had kept to herself enough that she was more like a passenger than part of the team. She had come to them in the usual way—basic training in a top Earth school, advanced work on the Jovian moons, research on a "safe" planet (in her case, Kruger 60-E), and two intern missions at the elbow of an experienced XB. Semu was her first solo mission, which Lanton saw as the reason for her reticence. Whatever the reason, Wells did not give much of herself away. Her small smile at being selected was comparatively revealing.

"Thank you, sir. Captain—" she began hesitantly.

"Yes?"

"I know it's difficult to tell with ET's, but they didn't seem very surprised."

Lanton's expression was sober. "I know."

The gig pilot set the tiny ship down gently within sight of the village walls, then lifted off again as the humans walked side-by-side down the knoll to the gate in the low village wall. A pair of Semu waited there; they seemed agitated, heads turning repeatedly through full circles. As the humans drew closer, other pairs appeared in the yard just inside the wall.

"*Bantroi,*" Lanton called as soon as he thought they would hear a normal speaking voice.

"*Bantroi,*" said one of the newly arrived Semu. "I am Gision Ah, Protector of the village of White-hill. We celebrate your safe arrival."

"We celebrate your continued health," responded Wells.

"Have those who are missing been found?" Gision Ah asked matter-of-factly.

"No. They are still missing."

Those Semu who stood watching muttered at this. "Slac/ /," one said clearly.

"Where did you last know of them?"

Lanton pointed east. "Three hills—two *kai* walk-time."

"And the missing are like you?"

"They are."

Gision Ah made a sweeping downward motion with his hand, the fingers coming together to touch at the tips—the Semu gesture for "gone," equivalent to a shrug of hopelessness.

"Have you heard anything of strangers in that area?"

"We know nothing of the world there."

"Your travelers—hunters—"

"Nothing."

Wells stepped forward. "We are *kiranchi*. We ask your help."

Gision Ah's *otati* spoke, a harsh, incomprehensible outburst. Looking back, Gision Ah answered with equal intensity, then said to Lanton: "You will wait for us. It will be so?"

"It will be so," Lanton said. Immediately a pair of the large Semu ushered the humans away from the gate and deeper into the village. Surprised, the humans let themselves be steered into a small, sturdy building. It was dark inside; the windows were mere slits in the wooden wall. "Prison?" Lanton wondered aloud.

Wells moved to the doorway and looked out. "Three pair of them standing close by, including our escorts. And this door is lockable—there are holes and loops for vertical crossbars."

"Come have a seat." As she joined him, he continued. "Some of those pairs are homosexual, correct?"

"Oh, yes. They seem to place no stigma on it—male-male and female-female pairs are as common as mixed ones. It was part of the report I submitted on the Semu social organization."

"Ah. Remind me of your conclusions." Lanton remembered the report clearly; he was trying to draw her out.

Wells nodded. "Generally, there is a strong correlation between the formal social acceptance of homosex and crowded niches. But that doesn't seem to be the case here—the food supply appears adequate for five times the population."

Lanton was mildly disappointed; her tone was professional and deferential, not personal. "So?"

"So the pairing patterns are just variation, not adaptation. Unless this *is* overpopulated for Semu sensitivities."

"Or their diet is more specialized than we realize." Lanton grasped the pinky of his left hand and pulled, as if he were unjamming a finger. "Nixon?" he said experimentally.

"Here."

"We're a bit isolated just now. Try to find out what's happening with the group that greeted us."

"Call when I have something," the tech promised. "Nixon out."

Gision Ah sounded the three pipe-sounds, and the room fell silent. "Nepion Tu has asked for a sharing-time concerning the *kiranchi.*"

"I wish to know what Protector Ah sees," Nepion explained.

"Protector Ah does not see clearly, and would accept the sharing of others on this question."

"Clarify."

"What is done? They are not slac/ /; they are not lessers. Are they Semu? They are two, and yet not *otati.*"

"They are insane," spoke up one of those who had watched the humans at the gate. "They wood-walk with eyes down and ahead." He made the 'gone' gesture. "They are insane."

"They are strangers," offered another.

"They speak language—"

"Like a poorly trained child."

"But still they speak."

Gision Nu rose. "Our ways permit only one response. They have demanded *kiranchi* with us. *Kiranchi* must be given."

"They are not Semu," protested Nepion Tu. "Would you grant *kiranchi* to a slac/ / if it demanded it?"

"It seems to be a meeting over your status, sir. I don't dare move the mobicom for fear of alarming them, so I've got the long mike on them—but the gain isn't too strong. Here, Quon wants you."

"I'd say we misread *kiranchi,*" said the linguist. "It's not 'visitor', it's more to a temporary communal membership—a reciprocal relation between villages, apparently."

"How are we doing?"

"Hard to say. Several 'In Question' terms have shown up already—brings an element of uncertainty into any analysis."

"Keep listening. I don't like uncertainty. And give Mandy a signal feed so she can help."

"Yes, sir."

"Where is their village, where we may claim *kiranchi?*"

"If they are from it, it must exist."

The argument went on, the alignment of delegates shifting on nearly every new point that was raised. "I could make more progress with a committee of snakes," grumbled Nixon, eavesdropping from *Cimara*. But Gision Ah seemed content, sitting back and staying out of the discussion.

Three hours later, the vigor of the debate undiminished, the door to the building opened and a young Semu poked his head in. *"Ginu,"* he called, and without a further word the delegates hurried from the building in the ubiquitous Semu pairs.

It was about that time that the signal from the mobicom died.

"What do you want me to do?" Nixon asked plaintively. "If I recall it for maintenance or send down another, they may not take it well. We've shown them a lot of technology for this point in the contact."

Lanton decided quickly. "Do nothing. The information hasn't been that valuable. We have to make things happen from here, and we've just been sitting."

"Good luck, sir."

"I'm a believer in making your own luck."

"Yes, sir. Uh—Captain? Think the Semu tampered with the 'com?"

Lanton exhaled heavily. "I don't know."

"Check in in three hours?"

"Yes. Lanton out." He looked expectantly across the room at Wells. "Ready to go?"

"More than," she said eagerly.

But this time, the door would not open.

Without benefit of clock or crier, as sunlight began to reach the village of White-hill, the delegates migrated back to the meeting house.

This time, however, Gision Ah reined in the wandering thoughts. "We know of only one thing that may be done. *Kiranchi* has been claimed, and will be granted. But there is more. They seek their missing in the open lands. If we permit them to search freely—"

Several of those in the front circle made the sign for 'gone'.

"Yes. More is called for from us."

"There must be a *tiranon,"* said Nepion Tu.

"There must be a *tiranon,"* Gision Ah agreed. "But because they are strangers, it is required of no one. Return to your homes and seek out those who will serve. Send them to me. When a *tiranon* has been found, we will proceed."

Aldis Lanton had taken a long time to fall asleep. He and Mandy had found out at the cost of bruised hands and shoulders that the door was strong enough to hold them, and at the cost of their voices that no Semu could be persuaded to release them. Nixon's offer to intervene tempted him briefly, but in the end he decided to wait until the situation was clearer. Still, he could not seem to close his eyes, his hopes for finding the Contact Team alive having reached a new low.

In the morning, the posts were noisily removed and the door thrown open by a young Semu. "*Ginu* ends," he said, then disappeared from the doorway.

When Lanton tried to follow and get an explanation, however, he found himself quickly surrounded by Semu—not threateningly, but purposefully.

"I will talk with Gision Ah. It will be so?"

"It will not," was the answer. "He is occupied."

Lanton frowned. "We must begin looking for our missing companions. Too much time passes."

"It will not be," said the Semu who barred his path. "*Kiranchi* has been granted, the *tiranon* forms. Wait."

His frown deepened, and Wells touched his arm. "We're not in danger," she said in English, "and it sounds like we've been granted a protected status. Perhaps we should give them more time."

"Time is the problem," Lanton said simply.

"I think it would be a mistake to force the issue now. There's no indication they don't intend to help us."

The forcefulness in Wells's voice was a welcome surprise. Perhaps, Lanton thought, she's starting to find her professional backbone. But he was not as convinced of their safety as she was.

"We will wait—two *kai*," he said to the Semu. "Come on," he said to Wells, and ducked back inside the hut. Sitting down, he signaled the ship, aware that the Semu way of doing things was wearing on his patience.

"Put Quon on."

There was a short silence before they heard the Lyraen's voice. "Yes, Captain?"

"A translation on *tiranon*, please."

"Repeat?"

"*Tiranon*."

"Must be a new word. Any contextual clues?"

"I was thinking it might be 'search party', Captain," offered Wells.

"Um. Translation on *ginu*."

"Still on the 'In Question' list," said Quon. "Best guess would be 'sunset', except we already have a word for it and they're very economical in their vocabulary—"

"I don't want might be, I want to *know,*" Lanton said heatedly. "Start doing your job." He looked up to see Wells considering him curiously. "What do you want?"

The look vanished. "Nothing."

Near noon, the Protector came for them.

"We are ready," he said simply, and they followed him out into the sun. Standing there were a dozen Semu, each carrying a sort of rigid sling that the humans had seen used in play—it was one of the three Semu tools they had identified. But the short five-pointed arrows that they were also carrying were new. It was clear that the arrow was intended to fit in the groove along the upper side of the sling.

The band moved off to the nearest village gate, where they paused while Gision Ah moved among them, rubbing a yellow-white cake across the arrow points. The Semu gabbed animatedly as they waited, then fell silent when Gision had finished. Offering the humans no explanations, the Semu leader moved to the front of the group and set the pace with long, smooth strides. His *otati* followed close behind him, stepping into his footprints with a precision that seemed practiced, her head facing back and sweeping slowly from side to side.

The other pairs arranged themselves similarly, spaced at regular intervals across the open meadow. After an exchange of glances, Lanton and Wells fell in behind them.

"We haven't seen that sling used as a weapon before," said Lanton.

"No. But I have seen them walk this way—the young have a kind of game they play," she said, watching them intently.

"That cake must be some sort of poison."

"Or it could have ritual significance—the Semu are big on ritual. I think this is what we wanted, though—a search party. Look at the way each one of them only scans a small part of the surroundings—but between them not a bit is missed. Remarkable example of social coordination, don't you think?"

"I think Gision is going too fast."

The countryside was gentle in slope, but the long-legged Semu were not dawdlers—they proceeded without pause at a rate awkwardly between human walking and running. For the first hour, the *kiranchi* kept up, breathless. But as they drew nearer to the landing site, legs tired and spirit flagged.

It happened then, in one terrible moment. A shadow flashed across the ground unnoticed. At a noise, no more than a breathless rush of air, Lanton's eyes flicked upward. There was not enough time to sort out the impressions—he smelled something pungent, saw claws, sensed *close,* and threw up an arm in self-protection. Something hard and sharp struck his arm with surprising force, glanced off, and raked his head.

Wells spun at the sound and saw Lanton spin slowly into a jumbled pile of limbs. "Slac/ /," cried a shrill Semu voice as the creature glided overhead on its sail-like wings.

A flurry of five-pointed arrows filled the air, and three came to rest in the flesh of the attacker. The slac/ /'s grasp on the heavy stick it carried in its lower claws weakened, and the stick fell to the ground; a moment later the creature folded its sails and followed it, thudding against the ground fifteen meters from where Wells crouched. With an effort she released the air in her lungs and hurried to Lanton's side.

Lanton's eyes were closed and his temple bloody; his left forearm made an angle of 40° where the designer had not intended one to be. But he seemed to be breathing regularly, and Wells took time out to signal the ship. "Lanton's been hurt—get the gig down here ASAP."

"Hold on." After a pause, Quon's voice returned. "Nephei's boarding now. Six minutes or so—will that do it?"

"Yes." She looked yearningly in the direction of the slac/ /. "You can cross slac/ / off the 'In Question' list—it's what the Semu call the flying species that attacked Lanton. About a meter long, wingspan about the same—ruddy orange color."

"With a pipe-sound, it should be a verb."

"For attack, maybe." Looking down, she saw that there was considerable blood on Lanton's face. "Nephei coming?"

"On the way," Quon reassured.

"Wells out." Kneeling, she wiped away the blood and found, to her relief, that there were no deep gouges—the blood was from capillaries torn open by the stick scraping across his face. Reassured, she checked his pulse and breathing again, then crossed the meadow to the circle of Semu. Shouldering her way to the inside, she stood beside Gision Ah and stared at the creature.

The slac/ /'s wings were simply loose flaps of skin connecting its upper limbs to its body, though in flight they had the shape of a parasail. Its legs had enormous extensor muscles, and ended in powerful claws that were not at all birdlike. Similar but smaller claws were at the end of each sailstrut.

"The stick it carried—" she said to Gision.

Gision Ah struck himself in the throat with his forearm. "The slac/ / neck-break."

Wells suddenly felt exposed. "No one is on lookout now," she said. "Couldn't there be another nearby? Are they never found in groups?"

"The slac/ / dislike each other's company."

"A *kiranchi* from Low-tree told once of a *tiranon* that slew two slac/ / in a single day," said Gision Nu.

"The people of Low-tree are known braggarts and liars," said Gision Ah. *"Beyta,"* he barked suddenly, and the Semu began to scatter in all directions. Two headed for Lanton, and Wells hastened protectively back to his side. But the pair continued on with barely a glance at Lanton, and disappeared into the woods as the others all had. Before Wells could wonder about it, the gig swept down and settled with a muffled roar a hundred meters away.

Nephei examined Lanton quickly and sniffed, "Nothing serious." Producing an airsplint, she worked to immobilize Lanton's arm. "Help me get him to the gig."

The Lyraen woman was strong, and Wells felt unneeded in the four-hand carry. The feeling was confirmed when Nephei changed her grip and carried him up the ladder and into the gig herself. Arranging him on a flight couch, she turned and poked her head back out the hatch.

"Coming?"

"I think not."

"Standard prac says not to be groundside solo."

"I'm not. I'm with them," Wells said with a jerk of the head.

Nephei glanced up. "Speaking of whom—what the hell are they doing?"

"My specimen!" cried Mandy, running toward the gathering. But she was too late; flames were already leaping up through the mound of brush the Semu had collected. Atop the mound was the slac/ /.

"Gision Ah," she called across the circle. "I need to—" She stopped, frustrated. They had learned no Semu word for 'study'. "To look at it."

"The fire will put the smell of death in the air—no slac/ / will come for days. It will be safe to feed here." The flames leaped up and hid Gision Ah's face from her.

Horrified, Wells watched the slac/ / writhe until its flesh turned black. Once she had seen a boy torment a Terran worm with a hand lens; the feeling of mixed fascination and disgust was the same then and now.

Though Wells pleaded with Gision Ah to go on to the landing site, he would not hear of it. "The *tiranon* has known fire, and darkness comes. At *ginu,* the world belongs to the slac/ /."

He strode off, and Wells hastened to fall in beside him. "The door to our sleeping-place would not open once." Semu was sparing with time words; anything past was *esu*—once.

"Yes," acknowledged Gision Ah. "A Semu forgets—the madness comes. He must be helped to remember."

"The slac/ / see well in the dark," Wells suggested.

"For slac/ /, there is no dark."

An odd speculation came into Wells's mind, but she dismissed it quickly. "We will look for the missing again tomorrow. It will be so?"

Gision Nu clucked reprovingly—an unnerving cross-species parallel—and said, "It will not." She looked to Ah.

"It will not," he agreed. "You must find a new *otati,* now that yours is lost."

"He's not lost. He was taken back to have his injuries attended to."

Gision Ah said nothing but exchanged a glance with his *otati.*

"We must look again tomorrow," Wells pressed. "It will be so?"

"It will not," Ah repeated. "You must find a new *otati,* now that yours is lost."

Wells took the Protector by the arm and stopped him. He looked at her blankly.

"Gision Ah, what am I?"

The blank look continued.

"Am I a Semu?" She held their forearms up side-by-side before him. Behind them, the rest of the *tiranon* had come to a stop.

"No—you are not Semu." Ah seemed disturbed.

"Then what am I? Where do I come from? What took Lanton away?"

Again the blank expression. "You are not Semu," he said slowly. "You are not slac/ /. You are not lessers." Then, as though he had solved a great puzzle, he pronounced, "You are *kiranchi.*" Satisfied, he resumed walking.

Wells stood and watched him go, astonished. The Semu had not asked them a single question about humans, had never reacted in the least to the coming and going of the gig or the mobicom. She had noted it, of course, and attributed it to caution.

Now she began to wonder—could it be that they simply weren't curious?

Mandy Wells squirmed uncomfortably on the sleep-bench and stared up toward the ceiling, somewhere above her in the darkness. The last few hours had been the best since they had left port—finally there was no one looking over her shoulder, ready to judge and find her wanting. When the gig had left, Wells had felt a wave of relief. For a while, at least, the pressure to prove herself was gone.

But she still could have been happier. She hated the guessing—pretending that it was possible to somehow make human sense out of alien strangeness. She hated guessing wrong still more—and she had a deep suspicion that she had been very badly wrong about the Semu.

On top of that, there was something troubling about the attack on the captain. The use of the neck-break stick could be overlooked; many more animals used tools than made them. But why had the attack taken place at all?

At first, Wells had dismissed it easily. Just as the Semu are sensitive to "mad" behavior, so too must be the slac/ /. She and Lanton had walked as a human couple, not a Semu *otati*—and they had been singled out just as any predator singles out the cripple in the herd. But now, under closer examination, that explanation fell apart. What would the slac/ / have done with Lanton had it been successful? It wasn't a flier, merely a glider; and couldn't have carried him away. Nor could it have fed, with a band of arrow-slinging Semu forty meters away. The attack defied survival instinct.

Then the scratching began.

It was above her in the dark, on the roof outside the shelter. Wells sat up and clutched the edge of the sleep-bench tightly in both hands. The scratching circled the roof twice, then stopped. A moment later another sound began at the door—the sound of the lock-posts turning in their holes in the ground. Finally the door itself came alive, shaking back and forth against the lock-posts and the frame. The shaking was almost frantic, and Wells had little doubt about what was outside the door.

At last, to her relief, the noises stopped. But it took a long time for her to relax enough for sleep to come.

In the light of her second dawn on Semu, with the visitation more tantalizing than frightening, Wells was determined to find a slac/ /

to observe. But Gision Ah refused to help, and when she tried to leave the village alone a small crowd of Semu converged on her at the gate, lovingly but firmly turning her back. When a second effort was just as fruitless, Wells retreated to the center of the village and contacted *Cimara.*

"Morning, Mandy," Nixon said cheerfully. "I wasn't five minutes from checking on you. Night pass uneventfully?"

"More or less. How's the Captain?"

"Out cold right now—Nephei's warming up the microknitter to fix that broken wing. As soon as she's done, she and Quon are coming groundside to start formal contact procedures."

"What about me?"

"You'll be staying—to concentrate on the slac/ /. The Captain wants us to give the Semu something to help them with that problem."

"Isn't that a bit premature?"

"He doesn't seem to think so—and you can't exactly discuss it with him now. Oh, and another thing—that mobicom that went out. Chip failure. Not tampering."

"What about Terry and Marisa?"

Nixon hesitated. "We've come to the conclusion that there won't be much to find."

"You're writing them off."

"Not exactly. But it's pretty unlikely they're going to show up alive, wouldn't you say? After all, without a little help from the Semu, you wouldn't be in much of a talking mood yourself."

"I'd be dead, you're saying."

"And the Captain. You disagree?"

Wells frowned. "No. That's probably right. Wells out."

Gision was playing *tiranon* with five young Semu when Wells found him. "I have to talk to you."

"I knew the need once—Nu is my third," Ah said, waving the young ones away. "Share."

"Protector Ah, I know what you're trying to do. You're convinced I'm insane because I don't fear the slac/ / every waking moment—and because I've lost my 'otati'. You're trying to save me from my madness. But it isn't necessary!"

The Protector waited patiently, and Wells continued. "It's become a problem—I can't do my work. I can care for myself. I'm an experienced—*kiranchi.*" It wasn't the word she wanted, but the maddening Semu language straitjacketed her. It had no word for exobiologist, of course, but it did not even have a word for explorer.

"Please tell your people to leave me be."

"When I lost my first *otati,* the madness stayed for fifty days," Gision said gently. "I did not gather food—I longed to kill slac/ / singlehanded. But my friends were good to me, and locked me in a sleeping-place, and I became well again. How can I tell your friends not to help? You ask me to take your madness and spread it among them."

"I'm not a Semu," Wells said heatedly. "Forget *otati,* forget madness. Look at me—if I'm not the same as you on the outside, why should I be the same on the inside?"

"The madness runs deep in you, *kiranchi,*" said Ah, ever gentle. "But we will help you, do not fear."

Wells stared at him, then turned and stalked away. Behind her, Gision Ah called loudly to the nearby adults, and Wells's steps became running strides. She headed unerringly for the nearest gate, meaning to test at last the strength of the slender Semu arms that barred it.

Though there were five of them, the struggle was brief. Wells broke free and ran for the forest, leaving the Semu dismayed and largely prone behind her.

Heading toward the nearest portion of the Wishbone, Wells ran herself to near-collapse through the wood. When she felt she had won enough time from the Semu's doubtlessly concerned pursuit, she slowed to a walk. Though finding a slac/ / would be, on the face of it, difficult, she had the idea that given a chance to they would locate her.

Protecting her back by resting against a trunk at the edge of a large clearing, Wells sat down to wait. The slac/ / would have to approach head-on, and an attack would be difficult.

A new vision of the Semu took form in her mind as she waited. *Tiranon* was not search party, but hunting party. *Otati,* the strongest relationship in their society, was not reproductive-mate, but partner, or buddy as in buddy-system. The slac/ / seemed to thoroughly dictate the Semu way of life.

As she mulled over the new observations, a graceful orange-red creature glided down to settle in the middle of the clearing. Its lower claws were empty.

"Now we'll find out what sort of creature you are," she murmured, leaning forward. "I prefer my specimens live, anyway." The slac/ / and the woman considered each other across the expanse of blue meadow. The gaze of the slac/ / made Wells uncomfortable in a way the Semu never had.

"Do you speak? Do you have language?" she said loudly, hoping not for understanding but to encourage the slac/ / to display similar ability. But there was no response.

"Are you the one that came last night?" she asked, standing. "Or is there a nest of you somewhere near?"

The slac/ / took two awkward steps toward her.

"A little test, then. It's easy, you can do it. Give me something I can show the captain." She extended a closed fist, then uncurled a single finger from it.

With what to Wells was painful slowness, the slac/ / unfolded its right sailstrut and flexed one, then two of the diminutive claws at the end.

Resisting a premature smile, Wells raised one, then two, then three fingers. She watched eagerly as the slac/ / uncurled its last two claws, then shifted its weight from foot to foot.

"Beautiful!" she said, applauding. "There *is* something behind those eyes. You gave me sequence, not simple imitation. Use of symbols and number sense. It's a start. God, if you could only talk to me." She tugged on her radio. "Maybe this is enough."

"Enough for what?" crackled a voice.

"Wells here. Is the Captain available yet?"

"Didn't know you wanted to talk to him," said Nixon. "He's a bit groggy—can it wait? Or can I handle it?"

"Not really."

Nixon sighed. "All right. A word of warning—he's been rather humorless since we picked him up."

"Noted."

"Problem, Mandy?" Lanton sounded tired.

"How are you, sir?"

"Skip the pleasantries, please. What's your difficulty?"

"I've been looking into the slac/ /—"

"Good. I presume Nixon told you what I want done."

"He did, sir. I'd like you to reconsider. There are some questions that should be answered first."

"Such as?"

"Such as why they're on the flatlands at all—they did *not* evolve there. Their exact relationship to the Semu—"

"*Cimara* is here to find and contact intelligent life, not write the final text on this planet's ecology," Lanton reminded her. "You can leave some things for those who follow."

"I know. But there are indications that they're intelligent."

"What indications?"

"Number concept, for one thing. And I believe they're trying to contact me—"

"The way they contacted me? Come now, Mandy, you're dragging your feet. Don't you want to give the Semu a chance to devote their energies to growth and development? We gave the k't'p'ch a selective pesticide, and the Mau vaccination. You did excellent work with the killflies on Kranh—how is this different?"

"We missed the slac/ / completely—what else might we have missed? Our planetary survey is suspect—I want to go back and review our procedures. In the meantime, we should hold off on any other contact."

"Contact's already begun, and we don't have the kind of time you seem to be implying. Mandy—don't lose confidence in your work because I don't know how to duck. *I* haven't lost confidence. Just think of the slac/ / as a natural enemy of an intelligent species, and figure out what to do about them. In nine or ten days we'll be on our way home."

"Nine days," she echoed hollowly.

"Yes—sounds attractive, doesn't it? Quon says they're progressing well. Report in at the regular time."

"Captain, I'm standing here looking at a slac/ / who—"

"Good. Find out how to kill it. Lanton out."

Wells looked unhappily at the slac/ /. "We have a problem," she said softly. She stepped toward the creature, and it turned and waddled away. Then with a boost from its powerful legs, the slac/ / launched itself into the air. As it rose, it filled its sails with air and glided downhill, holding an altitude near two meters. Dismayed, Wells watched it go.

At the bottom of the slope, however, it banked and landed, looking expectantly back at Wells. Opening its mouth, it filled the clearing with a modulated trill that said to Wells as clearly as if it had been in English, "Aren't you coming?"

Jubilant, she set off after it. The slac/ / waited until she caught up, then pushed off again to glide alongside her. As it lost momentum, it would near the ground and the powerful legs would lash out again. It was a strange feeling to run within arm's reach of the living glider.

But it was a good strangeness. Her legs were tireless, her breath came easily. She found that she did not even care where they were headed—to share this moment, this place, with it was enough.

Before long, it became clear they were headed for the isolated outcrop of bedrock known to the *Cimara* as the Boil. As they neared it, her escort sent excited cries on ahead. Answers came back in many voices, and when she was finally led into the rock-encircled nest at the base of the Boil, there were fifteen slac/ / waiting. At the sight of her the air became thick with trilling.

Wells walked to the center and sat, to bring her eye level down to theirs. A fuss was being made over her escort, but most were studying her and jostling for a clear view.

Finally one waddled a few steps closer to her.

" *'antroi, kiranchi,*" trilled the slac/ /. The voice was high-pitched and slurred, but intelligible.

Wells was stunned. "*Bantroi,*" she managed to say. "I am Mandy Wells."

"I am (double-whistle, click)," said the slac/ /. " 'andy 'ells—*what are you?*"

"Captain, there's something down here you should see."

"I'm not planning on coming back down. Can't you handle it?"

"It has to do with the slac/ /."

"Pass it to Quon then. I don't need to be involved in the details."

"I'm afraid you do. There isn't going to be any slac/ / control program."

There was a pause. "I think perhaps you'd better come on back up to *Cimara* and explain that."

"I can explain part from here. The rest you have to see. The slac/ / *are* intelligent, Captain—there's no question now."

"That's a conclusion. Give me the data."

"Well—they have language—"

"Many species communicate with sound."

"Captain, some of these creatures speak Semu."

"Mimicry is not unknown, is it?"

Gritting her teeth, Wells continued. "They're socially organized—"

"So are bees. Are they tool-makers? Do they have writing?"

"No. Not that I've seen so far. But—"

"Aren't those the prime determiners? It seems to me as though you're losing both your objectivity and sight of your goal."

"It seems to me that your mind is closed on the subject of slac/ /. Is it guilt over Marisa and Terry, or self-pity?"

"Don't try home psychotherapy on me," Lanton said ominously.

"I'll use anything I can to break through to you. Captain, I'm sorry you were hurt—but so are the slac/ /."

That took Lanton aback. "How do you know?"

"Come down and I'll show you."

"That's out."

"Then you're going to have to deal with me helping the slac/ / while you help the Semu."

"What are you saying?"

"I thought I said it quite plainly."

Lanton's voice was cold. "I don't like threats, especially from my own people. Come up here and present your case. That's all you have to do."

"Captain, remember that we said the Semu weren't surprised by us. We expected them to react to our alienness, to our display of technology—and they didn't. They *couldn't.* Does a cat wonder about electric lights? Is a shark impressed by a submarine? Is a baby awed by sleight-of-hand? The Semu lack the capacity for true intellectual disequilibrium. They didn't and don't understand who we are. But the slac/ / do!"

Lanton frowned. "Meaning what?"

"That we contacted the wrong species."

"That's nonsense."

"No—an educated opinion. And one you can't fairly contest until you see what I've seen—down here."

"Why do you insist I come down?"

Wells's face and sigh showed that she was perturbed. "Captain, I've always said that the true sign of an intelligent species is that when you point, it doesn't look at your finger but at the place to which you're pointing. *You* keep looking at my finger."

There was a pause. "You may be right, at that. All right—I'll come down."

Wells met the gig a kilometer from the nest.

"Stay inside," she said sharply when Nixon started to follow Lanton out of the gig.

"Why?" asked Lanton.

"It makes me uncomfortable to be one against your two."

"*You* make *me* uncomfortable," Lanton said shortly, but waved Nixon back. "Where are they?"

As though cued, three slac/ / burst out of the trees and glided down to settle beside Wells. Lanton shied back at their approach.

"Face of the enemy," he said. "How many times did you practice that entrance?"

Wells ignored the gibe. "The Semu's enemy, yes. But not necessarily ours."

"I realize now why I don't like them. They remind me of the witch's monkeymen from *The Wizard of Oz*. Know it?"

"Science fiction?"

"Old-time flat movie—saw it as a child. Not important. I'm here. You had something to show me?"

"I want to explain about the attack on you first. The one that went after us had lost a vote in conclave and acted on its own. It was one of the first to spot us, and urged we be killed to eliminate the threat."

"What threat?"

"What's my current assignment?" she asked pointedly.

"Um. But he lost the vote."

"The majority voted to 'wait and see'."

Lanton's hand went slowly to the heal-seal on the side of his face. (Double-whistle, click) advanced toward him.

"You are Protector Lanton," it said in Semu.

Startled, Lanton nodded.

"Why do you help your enemy against us?"

"*Our* enemy? The Semu?"

"Do they find your missing?"

"Can *you?*"

"I can take you to the place." (Double-whistle, click) launched himself, and the other slac/ / followed. Wells took a step, but Lanton grasped her arm firmly.

"How do they know?"

"They have the whole flatland under surveillance."

"Or because a predator can find old kills?"

"We'll see," said Wells, pulling free and starting after the slac/ /.

Lanton caught up to her in a few steps. "I don't know what to make of you, you know."

"What about the slac/ /? That's more important."

"I can see they have some intelligence," he said. "But so do most species."

"Not like this," she protested.

"But it's a sliding scale—there's no line that separates intelligent from merely instinctive. One graduates into the other."

"Admitted."

They ran in silence for a moment, then Lanton asked, "So what else have you found out?"

"They originally were highland creatures, capable of something approaching true flight using the updrafts. They're moving here not because they have to, but because they want to. In the highlands almost all their labor is devoted to feeding. In this richer habitat, that won't be true."

"They're conducting a war, then—they don't feed on the Semu."

"Yes. They have scout-soldiers everywhere, working alone but part of an organized web. The Semu are a race in garrison."

"My sympathies are still with the Semu—perhaps even more so now."

"I don't doubt that the Home Worlds would consider them our closest kin. But that's not the point, is it?"

Ahead, the slac/ / had come to a stop and were waiting. "You admit the Semu are intelligent," said Lanton.

"Yes—though I think it's of a lower order."

They reached the slac/ /, and (double-whistle, click) extended a sailstrut toward the ground. "Here."

There were two blackened circles, each a meter across. A few stalks of fast-growing grass poked up through the low mound of ash.

"I don't understand," said Lanton.

"The Semu have a ritual when they kill a slac/ /," Wells explained. "They immolate it."

"So two slac/ / were killed here."

"No." Kneeling, Wells raked her fingers through the ashes and came up with a slender bone. She handed it up to Lanton and continued sifting.

"This looks like a human radius."

"It is." From the ashes she plucked the blackened cylinder of an implant radio. "This is Marisa—or Terry."

"But the rest of the bones—"

"The Semu take souvenirs—trophies."

Lanton stared at her. "The Semu killed them? They thought they were slac/ /?"

"Not thought. They reacted to a particular set of stimuli—the color, diving—and ignored the anomalies."

"They ignored a lot, in that case."

"We've seen the Semu aren't very flexible conceptually."

Lanton turned the bone over in his hands. "But the biotelemetry—we should have seen they were dead. The EEG was normal—only the high temperature—"

Wells shook her head. "The substance Gision Ah used on the arrows was a tranquilizer. I don't think Terry and Marisa were dead until the Semu burned them. Your slac/ / wasn't."

Lanton drew a deep breath, then exhaled. "So little to take back," he said, staring at the ashes. "And now I have a problem, don't I?"

"I hope so, sir."

Lanton toed the ash and said nothing.

"There are *two* intelligent species on Semu, and they're competing for essentially the same niche. The slac/ / have the individual physical and mental advantages, and the Semu are countering with social adaptation."

"And whichever side we come in on, wins," Lanton thought aloud.

"Yes. With all respect, I suggest it's not a choice we have the right to make."

"Is there any chance the slac/ / can be persuaded to return to the highlands?"

"None. They feel as though they have finally discovered a food heaven."

"To leave the Semu alone, then."

"That calls for a moral development neither side has come close to achieving."

"Working with both, then. Your opinion."

"The slac/ / are in a better position to take advantage of the contact. And is creating and juggling a balance of power our role—like we were lords of the planet?"

Lanton did not answer immediately. Instead, he signaled Nixon, instructing him to ferry the gig to them. Switching off, he gazed at the circle of ashes with a troubled expression.

"Captain?" Wells said softly.

Lanton rubbed at his right eye, turning half away. Wells knew he was not thinking of slac/ / and Semu but of his two dead crewmen. Finally he turned back.

"You enjoy complicating my command, don't you?"

"In this case, yes."

"You flirted with insubordination."

"I'm a naturalist first. I thought it worth the risk. Or am I being premature—what are we going to do? Do I need to keep on flirting?"

Lanton smiled ruefully. "Please, stop. There is only one option that makes sense to me. We'll do what any polite human would do when he accidentally comes upon an arguing couple—quietly leave and come back later." The slac/ / scattered suddenly at the approach of the gig. "Would you say they'll have this worked out in, oh, a hundred years?"

Wells smiled back, relieved. "A hundred years ought to be just about right."

HEADLINES BY THE DOZENS (RIGHT IN MY OWN KITCHEN)

If even the smallest, very tiniest one of you—a speck bug, say,
Could somehow get yourself up to Mars,
Or Venus, say; or even the moon would do,
And wiggle your feelers just a little—
Just once up there would be enough—
And be found out doing it,
Oh WOW! how you would throw
The whole Scientific Establishment into such
A tizzy of glad discovery and madding sweet surprise
That it would take a boldface,
Giant lettering such as we right now
Don't even have the ghost of
To shout the headlines and exclaim the clues:
LIFE ON MARS!! VENUS IS VITAL!!! THE MOON HAS BUGS!!!!

But sadly, oh sadly, little exploring guys,
You're here and I don't have
Any way in all the world, that I
Can figure out, to get you,
Even the tiniest teeniest one of you,
Up to Mars or Venus, say;
(Oh, even the moon's too far!) So it's the Black Flag,
I'm sorry. And the Real Kill, I'm sorry.
And also a shot of Raid,
If you don't all leave soon,
Or anyway, pretty soon, and quit
Hopping around, across, and up and down
My eatables as though they all were somewhere
In the Sea of Tranquility and you,
Each and every one, were moon-based
Neil Armstrongs and Buzz Aldrins—headliners
With Collins—sashaying like kangaroos! SORRY . . .

—David R. Bunch

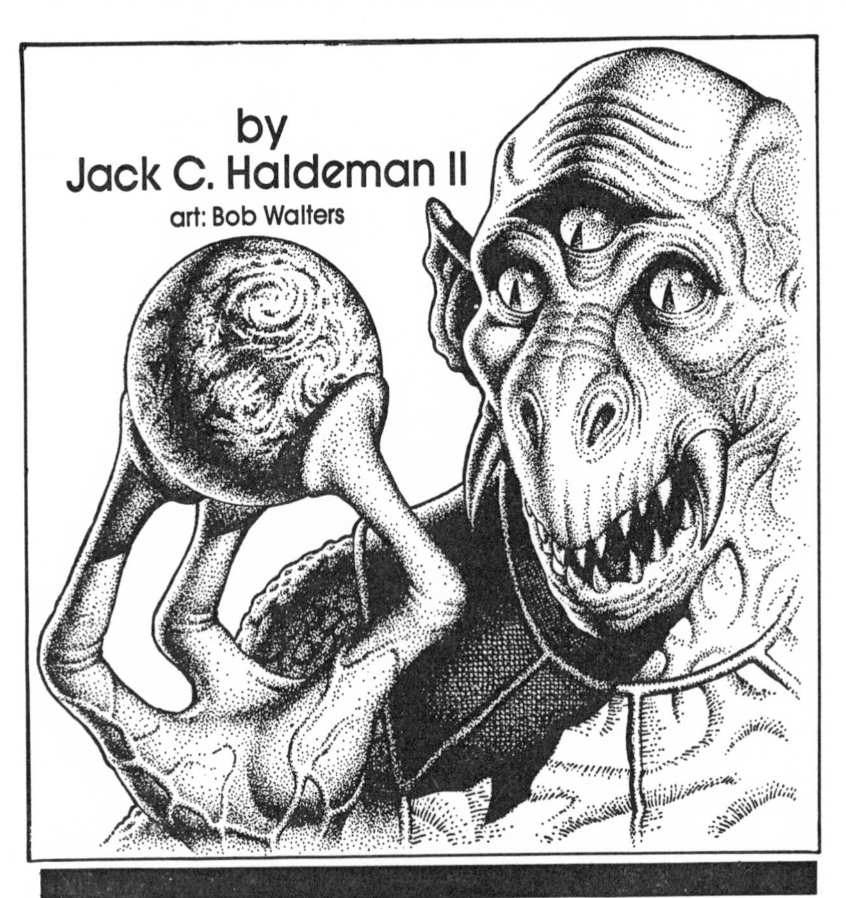

PLAYING FOR KEEPS

Jack Haldeman makes his home in Gainesville, Florida, where he tends his garden and follows the fortunes of the Fighting Gator football team. Between the cucumbers and the touchdowns, he writes science fiction.

Johnny Russell was playing in his backyard when the aliens landed. He was Tarzan in a land of giant ferns while they invaded Philadelphia, but had shifted over to Superman before Baltimore fell. Johnny was eight years old and easily bored. By the time his mother called him in for dinner, the aliens were all over Washington, D.C. Things were a mess. Ugly green monsters were everywhere. Lots of people were real upset, especially Johnny. They were having spinach for dinner.

Johnny hated spinach more than anything else in the world, except maybe brussels sprouts and creamed corn.

He made such a fuss at the table trying to slip the dog his spinach that his parents sent him to bed early. That was too bad, because there was a lot of neat stuff on television that night. Eight years old is just the right age for appreciating a good monster or two. Johnny slept through it all, dreaming that he was flying his tree house over the ocean in search of lost continents.

His parents, on the other hand, were totally immersed in aliens of the real sort. There was no escaping them. Even the 24-hour sports network was full of monsters. Specials followed specials all night long. Bert and Sara stayed glued to the tube, afraid they might miss something. It was an exciting time to watch television, even better than the time the dam burst at Fort Mudge. A good crisis brought out the best in the electronics media, no doubt about that.

They watched the national news for a while and then switched over to the local news. They even tuned in PBS and watched a panel of distinguished professors pointing sticks at an alien's picture. It was exciting. Sara made popcorn and Bert put another six pack of beer in the fridge.

"Don't you think we ought to wake up Johnny?" asked Sara, salting the popcorn.

Bert opened another beer. "No," he said. "We've got to teach him not to play with his food. A parent has certain obligations, you know." Bert had always been the strict one.

"But isn't that a little severe?" asked Sara. "After all, he's very fond of hideous beasts."

"No," said Bert. "Remember what he did with the brussels sprouts?"

Sara turned pale. "I thought I'd never get it all out. The air conditioning hasn't worked right since."

"And the creamed corn?"

Sara shuddered at the memory of the bomb squad marching through their living room in knee-deep water. "You're right," she said, passing him the popcorn.

They settled back and watched the early news, the special news, the update news, the fast-break news, the late news, and the late-late news. In between, they watched the news in brief and the news in detail. They were saturated with news and popcorn and all they got out of it was indigestion and no news at all. Nobody knew much of anything about the aliens except they were crawling all over the place and were meaner than junkyard dogs.

Their silver, cigar-shaped spaceships had simply appeared out of nowhere with a shimmering colorful splash of glitter not unlike the special effects of a once-popular TV show still in reruns. It was horrible. People fled in panic, especially when the monsters started coming out of the spaceships.

The aliens stood about eight feet tall with thick, stocky bodies. Their four arms had too many elbows and not enough fingers. Folds of wrinkled green skin covered their neckless heads, and their three unblinking eyes held what could only be interpreted as malice and contempt for the entire human race.

At first it was hoped that they might be a congenial star-roving race of beings, eager as puppy dogs to give mankind all sorts of marvelous inventions. These hopes were quickly dashed. The aliens seemed far more interested in vaporizing people. Helicopters and airplanes that approached the hovering ships vanished in white-hot explosions. People who were foolish enough to make threatening gestures or stray too close went up in smoke. It made for good television footage, but did little to aid any kind of mutual understanding.

Mutual understanding, as a matter of fact, didn't seem to be the aliens' strong suit. They just didn't appear to be interested. Some of the best minds on Earth had attempted to establish communication with the aliens. Some of the best minds on Earth had been vaporized, too. The aliens were obviously intellegent, but they didn't have much to say.

Bert and Sara were about ready to turn in, having watched the instant replay of the destruction of Washington for the fourth or fifth time. It was impressive, but not really all that great. The Japanese had done it better in that movie about the radioactive frog. Sara washed the popcorn bowls.

"I'll bet Johnny will be excited when he wakes up," she said. "Channel Four said they've even seen a couple aliens right here in town. Imagine that."

"I don't think we ought to tell the boy about them," said Bert. "At least not yet."

"For goodness sakes, honey. Why not?"

"The child has an active enough imagination as it is. There's no sense in getting him all riled up. Remember the time he thought he saw that UFO down by the river?"

Sara nearly dropped the bowl she was drying. That had been a near thing. Johnny had pulled every fire alarm in town, and only their friendship with the judge had kept their names out of the paper.

"Besides," said Bert. "What does a kid know about monsters? He's only eight years old."

Sara nodded. He was right, as always.

But Johnny wasn't completely fooled. When little Freddy Nabors didn't show up by twelve o'clock, he knew something was wrong. He and Freddy *always* messed around together on Saturday afternoon. Sometimes they went on dangerous secret missions, but usually they just played. By twelve-fifteen Johnny had decided a plague must have killed all the kids on Earth but him so he went out into the backyard to play.

He wasn't allowed to go out behind the garage, so naturally it was his favorite place. It was full of old lumber and rusty nails. Lumber was more fun to play with than almost anything. Sometimes he built boats out of the scraps, and sometimes spaceships. Today he built a Grand Prix car. It was low and sleek, faster than a bat. He pretended it was orange with black trim. Since he couldn't find any wheels, he used cinder blocks for racing tires.

Diving into the hairpin turn, he had just passed Fangio and was gaining on Andretti when he saw the monster. Johnny was not impressed. He'd seen better ones on television. Sticking his tongue out between his lips and making a rude noise, he downshifted with a raspberry and pulled to the side of the road. After taking off his imaginary helmet and racing gloves, he got out of his fabricated car and stared at the alien. The alien stared back. Three eyes to two, the alien had an edge; but Johnny never flinched. The Lone Ranger wouldn't have backed down, and neither would he.

In the distance Johnny could see one of their spaceships hovering over the river. It looked just like the one he'd seen before. He knew better than to head for the fire alarms this time, though. His father would tan his hide.

The alien grunted and pointed at his ship and then to himself. Johnny stood as firm as Wyatt Earp, his jaw set like Montgomery Clift's, playing for keeps his body held with the stern proudness of John Wayne. He didn't nod, he didn't blink. He stared at the monster with Paul Newman's baby-blue eyes, hard as ice. He wished he'd worn long pants, though. Shorts just didn't cut it when you were staring down a monster.

The alien started waving all its arms in the air, grunting like crazy. Johnny was frightened, but he didn't give an inch. He could have been Gary Cooper standing alone in the middle of a dusty street facing an angry mob with only the badge on his chest and the goodness in his heart to protect him. Johnny could almost hear the people scurrying for cover. The helmet and racing gloves were useless. He should have had his six-shooter.

The alien kicked at the dust, smoothing out an area between them. He bent over and Johnny hunkered down to join him. At least now he knew what to expect. They were about to talk, or *palaver,* as Slim Pickins would say.

The alien picked up a stick and drew a large circle in the dirt. From a fold in his tunic he removed a small golden globe, which he placed precisely in the center. He pointed to the sun and then to the globe. Johnny nodded, his face as deadpan as if he was trying to fill an inside straight.

The monster drew three concentric circles around the golden globe and placed another globe on the third circle. It was smaller than the first and covered with blue and white swirls. He patted the dirt, waved his arms in circles all around them and pointed to the globe. Johnny bit his lip. This was getting complicated.

The alien continued drawing circles in the dust and setting down the small globes. When he had finished, nine of them surrounded the larger yellow one. With a flourish he took one more from his tunic. This one was special; it was silver and seemed to glow with a light from within. He set it outside the farthest circle and pointed first to himself, then to the spaceship, and finally to the silver sphere.

Slowly he began rolling the sphere into the ring of circles. As he passed the outermost globe, he snarled and crushed it into the dirt beneath one of his massive thumbs. He continued rolling the silver sphere toward the center, snarling and crushing as he demolished each of the small globes. When he reached the third globe from the center, his lips drew back in a hideous sneer and he rose to his full height, towering over the crouching boy. The alien gloated, roaring with bone-chilling laughter as he crushed the small blue globe under his foot, grinding it into the dirt with a vengeance.

This, at last, was something Johnny could understand. It was a challenge. Without rising, he reached around to his back pocket. It was still there, as he knew it would be. He'd won it from Freddy Nabors two years ago and he never went anywhere without it. It was his talisman, his good luck piece. It was also his weapon and had never let him down. He gritted his teeth and took it reassuringly in his hand. It was blue with milky white bands, a perfect agate.

He dropped and took quick aim, oblivious to the ranting and raving of the alien. He'd been under pressure before, this was nothing new. With a flick of his thumb the aggie sailed across the dust, crashing into the silver ball, sending it careening out of orbit into the yellow one. They both flew outside the circle.

He stood—as a man would stand after battle—and retrieved all the marbles. He held them high above his head.

"Keepsies," he said and slipped them into his pocket.

The alien backed away in horror, babbling wildly. With a shimmer and a pop, he disappeared. An instant later the spaceship vanished in a similar fashion, as did all the spaceships and all the aliens all over the world.

Johnny climbed back into his Grand Prix car and accelerated through the gears. He was nearly a lap behind by now and would have to do some fancy driving to catch up. Besides, his mother was fixing creamed corn tonight, and the boy who had saved the world had important things on his mind.

As he took the checkered flag he wondered how Conan would have handled creamed corn.

COURSING

by Barry N. Malzberg

art: Jack Gaughan

Mr. Malzberg recently
played violin in a concert
of SF writer Somtow Sucharitkul's music,
conducted by the composer...
which really has nothing to do
with this strange story,
but does go to show
that SF writers are
a versatile lot indeed....

There was this woman and her name was Maria. She lived in a console of the great ship *Broadway* and whispered to Hawkins in the night, promises of love and fealty, warmth and connection. Hawkins could not touch her, could not consummate the promise because she was a simulacrum, a collection of electrons and impulses in the bottle but she made dark periods lively indeed and they had promised that at the end of the voyage, if Hawkins were to do what he was meant to, she would be waiting for him, the real Maria; and she would make all these things true. Hawkins did not really believe this, did not believe any of it but the light years were vast, the ship was vacant and full of the stink of antiseptic, and if he were not able to converse with Maria there would have been nothing at all. So he thanked them in his heart for their time and trouble, their cruelty and their manipulativeness, and let it go by. He let everything go by. The twenty-fourth century was all accommodation.

Hawkins, a felon interred on Titan, had been given a conditional release to go to the Pleiades System and negotiate with the King of the Universe. The King of the Universe, through pulsar, had advised the inner clusters that he would destroy them greatly unless every knee bent and every tongue did give homage. The King of the Universe might have been insane, but very little was known of the Pleiades Cluster and it was assumed that any culture with technology advanced enough to make possible this kind of communication could not be dismissed out of hand. *Half* a hand yes—send them a felon to do the negotiating—but the last time an alien threat had been entirely ignored brought about the Slaughtering Hutch of a hundred years. The King might have been a child given access to powerful communications *matériel* or a lunatic acting out for therapy; on the other hand he might be exactly what he said, in which case the inner clusters had a problem. Hawkins, a failure, was half a hedge against riot. Keep a civil tongue, the Advisors had said, evaluate the situation, and try to buy him off; if he refuses to negotiate or turns out to be what he seems then you know where the self-destructs are. Try to get near enough to take the King down. There's enough armament on the *Broadway* to take down the Pleiades themselves. And have a good time; after all, the Advisors concluded, that's what it's all about, isn't it? Thirty-three Earth days is nothing for a man who has done half a lifetime; think of it as front-loading.

Hawkins lay in the ship's abcess, just inside the probes, and said to Maria, "This isn't going to work. They'll wipe me out as errata; we're an unidentified flying object."

"I love you," Maria said softly; "I want to hold you against me.

You are the gentlest and most wonderful man that I have ever known and I want you to be mine, all mine."

"I have to get serious," Hawkins said; "there's no time for passion here."

"Don't put me off, you dark fool," Maria said. "Closer and closer. Touching in the night. You will pacify the King and return; we will meet on Ganymede and in the silence and the density we will hold one another. Oh, if we had only met earlier; none of this would ever have happened to you."

Hawkins said, "I don't want to think about what it would have been like if we had met earlier. I don't want to talk about that now." He reached for the volume switch and lowered Maria's voice to a soothing burble. For reasons which were quite sufficient the technicians had made it impossible for him to cut off Maria completely, but he was able at least to modulate; this made it possible for him to find some periods of sleep. In the intricate alleys of metal and wire he could still hear her voice, extract the shape of words. *Lover. Apposite. Breasts.* Hawkins felt a regret which verged on pity, but he urged himself to be strong. He could not listen to her now. He was scheduled for a confrontation with the King of the Universe shortly. The King had scheduled it all. Hawkins would be brought before him in the dock of an artificial satellite and explain his condition, offer his terms. The King had stated that he had not been surprised; he knew that it would only be a matter of time until the Inner Cluster sued for mercy. The *Broadway* had been tracked all the way with farsighted devices, had been under the King's mighty surveillance since it had torn free of the sun outside the orbit of Jupiter.

Hawkins huddled in the ship and awaited judgement. He thought of all the alleys and corridors of his life which, like the alleys and corridors of the ship, seemed to work endlessly and musically against one another, bringing him to this tight and difficult center. If he had done this then he might not, instead, have done that; if he had served his time penitentially rather than with defiance they might have sought someone else to deal with the King. But then again defiance was good because they needed a man who would take a position and most felons got broken within the early months of their confinement. Then too there was Maria who had been given to inflame and console but with whom, instead, he had fallen into a difficult kind of love. It was not her corporeality but the electron impulses themselves, the cleverness and sophistication of the device, which had hooked him in. Someday, if he lived through this, he would try to explain it all to the technicians. He doubted if they would listen; creating their wonderful devices they had come only to hate themselves because they could not be part of them. If the twenty-fourth century was for accommodation, then it was also for paradox. It was a paradoxical age. The *Broadway* veered and the grey abcesses colored to flame; the King of the Universe materialized before him in holographic outline. "I thought this would be easier," the King said. "Of course I am at a good distance from this image so don't think of anything foolish."

Hawkins was thinking of nothing foolish, concentrating instead upon the holograph. The King was a wondrous creature; the form was avian but like no bird that Hawkins had ever seen, and the beak was set of fierce design. The King half-turned, seemed to preen, displayed feathers. "Do you like this?" he said. "I wanted an imposing design in which to appear."

"Then this isn't how you look?"

"This is *exactly* how I look," the King said, "and this is no time for conundrums. Can you give me any reason why I should not sack and destroy the Inner Cluster?"

"I have brought priceless gems," Hawkins said; "if you sack and destroy there will be none of them left. Also, as a creature of some sensitivity you would not want to destroy ten trillion sentient and vulnerable souls, would you?"

The King winked. "You don't believe me," he said, "you think that only a lunatic would address you over the light years, threaten destruction, call himself the King of the Universe."

"On the contrary," Hawkins said, "we take you very seriously or why would I be here?"

"I can't answer that," the King said, "I merely run things, not try to account for them; and I must tell you that I am sore displeased. I think I'll appropriate your gems and dematerialize you."

"Don't do it so quickly," Hawkins said. It was impossible for him to tell whether the King was serious or capable of such action, but the entire mission had been predicated on the fact that he might be, and his own condition was humbling. "Don't do it," he said again, pleadingly. "We're not without a history. There are elements of our tradition which are honorable. If not science, art; if not art a certain damaged religiosity." *Why am I defending us?* he thought; this was the civilization, those were the technicians who first imprisoned me and then sent me out with the simulacrum of a woman to tantalize and to die. Truly, the situation is indefensible. Perceiving this, knowing that his thoughts were moving toward hopelessness and failure, Hawkins reached out and moved the volume switch. "Tell him," he said. "Tell him the things that you tell me, Maria."

"He is a good man," Maria said, "I love him desperately. We talk in the night; he tells me many things. When he returns to Titan I will dwell with him in holiness and fealty forever."

The King fluttered. "Who are you?" he said.

"My name is Maria and I am the lover of this man, Hawkins. He is a good man."

"Where are you?"

"I walk on this ship and to and fro upon it. Where are you?"

The King said, "That is not the issue." His speech had slurred; he seemed to have lost that edge of high confidence with which he had threatened destruction. "Show me yourself."

"That is not necessary," Maria said, "I am faithful to this one man."

"Abandon him," the King said, "and come to me instead. Perhaps we can work out something."

"I won't do that."

"Maybe something can be worked out," Hawkins said carefully. "It isn't absolutely necessary—"

"Offer him the diamonds, but don't offer him me."

"I don't want the diamonds," the King said. He sounded petulant. "I can have the diamonds *anyway*."

She is a simulacrum, Hawkins thought, a memory, an instance, unpurchasable. But instead he said, "If you return with me to the Inner Cluster you can have her."

"Why return? I want her *here*."

"Love is impossible in space," Hawkins said quietly. "The eternal vacuum, the interposition of organism upon the void makes love impossible. Accept my assurances on that."

"I cannot return with you," the King said after some silence, "I would burn in the vastnesses of space. I am unprepared for a journey of any sort, confined to my castle. Leave her here."

"I'm afraid not," Hawkins said. "She would perish."

"Yes, I would perish," Maria said coldly. "I would most surely perish, Hawkins, if I could not have you. I am not property; I am your lover, I cannot be treated in this fashion."

"You can be treated in any way I want," Hawkins said. "Remember the conditions. You were delivered to give me solace, not argument. Nonetheless," he said to the King, "as you see it is quite impossible."

"Nothing is impossible," the bird said, "not to the King of the Universe," and the bird turned, opened both impenetrable eyes and clawed at the floor. "That is my demand," he said, "leave her here and the diamonds, and you may go. The Inner Cluster will be spared.

Take the diamonds, in fact. I don't need them."

Hawkins said, "For the greater good, Maria, for all circumstance, I ask you—"

"I love *you,*" the simulacrum said. "I know that I was made part of the equipment merely to convenience, to give you solace, but I'm quite out of control and it's you I love. I don't want to deal with any bird."

"I'm not really a bird," the King said, "this is merely a form which I project. Actually I can be anything at all. You would be most pleasantly surprised."

"Appearances mean nothing to me," Maria said, "I'm sorry but it's quite impossible. This wasn't how the situation was supposed to be, but it's how matters have turned out, I'm afraid. No, Hawkins, I will not yield."

"Then neither will I," the King said, "I am not a paranoid Pleiadan but the true and invincible King of the Universe, and I will make good on my threats. I tracked you from Jovian orbit, Hawkins; I had hoped that it would be for better outcome."

Hawkins looked at the figure of the bird, the eyes and figures glinting in the tight spaces of the cabin; he listened to the continued murmuring of Maria, now plaintive as she explained why she could not leave him. Hawkins looked at one simulacra and listened to the other as the *Broadway* ebbed and dipped in station, thinking I am man, I am twenty-fourth-century man, era of accommodation and paradox, felon of the twelfth order; you are in a Hell of a spot now. A Hell of a spot for she cares.

But he wasn't. He really wasn't, after all. As he heard Maria begin to shriek in passion, as he heard her say *oh King o King o King* he came to understand that for some dilemmas there is, after all, resolution; if not flesh, then steel is all. *Oh Kingokingoking* Maria cried, and as the *Broadway* grandly broke stasis he began to see the light of eternity open up to him. *He's wonderful!* Maria cried, *OKing!*

There was this woman and her name was Maria; she loved Hawkins, she said, and first refused the impossible embraces of a mad Pleiadan but there was a grander design and she saw it saw it saw it *okingoking*.

Hawkins felt the tumble of paradox.

Just before the blankness he mumbled, *faithless bitch.*

O flawless faithless one.

CONVERSION

by Bob Shaw

art: Stephen Fabian

The author has written an array of suspensful, well-crafted novels, including *Orbitsville*; *Other Days, Other Eyes*; *Vertigo*; *One Million Tomorrows*; *Nightwalk*; *Who Goes Here?*; *A Wreath of Stars*; and *The Two-Timers*. He is also famed for his short story "Light of Other Days," which introduced the concept of "slow glass." Mr. Shaw is a splendid toastmaster and speaker at (mostly British) SF conventions, and one of the most celebrated fan-writers of all time.

When you love a woman you can forgive her for doing almost anything—but there has to be a limit.

And Sharly went way beyond that limit at 3:17 on the afternoon of June 12.

I know the exact moment it happened because the whole thing was recorded, though at a distance, by Arnie Archbold. He was making his scheduled round of Level Eight, pacing himself to be close to the coffee machine when it came to break time, and was so wrapped up in visions of burying his nose in a hot foaming beaker that at first he wasn't even aware of Sharly on the gallery above him. His recorder picked her out, though.

All members of Icewell Security, myself included, wear wide-angle buttonhole machines which serve roughly the same purpose as flight recorders on aircraft—if one of us gets himself totalled the investigation team can run a tape through afterwards and settle back in comfort and decide what went wrong. To be fair, the recorders often provide valuable retrospective evidence concerning accidents and equipment failures, and I guess I should have been grateful that there was no doubt, none whatsoever, about what Sharly did. I was off the island on a five-day course at the time it happened, but the tape showed everything. . . .

She came out of the Field Analysis suite on Level Nine and walked slowly in the direction of Structure Telemetry on the south side of the well. Nothing in her gait or manner suggested she was under any kind of stress. That was something to which I could testify because we had been lovers for some months; and, although she was wearing a loose-fitting heatsaver, I could visualise the fine lazy action of every muscle in her body. She even, and it hurt me every time I watched it on playback, performed one of her most characteristic tricks with her hair—pushing the curls upwards slightly from the nape of her neck with one hand as though they were little springs upon which she was carrying out a compression test. I had seen Sharly do that a hundred times in reality, always when she was relaxed and pleased with herself and feeling good about life, and that made what came next all the more shocking.

About ten paces from the door to Structure Telemetry she came to an abrupt halt and clapped her hands to her temples. She rocked backwards and forwards for a few seconds, then turned towards the centre of the well. The blow-ups from Archbold's tape gave us a good look at her face in that crucial moment, and I pray never again to see anything so close to "The Scream." Her eyes and mouth were circular black wounds, deep, incurable. She advanced to the gallery's safety rail, went up the four bars as though they were steps of a ladder, and walked off the top one into space.

Cold, empty, unforgiving, lethal space.

The sudden movement attracted Archbold's attention and dragged him around, with the result that all who studied his recorder tape got a clear view of Sharly's body plunging down into the well. There were lights down there, but they only had the effect of deepening the blackness in between, and her writhing figure disappeared into a complicated nether world of pipe runs, valves, ice bulwarks and pools of oil and oil-scummed seawater. She made no sound on the way down and the final impact was lost amid the massive heartbeats of the primary pump.

That's all there was to it.

Charlotte Railton had been part of the world scene as a warm, intelligent, humorous person for twenty-six years, and suddenly—for no reason that I could fathom—she was gone. They didn't even manage to find her remains. The investigators who arrived next day by copter concluded that the body had been drawn into one of the main drainage outlets and expelled into the sea. They only stayed a day-and-a-half before heading back to Port Heiden, and I received a distinct impression that if Sharly hadn't been a Grade One Engineer they would have taken off much sooner.

I resented that a lot. In fact, resentment was the driving force that got me through the following weeks. I felt other emotions, of course—grief, despair, anger, self-pity—but I was able to keep them in check by concentrating on my sense of outrage over all that had happened. One playback of Archbold's tape was enough to satisfy everybody concerned that they were dealing with a straightforward suicide, and from that point on the case was virtually closed. My testimony that Sharly had not been a suicidal type and had, in any case, been in excellent spirits immediately prior to her death was politely noted and dismissed as not being relevant. The evidence of the tape was all that mattered, and even I had to acknowledge it.

That was what helped crystallise my resentment against Sharly herself. Widows and widowers often feel anger—even though it is rarely expressed—towards their departed spouses for having spoiled everything by dying, and I came to know exactly what goes on in their minds. At times I actually hated Sharly for the pain she had caused me, then a reaction would set in and guilt would be added to all my other emotional burdens, and to help me squeeze out from under I would get out of bed, put on my uniform, sling the carbine on my shoulder and go patrolling the chill dark reaches of Icewell 37. I don't know what I was hoping to find. I wanted to blame *something* for Sharly's death, but the rational part of my mind told me there was no chance of encountering a convenient and suitable external agent. There was no malign ghost of Level Nine, and even had there been it was unlikely that it could have been exorcised by a spray of high-velocity bullets.

The well is a creepy and fear-making place, though, especially at night. It is an artificial island constructed from ice, and it's hard for a non-scientist like me to accept that the localised coldness which makes it possible is imported from interstellar space.

Sharly knew as much about the telecongruency warp as anybody and she used to waste hours trying to make me understand how the focal point of the warp generator actually existed in two places at once—one of them here in the middle of the Bering Sea and the other at some unknown location between the stars where the temperature was close to absolute zero. The position of the alpha-locus, the Earth-based focal point, could be accurately controlled; and it was automatically drifted all over the island to keep the ice structure hard and strong, but nobody had any idea of the spatial location of the zeta-locus. Apparently it could have been just about anywhere in the Universe. I never really got used to the idea of dangling a kind of cosmic fishing line in a distant part of space, but the notion held no fears for Sharly. It buoyed her up.

"This is only the beginning," she had assured me once. "The telecongruency warp is a powerful tool, but right now we're only debasing it. Using it as a heat sink to create ice castles in the ocean is easily the cheapest and best way yet of building deep-sea oil wells, but that's only playing with the concept. What we have to do is gain *control*. We ought to be able to reverse the potentials, make it a two-way thing. We should be able to pinpoint the zeta-locus anywhere we want it—and when that happens we'll be able to grow food or gather diamonds or pick flowers on any planet in the Galaxy."

When she talked that way I used to get jealous because the disks of misty white light appearing in her eyes were exactly the same as when we were making love and it was going well, but I had sense enough to keep my mouth shut about how I felt. Most people were surprised over a woman of her background taking up with a sergeant in Icewell Security, and as I couldn't quite believe it myself sometimes I knew not to strain my luck. And in the end it was Sharly's luck that ran out, not mine. She would never have the chance to pick those alien blossoms, and I desperately wanted to know why.

I even, and this shows how obsessive my thinking became, considered murder. Post-hypnotic suggestion was one method I dreamed up—it seemed to me that somebody could have implanted a command for Sharly to walk off that gallery railing. Then there were exotic drugs which could suddenly trigger a self-destructive urge, and sonic beams which might scramble the brain and produce instant madness. Far-out ideas like those clamoured through my mind for hours on end, accompanied by equally bizarre notions about possible motives, so I was in a pretty abnormal psychological state during those nights when I was up there prowling on the high levels with the carbine nudging me in the back like a secretive accomplice. And I guess that's why I sensed there was something badly wrong as soon as Lieutenant Oliver came through on my personal radio.

"Sergeant Hillman," he said in an irritated voice when I had identified myself and reported my position, "what are you *doing* there? According to the roster, you went off duty six hours ago."

"I know that, sir, but I couldn't sleep tonight," I told him, raising my wrist set to my mouth. "I decided to do an extra shift."

"You decided to . . ." Oliver sounded incredulous now, as well as irritated. Obviously the idea of a man choosing to walk the galleries at three in the morning when he could have been wrapped up warm in bed was hard for him to ingest. "Did you, by any chance, arrange to do Sergeant Dresch a favour and take over his shift for him?"

"No, sir."

"Then why can't I raise Dresch or anybody else in the duty room?"

"Don't know, sir. He was there okay less than an hour ago when . . ." I stopped speaking as it dawned on me that it had been quite a long time since I had heard the elevator shuttling between any of the lower levels. Maddern and Katzen were the two men assigned to do the inspection rounds that night, and neither was the type to use the stairs when there was any other option. I went to the rail and looked down into the well. The galleries below formed concentric circles, all of them beaded with lamps, surrounding the dimly-seen shapes of the wellhead equipment. A freezing mist drifted over everything, giving the most distant lamps the appearance of illuminated balls of lime-coloured candy floss. The primary pump was beating steadily down there, transferring oil to the outer tanks; and I could hear the faint sound of ocean waves coming through the ice walls, but there was no sign of any human activity. There was no waving of flashlights or bellowing of supposed witticisms—two favourite pursuits of men on night inspection.

I eased the sling of the carbine off my shoulder and raised my eyes to scan the one gallery remaining above me. Saboteurs often came in over the top when they were mounting an all-out showpiece attack on a well, but I could see nothing up there apart from a circle of unblinking lights and a few stars barely piercing the greenish haze. Not comforted, I allowed the rifle to slide into my right hand.

"What are you doing, Sergeant? Are you still there?" Oliver was calling from Field Control, more than half a kilometre away at the opposite end of the island, and he was sounding increasingly annoyed. He didn't seem unduly alarmed at that stage, but I was the one who had been living on nerves for three weeks. I was the one who was keyed up to see spectres of death in every swirl of mist.

"I've been looking around," I said, keeping my voice low. "It all seems quiet."

"It *is* quiet—that's what this is all about. See if you can raise Dresch on your ops band."

I pressed the priority call button on my wrist set and got no reply. "He isn't answering."

"*Damn!* You'd better get yourself down to the duty room and see what he's playing at. Tell him to contact me immediately. And Hillman?"

"Yes, sir?"

"Tell him he'd better have one hell of a good excuse for this."

"Right!" I spoke crisply to conceal my deep uneasiness about the situation. The fact that it was three in the morning had something to do with it—three in the morning was a bad time, specially for somebody in my frame of mind—but, also, it was not beyond the bounds of possibility that Icewell 37 was under some form of attack. A mental scenario unfolded before me. International terrorist group . . . approach by submersible . . . take out guards by knife, silenced gun or gas . . . plant bombs . . . I could walk into anything down there, anything at all.

Even the thing that killed Sharly Railton.

The thought heaved itself into the full light of my consciousness like some leviathan breaking the surface of a prehistoric swamp, bringing about an instantaneous and profound change in my outlook. It happens that way sometimes. You can be alone in spooky circumstances, alone but perfectly at ease, then a change takes place. Not in your surroundings, but inside you. An unseen hand is laid on your shoulder and an unheard voice whispers a few words of warning, and suddenly you're scared. And what makes it even more terrifying is that the silent voice is the voice of a friend. It is rueful, reproachful, concerned. Not only had you let your guard down, you had forgotten why we all need a guard in the first place—and that was oh so foolish. . . .

"This is crazy," I said, half-aloud, my gaze travelling on a circuit of Level Nine. The regularly spaced lights reflected off the backdrop of ice and from the prefabricated huts that housed an auxiliary power unit and some structural telemetry equipment. I knew that both huts were securely locked, and I had just come down from a tour of Level Ten, so the next logical step was to check out the gallery below and gradually work down to the duty room on Level Three. The elevator was only a short distance away, but it was a noisy, open-cage affair—a good way of advertising my exact movements to all and sundry.

I bolted a cartridge into the breech of the rifle, slipped the safety off and walked quietly to the nearest stair. The tower-like structure of the stairwell vibrated underfoot, and I cursed as I imagined it broadcasting messages about my position. I went down the four zigzagging flights that took me to Level Eight, then did a cautious circuit of the entire gallery. Everything was as it should have been, and it was the same story on Level Seven and the two below that. Icewell 37 appeared to be running itself with its usual efficiency and there was no real need for human beings to fuss around the place at all—which was the principal reason for the rather hefty consumption of strong liquor on the night shift.

Now that I thought of it, Bert Dresch had been somewhat red of face and pink of eye when I saw him an hour earlier. It was possible that he was out cold in the office—it had happened before—and that Maddern, Katzen and the others were labouring to get him fit enough to answer his calls. The idea perked me up considerably and

I was in a more relaxed mood when I began the circuit of Level Four. I even considered leaning over the rail and bellowing a few choice obscenities in the general direction of the duty room, which was basically a square hole cut into the ice on a level with the gallery below.

That was when I began to find small pieces of Dave Maddern.

I didn't even know what they were at first.

I was about a third of the way around Level Four when I saw that the metal floor of the gallery was badly cluttered up for a distance of about ten paces, as if somebody had spilled a couple of sacks of coal and had just let the pieces lie. Drawing closer, I saw that the fragments were deep red in colour, although it was difficult to be too certain in the artificial light. I disturbed several of them with my feet and found they were as hard as glass, and my next thought was that there had been an accident with some deep-frozen melons. Then I began to notice the whiteness of bone and a few seconds later saw three-quarters of Dave's face lying on the metal deck, like a discarded fright mask.

The shock seemed to clear my perceptions, for in that instant I became aware of other kinds of fragments lying around. There were irregular pieces of clothing—not with ragged edges, but as cleanly snapped as candy. There even were pieces of Dave's carbine, his helmet and his boots mingling with the glittering, dark-hued shards of what had been his flesh and internal organs.

"Oh, man," I whispered. "Oh, *man!*"

At that point I guess I should have radioed for some kind of back-up, and now I can't even remember for sure why I didn't. It may have been that my brain had been jarred loose by the nastiest shock of my life. Suddenly fastidious about what my feet might accidentally touch, I tip-toed through the human debris, going faster and faster until I reached the uncontaminated part of the gallery at a near-run. The only conventional way of utterly destroying a man, as Dave Maddern had been destroyed, would have been to immerse him in a vat of liquid oxygen and then go to work on the frozen body with a sledge hammer—but there was another possibility.

All icewell personnel were assured that it was impossible for the alpha-locus to wander from its prescribed path. A computer and triplex controls kept it moving in a regular and pre-ordained pattern through the island, continuously reinforcing the ice structure with the unthinkable coldness of space—but since when had men been able to build perfect machines? What if accidents sometimes did happen? We were busy sucking the last drops of oil from the Earth's crust, using new techniques that had been born of a desperate need; and no government in the world would draw back on account of a few operational mishaps. It would be perfectly natural to conceal the fact that every now and then there was a glitch in the telecongruency warp system, that every now and then the controls wavered and sent an invisible killer cruising through icewell living quarters. That bleak focus of interstellar cold would only have to brush through a man once to turn him into a crystalline statue.

I wasn't thinking as clearly as that while I ran for the stair that led down to the duty room. Shock, revulsion, and fear had numbed my brain to the extent that I could scarcely nail down a coherent thought; and to make matters worse silent voices were screaming at me, hurling confused questions. *Is this what you've been looking for? What have you really explained about Dave Maddern? Was Sharly, in some way that you don't yet understand, driven over that rail? All right, you've frozen Maddern to death—but who or what broke him up like so much peanut brittle? And why?*

I clattered down on to Level Three and sprinted a short distance along the gallery to the bright rectangle of the duty room window, but slid to a halt just before reaching it, all instincts of self-preservation newly alerted.

The place was *cold.*

Icewells, by their very nature, are chilly places; and our part of the world never warmed up, even in the middle of summer, but this was a different sort of coldness. It was hostile, totally inimical, far more so than the polar wind, and I sensed—even before looking into the room—that it was a bad omen.

Perhaps there had been three men in the room, perhaps as many as half-a-dozen. I wasn't able to say for sure, because the entire floor area was covered with a gruesome organic rubble, the redness of which was slowly beginning to disappear under a coating of rime frost. The furniture in the room was quite untouched, but its occupants had been pulverized, degraded, robbed of every last vestige of their humanity. Had it not been for the previous experience with Maddern I wouldn't even have recognised them for what they were.

And, reacting according to a classic human pattern, I had two virtually simultaneous thoughts: *Thank God that didn't happen to me;* and, *How can I make sure it doesn't ever happen to me?*

There was no room behind my eyes for anything but those two linked expressions of self-interest. I turned towards the elevator, determined to ride it up to Level Ten and the starlit surface of the island; and it was then that I saw the thing with many legs.

It was huge—easily the size of a car—black and nightmarish; and it was rushing towards me with hideous, soul-withering speed. There was no time to think, only to react, and so I did the most natural thing in the world.

I grabbed the gallery rail and vaulted over it into space.

For a second or so I fully expected to die—just as Sharly had done—but the remarkable thing was that I didn't mind. I had avoided being taken by the black obscenity, and in that first airborne instant nothing else mattered—then I hit a large-diameter pipe and caromed off it into a latticed stanchion with a force that came near to breaking my ribs. My carbine flailed away into the dimness as I tried to throw my arms around the stanchion, but I had gained too much impetus for that to work and I continued falling, slithering, bouncing, impacting with steel, with lagged pipes, and finally with sloping buttresses of ice. Seemingly a long, long time after clearing the rail at Level Three, I found myself lying on my side in a shallow pool of water. The surface below me was cold soft mud, and I knew I was almost right down on the seabed. All the complex structures and machinery associated with the wellhead towered up somewhere above me in a spatial confusion of shadows and areas of wan, misty light.

I lay without moving for an indeterminate period, not so much recovering from the fall as trying to construct a new version of reality in which there was a place for the horror I had glimpsed before jumping. I have been told many times since that I didn't actually see anything on Level Three. The theory is that human beings are naturally programmed, that we are incapable of perceiving any phenomenon which lies beyond the in-built limitations of our world-picture. I had faced a manifestation which inspired me with the ultimate dread, and I therefore had endowed it with the attributes of dread, which in my case happened to be a multiplicity of legs. All that might account for my impression that the thing, although black in colour, was transparent to some degree, like a badly done special effect in a movie; but I'm not sure if I really can accept all that stuff about the limits of perception. The people who are so positive about it have no idea what it was like to be there at the time, and I *knew* I had seen something big and black and with a lot of legs.

The trouble was that I wasn't certain of anything else. A kind of detachment had stolen over me as I lay there in the bilges of the icewell—waiting for my breath to return and for my body to give some evidence, one way or the other, about its general condition—and I was able to think more rationally than one might have expected. But I couldn't fit the pieces together. A number of my friends had died in a particularly horrendous manner, but to me the cause had seemed highly technical—I had predicted something like an intermittent fault in a computerized control system—and what had showed up was the worst possible embodiment of ancient nightmares and superstitions. Coincidence? Not likely. Impossible was more like it, but what sort of creature could or would turn its victims into ice and crunch them into a bloody slush? And where in God's name had it come from? There had to be something missing somewhere, a connection I had failed to make.

Still numb with sensory overload, I raised myself to a sitting position and tried to make a decision about what to do next. I wanted to get away from the well and reach Field Control at the other end of the island, and there were only two possible routes—through the service tunnel at Level Nine or along the surface from Level Ten. Both alternatives involved passing through the region of the well where the black thing stalked the galleries, and I had a powerful aversion to doing that. I put my wrist set to my mouth and tried calling up Lieutenant Oliver. There was no reply. Either the radio was broken, or the nightmare creature had roved further afield.

Perhaps I was the only person left alive on the entire island. . . .

Repressing violent spasms of shivering, I looked around in the cavernous dimness and tried to establish exactly where I was. Faint reflections marked numerous dark pools, and there was no way of telling which might be drain tunnels through which waste liquids were pressure-pumped into the sea. This part of the well was a Stygian no-man's land, visited very infrequently by maintenance inspectors, and to get out of it I would have to locate a ladder and climb it to the first gallery. I decided the most likely place would be near the automatic pumping station which was steadily pounding somewhere off to my left, rippling the reflected lights.

Turning in that direction, I lurched to my feet and immediately became aware of a pale object a few paces away. My eyes still hadn't adjusted properly to the darkness, but the object seemed to have human proportions. It was slumped against a discarded wooden box in much the same attitude as a rag doll would have assumed. I stared at it, trying not to cringe, as a terrible idea wormed into my mind followed by an equally terrible dawning of recognition.

Sharly!

I had found Sharly's body.

Extraordinary situations, I have learned, elicit extraordinary human responses. I was already far too shocked by what had been happening to react to the ghastly discovery in a normal manner—instead I felt a pang of rage, resentment, and hatred towards the so-called investigators from Icewell Exec who had been so careless, so anxious to get back to their warm offices on the mainland that they had allowed a thing like this to happen. Had they done their job properly, Sharly would have been found three weeks earlier and given a decent burial. She wouldn't have been left to bloat and rot down here in the oil well's stinking black sump.

I think it was with some notion of determining the full extent of the investigators' crime that I approached Sharly's body and knelt down before it. My gaze hunted over the human wreckage, recording the sickening distortions of the broken legs, the multiple seepages of blood through her clothing, the lacerations which had disfigured that beautiful face. . . .

Oddly though, *very* oddly, Sharly's head was upright, not touching the wooden box, apparently supported by a firm neck.

Stricken, bemused by new visions of horror, I slowly put out my hand and touched her cheek. The blackly contused eyelids snapped open.

"Hello, Jack," she burbled. "I've been waiting for you."

I screamed. Throwing myself backwards from her, I screamed as only a person who has been totally betrayed by reality knows how. There are some things that simply never should happen to a person, and one of them had happened to me and my entire being protested about it until the moment when screaming was no longer enough. Eventually I had to look at Sharly again and try to cope with the situation.

"Don't be afraid of me, Jack," she said in a voice which seemed to force its way through a larynx filled with water. "I can't harm you."

"You . . . are . . . dead," I accused, raising myself to a sprinter's crouch in readiness for the flight which might become necessary at any second.

She smiled, and to this day I wish she hadn't. "How can I be dead if I'm talking to you? Come on, Jack—take me out of here." She extended her arms, begging for my help.

For a moment I wavered. I *wanted* Sharly to be miraculously alive, and I was in no condition to think rationally. Perhaps she had survived the fall—just as I had done. Perhaps she had somehow managed to cling on to life down here in spite of her awful injuries and the cold and the wet. Then I noticed that the effort of speaking, of expelling air, had caused black fluids to spill down her chin. I backed off a little further, shaking my head.

She must have been able to interpret the reaction because she lowered her arms and the ghastly caricature of a smile left her face. "I wanted to die," she said. "I tried to die, but it was of no use. I may have to live a very long time . . . but I don't want it to be down here, Jack . . not like this. You've got to help me."

"I . . . I don't understand." That was true—and most of all I couldn't understand what was keeping me from running. Perhaps it was just that my mind had reached its saturation point as far as horror and fear were concerned, enabling me to hold my ground and carry on something like a normal conversation.

"Perhaps you understand better than you realize. . . ." Her throaty, bubbling voice was almost lost in the sound of the primary pump. "I was supposed to be the great warp engineer, but your instincts were better than mine, Jack. You said it was like . . . dangling a fishing line in a distant part of the universe. I laughed at that because I knew how empty space actually is . . . but we caught something . . . then it caught me."

I nodded because it seemed the only thing to do. A black multi-legged nightmare was roaming the icewell above me, presumably in search of new victims, and I was crouched in the throbbing darkness at the bottom of the well beside the undead corpse of the woman I had loved. And all I could do was nod my head.

"Zeta-locii are highly visible objects as they drift about the Galaxy . . . to certain kinds of senses, that is . . . I was being pursued . . . wrong word—a virus does not pursue its host . . . tried to escape through the zeta-locus, but found I was trapped . . . chose the most suitable instrument of change, but there was resistance. . . ."

The hissing beat of the pump was obliterating many words, words whose import was totally bizarre, but I was oddly—almost telepathically—in tune with what was being said to me. My understanding was only partial, but it came quickly because I was preconditioned. I had believed all along that Sharly's was not an ordinary suicide. She had been possessed by a disembodied life form that the icewell's warp had somehow dredged from out of space, and rather than submit to it she had walked off the top rail of Level Nine. The tragedy was that her bravery had been in vain. The life force that had locked itself on and into her was so powerful and tenacious that it could compel a ruined body to go on living. Sharly was now Sharly-Plus, and her main preoccupations were those of an alien being. . . .

"I can't walk on these legs, Jack," she was saying in her laboured gargling voice. "The bones are smashed . . . no longer work as levers . . . but the arms are all right . . . and you could get me to Field Control, Jack. You remember how I used to talk about reciprocity . . . the need for a two-way exchange . . . I know how to do it now . . . you can make it possible for me to escape. . . ."

"You're too late," I said harshly, marvelling at my ability to think and speak. "The thing you're running from—it's already here."

"But that's impossible!" Her head turned jerkily. "I would have *known* . . . my senses can't be so . . ."

"I jumped from Level Three to get away from it. They're all dead up there."

"So that's why you're here . . . I thought I had finally manged to get through to you. . . ." Her eyelids closed, wavered and opened. "But you couldn't have escaped from a Taker so easily. . . . Did you see it?"

"I saw it, all right." The memory made my present situation almost bearable. "Black thing. Legs."

"How big?"

"It was the width of the gallery."

"That means it's still trying to emerge . . . still tied to the alpha-locus . . ." Her eyelids flickered again, interrupting her blind white stare like signal lamp shutters. "Jack, you're going to carry me to Field Control. . . ."

I still think there must have been some element of mental control involved, in spite of all she told me about the nature of the Takers and what it would mean to this planet if one of them were to be set free here. Otherwise, I don't know how I could have borne to pick her up. She stank, my once-beloved Sharly did; and she was *cold* and the lower half of her body felt like pieces of miscellaneous junk in a plastic sack. Perhaps the worst thing of all was the way she slid her arm around my neck. The movement felt so natural it reminded me that Sharly wasn't truly dead, that her own original personality was trapped in the decaying shell, being used by an alien creature which had no right to be on Earth. For an instant I almost squeezed her, to try communicating across the gulf that separated us; but common sense reasserted itself just in time.

"The alpha-locus is programmed to pass through each region of the ice structure once in every two hours," came the throaty voice in my ear as I stood up with a dead weight in my arms. "It is now at the far end of the island and dropping to the lowest level. That means it will be back here at the well in less than five minutes, bringing the Taker with it. It will pass very close to this point, and the Taker will have emerged more fully by then, so it will appear to be much larger. We must reach Level Five or higher within the next four minutes." The engineering analysis of our situation made use of Sharly's knowledge, but there was a clinical quality in the phrasing which told me it was Sharly-Plus who was speaking. And she was informing me that I had to move quickly or die.

Guided by the sound of the pump, I lurched in that direction with my burden. The surface underfoot was hidden in a slurry of mud, oil, and water, and was made more treacherous by the presence of industrial detritus—pieces of cable, submerged metal bars, and slimed sections of timber. I kept falling to my knees and each time that happened it was harder to stand up again. Only numbness and shock kept me from realizing the extent of the punishment I had taken during the hurtling descent from Level Three. By the time I located the ladder which slanted up to the first gallery, I had serious doubts about my ability to climb it; but the thing I was carrying gave assistance, reaching for higher rungs with eager hands and pulling upwards with unnatural strength. There was no mistaking the urgency which galvanized those limbs and fingers. Sharly-Plus and I had one thing in common—we were both deathly afraid of the Taker and wanted to get as far away from it as was possible in the time available.

I had no check on how quickly our time was running out, but it seemed to me that four minutes had passed when I reached the elevator and found that the passenger cage was somewhere high above, lost in the alternating circles of light and dark. There was a dead silence after I thumbed the call button. For a panicky moment I thought the power was off; then the steel lattice enclosing the elevator shaft began to thrum. I instinctively glanced at Sharly, got my first good look at her face in adequate lighting, and turned away with my eyes closed.

Standing there in the self-imposed darkness, I could almost sense the alpha-locus racing back through the length of the island and carrying with it the night-black antithesis of life I had glimpsed earlier, still trapped and squirming, but grown much bigger now, more capable of destroying me without even being aware of my existence. A Taker, from what I had learned, was less of a malevolent being than an unconscious agent of entropy. It seemed to be a kind of materialised force which reacted blindly against organization in matter or energy, but the outcome was just the same as if it were a hate-crazed animal which had scented my blood and was coming to claw me apart. Every nerve in my body was telling me that I ought to be running for my life, and all I could do was stand there on the first gallery and pray for the elevator to arrive. It seemed to me that the air was growing noticeably colder.

When the cage finally clanged to a halt in front of me I grabbed for the sliding door, but Sharly was already dragging it open. The air *was* colder now, filled with a premonitory chill. Sick with fear, I stumbled into the cage and pressed the button for Level Ten. There was another silence, the machinery playing cruel pranks again; then the cage began its painfully slow climb. I counted the numbers painted at each level. Two. Three. Four.

It was when the cage was passing Level Five that the Taker went by not far beneath us. I didn't see anything this time, but a convulsion went through the upper part of Sharly's body and I felt the temperature in the cage momentarily dip to sub-Arctic levels. For a few seconds I was unable to breathe. I stood perfectly still and wished miserably that I could be somewhere warm and safe and very far away from Icewell 37.

"The alpha-locus is programmed to describe an ascending helix around the well shaft," Sharly husked. "Multiple passes may be required in some areas—I can't say without the hourly report on wave and tide action—but the entire operation is unlikely to take more than thirty minutes. When it is completed the locus will make a scan-pattern return on the surface of the island, terminating at Field Control. We must get there well ahead of it. Do you understand?"

I nodded, not trusting myself to speak. Field Control was actually a converted trawler housing all the essential telecongruency warp generating and control equipment. Two years earlier, working by satnav, it had taken up station near the drilling site and built around itself a rectangular island of ice. The well and the embedded ship were at opposite ends of the artificial island, and I would have to travel the length of it with Sharly. That in itself wasn't much of a problem, because there were Moke transports for communal use both on the surface and in the Level Nine connecting tunnel. My main worry was about what would happen at the far end. There was no way, especially in the time available, of explaining the facts to a man like Lieutenant Oliver, yet I couldn't see how I was going to get Sharly-Plus into the warp control room unobserved.

I was still trying to think constructively about the matter when the cage reached Level Ten and jolted to a halt. We were in a small machinery house situated on the topmost gallery of the well. When I opened the door I was very conscious of being on the surface. A strong, ocean-tanged breeze hustled noisily through the various superstructures; and the clustered lights of Field Control were visible at the far end of the island. The air was clear in comparison to the chilly mists that drifted far down in the icewell; and the moon was riding high overhead, looking serene and remote. Everything was deceptively normal.

"We must hurry," Sharly said in her rattling whisper. "There is very little time."

Trying to avoid looking directly at her, I turned my head and saw there were three open-sided Mokes parked only a few paces away. I went to the nearest and placed the undead body in the rear seat, wincing at the pain which needled through my side as I bent forward. With a considerable effort of will, I tucked one of the shattered legs inside the line of the vehicle and made to climb into the driving seat.

"Where are you going, Hillman?" a man's voice called. "What do you think you're doing?"

Lieutenant Oliver came striding towards me from the shadow of a crane shed, a borrowed carbine in hand. His oval face was pink with anger and exposure, and the overlong sandy moustache he had grown to make himself look more mature was bending this way and that in the wind. The winter-weight coat he had put on seemed several sizes too large, giving him something of the appearance of an extra in a low-budget move; but I'd had run-ins with him before and knew him to be an ambitious man who jealously guarded his career prospects.

"I've got to get down to Field Control right away," I said. "There's no time to explain now."

"*Sergeant!* Am I hearing you right?"

"You'd better," I replied heavily, "because I'm only going to say it once. Dresch and all the others who were on duty tonight are dead, torn apart. The thing that did the killing is still down there, around the lower levels; and there's only one way to get rid of it."

Oliver's eyes narrowed. "Are you telling me there's a bear or something loose on this well?"

"Not an ordinary animal." I hesitated, aware of how ridiculous I was going to sound, but with no alternative but to press on with the story. "It's some kind of alien thing the warp has sucked in from space. It killed Dresch and the others, and . . . Look, I've got to go." I reached for the Moke's ignition key.

"Don't move!" Oliver stepped in front of the vehicle. "I think you're drunk, Hillman. Falling-down drunk, by the look of you, and I'll bet Dresch is worse." He raised his wrist communicator to his lips. "Pilgrim and Dubois! Forget about checking out the galleries—go straight to the duty room. Pilgrim? Answer me, Pilgrim."

"If you've sent them down the well, they're dead. I can't explain any more now, but you'd better grab yourself a power boat and get the hell off the island, and that's the truth." I switched on the Moke's engine and in the same instant Oliver snapped his rifle up to point at my chest.

"Switch off and get out of the vehicle," he ordered, moving around to my side.

I clenched and unclenched my fingers on the wheel, afraid of getting myself shot, but even more alarmed about this fresh delay in reaching Field Control. Vital seconds were flitting past—and the Taker was on its way.

"I'm warning you, Hillman," Oliver said, drawing level with me, reaching a position from which he could get an unimpeded shot. "If you don't switch off that eng . . ." His voice faded out as he saw what lay on the Moke's rear seat.

"It's Charlotte Railton's body," I heard myself explain. "I found it down in the bilges."

"And you carried it up here! What's the matter with you, Hillman?" Oliver moved closer to the inert body, apparently repelled and fascinated. "Nobody in his right mind *carries* a thing like . . ."

Somehow I knew what was coming next and was completely prepared for it. Oliver wasn't. When Sharly snatched the rifle out of his hands he made a sound that was both a whimper and a moan, and which was drowned in the snarl of the Moke's exhaust as I gunned the engine. The wheels spun for a moment on the plastic mesh which covered the working areas of the island, then we were accelerating down the v-shaped perspective of lights which terminated in Field Control. I watched the mirror to see if Oliver would come after us in one of the remaining vehicles, but he simply stood there until I lost sight of him.

The ramp to the old trawler's main deck usually had a guard on it, but I could see from quite a long way off that it was deserted, and it occurred to me that reaching the actual warp control room might be easier than I had anticipated. Oliver could have taken all available security men to the well with him, and as it was a weekend there was a good chance that all the engineering staff had flown off to Alaska. If one or two had stayed behind, I had Oliver's carbine with which to keep them in line while Sharly-Plus did whatever it was she needed to do.

I have to admit that I had no real understanding of what her plans were. Even if I had been able to hear her properly down in the bottom of the well, even had I been in any condition for absorbing abstruse ideas, I still wouldn't have been able to understand. Sharly alone had always been able to think and talk rings around me—and now she was Sharly-Plus. There was another mind there, an alien mind accustomed to dealing with alien concepts; and in company with it my Sharly had travelled far beyond the bounds of contemporary human knowledge.

All I knew for sure was that the Taker was squirming through into my part of the continuum, and the only way to stop it was to get the dismaying object that was Sharly's body into the field control room without any delay. I broadsided the Moke up to the base of the ramp on locked wheels, jumped out and gathered the body up in my arms. Again it slid one arm around my neck, but I was too far gone to notice much. I struggled up the ramp, crossed an area of deck, and opened a door in the superstructure and got inside. The companionways in the trawler were narrow, certainly not designed for the carrying of awkward loads, but I caromed my way along them, bursting doors open with my shoulder until we were in the rebuilt part of the ship, the area which housed the warp controls. In contrast to the spartan conditions elsewhere, this was a region of thick carpet and indirect lighting, with one large window giving a longitudinal view of the island.

"Over there," Sharly burbled in my ear, pointing at a long console before which were three swivel chairs. I lowered her into the nearest chair, only then becoming aware of a disturbing new facet of the situation. Until that moment I had been under the impression that my plunge from Level Three had left me with nothing but a selection of bruises and perhaps a fractured rib, but all at once there came the queasy suspicion that something inside me was ruptured and leaking. I had always purposely avoided medical knowledge and so was unable to make any kind of diagnosis, but there was a definite wrongness at the centre of my being, and its effects seemed to be spreading. Holding a stanchion for support, I examined my surroundings and found them curiously distant and unreal. Horizontal surfaces appeared to slope, and solid objects tended to shimmy.

This must be what it's like to faint, I thought, bemused. *Or perhaps this is the way you die!*

There followed a period of blurry confusion. I clung to the stanchion, internally preoccupied, and was only dimly aware of what Sharly-Plus was doing. It meant nothing to me that she was moving herself from chair to chair by the strength of her arms, or that she was using the same physical power to strip cover plates from equipment banks and doors from cabinets. Other forces were at work too, because I know I saw drawers slide in and out by themselves, saw looms of wiring change shape like live creatures, heard the crackle of high-voltage current, smelt the ozone and the hot metal. I was in the presence of things far beyond my understanding. For a time Sharly-Plus was superhuman, perhaps supernatural; and she was imposing her unearthly will on artifacts of this Earth, changing their relationships and functions, moulding them to suit her own purpose. Stray currents of psychokinetic energy rippled the carpet, sent papers skywards like flocks of startled birds, tugged at my clothing. The very air hummed and crooned and was disturbed by strange flitting shadows. All I could do was stand there and try to endure.

The lull, the onset of silence, took me by surprise.

Fighting for a clearer picture of what was going on, I noted that Sharly-Plus, her head flung back at an unnatural angle, had ceased her labours and was staring at the window. I looked in the same direction and, in spite of all that had happened within and around me, I quailed.

The night-time scene was basically a familiar one—multiple rows of lights, flanking the helicopter pad and the STOL runway, converged on the accretion of greenish illuminated rectangles and points of brilliance which marked the head of the well shaft. The moon was too high to be visible from inside the control centre, but it sketched in a silver-grey background of ocean and cloud-vaulted sky pierced by stars.

And against that background something was moving. Something incredibly huge, and black, and with too many legs.

"Breakthrough . . . too soon," Sharly-Plus breathed. She reached towards a tilted and displaced keyboard on the console and began to tap instructions into it at high speed. At the far end of the island the Taker loomed high above the cranes and machinery houses, its legs slowly windmilling across the sky, quivering, questing. . . .

"Get away from here, Jack," Sharly-Plus said, or it may even have been Sharly, for in that moment her voice was almost human. "Take a boat and go fast."

I gaped at her back, nodded without speaking, then pushed myself away from the stanchion and ran, partially doubled over, for the ship's entrance ramp. Whatever it was that was damaged inside me reacted by producing spasms of pain, nausea, and weakness; and by the time I reached the bottom of the ramp I was sobbing aloud with every breath. It was only thirty yards to the jetty, but the crossing seemed to take a long time and all the while, at one corner of my vision, the night was hideously turbulent and alive.

I have no clear memory of reaching a boat, nor of starting the engine and casting off and heading out to sea. But in spite of being semi-conscious at the time, I can recall vividly what it was like when Sharly turned Icewell 37 into a miniature sun. I lay there, shielded by the gunwale, drowning in the sudden awesome wash of noontime brilliance.

It lasted less than three seconds, but when it was over the icewell and everything connected with it—including the Taker and the mortal remains of Sharly Railton—had vanished in a mile-high column of fire and steam. Clouds of vapour were roiling upwards to the stratosphere, and circular waves were racing towards the ocean's distant shores with their message that a battle had been fought and won.

I lowered my head and wept till I lost consciousness.

They'll never believe me!

The words of the old song kept mingling and merging with my own thoughts, interfering with all attempts at lucidity. I lay in that hospital bed for the best part of a day, fighting off the drugs that had cushioned my nervous system during the excision of the spleen, and my principal concern was that nobody would give my story credence. It was the kind of inversion of priorities which is typical of the semi-lucid state. I imagined myself to be in the situation which crops up so often in children's fiction, the one in which all evidence of a fantastic adventure is maddeningly lost and the protagonist, if he speaks at all, meets knowing smiles of disbelief.

But I had forgotten about my buttonhole recorder.

It had continued working through the entire episode, and its tape became one of the single most valued artifacts in history, even though the evidence was imperfect in many ways. The Taker, for example, registered only as a vague area of darkness—with no sign of the legs which I had seen so distinctly; and the scene in Field Control was obliterated here and there because I had been clinging to the stanchion. However, the scientific and technical teams got most of what they wanted from it. They were able to see something of what Sharly-Plus had done to the warp control complex, to deduce others, and to make inspired guesses about much of the rest.

That was three years ago, and they believe that before another three have passed the first of the new breed of power stations will be operational. It will employ much the same equipment as an ice-well, but with the big difference that the zeta-locus, instead of wandering blindly in space, will be positioned exactly where we want it. Instead of serving as a heat sink for the construction of ice islands, it will be used to import unlimited energy from the vicinity of the sun.

Visionaries, and there are quite a few of them in the scientific community, say it won't be too long until we achieve the reciprocity that Sharly used to talk about, that an advanced form of the tele-congruency warp is going to give us instantaneous travel to the stars. As Sharly once put it, "We'll be able to grow food or gather diamonds or pick flowers on any planet in the Galaxy."

I guess that's the sort of memorial she would have chosen for herself.